Problem Child

BLUE IVY PREP
BOOK ONE

HEATHER LONG

Copyright © 2022 by Heather Long

Cover: Vicious Desires Design

Editing: Leavens Editing

Line Editing: D. Jackson

All rights reserved.

This book is licensed for your personal enjoyment only.

This is a work of fiction. Names, characters, places, brands, media, and incidents are either the product of the authors imagination or are used fictitiously. The author acknowledges the trademark status and trademark owners of various products referred to in this work of fiction, which have been used without permission. The publication/ use of these trademarks is not authorized, associated with, or sponsored by the trademark owners.

Problem Child/Heather Long – Special ed.

ISBN: 978-1-956264-26-5

For Harley Quinn Zaler

Series so Far

Problem Child
Mad Boys

Foreword

Dear Reader,

Thank you for picking up this book, for taking a chance on a new series. If I'm a new to you author, welcome. If you've read my previous works, hello there, it's good to see you. I wanted to take a minute to discuss a little history behind Problem Child. A little context, if you will.

If you're reading this one for the triggers found in this book, go ahead and skip to the end of this letter where I will list them for you. If you don't mind giving me a couple of minutes of your time, I'd like to share another story with you.

This story is the history behind Blue Ivy Prep, the concept of KC, and a young, talented woman named Harley (Harley-QuinnZaler on Facebook).

Harley was a devoted reader and a talented cover artist. During one of her pre-made sales, I grabbed a cover that just resonated with me. A girl in denim overalls, dancing like crazy, and her hair was teal. From the moment I saw that cover, KC aka Kaitlin Crosse was born.

It was January 2020 and I was only working on the third

FOREWORD

book of my 12 book series Untouchable. (The series is now complete). The girl on this cover was everything I pictured for Kaitlin, who along with Aubrey Miller and Yvette Chanteur, formed the girl band Torched.

They were one of Frankie's favorite bands and they appeared on the page in book 5, Hangovers and Holidays. I'm not telling you all this to get you to pick up that series. Absolutely not. While KC and the girls do appear there, you do not have to read Untouchable to appreciate this series.

At the time, when I told Harley what I wanted to write, she was so stoked. We discussed cover concepts, art, the characters and more. She was so excited about the future books and the cover models I picked out. She couldn't wait to do their covers.

Then in 2021, unexpectedly, Harley passed away. Her loss was devastating for her family, her husband, her mother, her daughter... I felt that loss keenly because losing anyone is hard. Losing someone so young with so much future in front of her was just not fair.

Her family offered the covers already purchased and her team was working to get all of this sorted, but with three more covers needed, I made a different call.

Working with Stephanie at Vicious Desires Designs, we used the inspiration of the cover to go in a different direction. The cover that Harley made me for this first book, originally titled Party Girl, remains an inspiration and I wrote Harley into this book because she was so excited and I want her to remain a part of it.

As you can see by the dedication, this book... this whole series is for her and for the joy she brought into our lives with a light that was far too soon extinguished.

Thank you, Harley and I miss you.

If you have read this far, thank you as well. Problem Child is the first in a four book series following Kaitlin Crosse as she

FOREWORD

attends Blue Ivy Prep, an exclusive boarding, prep, and college school for the wealthy and the privileged.

The series is reverse harem/why choose. This means the female main character will not have to choose between the guys in her life. This series is also slow burn, and begins with bullying, secrets, lies, and complicated family ties.

There is some stalking, and I will give a warning for a severe health diagnosis for a side character. This book is also told exclusively from Kaitlin's viewpoint except for the prologue. Future books in this series will contain multiple points of view.

Thank you again for taking a chance on this series, I can't wait to hear what you think of KC and the girls. Be sure to join us in my reader group on Facebook where we talk books, book loving, some spoilers, teasers for the future, and bonus scene. Don't forget to sign up for news and updates on my website to get all the latest news, releases and more emailed right to you.

xoxo

Heather

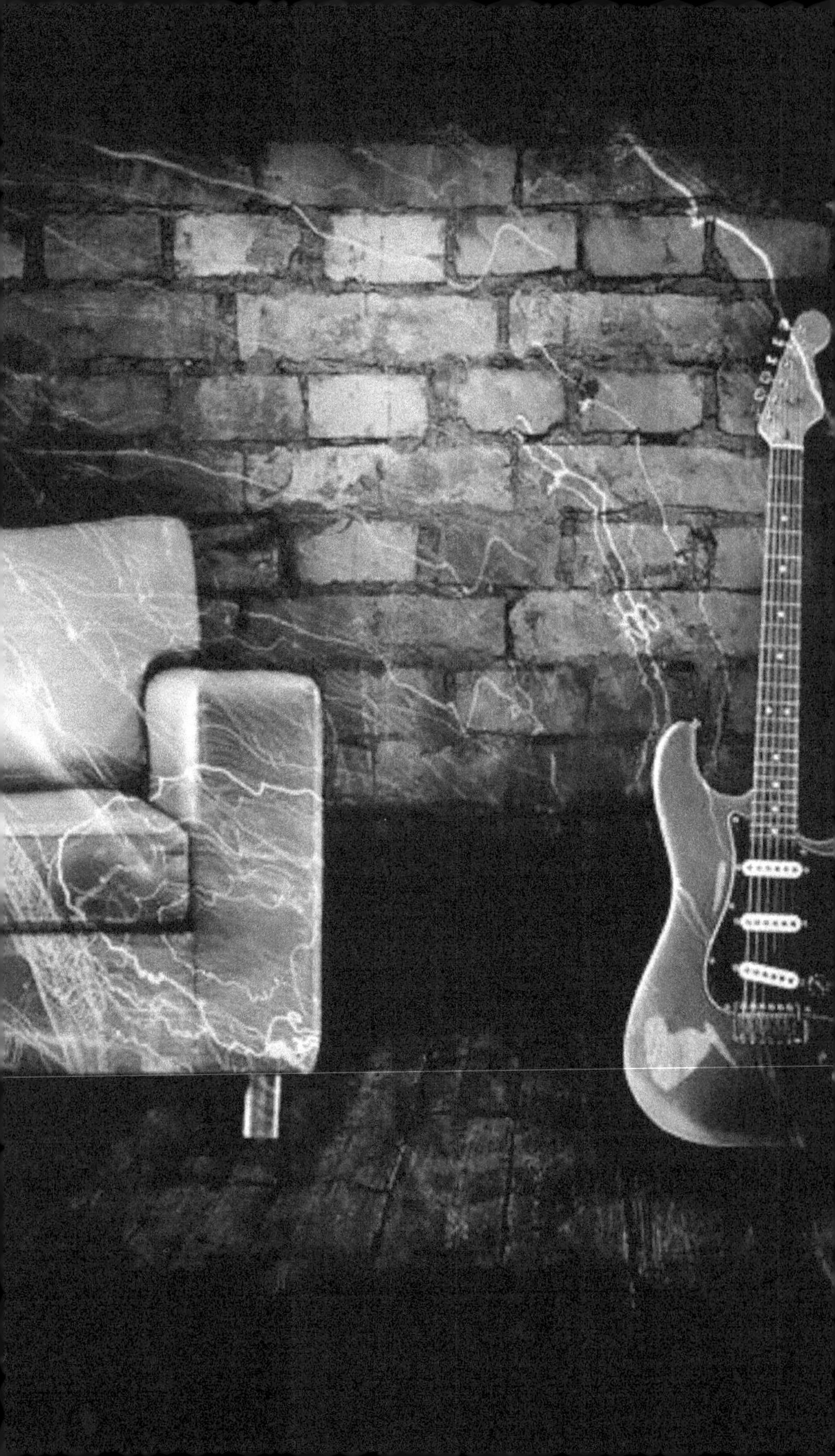

Prologue

When they handed out the new year packets, I wasn't expecting it to be quite so full of new student data, protocols, and security measures. The email blast we'd gotten earlier in the summer indicated Blue Ivy would be employing a number of new measures to crack down on all visitors traveling to and from the campus. There would be increased patrols. They'd also added new hires to the main administration to handle all publicity calls and public relations.

"Good morning everyone," Mr. Black said as he made his way around the large table in one of the executive conference rooms of the administrative building. The oversized cherry-wood gleamed, as did everything else in the Victorian-style room that boasted a large fireplace they even lit when the winter months buried us in snow. Like all the other RAs and TAs present, I'd dressed for the occasion. Even administrative meetings required a suit and tie.

"If you can all sit down," Mr. Black continued as he circled the table, handing out stacks of paper clipped together as one group but with five separate stacks in each set broken out by colored paper. "We need to go over the nondisclosures first. The school legal team has been in touch with each of you, and you should have copies of your updated signed agreements for your records. We're going to go over this together before our new students arrive because legal wants there to be no mistakes. Mistakes can lead to immediate dismissal, so I need all of you to be sharp and focused."

"Dismissal?" Harley said as she leaned forward. "Just from being an RA and TA or from the school entirely?" Not an unfair question; this was *our* education, too.

I spared a glance at the names on the blue sheets of paper. Media darlings were coming to the school, and there had already been an uptick in trespassing and press calls. It wouldn't be long before money changed hands to get the right photos and videos. Kaitlin Crosse. Aubrey Miller. Celebrities brought their own form of notoriety and problems. Celebutantes like Crosse and Miller brought even more issues because they craved attention. Didn't matter who they hurt along the way.

"First on our list is the son of the U.S. attorney general. He's coming in with the junior class..." Mr. Black went down the list of dignitaries. While the school wouldn't make any official announcement about the identities of the students attending here, residential advisors and teaching assistants were informed as well as the faculty because additional measures needed to be taken for both residential and academic halls.

Not that it was all that unusual for there to be special circumstances that impacted students *and* faculty for that matter. I'd been one such student once upon a time. We had students now, and we'd have students later, that all needed special handling. None of those required a meeting like this.

PROBLEM CHILD

While this was my first year as an RA, it was not my first as a TA.

We didn't even make it through the first half-dozen special cases before my phone went off. Granted, I had it set to vibrate, but two of the TAs closest to me flipped open their messages.

"How is having this girl band here not an insurance risk?" the guy closest to me asked, and I just shrugged. I didn't even know why she'd insisted on enrolling in this school. Of all of the schools out there, she chose ours. As annoying as I found her from a distance, I could ignore her. Frankly, I really couldn't imagine having to *endure* her presence all year. More than endure, I'd already seen her name on one of my class rosters. I was going to have to handle her attitude every damn day.

I really didn't *want* to have an opinion on this topic. Not about the politics of what their enrollment meant or the optics of having the hottest "it" girls in attendance. It was just asking for trouble, especially when you threw in the volatile mix of competitive academics and gossip. I wouldn't be human if I didn't have an opinion, which started and ended with: *pick another school and be their problem.*

"People," Mr. Black said. "I know some of you are excited, but we will be expected to set the tone for our new arrivals. That means whether you're fans or not, you make them feel welcome and treat them with respect and generosity while they are here."

"And if their tour bus follows them? Every single story involving them usually involves some form of recreational narcotics or worse... We're all aware of *her* background. Let's not pretend she's anything other than what her reputation has always been, a problem child. We can't afford to let that kind of disruption interfere with the academic atmosphere," Waldham said from the other side of the table, where he studied his nails like he hadn't gotten quite the right manicure. The prick probably didn't even possess a single callus because he was born with a ten-figure bank account. "It wouldn't be fair to our *real* students."

"They are real students. We will do no more and no less than we would for any other member of Blue Ivy Prep's student body. Is that understood?" Mr. Black's expression was implacable. He really did subscribe to the theory that who you were *outside* of school should have no influence on who you were inside of it.

Not all of us could live in that delusion.

"Yeah, but since when did the student body here come with a rap sheet? Or a smoking hot bod. Is she really sixteen?" the guy next to me muttered, and I shook my head. We did *not* need to be discussing her looks.

"Just remember," I cautioned him. "Hot or not, she's a problem."

The photos for each student would need to be updated. Blue hair was not exactly in the dress code. Neither were tattoos. I checked my watch and adjusted it to hide the tattoo around my wrist. Most students who had tattoos or piercings knew better than to flaunt them on campus. They dressed conservatively, kept their heads down, and followed the rules. At least, they made a show of it. It was how it should be. But I didn't think *Kaitlin Crosse* had ever done a single *quiet* thing in her life.

"In order to make things easier, we've moved them to one of the renovated buildings…"

I wasn't the only one who made a face. A headache pulsed behind my eyes. I could hear the complaints now. This wasn't going to make their immersion into the school year any easier. The new renovations were in high demand, and the school worked on a system of meritocracy and seniority. The fact the new students got the coveted space over students who'd been enrolled longer was already going to poison the waters.

Dammit, couldn't she have picked some other place to park her real-life reality show? I had plans, and none of them involved an entitled, self-important rock princess who wouldn't know hard work or dedication if it bit her in the ass.

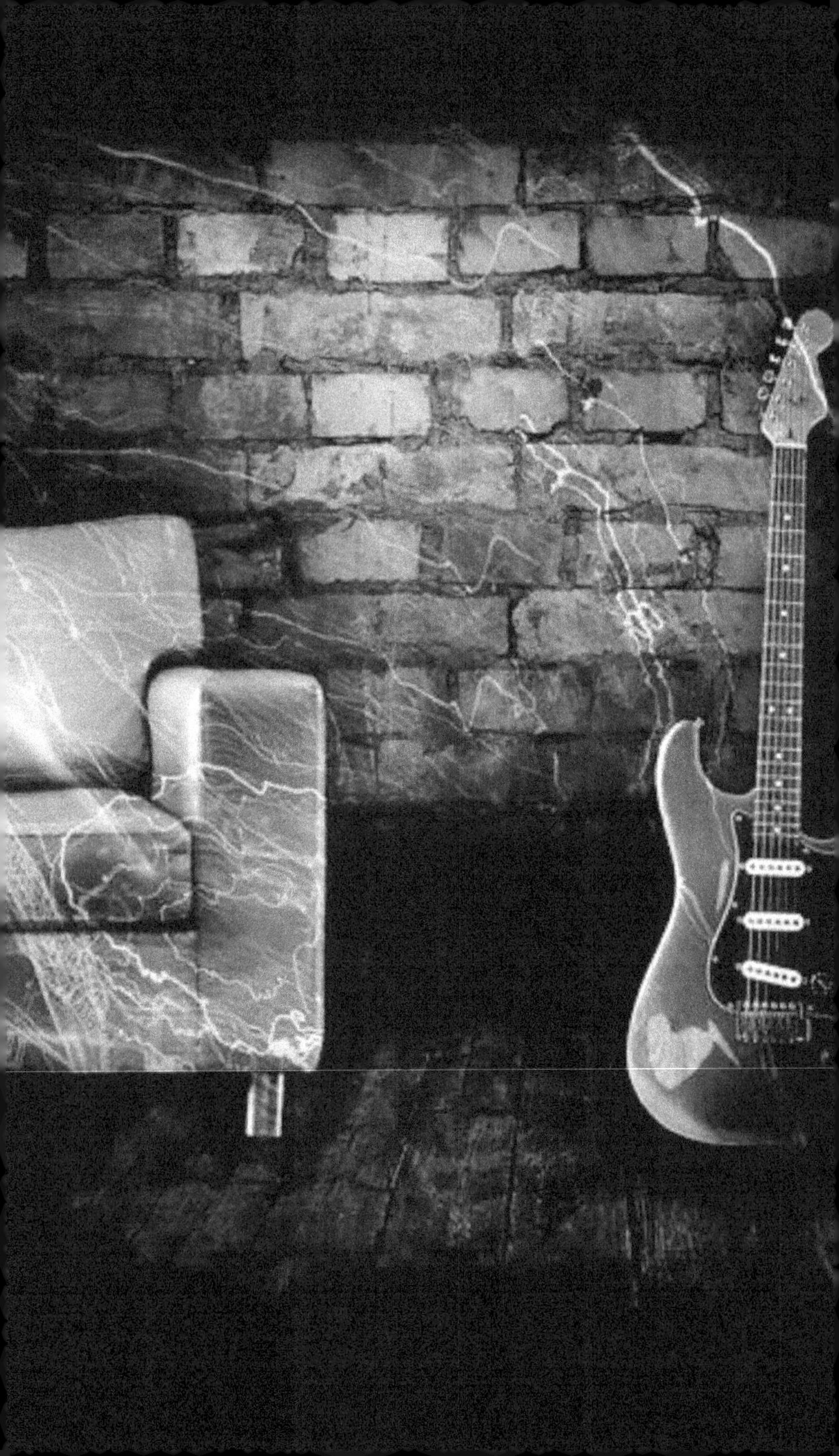

One

KC

Nothing said "good luck on your new adventure" like being the subject of an email blast. Especially one that read like a burn book from a mean girl who got jilted at prom to a few million of our closest fans and haters. *Haters are going to hate only goes so far to soften the blow.* I was used to the biting, clawing, and stinging statements. Right?

"Hey little Kissy Kats, did you hear that Torched's lead singer is going back to school? A little birdie told me that this isn't about education so much as leashing the problem child while she gets a certain *bad habit* under control. The prep school, of course, has no comment. They wouldn't. They can't even confirm she's enrolled. Who wants to get a picture for us so we can see where our favorite problem child is? Kiss. Kiss. More soon."

Aubrey made a face as she read the blast out loud. Somehow, despite years of exposure, she could still manage to be shocked by the tabloidesque commentary on our lives. At least they hadn't discussed the state of her virginity at twelve. Mine, apparently, vanished long before in a clearance sale, but hey, what did I know about my own sexual exploits?

"What a cunt," she muttered. "Why does this bitch hate you so much?"

I laughed as I held up a finger for each item. "Daddy. Mommy. Mom's big-dick boyfriend. Then there is my *drama* when I'm the so-called lucky one with the blessed life. I'm clearly a stuck-up, pampered bitch because I can't even be bothered to give her an interview."

Rolling her eyes, Aubrey slumped into the seat. "You realize she's just set, like, everyone and their brother out to take photos of you."

"Yep," I said with a shrug. "Nothing I can do about it."

"Stay on the grounds of the school," Dix said over his shoulder. I'd almost forgotten he was driving us. *Rude, KC, rude.* "Any press that trespasses, or fan for that matter, can be arrested. You should consider the bodyguard, K. I know you want normal, but I can stay. We arranged it with the school so you could have someone there to run interference."

Fuck, no. "Dix, I adore you for wanting to protect me." I did. "But the whole point of this is to be *normal*. Normal kids don't have bodyguards."

"Normal kids don't have drivers, million-dollar contracts, and platinum albums," he countered and Aubrey laughed.

I shot her a dirty look, but she looked less than impressed. "Can't hurt to have some backup," she coaxed, and I shook my head.

The minute I allowed it, I would be admitting defeat, and I might as well follow Yvette up to Boston and finish school with online classes. That wasn't what I wanted. We were going to an exclusive school in the middle of nowhere Connecticut. Yes, it wasn't precisely *normal,* but it was far more normal than the first twelve years of my life and a hell of a lot more normal than the last four.

"I don't want a bodyguard. I don't want to stand out." Another perk of the exclusive school. We would be like the other students. Their student population drew wealthy pools that included foreign dignitaries to politicians to old world aristocrats and the ever-expanding digital and social media conglomerates.

Aubrey twisted in the seat to look at me. "We're arriving in a type of limo, yes. Sure, it's almost black car service. A highly *secure* Cadillac SUV." Despite her description, it wasn't a stretch limousine. It was just a standard black Cadillac Escalade.

"But he's not staying with the car, and neither of us have licenses yet." I knew how to drive... sort of. Aubrey had taken lessons at one point, but we'd never been anywhere long enough to actually apply, take the tests, and get our licenses. That was on the list for this semester.

Then we could buy a car, or cars, if we couldn't find one we wanted in the collections of vehicles we'd received over the years. At least the ones I hadn't gone ahead and donated, since I couldn't drive them. A bridge to cross when we got there. I didn't know what car I wanted. Aubrey wanted a Mini Cooper, because she'd seen *The Italian Job* like five hundred times.

"KC, I love you, but—you're never going to be normal." Aubrey flopped back in the seat. "You didn't change your hair and got permission from the school to keep it that shade, even if we're supposed to be conforming with uniforms that have ties—why did I let you talk me into this again?" She tapped a manicured nail against her lower lip then grinned. "Oh, right, I wouldn't let you do this alone, despite Yvette telling us both to go to hell."

She really had. A laugh escaped me, and I shrugged. "We still have some commitments that we're not going to just be able to ignore. If I have to strip my hair and recolor it constantly, it's gonna fall out. The blue has been a signature for the group from the beginning."

"Very true." She reached over to stroke her fingers through the ends. "You do need to get a trim."

"Anastasia wasn't available when we were in the city, and she had a litter of kittens the last time I let someone else cut my hair."

"I'll do it," Aubrey volunteered. "Anastasia's hot when she's mad."

Dix laughed, and I grinned up at him. I appreciated Dix taking the time to be in New York while we'd been there. Especially since he was based out of the LA house. Mom had an apartment in the city. She'd planned to go with us for the drop-off, but a change in a film schedule meant she was on location. I hadn't even known there had been a change until Dix showed up. He'd volunteered to handle the driving and hauling.

There were easily six suitcases in the back of the SUV. You'd think life on the road would make us expert packers, but we weren't staying in a hotel. We had a dorm room, and there was some equipment I didn't want to leave in the city or California. My guitars, for example. Music. Clothes. We had six or seven sets of uniforms, winter gear, and more shoes than anyone needed—that was Aubrey, not me. I was fine barefoot or in my running shoes, unless we were performing.

My phone buzzed, and I dug it out of my bag to see a message from Yvette on it. Aubrey was already laughing. Yvette had sent the message to our group chat.

> Good luck with High School Drama Nightmare Fall Edition. You two are nuts, but I love you. When you need to escape, my door is always open. I've even stocked up on the liquor.

"She's the best," I said with a laugh.

"You know, she might have the right idea," Aubrey said with a hum.

"Still time to change your plans," I reminded her. "I love you for going with me, but you don't have to. This—crazy plan is all me."

"I know, but I'm exceptionally awesome, and you definitely don't deserve me. You need to be reminded of that daily. Besides... friends don't let friends walk into a horror movie on their own."

"You're the brunette," I reminded her. "You would survive."

Her grin was pure mischief. "You're the quirky one who either dies in the first five minutes or barely makes it out."

"Helpful." But I was still laughing. Some of my nerves evaporated. Or at least, bubbled to a place I didn't have to focus on right now.

"Ten minutes out, ladies," Dix said. "Do you know what building you're in?"

Blue Ivy Prep was so huge it had its own app with a map and locator so we could get directions on campus. Very helpful, if you asked me. We'd also gotten a welcome packet with paper maps and booklets that included everything we needed to know as first-time students.

Our orientation would be different from the others in our class because we were *new arrivals* joining in our junior year. We'd almost had to settle for sophomore, but our scores qualified us to begin as juniors.

I liked that plan *much* better.

"We're in the Apollo-Volusia complex." It was one of the newer dorms. Blue Ivy Prep included an on-campus college that was affiliated with one of the bigger universities. Several endowments had let the school expand. Students began enrollment there as early as the third grade, but housing and classes for the younger kids were in separate buildings. We would be in the high school dorms with access to our various lecture halls and libraries.

Collegiate dorms were located not far from the "high school" buildings, because at Blue Ivy Prep, we would be taking college-level courses alongside typical high school curricula. I couldn't wait. It was going to be a blast. We were going to be discussing the books we read, the assignments we'd done, and we would all survive this experience together. It was everything I wanted. The sudden palpitations and the racing of my heart kind of called me a liar, but I could fake it until I could make it. All of life was a stage, and we were but the actors on it—or however the Shakespeare quote went.

"South side of the campus," I told Dix as the huge iron gates appeared ahead of us. The closer to the campus we'd come, the more rural the area seemed to be. The school had everything and covered several acres. Far from California glitz and sunshine as you could get, the campus also seemed even more remote amidst the gray day with a hint of rain. Despite being August, the temperature barely seemed to hit eighty-five.

It was just about perfect. The leaves were going to be changing soon. We'd get *real* seasons and time to savor them rather than see them outside of the tour bus window as we drove in and out of various towns. That was if we saw them at all, usually. So many times we were asleep on the bus when it was on the road.

A huge banner was up welcoming new and returning students. Dix slowed down as he passed through the gates and then stopped to talk to the girl with the iPad and the no-nonsense expression.

"Welcome home to Blue Ivy Prep," she said. "Names?"

"Crosse and Miller," Dix said as he handed over a card. It was a temporary ID card for campus. We were going to have to go and get all the real things once we got to our room. But we also had our dorm assignments and keys. They'd sent those ahead of time. Once we got registered, though, everything would be coded to our ID cards.

"Wait for it," Aubrey murmured.

"Crosse and Miller," the girl repeated, then did a double-take at the screen. "For real?"

She glanced toward the back of the Escalade and I rolled the window down to smile at her. We didn't have to hide back here, even if ice slicked over my skin and sweat dotted the back of my neck. The sunglasses hid her eyes, but I had on my own pair. "Yes, for real."

"That's really awesome," she said, tapping a couple of things on the screen before handing the card back to me rather than Dix. "You're already assigned to Apollo One, third floor. That's the brand-new renovated building, so you've definitely got a sweet suite."

The genuine warmth rolling off the blonde girl helped settle my nerves.

"I'd be jealous, but my sister Olivia and I also got a suite in that building, so we'll see you there. I'm Sydney, by the way. We're on the second floor, B wing. Room 2205. If you need anything at all, come grab me. We know everything on the campus."

"Thank you very much," Aubrey said. "We'll do that."

A car honked behind us, but Sydney didn't miss a beat as she held up a hand to them indicating they needed to wait.

"Once you get to your room and get your stuff inside, I'd head down to the admin building to get your actual ID cards. They will load it for your food account, library privileges, and access to WiFi, as well as let you pick up everything you need from the bookstore. Today's upperclassmen move-in day, but the underclassmen tend to flood in as soon as they can because they want to get the good assignments."

"Thank you," I said. "We'll definitely check it out."

"Great—I promise not to fangirl too much, but I'm pretty sure Olivia is going to have an aneurysm. There was a rumor that you girls were enrolling, but I didn't think it was true."

"Just going to school," I said. "Don't be a stranger."

She waved us on and Dix chuckled as he glanced at me via the rearview mirror. "Totally normal."

"Bite me," I muttered, setting him *and* Aubrey off laughing. The driveway was long, lined with trees, and everything the handbook promised it would be. Despite their earlier teasing, we weren't the only limo. There were parking areas marked off that were tucked behind trees and hidden by the landscaping. Instead of heading to the right, we went to the left and followed the signs for the Apollo-Volusia buildings.

The closer we got to the old-world brick buildings, with their decades of history and links to the past as well as promises of the future, the more nervous I became. I'd stopped throwing up before performances a long time ago, but this was as close as I'd been in years.

Look out, Blue Ivy Prep, here we come.

Dear KC,

I have been a fan of yours for years, and have enjoyed every single album and all of your songs. My favorite is Blue and Yellow. I love how you show that truth and fact are not the same. How we see someone is more about our own truth than it is about facts.

I would love to get your autograph or see you in concert again. I couldn't make the last tour, so I'm really hoping Torched isn't done for good.

Thank you for being a rock star!

Joy Diamonte

Fan Mail

Dear KC,

I have been a fan of yours for years, and have enjoyed every single album and all of your songs. My favorite is Blue and Yellow. I love how you show that truth and fact are not the same. How we see someone is more about our own truth than it is about facts.

I would love to get your autograph or see you in concert again. I couldn't make the last tour, so I'm really hoping Torched isn't done for good.

Thank you for being a rock star!
Joy Diamonte

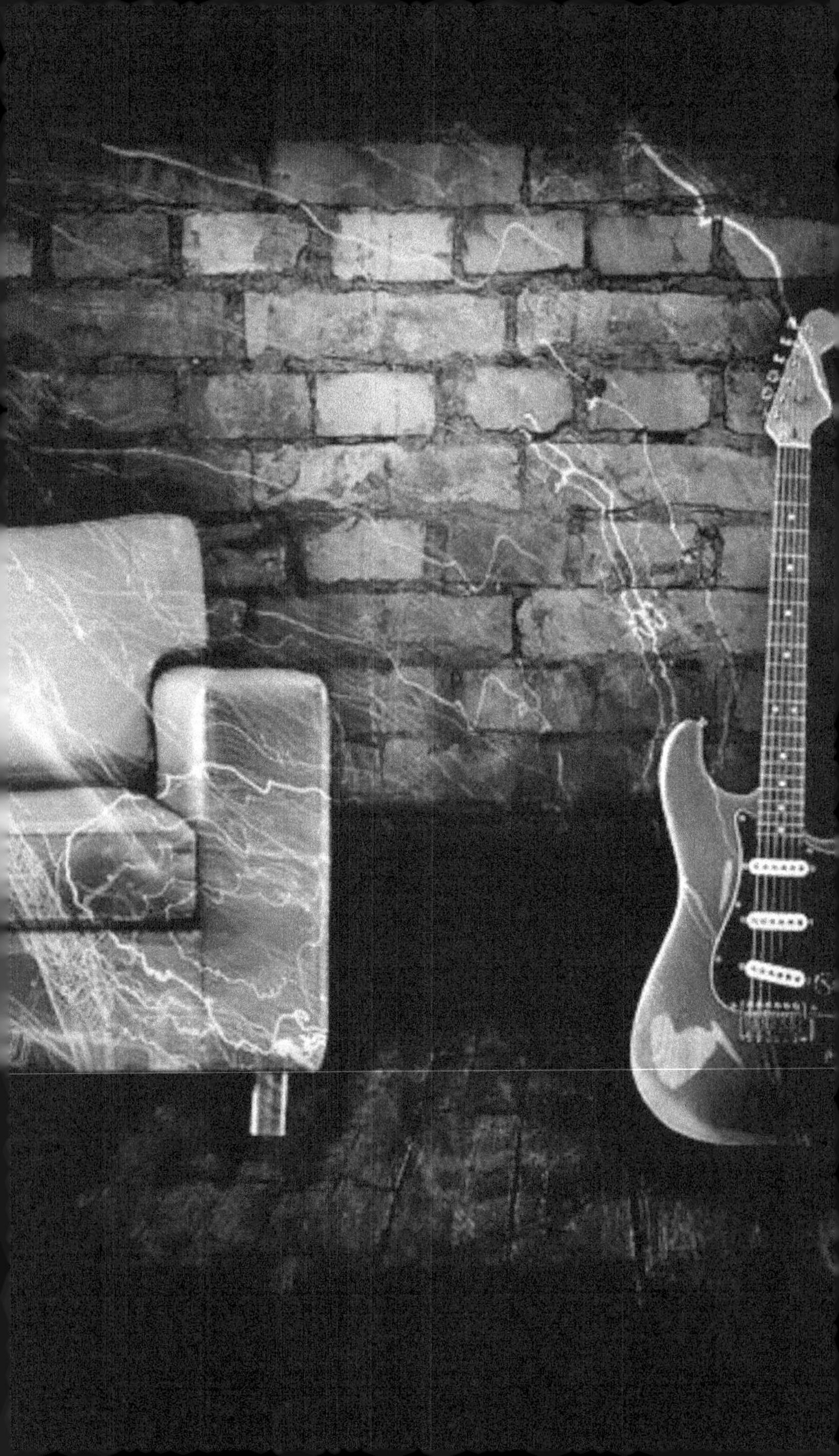

Two

Getting our new cards was a fuck ton easier than getting all our shit up to our room. I'd forgotten for a minute that we were on a historical-landmark campus where you climbed stairs to all the different floors and the only place with an elevator was the new administrative building on the far side of the campus. Why not put one in the newly built dorm?

Dix just laughed at us as he parked the Cadillac right in front of the building, even though a half-dozen signs clearly marked a path to the parking lot. We weren't the only car parked out front, though the other car was a convertible and there was an actual moving truck parked behind it.

"I thought we weren't getting movers," I said as we climbed out. Most of our things, including suitcases and musical instruments, fit in the back. We did have a couple of boxes...

"I told you," Dix said, giving me a firm look, "I will take care of everything. Let's get you up to your room first, shall we?"

Right, no arguing, especially when it came to hauling all

our shit up *three* flights of stairs. Even though he offered, I refused to let him or the movers carry either of my guitars.

By our last trip, it didn't matter how "cool" it was here, I'd soaked my shirt with sweat and Aubrey had piled all that black hair of hers up into a messy topknot. My hair refused to stay tamed; the hotter it got—just like when I was under the stage lights—the wispier and wilder my hair became. Still, I dug out a big fat clip and got the weight of hair off my neck.

"Home sweet home," Aubrey declared as I set my guitars down on the unmade bed that would end up being mine. We had a sweet *suite* indeed. Our accommodations were a lot bigger than I'd been thinking. We had *two* bedrooms and a common room. The bedrooms were two steps up, and we shared a bathroom in between them. I'd actually thought our "dorm" would be a single room with two beds and maybe corner desks if we were lucky.

No, this was a lot more like a mid-level hotel's business suite, right down to a kitchenette. We had a standard fridge, slightly larger than a hotel size, with decent freezer space. Perfect for ice packs, ice cream, and frozen meals. A good-sized microwave. A rather sad looking coffee maker had occupied the minimum amount of counter space next to the sink.

Aubrey had already put it away into one of the cabinets. If we'd known we had this waiting for us, we'd have already ordered our upgrade. As it was, Aubrey was scouting all the nearby stores on her phone. If we had to order one, well, we could do that, too.

Standard furniture had been assigned to us, including desks for each room, along with beds. We could replace the mattresses if we wanted. If we did, we were responsible for hauling out the old ones. I didn't see why we would. At least, not right now.

When they said "new," they weren't kidding. I could still smell the paint. Thankfully, Dix hadn't bailed on us yet. The

PROBLEM CHILD

suites were great, but we needed to open the windows and air it out, and that required arm strength we didn't possess. The movers were efficient; they carried up recliners and a ginormous television.

"We don't need a—" I started to protest, but he just pointed his finger at me then mimed zipping his lips. Yeah, yeah. He could be so bossy, but it was also kind of fun.

Dix took care of shifting stuff from the sitting room to our respective rooms, including our larger travel trunks. Then he volunteered to run into town for supplies we hadn't thought of...like ice packs for the freezer, some frozen meals, and yes, the ice cream we both preferred. Score, he'd even picked up the espresso machine we wanted. Dix was the best.

"Need anything else?" He checked the list he was making on his phone. "Extra power strips, phone cables? Space heater? Backup generators for the space heaters? I can pick up contraband, too."

The clearing of a feminine throat had me sticking my head out of my room to meet the gaze of an elfin-like girl. Well, woman. She was definitely older than us, but she was one of those ethereal looking beauties. Classically beautiful features, alabaster skin, hair that fell in a perfect line from her scalp and didn't have any stray hairs out of place.

Yvette would absolutely hate her and lust after her in the same breath. I was pretty sure Aubrey already was. Even Dix had gone so still I was worried he wasn't breathing.

"Hi," I said, letting those two collect their brain cells.

"Hi," she greeted me. Like Sydney by the gate, the girl at the door held a digital tablet in her hand. "I'm Harley, the RA for Apollo One. I saw you moving in and I wanted to introduce myself and answer any questions you might have. Also, to let you know that while I definitely don't *try* to eavesdrop on conversations taking place in front of wide-open doors to a public hall," Harley said, pausing to give us and then the open door a significant look. There were people moving in the hallway beyond. A couple of guys cursed as a large piece of furniture thudded against the wood. Right, we did have to close up behind us. Needed to remember that we didn't have a staff here and the plan was to keep it that way. "I do periodically have to do inspections for all dorm rooms and contents being stored in them—contraband included."

"Right, so I'll make sure we hide all the chocolate in a safe stash." That should be simple enough. "I'm KC, by the way and that's Aubrey. Dix isn't a student, but he is a friend." Aubrey lifted a hand as she went to the open door and glanced out for a moment before she closed it. The action quieted the hum I hadn't even noticed earlier.

Harley laughed. "Excellent. Dix—if that's your car downstairs parked out front, you probably have another hour before someone gets irritated and calls campus security. They'll poke me first, but you're almost done here."

"Got it," Dix said. "I'll use the guest parking on the other side after I bring back supplies."

"You can totally pull up out front and leave the items with me. My suite is on the first floor, closest to the door. Then the girls can come down and get it if you don't want to haul it all over from guest parking, which is by Administration."

"I like her," Dix said before he dropped a kiss on my head. "Be good, Problem Child. I'll be back."

"Jackass," I grunted, thwacking him as he danced backwards laughing. I *hated* that nickname. Considering the paps' love affair with the moniker, I usually said nothing because why feed the beast. But Dix should know better. "That's *Ms.* Problem Child to you."

"Yes, ma'am, Ms. Child," he snarked with a grin before ducking out the door. Aubrey's soft laughter was far more polite than real. She happened to be one of the small handful of people fully aware of my dislike of that name. At least she'd managed to rouse herself from the gawking stupor Harley's arrival had thrown her into.

"Didn't mean to chase him off," Harley said. "But if you have a couple of minutes, I just need to go over a few things with you regarding dorm rules, how to handle visitors, curfews, and scheduling."

"Do you mind if we keep unpacking while we talk?" I asked, more because if I stopped right now, I'd probably collapse. I did better on the move.

"Perfectly fine. Just do your thing and I'll run through my spiel, stop me if you have any questions."

Worked for me. I gave her a thumbs up then headed to the open door of my room. Aubrey followed me rather than head to her room, so that made it easy. Putting the mattress protector on the mattress would be easier with the two of us. So I started there...

Harley wasn't kidding about being quick. The rules were pretty straightforward. We were a high school dorm, no underclassmen—students below tenth year—were allowed in Apollo One. Our library was actually shared by the whole of the Apollo-Volusia dorms. "I'm in the undergraduate program —all resident assistants are graduates of Blue Ivy Prep and currently enrolled in the college-level courses. We have to be in at least our second year to qualify as RAs."

"Means you're legal to buy alcohol. Did they think that all the way through?" Aubrey asked. Despite the bluntness of the statement, it would be hard to take offense at how genuinely amused she sounded as she voiced the question.

"Probably," Harley said with a grin. "Being able to do something and *actually* doing it are two different things. They made sure I could walk and chew gum at the same time."

"Yes, a rocket scientist," Aubrey declared, two fists up before she turned back to help me make the bed. "We like you."

I laughed and so did Harley, thankfully. "Couple more things. This is move-in week. As new enrollment and upperclassmen, you got a head start for moving in. More students will begin arriving tomorrow and every day of the rest of the week. While classes don't officially start for another eight days, there were summer assignments. You got those when you finished enrollment, right?"

"Yep," I said. "Actually, we didn't get them officially until we picked up our class schedules about an hour ago, but they did tell us we would have them and that we would have time to do them. Honestly, I expected there to be a longer line, but everything seemed to be running smoothly."

"Great. If you have any questions, please don't hesitate to ask me. It's not super rare for us to have new students enrolling over the years, but the vast majority have matriculated up through the ranks of the school, and some of us never leave." She double-checked the screen on her tablet. "One last issue: I did receive notice about the potential for press intrusion. Blue Ivy takes the privacy of our students very seriously, so we also have our own on-campus security service that links with the local police department and also shares resources with them."

This was always the fun part, but if Harley was a fan, she never let on. By the time she handed us the tablet to sign that we'd done the meet and greet and received the various bits of information, we were definitely fans of her. I liked that we'd added her contact info to our phones along with her schedule of hours. It was like finding a new friend.

"Honestly, you *can* call me twenty-four-seven. I'm always here, and my phone is always on. That said, I do like to sleep and I'm usually crashing out by eleven most nights, midnight at the latest, and if I'm up before the sun, just bring coffee with you if you're knocking on the door."

"Sounds great," I told her as we walked her to the door. "Thank you for everything."

"We're going to have a great year!" Then she was out.

After I closed the door behind her, I slumped back against it and let out a breath.

"Don't," Aubrey warned. "We still have a ton to do before we can sleep, and if you stay there, you're going to collapse."

She wasn't wrong. "Last one done has to wait to shower," I declared and Aubrey let out a squeak. But fair was fair. I followed her to her room to get her bed sorted out before we split up to unpack.

Dix got back just as I stepped out of the shower. I had the towel wrapped around my middle and another around my hair when I heard Aubrey greeting him. The shower wasn't huge, but the water pressure was kickass and the heat was perfect. The smell of pepperoni, olives, mushrooms, and red sauce with a kiss of garlic hit me all at once and my stomach growled.

Food.

Dix brought pizza back.

"I love you!" I called through the closed door.

"Come out here and say that to my face," he threw back and I laughed.

"Give me five." I toweled off and dragged on an old movie t-shirt from the eighties—I happened to freaking *love Goonies* —and some shorts. Aubrey was already ducking into the bathroom when I was hanging my towels on the door. Too many years of traveling together nipped the need for serious privacy in the bud.

"He got us both our favorites," Aubrey said with a smug grin. "Are you sure we can't bribe him into sticking around as your bodyguard? And by bribing him, I mean you asking. He already said he wanted to be here for you."

I flipped her off and she laughed.

The bedroom was coming together. We still had a few more things to unpack, and we'd probably send for some things now that we had a solid feel on the size of our space, but I was just happy to be here. Dix was sitting out in the living room, in front of that enormous television.

"You know," I said as I stared at the monstrosity. "We really didn't need a sixty-five-inch television."

"No," he said, agreeing with me. "You didn't. That's why I got you a seventy-five inch." When I opened my mouth to protest, he pointed a finger at me. "You will accept it, you will enjoy it, and you will watch all the good things. It's a smart television. I already programmed it and logged into all of your favorite services. You might be going to school here in the sticks, but you deserve to have some high-quality television. Also—I found the espresso machine."

Okay, it was really hard to hold onto any kind of irritation at the high-handedness of getting us a television when he had indeed found the producer of heavenly coffee. I bounced once and then gave him a quick hug.

"Accepted. You're the best."

"I am, in fact," he said with a hint of smugness, "the one and only best, because I also got you both pizza *and* ice cream. You two should be celebrating academic hell—I mean higher education."

"You're hilarious."

"Thank you." He waved me toward the sofa to sit while he carried the pizza boxes over.

Dix hung out until Aubrey finally emerged from her own shower, dressed in comfortable PJs and a smile on her glowing face. I hadn't intended on getting ready for bed this early, but with the pizza, ice cream, and sodas, not to mention everything else, we didn't *have* to leave our room to deal with the dining hall. While I craved the whole experience, I was tired and the experience would be there tomorrow.

All too soon, Dix had to go. "I grabbed a hotel room about thirty minutes away," he said. "I know you wanted me to just drop you and go, but it's only for one night. I'll be close enough to do a run for you tomorrow if you need it, and I'll text before I head back to New York. You sure you don't want me to stay closer?"

I didn't deserve him. Dix rarely got to spoil us, but whenever I was at my mother's in California, he was always there. He was a driver and looked after the cars, but he and Davina were practically family. They were definitely the people I missed when I was on the road.

As much as I'd like it if he stuck around, I couldn't let myself be dependent on it. School was the goal here. School and a sense of normality. "We'll be good, but if anything changes, I absolutely promise to call."

"If she doesn't," Aubrey declared, "we all know I'm not shy."

"I'll walk you down," I volunteered and Aubrey gave a thumbs up.

"I'll find us something to watch," she called. "Don't take too long; it's shark week."

Dix frowned as I closed the door behind us. We'd heard other students arriving, but the hall wasn't busy, thankfully, as we headed to the stairs. "Shark week—should I have—"

"She means actual *Shark* Week," I told him as I grimaced. There were some conversations we *never* needed to have. "You know, like on television with sharks?"

"Thank fuck," he muttered and we both laughed. Downstairs, the air was cooling, but the sun was still up. Probably had another hour before it was full sunset. "All right, kid," he said as I followed him along the path to where he'd parked the dark SUV he'd acquired for the move in. "You have my numbers. You know I'm a phone call away. I'll probably be in the city for another couple of weeks before I head back out to the best coast. You sure about all of this?"

Out here there was still movement. I caught sight of Sydney from earlier heading down a path between buildings, and there was another girl coming in with what looked like her parents. They were all talking animatedly and didn't give us more than a passing glance.

"Nope," I said finally, being honest with both Dix and myself. "But, this is where I want to be, and I'm excited." Despite all the trepidation setting in over the course of the day, I still wanted this. Even more, I wanted to want this, and I'd turned our lives upside down to make this happen. It had been a driving goal for more than a year and we were here, finally! I was going to make this work, and I was going to have a great time doing it.

"Well, when—let's go with *if*—you change your mind. Call me and we'll get you taken care of."

"Thank you, Dix," I said as he paused to open his arms. I accepted the hug. I didn't appreciate him enough. He always picked me up for these hugs. He definitely had several inches on me and in moments like right now, it just made me feel safer. "If you could do one thing for me," I whispered.

"Name it?"

"Bribe Davina into sending me care packages?"

He laughed, then pressed a kiss to my cheek before he set me on my feet. "You got it, gorgeous. Now get that beautiful little ass back inside, and get some rest. I expect you to stay a hot mess while you fine tune that academic brain."

I shot him a cheerful middle finger and he was still grinning as he headed to the car. I folded my arms, waiting for him to get in the car before I turned around to go inside. He honked as he pulled out, and I glanced back to wave.

As the car passed, I locked eyes with a guy standing next to another car in the little lot that I hadn't noticed prior. He was older, had gorgeous blond hair that looked like he'd been raking his hands through it, and held a pair of glasses in hand like he was cleaning them. The fierce frown on his face smothered any need I had to say anything. But since we were literally locking eyes, I summoned up a polite smile.

That just seemed to irritate him more. Right, not my circus or my monkey. I pivoted to head back inside. I didn't know who pissed in his cereal, and I didn't care. Tonight was the first night of the grand adventure.

Thank fuck Dix brought us ice cream.

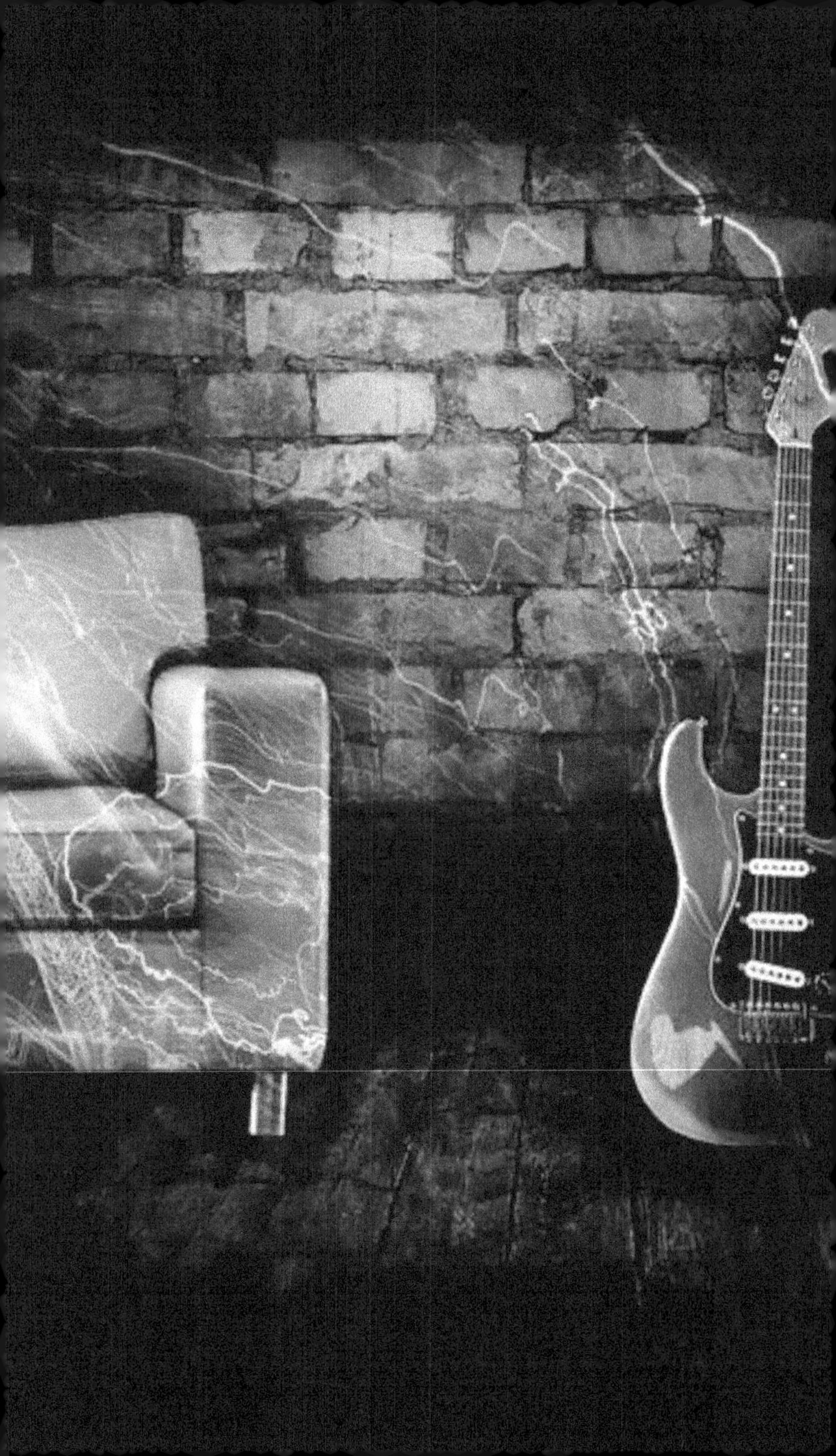

Three

A thudding sound vibrated through the walls. Hammers? Drills? A party? Wait—not a hotel. So probably just movers. Maybe. Despite the day before being the first of a couple of exclusive move-in days for our building, I hadn't paid a lot of attention to the others moving in.

Fuck me, why was I even thinking about this? I needed to pay closer attention. I'd been developing blind spots like a callus to keep me immune to the more abrasive elements around us—particularly the press. I needed to do better here.

That thought kind of dented my psyche like its very own scar, then faded into the background when laughter floated up from the ground via the open windows. I hadn't closed the window in my bedroom the night before. The smell of paint and cleaners wasn't my favorite, and the fresh air had been nice. I wasn't even sure what time it had been when Aubrey and I called it and went to bed. Probably after Aubrey fell asleep and I nudged her.

Rolling onto my back, I stared up at the ceiling. The popcorn texture of the paint job made the white color seem almost gray. The sun was up, but it was still early. I'd been awake until four chatting with my brother, Bronson, in our group message, and now I was up again. Bronson was one of the members of our exclusive "We Could Have Been in a Condom" club, our family chat for all of Dad's spawn.

None of us shared the same mother, and I'd argue we didn't really share a father beyond biology, but I actually liked most of them, even if we were all so very different. There were five of us, well six counting Penelope but she was hardly old enough to have a phone much less be in the chat.

I lost the debate with myself about whether to pick up my phone and check the time. It was almost nine. Had we missed breakfast at the dining hall? Another burst of laughter carried up from outside, and I made a face. They were *loud*. Having entirely *too* much fun. It was early. I needed coffee.

Once my brain decided on that, no way in hell we were going back to sleep. I rolled out of the bed. It was so weird to walk out of the bedroom and into—our place. I paused and looked around the room. We'd arrived with stuff, but it was what we traveled with mostly. Clothes, instruments, a couple of knick knacks and—a handful of photos. There were two that were already hung.

Dix had gone above and beyond while he'd been here. I should probably send him a fruit basket or something. That sounded weird. Still, he'd hung our two favorite photos on the wall. The top was a framed photo of Yvette, me, and Aubrey at our first concert when we were amoebas. The one at the bottom though? It was the three of us at our final concert this past summer.

I loved those photos. I had pics of Bronson, Penelope, Allie, Cam, and Zeke on my phone. But Yvette and Aubrey were the sisters of my heart, my best friends, and the absolute best partners in crime—ever. I would not have survived the last few years without them.

Something banged out in the hallway and it jerked me out of my melancholy thoughts. Right. Too damn early to be getting weepy. It took me about ten minutes to set up a couple of shots of espresso. I was gonna make a real coffee, but fuck it, I was up and it was early and the first day of *normal,* so I was going for a run.

I knocked back the first shot of espresso and headed back to my room. Running was a habit I picked up on our *first* tour break. Six weeks being stationary *anywhere* left me restless as fuck. I couldn't sleep. I couldn't eat. I couldn't—pretty much do anything. I learned that running helped. So, when we weren't on tour, I ran.

Lacing up my shoes, I glanced at the whiteboard we'd attached to the back of my door. Class schedules were already available. The list of books I'd need would be in the bookstore. It opened at—nine. Oh, good, it was already open. Cool, I could stop there *after* my run and grab my books.

Aubrey's schedule was lighter than mine. I'd filled all eight class periods. Her last comment had been, "I'm not taking one thing more than I absolutely need to. I'll be here, we'll party, we'll hang out, and I will absolutely cheer you on, but me and academia do better if we're friends and not trying to be hate lovers, you know?"

I adored her.

Shoes tied, I grabbed my ear pods. Phone in my arm band, I checked my watch and made sure everything was synced. Then I put my hair up. After leaving a note for Aubrey on a sticky attached to the coffee maker, I knocked back that second shot then let myself out of my room.

The hallway was jammed with stuff. Like, legit jammed. There were boxes *everywhere*. A guy exited the room across the hall but he was *way* too old to be a student and the fact he wore "Three Guys All Your Boxes" as a shirt said he was definitely a mover. He grinned at me and I lifted a chin to say hello as I headed for the stairs. There were more movers coming up the stairs.

Seriously, the place was *hopping* with movers. So maybe this was why we had assigned days to move in. I cranked up the music as I played dodge and evade with the guys in the stairwells hauling up televisions, refrigerators, furniture, and more. Didn't they have their own fridges like we did? Then again, some of these seemed bigger.

Outside, the source of the laughter I'd heard lingered around the huge moving trucks that were parked in a row. The movers weren't just for one student; it looked like they were offloading for a lot of them. Huh. A couple of girls were leaning against the rail on the steps, and they both paused when I came out the doors. I summoned up a smile, but they both stared at me with these askance looks. Right, okay. I nodded and focused my attention on my music selection like I hadn't meant to make eye contact.

Finally happy with my music option, I set out away from Apollo One. The campus maps we'd gotten in email told me there was access to a running path not even thirty yards from the dorm's front door. Cars honked as they came up the driveway. The sound cut through the music briefly.

I glanced back at the Mercedes-AMG One that swung around a couple of the trucks. The guy behind the wheel wore a frown and I swore he looked right at me, but after the girls on the steps, I settled for keeping my attention to myself. Run first, make friends later. The guy navigated the tight spots like his vehicle would melt right through them.

Not that I knew shit about cars, just Mercedes had been a tour sponsor and we'd featured that car—in a perfect shade of blue—in one of our videos. Cars were Yvette's thing. I was already jogging before I hit the path, mostly to avoid the sea of people. The fact they all just seemed like staff to move people in was weird. But I was used to a lot of moving bodies during tour setup and breakdown. Roadies were the backbone of a successful concert tour.

Once I was on the path, the sound of cars, laughter, the backup beeps of trucks moving, and the thumping of heavy feet on stairs all faded behind me. Tired faded as I let myself warm up. The music set the perfect rhythm to run. I switched my low on sleep, broken biorhythm, and espresso-fueled brain to autopilot.

The school had five or six different running paths, including an indoor track that was available for students as well as a fully equipped gym. I'd just picked the one closest to my dorm. It peeled off away from the campus and into the trees.

Honestly, I was in love with the trees. It was hard to even see there *were* any buildings once you were on the path. Every now and then, I registered a pole with a light at the top of it and a hot button. Security features. I was picking up speed as a cut from our last live concert album kicked on. I didn't usually like listening to our stuff, but this had friends performing on it with us.

It made me grin as their voices blended with mine. Frankie and Ian were great performers. They were also super nice. Giving them a chance to perform with us at one of our final concerts was a chef's kiss of a moment. I'd never been able to give anyone that kind of *raw* joy before. I lived for it. Riding that memory, I almost missed the stairs ahead of me. The trail actually had *natural* stairs created by roots from the trees and I assumed someone was cultivating, because they were wider than normal stairs and a little shallower, but I picked up speed as I descended them.

Blue Ivy Prep wasn't my first boarding school, but it was the first one *I* picked. The brochures, their website, and the student interviews, had all described such an amazing place that would be perfect for me. I wouldn't stand out here.

Academic performance and achievements unlocked by the school? They had graduates in all walks of life, from entertainment to politics to international finance—whatever, I wasn't gonna recite the whole thing, I wasn't even sure why the videos we'd watched popped into my head, but there'd been one thing I'd seen in a lot of those promo materials that I was feeling right now.

Freedom.

My lungs burned as I pushed myself. Being a singer and a performer, lung capacity was everything. If this run was making me burn, I needed to run harder. The burn worked its way from my lungs to my core, to my legs and finally, the discomfort burned away entirely.

Runner's high was the closest to performance high I'd ever found in "regular life." The mile marker said 3.4 miles as I passed it. Not stopping now.

It was almost two hours after I started the run before I was done. Sweat soaked through my shirt and my shorts. The cooler air under the trees barely touched the heat pouring off of me. I needed food, water, and more coffee. Definitely a shower.

The chaos I'd forgotten about while running seemed to have intensified while I was out. There were cars, trucks, and people just everywhere. I had to do more than dodge to avoid folks, and there was a half-line at the stairwell as people queued up to head inside.

"It's in!" someone yelled from above, and there were shouts and cheers. Okay, I didn't know what it was, but it sounded great. My legs were spaghetti as I started up the stairs.

"Hey!" The blonde girl from the gate said as she paused in her descent to switch and head up the stairs with me. The exhaustion from the run had taken the edge off for real. The smile came naturally. I was genuinely happy to see her. "I just left a note on your door to see if you wanted to grab food."

"I would," I told her, still panting a little because I hadn't fully gotten my breath back. "But I need to go to the bookstore." I'd forgotten to stop before I was back at the dorm. Still, it was such a sweet offer. "I know this will sound dumb," I admitted as we got out of the stairwell and into the hall. The girls who just sort of pushed past us and shot impatient looks suggested I needed a shower maybe even more than I thought I did. "If I don't get on my to do list, I won't, and then one day becomes two and I'm behind and never catch up. So—maybe we can—do it tomorrow?"

"That sounds great." She motioned to my phone. "Can I put my number in? The school app lets us message each other, but I'd rather just text."

"Yeah, sure." I unlocked the phone, then fanned myself. It was warmer inside with all these bodies and no breeze. "Sorry, sweaty."

She laughed. "No problem. Olivia still thinks I'm lying, so I'm going to let her see us at lunch tomorrow."

I couldn't remember who Olivia was, so I just smiled. "Sounds great. Thanks. If I can't make it, I'll text—oh..." I hesitated. "Where is the dining hall from here?"

Sydney—thank fuck she put her name in with her number—laughed then tapped her nose. "I'd say follow this but sometimes it smells awful. Just remember, pizza day? Eat *anywhere* else. I don't know who taught them to make pizza, but it wasn't anywhere in Brooklyn or Chicago. You go out front, hang a left, then head up the hill. There are signs, just follow it to Grayson—mailroom, dining hall, and the commons are there. They also have a dining court with a mini-mall on the other side of the commons, but if you want coffee from the shop, get the app and order it there. The line is a joke, but Dancing Goats has the *best* coffee."

Sounded good to me and a lot of info. "Thanks!"

"Sure thing. See you later!"

Then she was gone. Pivoting, I reached for my key card and slammed right into a guy. It was like impacting a wall even if he didn't seem that much bigger than me. Definitely taller, but he wasn't built all big and muscly, leaner. The art on his left arm caught my eye as I tried to get my breath back. Outside of myself, I hadn't noticed a lot of tats on the other kids.

"Sorry," I said. "Didn't see you."

"Try turning around before you move then." The comment was so dismissive it caught me off guard. "Not everyone is going to move *for* you."

The fuck? I hadn't even said anything. Not to mention, dude *didn't* move.

"Like I said," I tried again. I mean maybe he hadn't had any coffee. His pale gray eyes seemed like something right out of a watercolor painting. The dark hair really made his eyes pop. So did his sun-tanned skin. "Sorry, I was distracted and didn't see you."

His eyes narrowed as he stared at me. "That's it?"

What the hell else did he want? "Did you want an autograph?" I mean hell, I apologized. Did he need it in writing?

If anything, his expression turned even chillier. Right. It was a pity, too. The guy was gorgeous in that pouty, bad boy kind of vibe that worked so well in movies and television. Pretty but an asshole. Good to know.

"Okay, Hot Shot, you do you. I need a shower." I gave him a salute and then walked around him. I narrowly missed colliding with another guy coming out of the door of the room next to mine. To be fair, this guy had his face locked to someone else's and neither of them were looking where they were going. Public PDAs were a go here. Good to know.

I snagged the notes off the door as I let myself in and crumpled the paper up. Since I'd already run into Sydney, I could just toss it.

"Girl, please tell me that hot and sweaty look is because you had sex or something?" Aubrey said on a yawn from where she leaned against the counter next to the coffee maker. The sweet scent of nirvana greeted me and I laughed.

"Yeah, cause that's what I get up early to do," I retorted as I shut the door. "Make me a cup?"

I jogged right toward my room. The more I cooled down, the stickier and ickier I felt. I desperately needed a shower.

"You need sex," she yelled after me. "Or a therapist." That joke was old, but familiar. It wrapped around me with the familiarity of a hug. A hug that slapped you on the ass and pinched you, but still a hug. It was a movie quote, but for the life of me I couldn't even remember what it was from or where we'd heard it.

I was still laughing as I shut the door. I needed something, but it wasn't either of those she just mentioned. First it was a shower, then it was coffee. After that, we could take over the world. I tossed the crumpled paper into the trash and stripped.

Go normal me! Day one, winning.

Kissy Kats

Kissy Kats, did you hear the latest about Torched's fall from grace? Turns out that *break* of theirs may not have been their idea after all. Their label, it would seem, is already on the hunt for the next big thing, something clearly the problem child and her BFFs aren't any longer. So ask yourselves, are they taking a "break" or were they just cut loose? Kiss. Kiss. More soon.

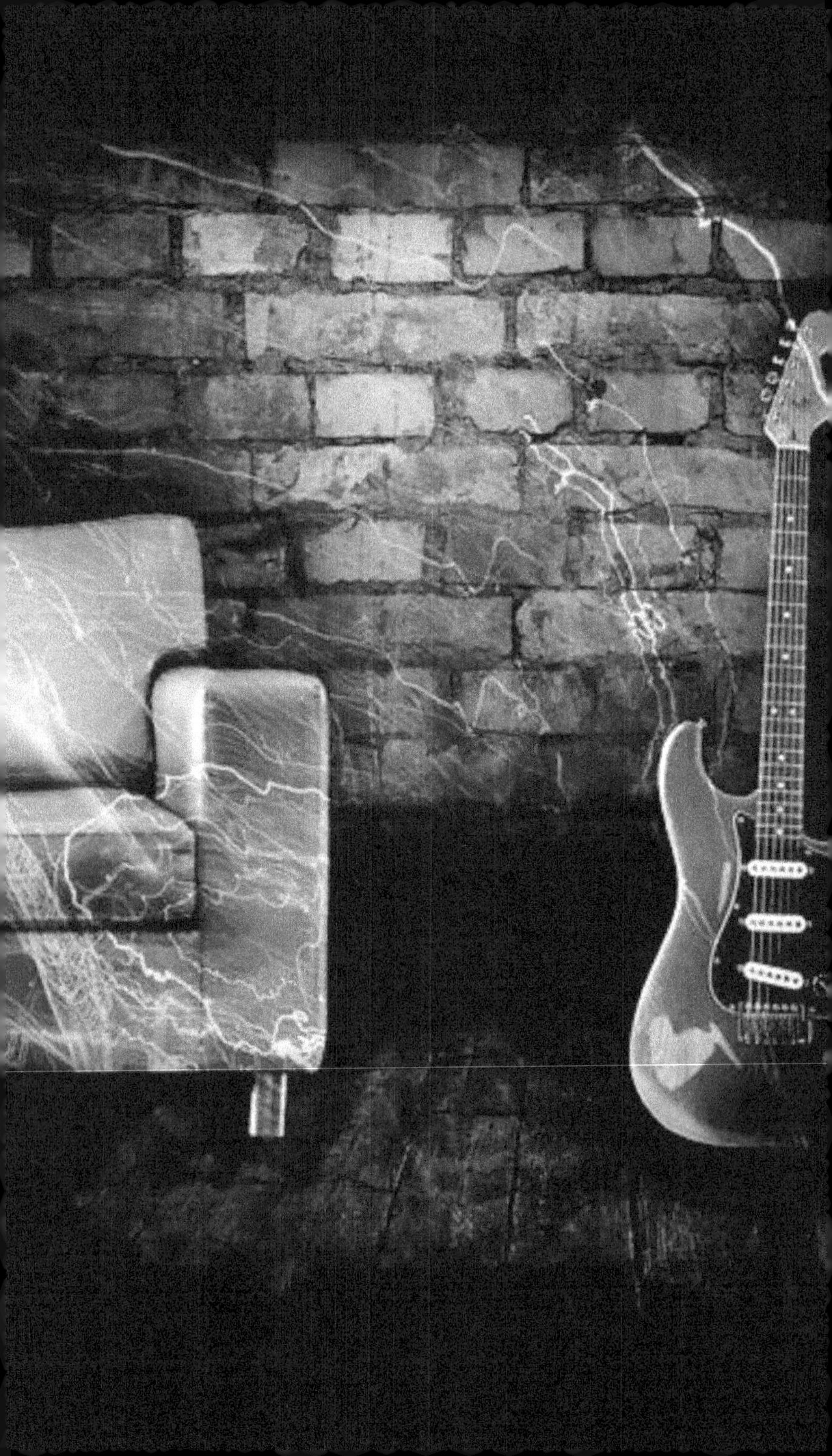

Four

Two days before classes officially started, I dragged Aubrey with me down to the dining hall.

"I hate you right now," she announced as we descended the steps. She was still in her pajamas.

Not that I could say much; I was in shorts and a tank top. It was a warm day and I'd debated going to find a tree to read under, but there were so many people. Reading under a tree sounded great for a movie, not so much in real life. I'd tried the day before and I swore every other person paused to stare at me a moment. Worse, they didn't seem to like what they saw.

It was one thing to be under observation. I was used to it. But I didn't like it *here*. Not...not when I wanted to be "normal." Maybe I should have dyed my hair back to blonde. Yeah, that was a wrenching feeling I didn't like.

"I don't care, I've tried to have lunch with Sydney three times so far. She's canceled once and I had to cancel to meet with the guidance counselor, this after I *forgot*." I still couldn't believe I'd just passed out and forgotten all about that lunch. I'd managed to make one possible friend and I was *failing*.

"You were up all night, then went running like a freak, then back on the phone with Bronson." Outside, Aubrey raked a hand through her long dark hair. I love that she could do "rolled out of bed" tousled so perfectly and I looked like a shit show.

A shit show with bright blue hair, so yeah, I got looks. But I could pretend that those stares didn't faze me. On the road, I learned to tune it out. If I needed to do that here, then I'd do it here. Not that it helped the unsettled feeling from earlier. "Classes start soon and we've barely done anything together," I retaliated.

"And you don't want to sit by yourself if she cancels." We weren't really hurrying, but the languid comment stopped me in my tracks and I made a face at her. "Yeah, that glare doesn't work on me." She wagged a finger playfully. "And I don't hear you arguing with me."

"Ugh." I pivoted. "I'm not saying you're right."

"You're not saying I'm wrong either." Aubrey's laughter warmed the air. Then she slung an arm around my shoulder. "Don't hate."

"I'm not hating. I just—this is a little harder than I thought it would be. Like, how do you decide *where* to sit?" For the most part, I'd been chickening out of going to the dining hall. Or just running in and grabbing takeout. Most of the time I'd had a good reason, but the first day I went in and everyone stared at me made the idea of lingering just...no. Then I found out we could get delivery, as long as we let Harley know it was coming.

I might have never come down here again except, I felt *really* bad that I slept right through lunch the day before. The day before that she'd had to cancel at the last minute because of something with her mother. She hadn't gone into details and it was none of my business, but I was already down there and it was like eating in a fishbowl.

Ugh.

"You pick a table and sit down. If you want to sit with people you sit with people, and if you don't—you don't." She bumped my hip with hers before dropping her arm from my shoulders to thread her arm with mine. "C'mon, you and I both know you've done this before."

"Yes, but that was before, and I hated it then. Most of the time I'd read a book, especially when I got old enough to understand all the bullshit gossip."

"I get that, been there and done that." Yeah, Aubrey's and Yvette's parents had their own issues and scandals that had been featured in gossip columns. It was one of the reasons we'd *bonded* in the first place. "I remember the first time I sat at your table, you know."

Nostalgia unfurled in me at the memory. "I think you were already sitting there when I got to my table."

"But it was your table. Like, three whole people warned me it was your table and I was like, she isn't here *now*."

"What did you say to me when I got there?" I had to think about that for a minute. "Oh, right, 'I heard this was your table,' and I said, 'Sure is, even has my name on it.'"

Aubrey laughed. "Yep, under the table, so I said, 'got it.' Then I slid down and wrote my name under yours and said, 'Guess we have to share.'"

"And I said, 'Yeah, guess so.'" And that was that. Aubrey and I were pals. We had been since like six, but still. It was my third boarding school and my first real friend. Yvette enrolled later that semester.

We arrived at the door to the dining hall, and I looked out over all the scattered tables. There were two seaters, four seaters, places where they had round tables, square tables, and tables that had been jammed together for larger groups.

There were literally tables every-fucking-where. There were also more people in the dining hall than I'd seen at any other time. Holy shit. This dining hall was for the junior and senior classes, right? There had to be two hundred people in here. Then again, the dining area was L shaped and I couldn't see around the corner.

"See your friend?" Aubrey asked and I blinked. Right. Sydney. I'd almost forgotten. Maybe we could just live on takeout and then never come here again.

That would be normal, right?

"No, but let's grab food and then we can walk around." Anything to not look at how many people were in here. We'd had concerts with thousands in attendance, so a few hundred should be fine?

Only I didn't have to *talk* to the few thousand. Just—sing and perform. The jitters in my stomach had jitters. As it was, we headed for the kitchen line and studied what was on the hot plates and ready for serving. Today was chicken and chicken.

Oh, and apparently there was chicken.

Chicken strips and French fries. That sounded amazing. Aubrey got a salad with grilled chicken. Right, the healthy choice. I went for the artery hardening. Live hard, die young, and leave a beautiful corpse.

The phrase popped up in my head. Probably not the thing to do.

"Hey!" a familiar voice said happily behind me, and I pivoted to see Sydney, panting and out of breath. "Oh man, I thought I was going to miss you and then I'd have had to show up at your door with pizza and apologies. That might be weird. I figure we shouldn't dorm pizza date until at least we've had a few regular meals."

I laughed. In some ways, Sydney reminded me of Frankie, and it wasn't just the blonde hair. "Come on and grab your food," I told her.

"She was worried we would miss you, too," Aubrey offered as she scooted forward to make room for her.

"Man, I would have been bummed," Sydney admitted as she got the same thing as Aubrey. The healthier ration. Right, I'd worry about that later. I was running, which meant I could eat the deep-fried food.

We got drinks, swiped our cards to pay for food, and then turned back to the tables. There didn't seem to be any empty ones.

"Come on," Sydney said. "I see a spot." She plowed ahead and probably assumed we'd just follow. To be fair, we absolutely did. More than one pair of eyes seemed to track us, and I did my best to nod whenever I accidentally caught someone's gaze.

"Make way," someone commented behind me. "Royalty has arrived." The tone was so derisive that it stung. Better to not look. They could totally be talking about someone else.

The hum of conversation rose and fell as we passed, and it wasn't until Sydney stopped at a pair of square tables jammed together with four other people already sitting there that I blinked.

Oh.

"KC, Aubrey," Sydney said as she slid her tray onto the table and the four people we interrupted all looked at us. Two of the four were male and the other two female. One was blonde and looked enough like Sydney that they had to be sisters. "This is—in order—Olivia, Lily, Soren, and Finley. They're mostly cool when they aren't staring like gawping fish."

Olivia was the first one to shake it off and she glared at Sydney. "That's really them."

"I *told* you," Sydney said in a serene voice. "Now, stop embarrassing me." She glanced at us and thank fuck I wasn't the only one standing there a little uncertainly. "Seriously, ignore them. They will be fine once they process. They just thought I made it up that I'd met you."

I chuckled. "She definitely did meet us, and I don't get the impression that she makes stuff up like that." Sure, I'd just met Sydney, but she'd been nice so I'd stick up for her.

"I can't believe you're actually going to school here," Lily said, her expression faintly puzzled.

"Had to go somewhere," Aubrey told her as she opened her water before taking a bite of her salad. "It's been a few years since we've even been in a school, so be prepared for some social faux pas. In fact, I say we make socially awkward and inelegant the new 'it thing.'"

Finley laughed. "That would be cool, though I don't see it happening. There are people who go here who grade their cool factor by how many followers they have on TikTok and Instagram."

"Not something they're going to have a problem with," Olivia retorted. "Also, no offense, not a huge fan of the music. I liked your first album but not the next two."

"Olivia," Sydney muttered. "Rude."

I laughed. "Actually, I kind of like the bluntness. We didn't like our third album that much either. The fourth was much better."

"Haven't really listened to it," Olivia said. "I'll check it out. Soren, stop staring."

"Sorry, I'm trying to figure out who they are. The blue-haired chick looks familiar. You guys are all acting weird."

There was a beat of silence and then all of us cracked up, even Sydney.

"We're just KC and Aubrey. First year here." I kind of liked that anonymity.

"Clearly, you're way more interesting. Also, that hair is gonna get you in trouble in a couple of days." He dug into the barbecue chicken in front of him. "Is it a wig or the real thing?"

"Real thing and it should be fine, I got permission."

"Oh man, I want permission to have blue hair." Sydney sounded wistful, but Olivia laughed.

"Tell Mom. I'm sure that would go over real well."

Sydney flicked a lettuce leaf at her, and something in me unclenched. It was normal, and after that bit of awkwardness, they switched to discussing upcoming schedules, sports, and more. They included us like we'd always been sitting there.

It was nice.

Later, back in our room, I made myself pull out the laptop and set it up so I could work on the summer assignments, but I couldn't seem to keep my attention on the reading.

So, I opened my email because that was conducive to getting work done. There was an email from Bronson, a forward of raunchy memes that just made me laugh. I had a few other emails including one from the school counselor.

She'd sent it to my personal and academic addresses. It had a new class schedule in it and an apology, but they'd had to shift some of my classes around. It didn't look like I'd lost any classes. If I had any issues, I could contact her office, and all future communications would come through the academic email.

Right, I needed to remember to add that one to my phone. The next email made me grin. "Hey Aubrey," I yelled. "Frankie sent us another recording."

"Cool," she called through the open doors of our shared bathroom. "I'll be there in a sec."

I couldn't wait to hear what the new recording would be. I'd meant it when I told her and Ian to send me music. We'd made similar offers in the past, not everyone took us up on it and fewer still had the chops to keep going.

This was fun. The first notes from the new song were truly

angst-filled; the ability to make a guitar *cry* was intense. Ian's voice was always strong, determined, and supportive. I kind of loved that about their dynamic. Frankie seemed to be gaining in that strength. She had a really great voice, a perfect counterpoint to Ian's. When she wobbled, he lifted. When she soared, he was right there.

Fuck, it was such a beautiful song.

Music really was my happy place.

Two days later, I groaned at my alarm going off at too fucking early in the morning. It was the first day of classes and I'd been up half the night again. I'd video-chatted with Bronson for an hour and finished up the last of my assignments.

Rolling out of bed, I staggered into the bathroom and then got dressed on autopilot. It didn't matter that I had just woken; mentally, I flipped off my brother. Bronson had said I would be too wired to turn off the alarm and go back to sleep.

He wasn't wrong. The dick.

I'd be more charitable about him later. Like, after coffee.

I made one shot of espresso and knocked it back before I put my headphones on and headed out to the trail. The sun wasn't up yet, but it was a ribbon on the horizon.

Today was going to be a great day.

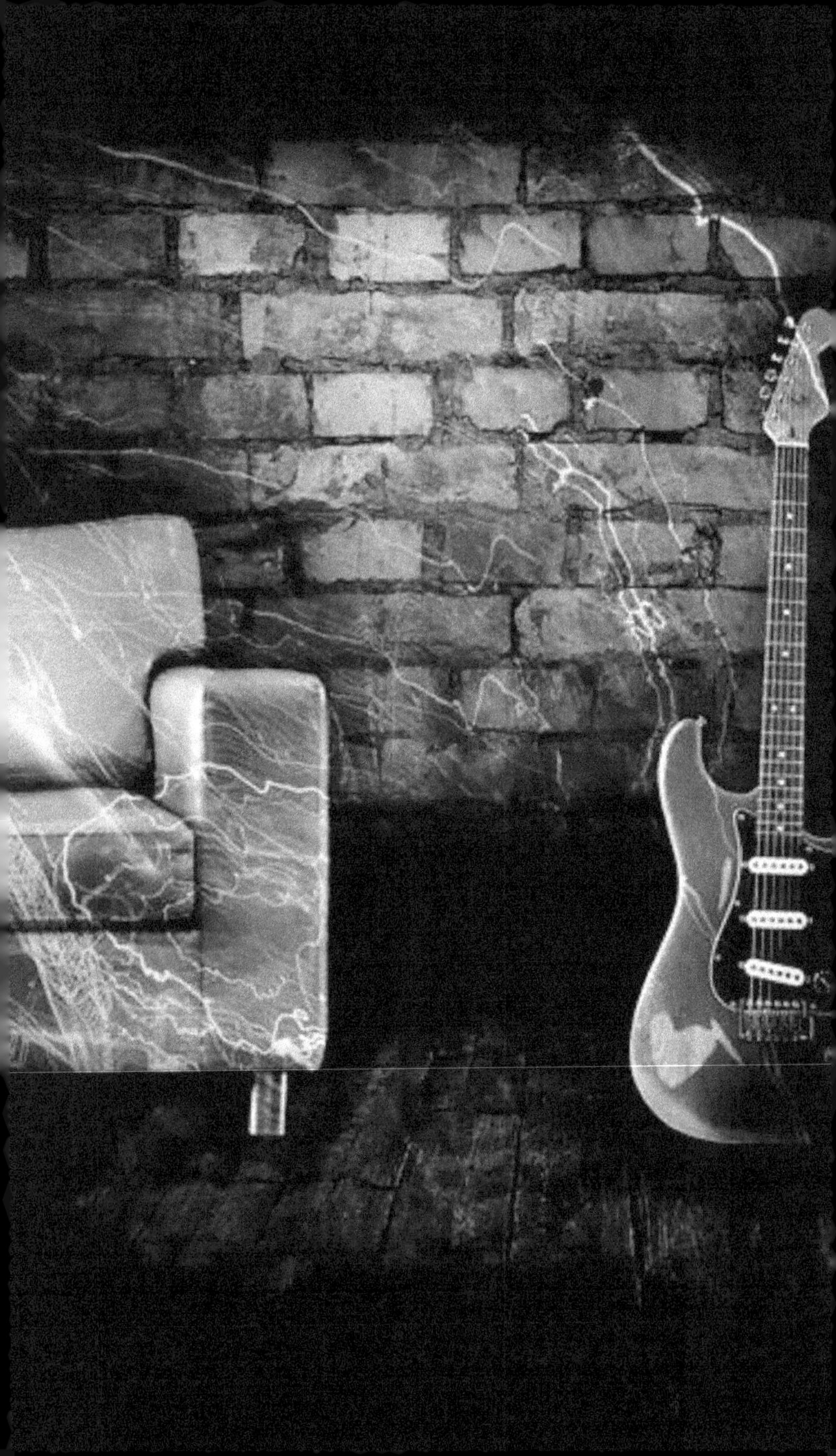

Five

I cut my run short at three miles. I wanted time to shower and do my hair before I put on the uniform. Excited and terrified pretty much defined me. The lack of sleep the night before, coupled with the early waking, just added to the twisty feeling in my gut. It didn't matter how much I reminded myself that I wanted to be here.

Back at the dorm, I took the stairs two at a time. I went straight for the water to hydrate. Aubrey was still dead to the world when I climbed in the shower. I took a little extra time to shave everything, scrub my face, and not to mention wash and condition my hair.

The hot water had worked out most of the muscle soreness from the run, not that the exertion had done much to help with the wired sensation invading my soul. I was more hopped up than I was an hour before a show.

Coffee. Food. But first, I needed to do my makeup and then my uniform. The internal debate of how much was too much in the cosmetics department raged in my head. I'd gotten some navy blues to go with the uniform rather than the hair or the Torched aesthetic. No gloss or glitter here, sober, a little more serious—academic and shit.

Maybe I should have gotten glasses. I didn't need to wear them but...no that was fake. It was good I didn't get glasses. I'd skip the cosmetics altogether except I would be too pale in the darker colors of the uniform. There was a teal stripe to offset the navy one on the tie, which was perfect, but everything else was pretty sober and serious, from the white button downs to the dark navy slacks and skirts.

I went with a skirt for day one and because it was still warm enough. Thankfully, I could skip the hose or socks and just slid my feet into a pair of black ballet flats. Apparently, you could wear heels, but they didn't recommend them, especially on the uneven hills of the campus. Fine by me, I had a lot of hustling to do.

I was ready a full ninety minutes before class. Plenty of time to get breakfast. Did I go ahead and go get it or make coffee and wait for Aubrey?

"Girl, anyone ever tell you that you needed to take a chill pill?" Aubrey's sleep-laden voice held more than a little humor. "I can't believe you're up and ready—also, the hair looks fucking fantastic. Nailed it."

I put a hand up to touch it. "I was trying to go for neat and presentable, since, you know—blue."

She laughed. "I do know blue. Give me fifteen minutes to get dressed. Perks of showering last night and not running my ass off at dawn."

Since we had a plan, I got our coffees made while she got dressed. When she descended the short steps, I grinned so hard it made my face hurt. She looked fantastic. "Let me fix the tie," I murmured, correcting the knot so it lay flatter.

"Thank you," she said with a huffed sigh before she claimed her coffee. Like me, she'd chosen a skirt and had similar black ballet flats. "Tell me you feel weird in this outfit. It's so...conservative."

"I dunno, I kind of like it, and there's something cool about being in a button-down shirt with a tie on." I smoothed my own down. "And not having to worry about *what* to wear."

While the button-down shirts were a requirement, we had our pick on sleeve length. I'd gone with long because it covered up my tattoos. While I loved body art, it wasn't exactly legal in most states for kids my age to *get* them. I got my first one when I was twelve. Every single one had a story.

"You are so weird sometimes," Aubrey commented. "But I love you."

"I know," I told her with a grin. "You're here."

"Yes, I am. I'm sure I will hate you by the end of the week."

"Wow," I said slowly. "I figured it would be at the end of our first day."

We both grinned and finished the coffees before heading down for breakfast. Even with my book bag over one shoulder and aware that today was the first day of classes, I was *not* ready for just how freaking packed the dining hall was. What I'd thought was busy at lunch the other day had nothing on this.

"Yogurt?" Aubrey was throwing me a lifeline because we did need to eat, but all at once my appetite was just gone. It happened before shows, too.

"And some fruit." Keep it healthy.

"Granola." That would keep it filling. Aubrey had all the good ideas today. I pivoted to follow her to a different line. It took effort to keep from colliding with other students who were also hustling to get their asses from one side of the room to the other. If Sydney or Olivia or—fuck what were the guys' names? An S one and an F one... right? *Note to self, make a list of the names so I can learn them.*

Anyway, if they were here, I wouldn't find them in this mob. Even though we'd gotten to the dining hall with an hour until class, it took another twenty-five minutes to get food, swipe our cards, and get out. We weren't even getting anything huge.

"I'm buying supplies for the room," Aubrey declared as we slipped outside to eat our yogurt. "No way in hell I'm going to get up a whole hour early to come down here and eat. I have to draw a line somewhere."

"That's your line?" I asked, amused, as I dipped the eco-friendly spoon into the yogurt I'd swirled with granola and raspberries. The food was good; the insanity in that dining hall, not so much. I thought anonymity would be easier with more people. Wow, I'd been wrong.

"That is my line," she told me firmly. "One of us has to be the brains."

"Clearly, that isn't me." I absolutely agreed with her. Brains were not my strong suit right now. Even eating hurriedly, time seemed to rush past us like we were dawdling.

"You ready for this?" Aubrey asked after we disposed of our containers in the recyclables bin. Another neat feature of the campus, every trash can also boasted a recyclable container next to it.

"I should be," I said, more hopeful than not. "This is what we wanted—I mean, I know I started it, but you agreed and it's what we worked toward." I swore my heart was hammering at a breakneck pace, and it was a lot warmer out here than it had been when I was running.

"It's absolutely what we worked toward," Aubrey said, then she opened her arms and I met her hug with one of my own. "You got this. I'll see you at lunch. Don't go nuts."

"Right," I said. "You're the one who likes it when things go nuts."

She laughed. "Break a leg."

"You too." I adjusted my book bag then checked my schedule against the map. My first class was three buildings over. We'd had a couple of classes together *before* the abrupt schedule change. Now, we had none. I hated that. But then I was also taking more classes than she was, and she'd put two study hours into her day.

I could have done that, I supposed, but I got excited when I went over the options. I was almost to the building when my phone lost its damn mind and alerts blew up over my screen. Sliding to the side so I didn't block the doors, I flipped to the newsfeed.

The photos were classy. Mom and her boyfriend photographed somewhere on a beach in the Caribbean, if I had to go by the water. Mom was clearly topless in a few of them, though most of the sites had that part blurred out. Well, it was hardly the first time the gossips had a blast with Mom's antics. Nothing for me to worry about...

Then the next article in the list, six down from the first caught my eye. "Starlit Mom cavorts while Problem Child enrolls in rehab center?"

Kill me.

I closed that screen then fired off a note to our manager. He wouldn't be thrilled, but I'd rather they ran the interference with the press on this one. The last thing I did was send a note to Yvette and Aubrey in our group chat before I put my phone on do not disturb. Not only did I not want to get interrupted in class, I really didn't want to see any other newsfeeds today.

I had a minute to spare when I slid in the door of my first class. Thankfully, I wasn't the last person to arrive. Hot Shot, the asshole from my dorm, came in right behind. I fumbled for a quick smile, but he didn't even glance at me. Right, asshole. Good looking asshole, but still an asshole.

The teacher glanced over from his desk. "Take the last of the free seats," he instructed. "Everyone get comfortable. Where you are sitting is where you will be for the rest of the year."

Back row worked for me. I was still a little too hopped up, and the galloping pace of my heart made it hard to just slow my breathing down. If I thought the back row would buy me some space from Hot Shot, I was wrong. He took the desk right next to mine. The fact he never *once* glanced in my direction seemed almost forced. Like he didn't *want* to see me there.

The teacher rose and crossed to the door, which he closed. "I'm Mr. Baer and we are going to be studying macroeconomics this semester."

He was passing out stacks of paper as he spoke.

"We're going to go over our syllabus today for the semester. Please note that every single due date for projects, papers, assignments, *and* tests are listed on the syllabus. There will be no excuses accepted for turning work in late or missing a test. If you are late, you will lose a full letter grade for each day you fail to turn something in. Plan ahead, plan well, don't be a statistic."

Oh. The stack of paper that made up the syllabus was several sheets long, and he wasn't kidding about the assignments being detailed, including all of the reading material. By the time we were dismissed to move onto our next class, my nerves had ballooned to full-blown panic, then deflated to exhaustion.

That was just one class.

I had seven more to go.

While I'd hoped to see at least one or two friendly faces in my classes, I'd been doomed to disappointment. The only person I recognized so far was Hot Shot. Not sure I'd call *him* a perk.

He popped up in my second and third classes but appeared absent from my fourth. The lit class should at least be fun, even if we had a shit ton of reading to do. It was also the next class where I actually recognized someone. Only instead of being a student, he actually seemed to be one of the teachers. It was the pissed off guy from our very first night here.

Great. A grumpy, sexy teacher. He seemed almost too young to be one, but his attitude disagreed.

Another man entered with a fairly easy smile and salt-and-pepper hair. "Sorry for almost being late," he said as he came in. "I'm Mr. Cohen. This is Mr. Malone—though he will tell you to call him Ramsey. Mr. Malone will be my assistant this semester. He's excellent at languages and literature, so be sure to pay attention. Before we get started today, though, let's see how much some of you remember from last year and where—" He paused for a moment, his gaze on me. "Where some of our newcomers are at. Books and bags under your desks. Pens only."

Pens only for—oh. Ramsey was handing out large sealed booklets.

"Be sure to read carefully, apply your knowledge, and then write clearly and coherently. You will not get any credit if we can't read your answers." He checked his watch, and I tried to summon a smile for the blond assistant, but he barely gave me a look as he slapped the booklet down on my desk.

He could be Captain America with that chiseled jaw, but he seemed to be more Iceman in his demeanor. Damn. This school had a lot of pretty people in it.

"Everyone has a book?" Mr. Cohen asked. "Excellent. No talking. You may begin. Turn in the booklet when you are done. You have until the end of the period."

There were more than a few groans as the sealed booklets were slit open, and I was probably one of them. The very first question on the test was about a book they'd read the previous year. It even said so. There were no instructions on what to do if you hadn't read it.

Then again, he said it was a test to assess where I was *now*. With that in mind, I squared my shoulders and wrote, *I have not read this work, so I cannot formulate an answer to this question.*

The weight of a stare pressed in on me, but I kept my head down. I didn't have time to wonder who was looking at me. By the end of the first page, I'd forgotten about the sensation. By the end of the third page, my brain hurt and my fingers protested, but I kept going.

I'd barely finished the last question when Mr. Cohen called, "Time's up."

Ramsey claimed the booklet from me. The sounds from the room rushed back in as students stood and began to filter out. My head hurt and my hand protested, but I made myself stand up. I'd gotten stiff from how focused I'd been.

It took me a minute to get my stuff together, and it wasn't long until I was the only student left. It was lunch and I wasn't even sure I was up for heading back to the dining hall. The clearing of a throat reminded me I wasn't alone.

Ramsey stood at the door, his expression flinty. "If you wouldn't mind, Miss..."

"KC—I mean Crosse. Sorry, Crosse is my last name but KC is fine."

"Miss Crosse, I have a short window for lunch, so I would appreciate it if you didn't waste it." He motioned me to the door.

"Sorry, just trying to get my stuff together." The apology was automatic, but the impatience in his expression as he gave me a pointed look had me raising my hands. "I'm going. I'm going."

Apparently, whatever pissed him off the day I moved in was still pissing him off. Pity. He was kind of cute, if you could ignore the glaring and sour attitude. Pretty people who were also pretty awful were better seen and not heard. Which really sucked, 'cause I could so crush on him. Crushing on a teacher was pretty cliché though, but I could work it in as a lyric. As soon as I was out the door, he brushed past me like the room behind us was on fire. The door half-slammed, or maybe it was just heavy.

Whatever.

I legit did not have the energy to even worry about him or his attitude. I was supposed to meet Aubrey for lunch, but I needed *time*. Time to just shut down and reset. I sent her a text then went to find where my next class was. I sat down on the floor, hugged my book bag to my chest and closed my eyes.

I'd taken longer naps in worse places. Thirty minutes of shuteye and then I'd be ready to deal with the afternoon.

Today wasn't so bad.

Nope. Not so bad at all.

Something hit my foot hard, and I jerked my eyes open to stare into the most devastating pair of green eyes. They were like a haunted forest, shrouded in mysteries and shadows. All I wanted to do was be *that* girl and plunge into them to see —everything.

"You do know that this isn't a park bench, right?" A cutting, feminine voice dragged my attention away from those gorgeous eyes to stare at the perfect girl standing next to him. Dark hair, stunning amber-colored eyes, perfect tan, and her cosmetics absolutely on point. She was as stunning as a model, but lusher with generous curves. Her lips, however bright red they were, twisted into a superior smirk.

"This is a school," she continued, enunciating each word

clearly, "not the back row of your low-rent concerts. You don't just go to sleep out here. That's what your room is for. Idiot."

My sleepy brain reacted to the verbal slap with a curled lip. "Bitch, our concerts have never been low-rent. I guarantee you the tickets cost more than that red whore lipstick you're sporting."

Right, I shouldn't have lost my temper. I knew better. Say nothing. Respond to nothing. Don't let them make you sweat. I caught the phone from the corner of my eye. Yeah, the little light told me they were filming. Great.

Something wet splashed against me. "Oops," one of the other girls with them said. The wet and sticky clung to my jacket and spilled onto my white shirt. Fuck, it was red. Which just spread the stain out.

The dark-haired girl laughed, and nothing humorous or kind existed in that laugh. "Remind me to call the janitors next time," she said to the green-eyed guy at her side who watched me with narrowed eyes and an almost unreadable smile that did nothing to lighten the rest of his expression. "They know better than to let the trash just lay in the halls..."

Wiping the expression from my face, I gave her a perfectly bland smile as I rose and peeled the jacket off. I was going to have to do something about the shirt. "You really should be kinder to yourself. Calling yourself trash is a negative affirmation, no matter how accurate..."

Shock registered in her smug eyes, but a sound echoed down the hall: the chime indicating time to go to class. The door to the classroom I'd been resting outside of opened.

"Good afternoon," the teacher said, then glanced down at me. "Are you all right, Miss Crosse?"

Fake it until you make it. "I'm great," I told him with a smile I definitely didn't feel. "Just need to get cleaned up."

I ignored my audience and the phone still pointed right at me.

"Excellent. Miss Webber," the teacher said. "You know better than to film on campus. Let's see it…"

It was too late though; there was a sucking sound that happened when an upload completed, followed by the little ding. Yep, that footage was out there. But it was nice of the teacher to try. Since my audience didn't seem to be moving on their own, I pushed between them and went toward the bathrooms, aware of a set of green eyes that tracked every move I made.

I was three for three with the good-looking jerks so far.

Tattler Blast

One thing's for sure ... **Jennifer Crosse** is definitely carrying a few extra pounds—not sure if it's a baby, then again, we haven't gotten to see much of her in form-fitting outfits lately.

Crosse was spotted leaving a Pilates class in a form-fitting outfit (see right), and from the side view, there are even odds on her uterus being sold out this summer.

To be fair, it's the first decent shot we've gotten of the actress's belly since we caught sight of her leaving her physician's office in Los Angeles with what looked like a sonogram in her hand (see below). The actress has been in a relationship with adult film star, and *much* younger man, Johnny Pound for the last three years.

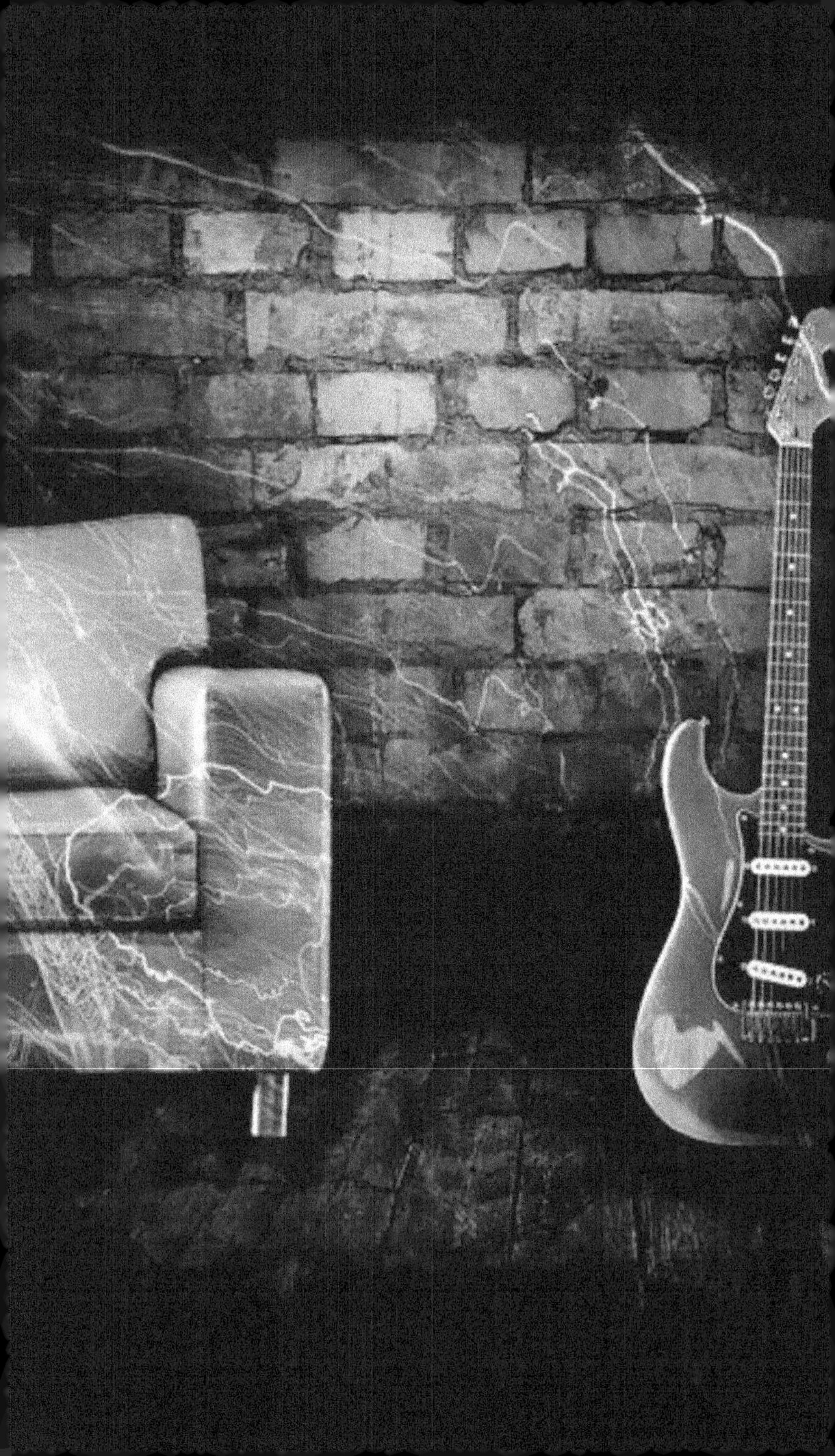

Six

Today *sucked*.

All it lacked was someone putting gum in my hair or the skies opening up to rain on me dramatically as I walked back to my dorm. I ran a hand through my hair as I headed up the stairs just to be sure. The sunny, gorgeous weather seemed to be mocking me *and* my mood.

The red crap had come off of the jacket all right, but the shirt was ruined. I'd buttoned my suit coat to cover the stain to the best of my ability, but it still felt icky against me.

Resisting the urge to flip the sky off, I just kept climbing. When the final class ended, a lot of kids had all moved like they were in a hurry to get—somewhere. I lingered at the end of the last class so I could ask Ms. Dunham about the psychology reading, only the longer I waited, so did Hot Shot from the hallway with the pale gray eyes and the shitty attitude.

I motioned for him to go first, but he waved me onward. No, I'd rather *not* have this discussion in front of a stranger. It grew clearer by the moment that he wouldn't be leaving before me. When Ms. Dunham glanced at me, I mouthed that I'd email her. Then I just left while she talked to the other student.

Once in my room, I let the book bag slide off my arm and hit the floor. I kicked off the ballet slippers and padded barefoot up the short steps to my room and fell on the bed. Taking off the uniform would probably be a good idea, but I was too fucking tired to care. The shirt was toast anyway. I also had extra uniforms in the closet.

Face down against the comforter, I screamed. The day had just sucked. Not only had there been a test in the lit class, there had been another in calculus and a *third* in biology, and that one included labeling internal organs on a rat.

So, so, so gross.

Why did I think this was going to be so easy? After my second scream left my throat hurting, I caught the sound of the door opening. A thud indicated that Aubrey had dropped her bag too, and then a couple of minutes later, she bounced onto the bed next to me.

"Bad day?" I could almost *hear* the smile in her voice. If I had the energy, I'd flip her off.

"It sucked," I mumbled, not lifting my head. My voice was muffled, but I was pretty sure Aubrey would understand.

"Aww, tell me who I'm killing and in how many pieces." She made the offer in that same even tone she always had when it came to me or Yvette complaining.

"No one really," I admitted after thinking about it, and I had to think about it. Even my *thoughts* were tired. Could brains get tired? Sure, of course they could. It made sense that brains would get tired. "I hated today."

Humming softly, Aubrey stroked her fingers through my hair. In no time, she loosened the clips where I'd pinned the top back in a little flip roll thing that had been super cute this morning. Now it made my scalp just fucking ache. The light stroke of her nails against my head threatened to knock me out.

"I'm sorry today sucked," she said gently. "Mine wasn't so bad. Lot of work to get caught up on, and I legit forgot how fucking boring it is to sit in a classroom and focus when the teacher talks in a monotone voice and takes their time to pronounce each word exactly."

I swore each word after *monotone* dragged out and elongated like she spoke in slow motion. "Ugh," I managed to grunt. "I'd have passed out." It probably came out mmmph, mmmph, mmmph, which was a little rude, so I rolled over and looked up at her where she sat against the head of the bed. Like me, she'd kicked off her shoes but was still in her uniform.

I'd probably just gotten makeup on the bed covers. Oh, I didn't fucking care. They would wash. If they didn't—I'd buy new ones.

"That sounds awful," I admitted. "I would have gone to sleep." Most of my teachers had been engaging. Even if the assistant in one of the classes was crabby, he was at least yummy to look at.

"You skipped lunch," Aubrey said, using her nails to comb my hair back. The scalp massage was heavenly. "You can't do that."

"I wasn't hungry." I still wasn't. I barely remembered the yogurt from earlier. "I feel like I just played a sold-out stadium on the fly for hours. The worst part was, you and Yvette weren't there."

I wasn't a solo act. Never wanted to be one. It had always been the three of us. It would always be the three of us.

"I had a few moments like that," Aubrey admitted. "Think maybe you should drop a class or two?"

"No, I'm a little further behind than you are. I need..." What? What did I need? Why the hell did I need this? This wasn't about need. We had plenty of money. Homeschooling was still an option. But I wanted—this. I wanted to be at school and around people our own age and be *normal*. "Am I crazy?"

"Yes," Aubrey answered with an easy smile. "Absolutely nuts. Totally gone round the bend."

"Thanks," I said, with a rueful laugh. "Tell me how you really feel."

"Girl, you wanted to do this because you wanted the experience. I just think you got a whole lot of experience today, and it wasn't what you thought it would be."

"No," I admitted with a long sigh. "It really wasn't what I thought it would be. I thought…"

She raised her brows but she didn't push me to answer. Yvette would already be impatient and start filling in all the gaps, but Aubrey would wait. She'd let me figure it out then when I did tell her, she'd decide what to do. Except…

"I feel so dumb," I said and then sat up, loosening my tie. "The first couple of classes weren't so bad, but then I got into the lit class and there was this whole test and it was essay based."

Aubrey cringed. "Ouch."

"Yeah, the teacher is kind of arrogant and snotty." Or maybe I was projecting? "His assistant though, was a dick."

"What did he do?"

"He scowled. A lot. He was kind of rude, impatient, and had a stick so far up his ass, he was probably its personal sock puppet." Dragging the tie off the rest of the way, I slid off the bed. I could go ahead and get changed while I filled her in on my day. "The thing is, I didn't realize how much I didn't know. Those classes were *hard*. It was like I knew some of the words, but not all of them. I had the melody, but then the refrain would switch it up or they'd remixed the song."

"That happened to me, too," Aubrey said, pulling off her

own tie and heading toward the bathroom to walk over to her room. "I think it happens to everyone. It's the first day, so they probably want to see how much people forgot over the summer."

"Or never knew in the first place?" I called as I dropped my uniform into the bag for cleaning. One perk of not eating after breakfast should have been I wouldn't get any food on my clothes. Unfortunately, that hadn't been the case. Dammit.

I ditched my bra, because fuck leaving the room tonight. We had snacks. Then I pulled on an old band t-shirt and shorts. It was one of our earlier band shirts, before we'd added roses to our symbol. The design involved the three of us posed back-to-back, all of us wielding guitars. It hadn't lasted long, but I loved how soft the shirt was.

So where I went, it did.

Besides, I needed a little band support tonight. Aubrey had switched out her uniform for pajamas, too. I headed for the coffee maker while she grabbed our bags. She made a grunting sound as she mock-dragged my bag over to our sofa.

"Ha, ha," I said, and she grinned as she set them on the sofa.

"What did you put in yours? Bricks?"

"Yes, I grabbed a brick from each of the buildings I went to today and added them to my bag just for you."

"I believe it." She pulled out her phone. "Pizza?"

"Yes please."

"Letting Harley know we're ordering and that I'll be down to get it." Aubrey was already typing our order into the phone. We'd found a good pizza place on our third try of testing what we could get sent to the school.

Coffees made, I carried them over for us. My legs hurt. My feet hurt. I still maintained that my brain hurt the worst. "Thanks for sticking around, though you could have gone down to eat if you wanted."

"Sure I could, but leaving you up here alone would have been pathetic. Besides, I'm a bit peopled out."

"Oh my god," I said with a groan. "When you read the brochure, did it say there would be eighty bajillion people here?" It wasn't just the students, it was the teachers, the staff—hell, there were gardeners outside that I'd seen.

"Well, no," Aubrey said before she took a sip of her coffee, "but there are something like two thousand students in total here. I think. It might be more if you take all the different grade levels into account. I was just looking at the high school portion."

"So many people. Tests." I groaned. "And they gave homework on the first day." I hadn't missed this part of boarding school. I barely remembered it some days, but I definitely didn't miss homework. "Did they give you the lecture?"

"That you have all your due dates now, so plan accordingly because nothing will be excused unless you're dying, and they might not even then?" The roll of her eyes said it all. "You picked this place."

Making a face, I said, "You followed me."

"We're going to be just fine. Our first tour was a disaster, remember? All the ratty hotel stops and sleeping on the bus, the fact that we played places that smelled like something died there?"

"Or when we did that series of outdoor concerts. In summer."

"In the southern half of the U.S." Aubrey pointed a finger at me. "Now *that* was crazy."

I laughed. "We had fun though."

"Yes, we did," she said. "We'll have fun here, too. It's just a matter of getting used to all the demands."

I glanced at my bag. "That means we really do have to do the homework."

"You bail, I bail," she offered. "I bet Dix would drive right up here if we called him."

"He should be back in California. Oh crap." I swore and went for my phone. "I forgot."

"Oh, about your mom's pictures?"

"Well, that too, but I forgot that I sent a note to Teddy about the pictures and the press inquiries."

"We're not doing a statement," Aubrey said.

"Oh, hell no." I opened my email and there was a response from Teddy. Just two lines.

Don't worry about it. We'll take care of it.

"See, he's on it." Aubrey squeezed my arm.

"I mean, it was bound to happen. Or something anyway, but did it have to be on the very first day?"

"No one said anything to you, did they?"

I shook my head. "I don't think so. But I've been in a bit of a fog all day." I'd talked to some, but I didn't think the bitch really counted, except... "Well, there might be a video."

Aubrey turned her own phone around and I sighed. Yep, there was a video. She gave me a sympathetic hug. "You need to sleep tonight." She plucked the coffee out of my hand.

"Hey..."

"You live on espresso, lyrics, and long-distance running. You need to sleep or your brain is not going to survive. So, homework while we wait for pizza. I'll help you, you help me. Then we can call Yvette and make her watch a movie with us before we sleep."

"I haven't been sleeping that well."

"Oh, I know," she said, pouring out the rest of her cup in solidarity with me, though it was a waste of good coffee. "But you're already wired and jammed up. You need to be able to relax."

I glanced at my book bag and then twisted to look back at

the kitchenette. "I don't think I'm relaxing again for the rest of the year."

"You will. You learned to play left-handed in two weeks when you broke those fingers on your right hand. You can do this."

"I love you, Aubrey," I said and made noisy kisses in the air. She laughed.

"It's a good thing I love you too, or I'd smother you in your sleep."

"Well, then maybe I'd get some sleep." It could work. "And sorry about the video."

She rolled her eyes but brought water back over with her. "I'd have punched her in the tits. You're fine." We had almost an hour before the pizza got there, which turned out to be a lot of time. I got quite a bit done, but I had another hour's worth to do after the pizza.

Aubrey hung in with me, even when she'd finished hers. We got Yvette on the phone and found a movie to watch. It was barely nine when the movie was over, but I was sleepy and more than ready for bed.

My phone lit up with a message from Bronson when I laid down. Time zone surfing was always fun. He wanted to know how my first day went. By the time I'd finished telling him, I yawned so hard my jaw cracked. I asked about his day, but he said to go to sleep. He'd fill me in later.

I was a terrible sister: I listened to him and passed out.

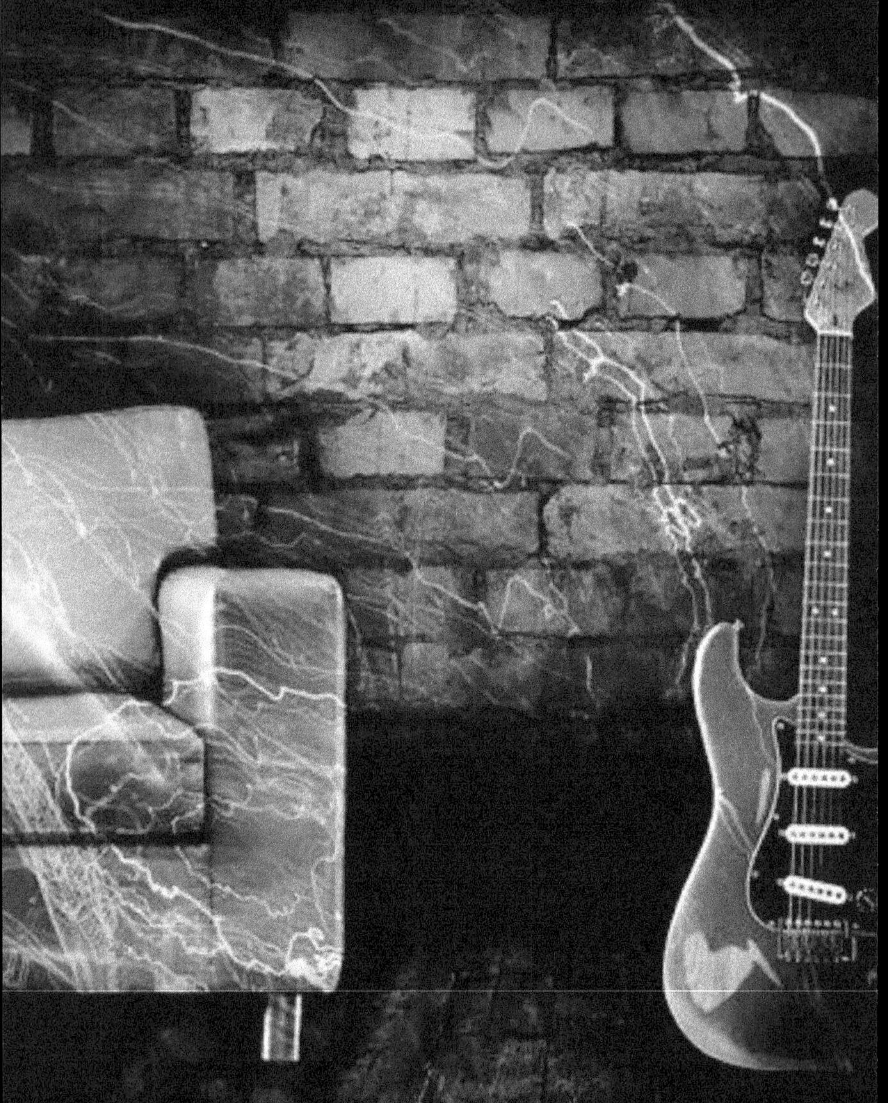

Seven

Day two wasn't much better than day one, but I was ready for the grueling schedule, and the tests were in different classes. I was already behind on the reading, but I'd get caught up on the weekend. I had a couple of granola bars in my bag and ate those over my lunch hour while I worked on the reading. Mr. Cohen wasn't actually in our lit class today. No, we got TA Malone. He seemed pretty warm and friendly, when he engaged the *other* students in conversation.

The questions all seemed focused on the books read over the summer. I still had two to finish, but I thought those last two were optional. Frankly, most of them had been dark, grim, and kind of hopeless.

"What about you, Miss Crosse?" TA Malone said, turning the attention of the class on me. I rewound a few seconds. What about me... what?

"I think I missed the question," I said slowly, as I tried to track back over what he'd been discussing with the redhead on my left. She snickered, and she wasn't the only one.

The faintest of smirks touched his face, but it wasn't

friendly or warm. If anything, it was dismissive and assholish. "We were just discussing which of the summer reading affected you the most?"

They were? I must have checked out way more than I thought. "All of them."

"All of them?" Surprise *and* disdain. I was almost impressed. Though, I think that had more to do with the fact it felt like he was looking down his nose at me. Removing his glasses, he made a show of cleaning them, and that distracted from the cut of his jaw and the serious jeweled-intensity of his eyes.

Jeweled intensity? That was a good line, I needed to write it down. "Well, 'all of them' was hyperbole—I read all but two of them. Of those that I read, they were depressing as hell."

"Language." The correction seemed almost automatic, so I ignored it and the titter of laughter it aroused from the other students. "In what ways were they depressing?"

Was he for real? "Cormac McCarthy's *The Road*?" I shot him a skeptical look. "*Crime and Punishment*? *The Book Thief*? *The Crucible*? What the hell was on that list that *wasn't* depressing?"

After putting his glasses back on, he folded his arms. "As colorful as that description is, you didn't answer my question. In what ways were they depressing?"

"Death. Abandonment. Mental anguish. Physical cruelty. Did I mention *death*?" Then before he could point out I hadn't been specific, I said, "I could go into more specifics if you'd like, but honestly, beyond reminding people life is horrible, I'm not sure what their point was—well except for *The Book Thief*, maybe."

Sure, who wouldn't want to make time to add these depressing-as-fuck books to their list? Breaking news, I sure as hell wasn't counting down the hours to add the last two. The fact I'd forced myself to slog through them at all had just been a discipline exercise. I'd play a song five hundred times if I had to in order to get it right. Pushing through a depressing book wasn't that much more difficult.

"I see." He studied me a moment longer before he moved on to another student. The minute his gaze left me, I felt the absence. Keenly. The frosty tone he'd used with me vanished as he continued to offer challenges to the other kids about their reading.

By the time class was over, I threw my shit into my book bag and headed for the door.

"Miss Crosse..."

Yeah, I pretended to not hear him as I sailed out into the hall and the throng of kids. The headache I'd been nursing all morning pounded behind my eye. Everywhere I looked kids moved together, they talked, they laughed. The walls practically vibrated with their conversations. I didn't know any of them, and most didn't make eye contact. Those that did? Well, there was a thin veil of contempt.

Then there were the fuckboys. "Damn, you really are hotter in person," a guy said as he fell into step with me. "You're burning me up."

"That's the crowd around us. Too many people. See ya." I cut to the right and down the stairs. If I picked up my pace, there was a fifty-fifty chance this guy would still follow. Some of them did. At the bottom of the stairs, I encountered an obstacle in the form of two kids locking lips and leaning into the wall on the right side of the stairwell.

I rolled my eyes. I'd call them cute, except it was the bitch from the hall with Mr. Green Eyes. Maybe they could move the PDA to a less populated area. Even as I cut around them, I nearly collided with Hot Shot. He paused a step below me. Technically, I probably should squeeze over to the sucking face couple, but he glared at me like I'd kicked his puppy or something.

Instead of taking any action in that direction, I glared right back at him. He could back off and get out of the way. Several seconds passed as we maintained the standoff.

"Goddamn," someone said behind me as they shoved forward, colliding with me and the kissing couple. I would have staggered down the step, but the push landed me against Hot Shot instead.

He steadied me and my bag. The bag was the much better save, because I hadn't closed it all the way. Dumping all my shit in the hall did not sound like a great idea.

"Thanks," I said.

Like the word burned him or something, he jerked his hands off of me. "Next time just get out of the way," he told me.

"Okay, asshole," I muttered. "What crawled up your ass?" Why did I even bother? Guy had the worst temper. He scowled in class. Out of class. In the dorms. In the education halls. Fortunately, the tide of people sweeping into us helped push me along as it also dislodged the kissing couple.

I had a date with granola and still needed to finish going over the biology lecture notes. Today was gonna be a lab day, or whatever. I'd have to deal with Hot Shot in *that* class. Thankfully, of all the classes we shared, he wasn't in my lit or my visual arts one. That meant I got breathers from his broody staring.

Imagining having to put up with Hot Shot *and* TA Malone in the same class just gave me hives. No, thank you. I found the quiet hall where I'd eaten lunch the day before and settled in with my granola and notes.

I *would* survive this day.

While day two ended about as terribly as day one, we still had leftover pizzas and made time to do mani-pedis for each other before we went to bed. Day three made me think I almost might get the hang of this. I'd also had a couple of students in the visual arts paired up with me so we could all work on an assignment together. Amanda and Jacques had been pretty cool. They also didn't treat me like I was either an alien to be examined or a snotty princess to be ignored, challenged, heckled, or sucked up to—whatever the latest tabloid claims were. Oh right, I was a drug addict.

The angst I could write about from these halls soaked in the scents of loneliness and despair, with a distinct undertone of disappointment and desperation.

That actually wouldn't be a bad set of lyrics. Taking the next couple of years off touring didn't mean we stopped thinking about music. I lived and breathed it for most of my life. Used to think it would make me and my father close, but I wasn't even sure he knew I was *in* a band.

When I turned eleven, he informed me that he and my mom wouldn't be haggling over holidays or birthdays anymore. If I wanted to see him, I could come to him. Then he went on a world tour for seven months and Mom picked up a movie that was shot on location in Africa. I went back to school and recorded the first video with Yvette and Aubrey for what would become Torched.

That memory helped to chase away the melancholy. I dug out my phone and fired off a text to Yvette.

> ME
>
> Miss your face.

I really did. We were so rarely apart the last week and a half seemed like an eternity. It could be months before we got to go visit her. But trust Yvette to know what I needed. She blew up my phone with a dozen selfies all of her making the stupidest faces.

I returned the favor and she sent back some laughing face emojis.

ME
Movie later?

YVETTE
Can't. Have a hot date.

Wait. What?

ME
Details.

YVETTE
Tomorrow. Maybe. Gotta run. Love you.

ME
Love you too.

I switched out to my message with Aubrey.

ME
Yvette has a date?

The goggling eyes would do it.

AUBREY
What? She does? With who?

ME
She didn't give me any details.

AUBREY
Oh, I'll find out the deets. Stand by.

I bit my lower lip to keep my laughter contained. I loved them both. Aubrey would get it out of Yvette. I couldn't wait to hear it all. Until then, more class.

Day five, I ran into the next major obstacle in my path. There was a guy warming up at the top of the trail that I used. With my earbuds in, I lifted my chin as if to say hello as I stretched through my own warm-up.

The guy straightened and raked his gaze over me. It was dark so I couldn't really read his expression, even under the lights stationed along the running trail. He seemed *vaguely* familiar but I'd seen a *lot* of people the last few days. I'd also not had any coffee yet. So, I was definitely not fit for the company. But that clearly didn't deter the new guy from continuing to stare at me.

"Why don't you take a picture," I suggested after I hit the button on my earbud to turn off the music for a sec. "It'll last longer." Because seriously dude, stop giving off the creep vibe.

He snorted. "If I wanted a picture of you, there are plenty out there I could grab."

"Great, then you can stop staring at me." I rolled my head from side to side, then gave him a half-wave before I started my jog. I didn't even make it a yard before the sound of him running reached my ears. I hadn't turned the music back on yet, but he didn't know that.

"You know," he said, "that hair is against school policy and our code of conduct. Someone could turn you in for it."

"Who are you? The fashion police?"

"If I was, you'd have been under arrest a long time ago."

"We don't know each other well enough to bring cuffs into the conversation."

"Police or not, someone should put a leash on you."

A leash? For fucking real? My face heated and I floundered a little for a comeback.

"Whatever." Right, strong burn there. I didn't want to talk to him anymore so I made a show of turning my earbuds back on, only I didn't actually activate them. He was matching strides with me, and I did not want to lose any of my senses with him being so weird.

"You really are a stuck up little pop princess, aren't you?"

No way he thought I heard him. Or maybe he was testing to see if I could. I forced myself to not react, so maybe he'd get the point. But he didn't drop back or speed up.

Nope, if I went faster, so did he. If I slowed down, he dropped back almost immediately. By mile three, my legs were burning. I'd been up super late the night before, but I had to get a handle on this homework and then Bronson was telling me about the volunteer program he was doing through his school's dual credit offerings.

"Looking a little flustered there, Ace," the jackass cracked the remark in the most dismissive way. "Maybe you should stop partying and start working out more."

The lack of music was grating on me, but that comment just made me want to wheel around and come out swinging. Then I would prove I had been listening. The guy had to be testing me.

Or maybe he was just a dick.

While I'd considered slowing to walk the last two miles on the circuit to cool down—fuck that. I pushed myself harder, I wanted to stretch out the minuscule lead I had. Hopefully, if I finished this run swiftly, I could get away from the new pain in the ass. Pop princess. Partying.

Ugh. Fuck off.

Not that I said any of that. Nope. I wouldn't give him the satisfaction. When we got close to my dorm again, I slowed to a walk and left the path to angle up the hill, and I got a better look at him from the corner of my eye. It was the gorgeous guy with the haunted forest for eyes. Great, not only did he date a bitch, but he was one, too. Awesome.

The air was crisp, which felt good against my overheated skin. I swore he followed me all the way back to the dorm building. I detoured toward the dining hall and their shitty coffee rather than let myself in. I didn't need him following me into the building. I used my card to let myself in and headed for the urns of coffee we'd discovered they put out each morning. It wasn't great, but it was better than nothing.

Braced to deal with him, I turned just as I got to the coffee urns. Only he wasn't there. He wasn't anywhere that I could see. I glanced around for a minute, but there were only a few students in here at all. Most of those had their heads down over books or their laptops.

Huh.

So weird.

After I got my coffee, I stuck a lid on the recyclable to-go cup and headed back out. It would look weird if I just went in and did nothing. Though I kept an eye out, I didn't see douchebag number three. Instead of Thing One, Thing Two, and Thing Three, I had Hot Shot, aka Douchebag One, TA Malone aka Douchebag Two, and now this guy—Douchebag Three.

Good. I had a hundred and one other problems, I didn't need him.

Fan Mail

Dear KC (and the girls),

I got the letter you sent! I'm still stoked over the fact you sent a hand-written note and you signed it! I've read it over and over again. I take it with me everywhere.

As long as I have that note in hand, I know you're close. Closer even than the music. Tell me we're getting a new album soon!

A Forever Fan

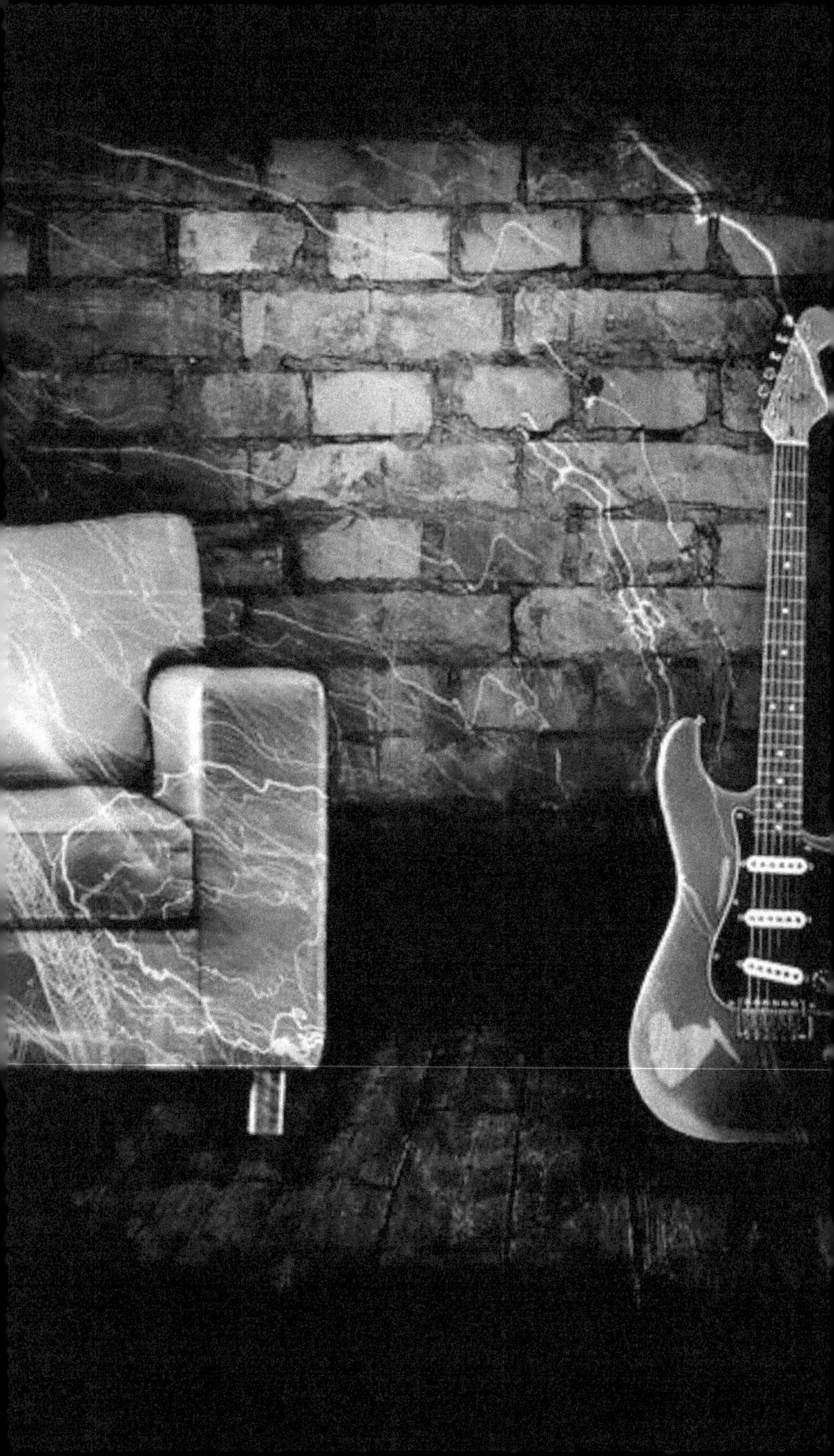

Eight

Few more hours and we'd be free—well, relatively free—for the weekend and would have survived our first official week back at school. Talk about achievement unlocked. I was dead on my feet, but the running was helping to keep the agitation and anxiety down.

Imagine my thrill when I got to lit to find TA Malone absent. I kept my mental fist pump to myself. Mr. Cohen was already writing on the large whiteboard. Before I could take my seat, though, Mr. Cohen said, "Miss Crosse."

I pivoted to face him and he beckoned for me to join him near the desk. "Yes?" I asked when I got there.

He glanced over the top of his glasses at me before he picked up a sheet of paper. "If you could go across the hall for the first half, TA Malone has some notes for you."

Wait. What?

I glanced down at the paper, and it was a copy of the test I'd taken on the first day. My heart sank at the red slashes all the way down, marking nearly every other answer as incorrect. The next pages in the booklet were worse. The scrawl all over them in red gave the impression the pages were bleeding.

They were going to kick me out of this school. I swallowed hard as I lifted my chin to meet Mr. Cohen's gaze. Performance face got me through some of the shittiest times. We'd marched out onto a stage in the middle of the worst cramps, head colds, and after celebrating birthdays our families fucking forgot.

The grade *sucked*, but I'd come here to learn so I'd take every drop of knowledge and run with it. "Across the hall?"

"Yes, it's the study lab. He's working over there today with a few of the students. Go on over. This is all review on some of the reading, but I heard you were very familiar with *The Road*, so I'll just send you a copy of the notes later."

"Thanks." Heart still sinking, I shouldered my bag and ignored the smirking pair of brunettes sitting in the front row. One of them crossed her legs as I passed her. While she came close to kicking me, she was going to have to work harder than that.

I'd danced through throngs at concerts and music festivals. Some chick in her knockoff open-toe, Gucci python sandals needed to work a lot harder to get me. I kept my expression in check as I carried my booklet and grade, along with my attitude, across the hall.

Just because I didn't like him didn't mean he couldn't be useful. Hopefully, this would be a "How can we make this work?" scenario and not a "Why did anyone let you into this school? You need to go back to junior high."

Through the narrow window, I could see Captain Ramerica—yeah that didn't work. Cap. I'd just go with that. Cap was talking to another student. Despite the fact she wore the same uniform as the rest of us, she had worked a ribbon through the braid in her dark hair and kept tugging on it as she smiled at him.

The sugary sweetness threatened to rot my teeth all the

way over here. 'Course, her tie wasn't quite straight and her shirt buttons seemed to be straining. Someone should tell her parents that she was wasting her uniform budget on too-tight clothing. Or maybe her boobs just came in.

Late bloomers were a thing.

Rather than stand there like a creeper watching them, I knocked on the door before I pulled it open. The girl jumped and glared at me as I came in.

"Do you mind? We're in a private session." All that sweetness she'd been oozing earlier evaporated in the fire blazing from her angry stare. "Oh," she said. "It's *you*."

It was Douchebag Three's girlfriend from the hall the other day. Right, I'd already been rude to her, and I didn't need to play nice. Which was even better 'cause I didn't want to be. "Actually, I do mind. Mr. Cohen said the TA was over here working with students today. So, if this was an exclusive booking, I don't think our teacher got the memo."

A flush turned her cheeks deep pink. The glare she leveled at me climbed from subzero to burn in hell. A for effort, but she wasn't even going to make me sweat. Stage lights were a fuckton hotter.

"Miss Webber, I already told you that these tutoring sessions won't help you. You've accomplished a great deal since last year, and your scores are solid."

So, she didn't need the time but was in here making eyes at the TA. I half expected a shiver of revulsion. But it irritated more than sickened me. Like you do you, boo, and all that, but don't do it right in front of me.

"Unlike Miss Crosse here, who will require several hours of guided tutoring to even get caught up with our first-years." He delivered the information like it wasn't revealing anything personal about one student to another. Or discussing something potentially embarrassing about me *right* in front of me.

Chin up, I pretended the hot face had nothing to do with his comments. Douchebag Two was in great form.

"Lucky you," she said with a sneer. Somehow, she sounded both genuine and disgusted. Genuinely disgusted? "Try not to waste his time if you're not even going to show up promptly."

I really needed to revisit the student handbook. I rather suspected ripping out her hair by the roots would be frowned upon. If not by the school, then by the press. 'Course they were salivating for a page-six story about me.

Right, stop imagining fisting that hair and slamming her head against a wall. The brief satisfaction would not be worth the following PR nightmare. Not when I really wanted some of the spotlight to fade.

Rather than respond to her verbal jabs, I just dead-eye stared at her. It had the same effect on her as it did on the press. At first, she attempted to keep her supercilious chin up. She shifted uncomfortably under the scrutiny, then finally snapped her gaze away.

Fresh heat bloomed in her face when she realized I won the stare off. The red flush just seemed to add to her general irritation. If I had five bucks and a mental link, I'd bet she was cussing me out in her head.

Cussing me out... needed to write that down. The lyric fragments were becoming the one really good part of this whole experience. But I was only on week one. Wait until I'd been here a month.

I'd either have a full song or my muse might drink herself under the table.

Fifty-fifty chances there.

"Payton," the TA interrupted and fixed a stony look on me. Oh, what happened to the polite address? "As provocative as Miss Crosse is attempting to be, we have a schedule to keep.

Return to class and we'll speak about your project later. For now, you have a firm grasp on it."

She had a firm grasp on something. From huffy to all sugary smiles, Miss *Webber* focused her attention back on the TA and didn't quite swoon when she said, "Of course, Ramsey. I have your number, thank you."

Yeah, that sounded academic. I waited a beat when she faced me again just to make her think I wasn't going to let her leave. Then with a mocking smile, I stepped to the side to *graciously* allow her passage.

I almost laughed at the second explosive breath of irritation escaping her as she stalked out. Hard to be cool and superior when your blood boiled... Girls really were the worst.

At least in school. I liked our fans. She clearly wasn't one.

The door didn't slam behind her, but I had to imagine that was more to do with the fact that they were weighted. Or whatever. I switched my attention to Cap, he with the chiseled jaw, the glasses that emphasized the sharpness of his cheekbones, and the suit that seemed to fit him like an illegal activity.

We cannot develop a crush on the hot teacher. Give him five minutes to open his mouth. I was sure it would break whatever fever being in close proximity to him provoked. Also, with Miss Webber and her heavy-handed floral bloom spray gone, I could just enjoy the more masculine undertone of some cedar-based shampoo or soap or whatever it was.

"Have a seat, Miss Crosse," the TA said, yanking me out of the sensory stimulation of trying to identify his cologne. Was it cologne anymore? Or body spray? Or did I have that backwards?

"Mr. Cohen said you were going to be working with some of the students." I set my bag down on the floor next to the chair before I took a seat at the table in front of him.

"If you'll recall on the first day of class, you received a booklet to complete to measure your current skill levels as well as reading comprehension and how prepared you were for this class."

And apparently, I'd bombed it. "I'd like to say that a test on day one to measure how much we know is a little unfair when you take into account it was literally my first day here." Definitely unfair. "I get that you need to test where we are because of the curriculum." I wanted to protest more, but I kept it to myself.

"Correct. Also, to see where the weak links are in the class. The material here is delivered at a brisk pace. We don't have time to slow the whole class down for the majority when it is only one, perhaps two, students who are holding them back."

Ouch.

Nice to be in the "one or two," apparently. I had no illusions, just… "I take it that's what this is for? To let me know I need to move classes?"

"Yes," he said, focusing his intense blue eyes on me. Something about their color seemed to shimmer via the lens of his glasses. Or maybe I was trying to write lyrics to distract myself.

Could be both.

"And no," he continued. "Based on your tests for placement, you are at the right grade level, but you lack the primary tools needed to achieve at this level. In order to keep you on task and in line we are going to need at least an hour a day, in addition to class time. The first week, we're going to take two hours, both the class period and a study hour in the library…"

Study hour in *addition* to class? "I don't have an extra hour in the day. So, is this going to be at the end of class?" Or fuck, would he make me get up even earlier?

"No, you need a tutor, and I'm the one who will be doing this, so you're going to have to do it on my schedule. I'm not available after classes, so we're going to make time for it during the day. I'll shift your schedule around this weekend to accommodate a study hall."

"I have a full load of classes," I protested. All of which I liked. "I can't just drop one."

"You're going to have to," he informed me.

"What if I just made extra time over lunch?" I didn't really go to the dining hall anyway.

"I'm not giving up my lunch hour because you think your time is more valuable." He wrote something down on a slip of paper. "These three classes are not required in order to graduate. They are also the best times to set up a study hall." He slid the paper over to me.

"The dean's office will be in touch with the class shift. It will come via email." He wrote something else down and slid the paper over. "That has my email on it and my phone number. Only text the number if you're going to be late for class or a session. You will be responsible for making up for any lost time."

I stared at him. Was he for real? "If I need a tutor," I said. "I can probably hire..."

"You need *more* than a tutor," he informed me. "You need a revisit to your basic education steps. Someone was seriously lacking in some key points of your academics. Let's start with your test booklet."

Did we have to? Every word that came out his mouth seemed bitten off, like he had to tear into the most overcooked, tasteless steak and it actively hurt to chew on the meat.

I barely had it on the desk before he dragged one of the chairs over closer.

"Page one," he said, tapping the sheet of multiple-choice answers. "You were given options for how best to complete a sentence." He opened the test booklet and went to the third one, the first one I'd missed.

"Tell me what you wrote and the reasoning for it?"

The fact it looked prettier was probably not the answer he was looking for. Frowning at the words, I tried to put myself back in the headspace I'd been in for the test. If he wanted the reasoning for that specific answer. That might take a minute.

We barely made it through all of the first page before the bell indicated it was time for lunch. I had a headache and a vague sense of nausea cut by dread. My Friday went from being a hell yeah to fuck no.

"Spend some time this weekend, revisiting *The Road*," he informed me as I stood. "There are ten possible discussion topics that we might be covering next week. Prepare for at least three of them, your choice, and be ready to defend your answers in class. We'll continue on the rest of this during our study hall."

My bruised brain just gave a careless shrug so I emulated it. At least I had Saturday and Sunday to try and recover.

I was almost to the door, when he said, "Miss Crosse?"

Tired, annoyed with myself, and trying to think which class I would be the least disappointed in having to give up, I spared him a look. "What?"

His expression went neutral and his eyes flattened. "Try to dial back on the partying. Lack of sleep contributes to cognitive issues. I'd rather you didn't waste anyone else's time if you aren't going to at least try."

I was still staring at him, mouth agape, as he stalked past me. What the fuck was he talking about?

Waste *whose* time? And I didn't ask him to do this. If he didn't like it, blame Mr. Cohen.

I certainly intended to.

Uh. My phone vibrated on my way outside. The sunny morning had given way to grayness and light drizzle. Honestly, a little rain suited my mood. Four days a week of non-negotiable tutoring with the hot TA that hated me.

Yum. Couldn't wait.

Yvette sent me a sticker flipping me off and I laughed. Nothing else. Just that.

Man, I missed her.

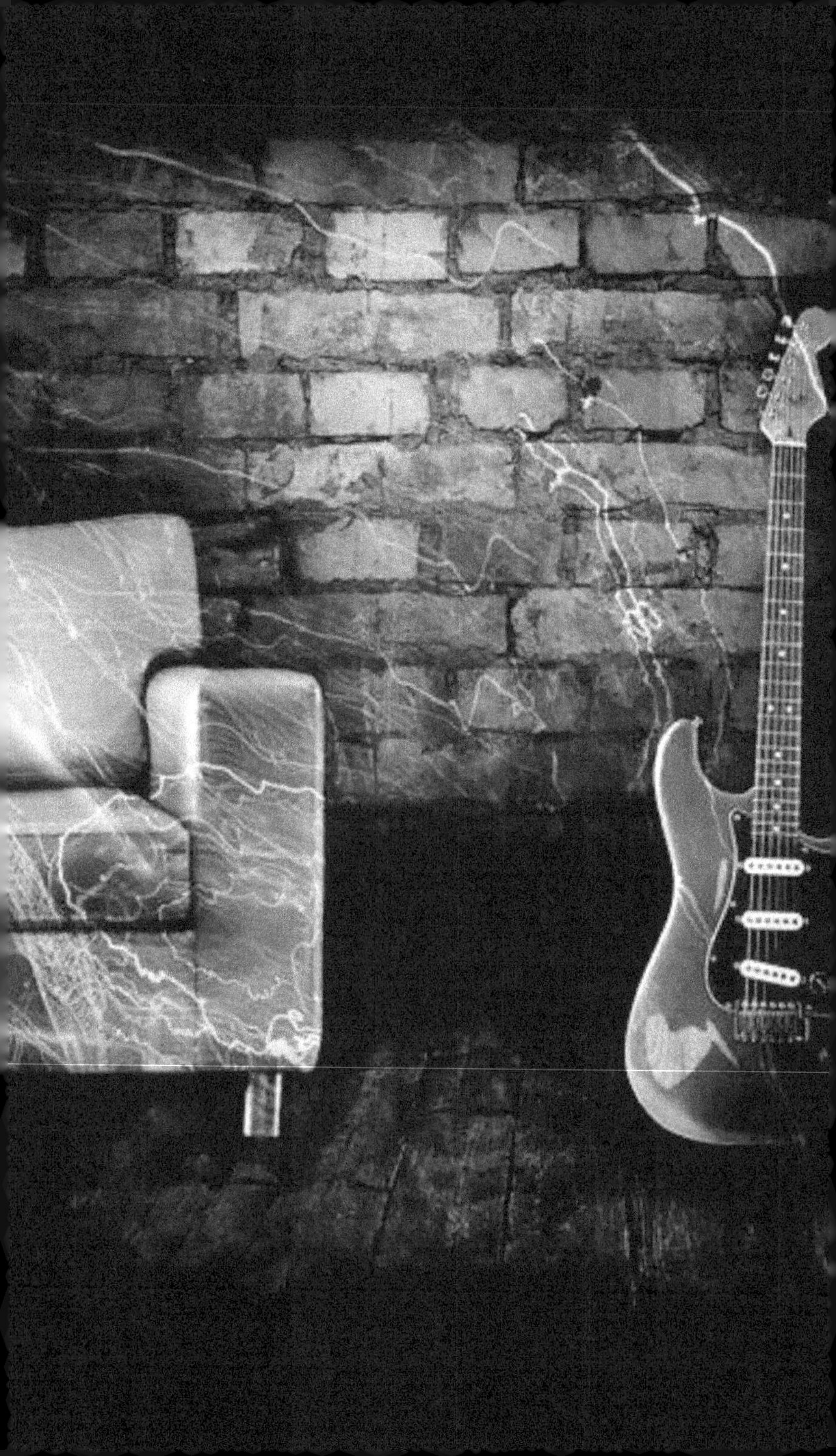

Nine

"C'mon," Aubrey said, dragging me by my feet from where I'd thrown myself into the pillows. "We are not spending our first party weekend sulking in this room. In fact, we've seen more of these walls than we have of each other and it's unacceptable."

I groaned. "Just let me die in peace."

Her inelegant snort derided my complaint, and I flopped over to try and glare at her. Only, it required too much energy to open both eyes, so I kind of squinted one. Like a pirate. Okay, like some child's cartoon character playing a pirate.

"I don't like you very much."

"Well, fuck me, at that level of epic insult, I don't know what I'll do. Get up." She grabbed my hands and hauled me upward. "We're going to put on some relaxing clothes, slap some cosmetics on, brush our hair. Then we're going out to enjoy the cool, crisp air, the bonfire, the music, and the party."

"Oh, that's what we're going to do?" Why was I arguing this point? Oh, yeah, I remembered. Nothing about this place was how I imagined it. Nothing.

"Yes, it is." Then she got right in my face with her minty fresh breath and sharply defined eyes.

"Pause," I said, holding up a single finger. "That new thing you're doing with your eyeliner. I really like it."

"Yeah?" She touched a finger to the corner of her eye. "It's this inkier charcoal, more gray than black."

"It's fucking gorgeous is what it is. I love it." I grinned.

She grinned back.

"Okay," I added after delivering the compliment. "Please resume yelling at me."

"You need a break. You need it like you wouldn't believe. You have been busting your ass. And while we both have very cute asses, it doesn't help if we never show them off." Aubrey raised both of her eyebrows. "Tonight, tonight we get to embrace that other part of being normal…"

I made a face. "You are not gonna let me skip this, are you?"

"Hell no," Aubrey said flatly, then folded her arms as she gave me a disappointed look. "We are too young and too beautiful to be going to bed at nine. You have the sex life of a nun, and the social life of a hermit."

"Hey!" I stuck my tongue out at her. "Don't act like you're any different."

"Well, then I know what I'm talking about, and I don't know if I want to be compared to a dirty nun." At her playful look, I laughed. "Now, make yourself presentable. We are gonna bonfire, and music, and socialize, and we're gonna like it."

I blew out a breath after I gave her a crisp salute. She just grinned as she crossed the bathroom to her room. "What do you wear to a bonfire?"

We'd left the flashier stuff back in New York. We'd packed for practicality at school, and for the idea that we would be wearing uniforms most of the time.

"Something comfortable! Maybe the cute blue crop top you got right before we came."

Oh, that would work. I pulled the little blue crop top out and then added a pair of blue jean overalls with shorts. It was a little baggy on me, but it worked, and when I snapped one of the straps into place, I liked the comfortable effect.

So yes, my abdomen was a little on display but also hidden by the overalls on a couple of sides. I shook out my hair. Dancing meant leaving it free because it would collapse out of most other styles.

Finally, I slid on the chunky hiking boots. They looked stylish and added to the goth Tinker Bell vibe. Gloss, maybe a little powder to touch up the shine. A flash of green caught my eye and I twisted to let out a wolf whistle. Aubrey looked *amazing*.

"I don't remember that top," I said, nodding to the green faux-sequined halter she sported.

When she turned so I could see the zipper on the side, I shifted gears to finish zipping it up.

At her huge exhale, I eyed the top and her. "You good?"

"I'm fine," she said with a laugh, then patted her tummy. "This shirt fits like a glove, like it's almost too tight, but everything stays where you put it and it's fine *once* it's zipped up."

It did look a little on the spray-painted side. Frankly... "That green is stunning with your skin tone."

It really was. It gave her skin a richer golden sheen to her tan.

"I love this," Aubrey said, tilting her head to look at me. "You need feathers. Come on."

"Feathers? You brought feathers?"

"I brought a little bit of everything." Aubrey gave me the "Did you take a shower in crazy this morning?" look before she opened up the old cigar humidor that she'd inherited from her grandfather. She kept some of her favorite pieces of jewelry in it. I spotted the dark and light blue feathers dangling from the silver ear cuffs. "Here we are..."

She held them up to my ear and then we both looked in the mirror. "You may not get these back," I admitted. The silver wire cuff was stunning and the feathers were the perfect combination of dark and light blues, with a hint of teal as well so they complimented my hair. "Like ever."

Laughing, Aubrey hugged my neck and pressed a kiss to my temple. "My shit is your shit."

"Same," I promised as I tucked the ear cuffs into place. Ready, finally, I did a triple-check. But we really didn't need our wallets, just our dorm keys, and I skipped a jacket, though Aubrey tied a sweatshirt around her waist. I grabbed a grunge-style flannel from the closet and tied it on too, just in case.

Stylish and comfortable. Besides, if there was dancing, we wouldn't get cold. Excitement began to thrum through me. Maybe going to the bonfire was a better idea than I'd thought. It was a chance to get some more of the normal experience. After a week of being on display, maybe they wouldn't notice me so much tonight and we could just *blend* in and have fun. Be normal.

That or maybe I was getting a second wind. "Shots?" I asked and Aubrey shot me a thumbs up. I left her to finish her cosmetics while I half-danced down the short steps to our sitting room. Espresso shots were definitely a way to kickstart our evening. I did double-shots 'cause it was Friday and we didn't have to be anywhere in the morning.

Not that we'd had a required bedtime in years, until this autumn, and no one told us we *had* to sleep. Thank fuck, 'cause I was having enough issues without my stubbornness rearing its ugly head.

As soon as Aubrey joined me, we saluted each other, downed our shots, laughed, and headed out. "We're going to have a great time," she reminded me.

Downstairs, Harley glanced up from her sofa. Our path to exit took us directly past her suite. The blonde grinned. "Technically, the bonfire is a junior and senior mixer with a curfew of midnight. I won't be doing bed checks until two. So have fun. Also, word of wisdom, you don't want the home team brew when they offer."

"I'm almost afraid to ask," I admitted as I braced a hand on the open door and we both studied her. Mostly because of how she worded "home team brew." It was bad, right? Like a sexual thing?

"It's usually hard liquor," she warned. "Everclear was popular for a while and so were some hallucinogens. Now the school will never admit it, but beware that some of the seniors think getting juniors plastered then hazing them is a good time."

"Fuck that," I said. "How is that even legal?"

"It's not," Harley said with a wry smile. "Privilege has its perks, you know?"

Apparently. I glanced at Aubrey, who shrugged, then back to Harley. "Is it safe to go?" I didn't really want to accidentally or otherwise get doped. I'd tripped once and that unplanned pharmaceutical journey still gave me nightmares.

"It is as long as you exercise caution," Harley said with a grin. "Really, I just know that who you are is going to be a lure for some people. Better to be aware ahead of time."

I glanced at Aubrey. "So, concert rules."

"Yep," she agreed with a nod. "We'll see you later." We both waved at Harley and headed out. It had grown steadily darker outside while we'd been in our room.

The chilly air felt good compared to the warmth from inside. It was just a bit cooler. It chased away the flush on my face. The hiking boots were a good call, 'cause the bonfire was located deeper in the woods and away from the main campus.

We followed a few other students heading on their way.

Aubrey had apparently gotten a map off the school chat she'd already plugged into.

"Have I ever told you how much I envy your ability to just blend?" I asked her as we crunched our way along the path with our phones as flashlights.

"Several times," Aubrey teased, bumping me with her hip. "But I always love it."

Shaking my head, I laughed. "You are a rock star."

"Don't look now," she replied with a flash of a smile, "but so are you."

"Damn, my secret is out."

It took us a good fifteen minutes to get to the party spot. We'd definitely warmed up, and there was no mistaking the wild heat coming from the enormous fire.

They set it up in the middle of a huge clearing. They'd even scraped the dirt around it so there was no grass near the sparks that occasionally fluttered off the tall logs stacked into each other.

The combination of woodsmoke, cedar from the nearby woods themselves, and that crispy pine smell was heavenly. Music filled the air from a series of speakers. I paused to identify the song playing; it was some Imagine Dragons.

Oh, I liked their music. Around the clearing there were tables with pitchers, and instead of plastic cups, they actually had some real tumblers. Huge ice buckets framed the tables filled with various bottles, some identifiable and others not.

What got me more than anything else was the fact the people "manning" the tables didn't look any older than us. Oh, that was probably where the doctoring of drinks happened.

Wandering past the drinks, we followed a circuitous path around the fire to where the music was louder. I spotted a couple of people I recognized. More than one raised a hand toward me or called out to Aubrey. When the music changed abruptly to one of our favorite dance bands, I let out a cheer and grabbed Aubrey's hand.

We half-ran, half-danced our way toward the others. They welcomed us into the throng, and I threw my hands up as I began to rock to the music. Aubrey let out a shout too, and we were both singing along to the lyrics.

This—holy shit—this was what I needed. Just letting the music wash over me as we let our freak flags fly. Whenever a guy danced toward us, we paired off. We'd dance with the guy, but we wouldn't let him curve around either of us. It was easier to dance with each other, roll our hips, and just get funky but also make sure the guys wanting to dance with us kept their hands to themselves.

I had no idea who was in charge of the music, but it was amazing. We ran through a series of some of the best releases of the last couple of years. The more I threw myself around and let go to the music, the more tension melted off me.

Music was life.

More people joined the dancers, and between the music blaring, the fire roaring, and the crowd thrumming around us, sweat slicked my skin. A buzz rolled over me, the high of performing for the crowd was right there. It splashed through the dried-out cracks created by digging down to be normal.

Right now, I wasn't a student or a performer, I was just the music. I rode that euphoric wave. It was so much better than anything you could cook up in a lab. At one point, awareness prickled over my skin. It was like a discordant note interrupted the hum ricocheting through me.

I twisted mid-dance-step to scan the area and locked gazes with a pair of pale gray, judgmental eyes. Oh, joy. Hot Shot stared at me from where he leaned against one of the tables, holding a bottle of something in his hands.

A bump from Aubrey broke the connection, and I blinked as I found my footing. It was like everything took a hard step to the left. The music wasn't as loud, the fire wasn't as warm, and the simple effervescence of being in the crowd evaporated.

Ugh. I shoved him out of my thoughts. I'd been having a great time and now he was—still staring at me. No matter when I turned to look or how I moved, Hot Shot kept those gray eyes pinned on me.

What an ass. I didn't stop or slow my dancing. If he wanted to be a creeper and watch me shake my ass, he could. It was a party. Aubrey had vanished when I'd been distracted. It took me a moment to track her down, and I found her grabbing water bottles.

I waved and she lifted her chin. Pivoting, I damn near collided with Douchebag Three from my run the day before. He was right there, dancing next to me. Fuck, the man needed a bell. Not that I could have heard *that* over the volume of the music.

He said something, or at least his mouth moved. I pretended for a moment that I hadn't noticed, especially since I hadn't been able to make out what he said.

The second attempt was harder to ignore, because he danced around me and got right in my face. This time, I caught his voice but not the words. Though the last thing I should have done was back up a little, I still gave ground.

His smirk told me he noticed. The move separated us out from the throng. My choices were full retreat or dig in and hold my position. When he made it clear that he would keep pursuing me, I stopped dancing to stare at him.

"What?"

Chuckling, then this fuckboy gave me a firm, thorough once over that left a sense of physical touch in its wake. When he closed the distance, I had to tilt my head back to hold his gaze. His smirk only grew as he leaned into me.

"You know, even when you're out of uniform, tattoos are against the rules."

Was he for real right now?

"Don't think the rules apply to you?" He raised his brows.

"Don't think I asked you." I put my hands on my hips, though I was seriously tempted to give him a shove. What a dick. "Also, maybe learn to respect people's personal space. You aren't that good looking or that interesting."

The insult was an easy quip. The dismissive tone and the cool look were well-perfected to chase off guys we didn't want to deal with.

He snorted, but then clacked his teeth together when Aubrey slid up next to me and draped an arm over my shoulders. "Who's our friend?"

"Not a friend," he commented before I could. The fact he spat out the last word like it was distasteful said a lot about the whiplash this guy was giving me.

He hadn't stopped staring since he got into my space, and only Aubrey's arrival seemed to nudge him back.

"Well, then you just became a non-issue," Aubrey fired back. "Shoo little nuisance, shoo." The fact she kissed her fingers before she made a sweeping motion didn't really sweeten her tone.

He glared a beat longer then turned away abruptly and stalked off. Honestly, I don't think the guy could have looked more annoyed if I'd spit on him. What a jerk.

"Having fun?" Aubrey asked as she handed me one of the waters she'd claimed.

"Actually," I said as I twisted off the cap, "I am."

With that, I tilted the bottle up to my lips to drink. The cold liquid felt good sliding down my throat. My gaze snagged on the pair of gray eyes that still fixed on me. Apparently, Hot Shot was here for the night...

Fine. If he wanted a show, I'd give him one. We drained our water then headed back out to dance. I shoved douchebags, haunted forests and hot, intense gray eyes out of my mind.

They could be tomorrow KC's problem. Today's KC needed to dance!

Forever Fan

I really hope you're okay, KC. The news stories have been pretty concerning. I get that a lot of it is gossip and absolute bullshit, but not all of it.

You're all I think about. You're all I dream about these days. I feel like I'm starving and every little morsel of news about you is what I am desperately craving.

One thing you should know, I don't care what the tabloids say about you: don't ever change. I love your wild hair, your sweet lips—especially when you smile, and your gorgeous eyes.

What do your tattoos represent? I hope you don't mind, I got one just like yours so I could have you on my skin.

Yours forever,
A Fan

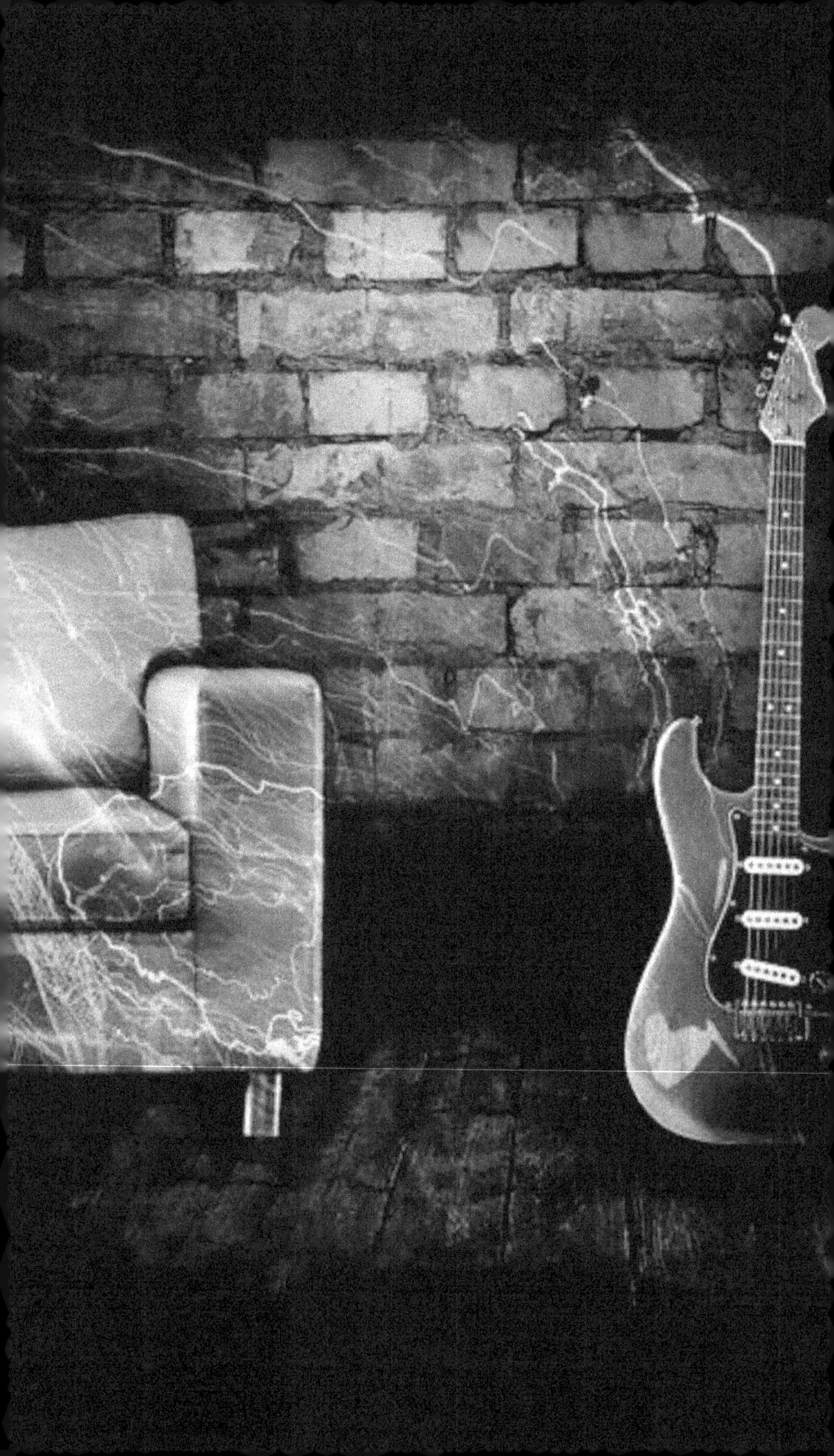

Ten

The weekend blew past us, but it wasn't until after I'd climbed into bed on Sunday night that I got the notice of my schedule change. I'd been given an afternoon slot for tutoring, which would send me back to TA Malone for the last class in the day.

That meant I also lost my art class. What a dick. It wasn't on required curriculum but it had been fun. Fun and something to look forward to each day, especially since I'd actually found a couple of people who seemed to like me for me and not for who I was. On that sour note, I'd gone to sleep.

I stewed on the class change all day. The other shift in my classes meant now I had Hot Shot in every class, save for TA Malone's. My mood was definitely not my best when I headed for the main library two buildings over. It had a lot of study spaces and tutorial areas, apparently.

It was also the location for tutoring that he hadn't bothered to share until *after* class. Despite my attempts to avoid any mention, he wasn't to be deterred. At the library, I used my ID card to get in.

I wasn't the only student in the library. Despite the time of day, there were quite a few students present, both younger and older than me. I checked the text message from the TA again. We were in room twenty-seven.

It took me a hot minute to find the room, since it was upstairs on the second floor and in a corner of the library behind the books on botany. The door wasn't closed, and a light cut through some of the shadowed gloom. I followed it like a beacon to find TA Malone waiting inside.

Leaning against the wall, he had his forearms on display thanks to rolling up the sleeves of his shirt. The white blond hair on his arms was a fine sprinkling, but it did nothing to hide the tattoo. Rather than stare at it, I set my bag down and pulled out the chair.

"You're late," he said, by way of greeting.

"Someone told me where we were meeting rather last minute, and I haven't been here yet." Rather than be flippant, I addressed his statement calmly. "It won't happen again."

"Unless I change where we meet, is that the potential threat, Miss Crosse?"

Potential threat? "No threats at all." Since he was still looming over his side of the table, arms folded to show off those glorious muscled arms and his even more spectacular ink. Ironic, considering the school "policy," but then I'd gotten away with my hair by personalized request and I kept my arms covered during the school day. So did he, I guessed. Still, between the hard lines of his frame and the chiseled nature of his jaw, I wasn't sure if I wanted to be hunter or prey.

She's a cheetah hunting a gazelle...

On that note, stop trying to write songs about his face. Not even the mental kick was enough to dissuade me from admiring his posture, his frame, and his whole—*vibe. Who makes the hunter swoon?* Swoon? Really? Ugh.

Without saying a word, the TA stared at me and there was

this—expectant air about him. Folding my hands together on the table top, I waited him out.

After an excruciating pause, I finally said, "So this is tutoring? A staring contest?"

The words did what nothing else had, jolting him into action. He moved to the table, pulled the chair out opposite me, and took a seat. After he retrieved a packet of paper from a bag near his feet, I grimaced.

I recognized the booklet. It was the test booklet from day one. The test I apparently bombed so bad, I ended up needing his attention.

Go me.

"You're going to want a pen and notepaper," he told me as he flipped the booklet open past the multiple choice answers and to the first set of essay questions. The sheer number of red marks visible from this angle made my stomach drop.

He waited only long enough for me to get out the pen and notepaper before he slid the booklet over. "Let's talk grammar..."

What about it?

It took thirty minutes for everything he was saying to trickle down into my brain. The content in the essay seemed solid, though hard to digest. Did I have no idea how to use an adverb or a comma properly? He would swap from explaining to interrogating to berating before circling back again.

By the end of the hour, I'd diagrammed my first simple sentence. He gave me more homework to go with it. Twenty sentences total.

"Bring them with you tomorrow and don't be late." The snappish note at the end of his statement almost felt like being slapped *again* for being late earlier.

Okay, asshole. If you want to play it that way. "Will it be here?" Two of us could be belligerent.

He cut a glance at me as he closed the test booklet. "Yes."

"All I need to know." I didn't rush or dawdle, I just got my shit and walked out like I had better places to be. As much as he annoyed me, he was right. Which was more annoying.

I did need a tutor. Needing one because I didn't have basic grammar concepts down that were taught in school wasn't humiliating me at all. Nope. It was a thrilling experience to have him look down his nose at me while giving me instructions in a tone so bored I was half-tempted to apologize to him.

Thankfully, I hadn't lost my mind, so I skipped that part. I went straight back to my room. Aubrey texted just as I got there that she wanted to hitch into town with a couple of seniors who had a car. Did I want to go with?

Yes. I wanted to run down the hall with my crap, go to town, then call Dix to book us flights and come get us. I wanted to run like hell. I had a headache.

But no, I wasn't going to bolt. The TA was really doing me a favor, grudging or not. So, I'd listen to him, do what I could, and soak up what he had to say. On that note, I looked at the homework.

I messaged Aubrey not this time, but I'd see her when she got back. She blew kisses then she was gone. I glanced at the homework then at the kitchenette. Clothes. Coffee. Homework. In that order.

The next day, he took my diagrammed sentences, red-marked them, then gave me another twenty to diagram.

I was in hell.

But I would not let him or *this* get to me.

Friday morning, I discovered the perfect perk to having endured TA Malone all week—the last day of the week presented me with freedom early in the day. I warmed up for my run. The last two days had been rained out, and frankly I'd been exhausted. Today, however, I needed my run.

It was still dark, and there was a guy stretching where I

usually warmed up. Shaking off the reticence, I squared up and just got to my stretches. We were at a big school and didn't need to fight over one running trail.

Only the guy who straightened was not Douchebag Three. Instead, it was a guy who had at least seven inches on me, red hair, and an open grin. "You're in my spot," he told me as I dipped into a lunge.

"Really? I was going to say the same thing. That's my spot."

"Oh, then I really did pick out the best spot on the campus to go for a run, especially if this is *your* spot. What are the odds?"

Rolling my eyes, I grinned. "Probably better than you'd think."

"RJ," he said, holding out a hand.

Rising from the lunge, I gripped his hand once. "I'm KC."

"RJ," he tapped his chest. "You're KC. It's fate, my initials for yours… magical."

I couldn't help it, I just snorted.

"Damn, that's some good material right there," he told me with a wry grin.

"You might want to work on your delivery," I suggested. When he gripped his chest as if I'd wounded him, I started to jog, turning long enough to add, "And your material."

"You're killing me," he called out, but I turned to focus on my run. When RJ caught up. I gave him a polite smile but motioned to my ear buds in the hopes that he would take the hint. It worked with Douchebag Three. Sorta.

The guy gave me an easy smile and a thumbs up. Cool. Despite the indication that I was listening to music and my absolute lack of conversation, RJ stuck with me. He didn't stare or loom, though he did kind of seem even larger in size running alongside me.

For the first couple of miles, he just paced me. When he

began to pull ahead, I let him go without comment. But he didn't get so far ahead I couldn't see him, and finally he jogged in place until I caught up with him again.

The wide grin and playful look pulled a grin from me, whether I liked it or not. As we neared the end of the last mile and the trailhead was in sight, I pulled one of the ear buds out.

Before I could say anything though, Douchebag Three appeared, a disdainful expression firmly in place. "If you're going to go slow, stick to the side of the trail."

Not that he stuck around for more than that comment. As soon as the dick had his back to me, I reacted maturely and rationally. I stuck my tongue out at him.

RJ laughed and I made a face as I glanced at him. We'd both slowed to a walk to cool down. Crap, I'd half-forgotten he was there but he just pulled his own ear buds out. His phone remained strapped in the armband he wore.

"Clearly, Lachlan needed to push it."

"Yeah?" I asked. The guy's name was Lachlan? Ugh, gorgeous guy with a gorgeous name was a complete prick. "Pretty sure he was pushing it by being a dick."

"To be fair, we are supposed to move to the right," RJ said. "But he can suck it 'cause I was enjoying running next to you."

"Nice," I chuckled. We were almost to the hill where the path split to head back to the dorm. "Well, this is where our partnership ends."

"Partnership?" RJ swayed a little from side to side like he was judging the term. "I like that. How about, this is where we part ways *physically*, but we keep the partnership…"

I laughed. "You know what—you got a deal." I threw up a hand to wave at him as I headed up to the dorm. The guy was nice enough company, and he seemed to be talking to *me* and not about who I was.

So much better.

RJ appeared in my fourth period class with TA Malone.

Check that out, he was returning to school and came in on late enrollment. Cool.

"Think I can get some notes later?" RJ asked, but the TA joined us before I could respond.

"You need to take your seat Mr. Wallach. Miss Crosse has enough problems with focusing, she doesn't need you fawning over her and distracting her even further."

RJ made a face behind TA Malone's back, and I had to swallow a grin. Still, it was fun to have him in the class, even if we weren't talking or even sitting near each other. He waited for me by the door then fell into step as we left the class.

"Wanna grab lunch?"

I blinked at him. "I don't usually do lunch."

You would have thought I said I hate puppies or something, because his whole face collapsed into an incredulous frown. "Don't do lunch? Please tell me you aren't into famine diets—you know that fasting during daylight or whatever it is."

I could have blown off the idea. I really could, but instead I just gave a little shrug. "It's nothing really, but I study over lunch."

"You can study in the dining hall..." He motioned to where the other students were heading. "I bet you can even eat and study. C'mon, we didn't get to sit together in class, and I think you like talking to me."

"You do?" I raised my brows. "What would give you that idea?"

"You're still talking to me," he told me with an even cheekier grin. "Now, c'mon, take pity on me, it's my first day back at school. If you don't come sit with me at lunch, who will?"

"Going for the sympathy card?" I dared him and he spread his arms with an unapologetic look.

"I like to do what works," he told me. "So, what do you say? Charm or sympathy?"

"You could try bribery," I offered, "if you wanted to be different."

He laughed. "Bribery can definitely be added to the equation. Come eat with me while we figure out the terms."

It was a stupid and silly conversation. My cheeks kind of ached from grinning. RJ was arrogant and a little smug, but he also seemed utterly aware of that fact, and I liked that about him.

The blow off died unspoken when I caught the TA watching us from the open door to the room. Oh goody, probably waiting to scold me for more distractions.

"Tell you what," I said to RJ. "I'll give you one opportunity to prove to me lunch with you is worth some study time."

"Oh, I like a challenge," RJ said, offering me his arm, and I rolled my eyes as I shook my head. "Right." Instead of being offended with my brush off of his offered arm, he seemed intrigued. "You know, KC," he continued as we fell into step together. "I think this is the start of a beautiful friendship."

I groaned.

"So," he said conversationally. "Movie quotes are not going to be our thing?"

"I'd prefer not," I told him. Growing up in Hollywood had long since given me a bird's eye view of the men and women behind the curtains for far too long. Glamor and romance didn't come without a heavy cost, a lot of make-up, and more special effects than people realized. CGI did more than cover up wrinkles and mustaches. "Movies are about fantasy. I like... to get to know people for who they are first before playing games."

"Oh, so like me be me and you be you?"

"Exactly," I said, not that it was ever that easy.

He grunted. "You strike a hard bargain."

"Do I?" I didn't think we were bargaining.

"Absolutely, but don't worry. I've got this. We're going to make the most of this one opportunity, and hopefully I don't have to charm a second chance out of you."

"Do you think I'd go for it? Letting you convince me to give you a second chance after I already decided against it?"

"You don't want to even leave me with the hope that you would *think* about it?"

Probably not, but I had to admit, he entertained me. "Would it help if I told you that you're already doing well and we haven't even gotten to the dining hall?"

Grinning, he pulled open the door for me. "Well, let's see how we can top that..."

I was looking forward to seeing if we could.

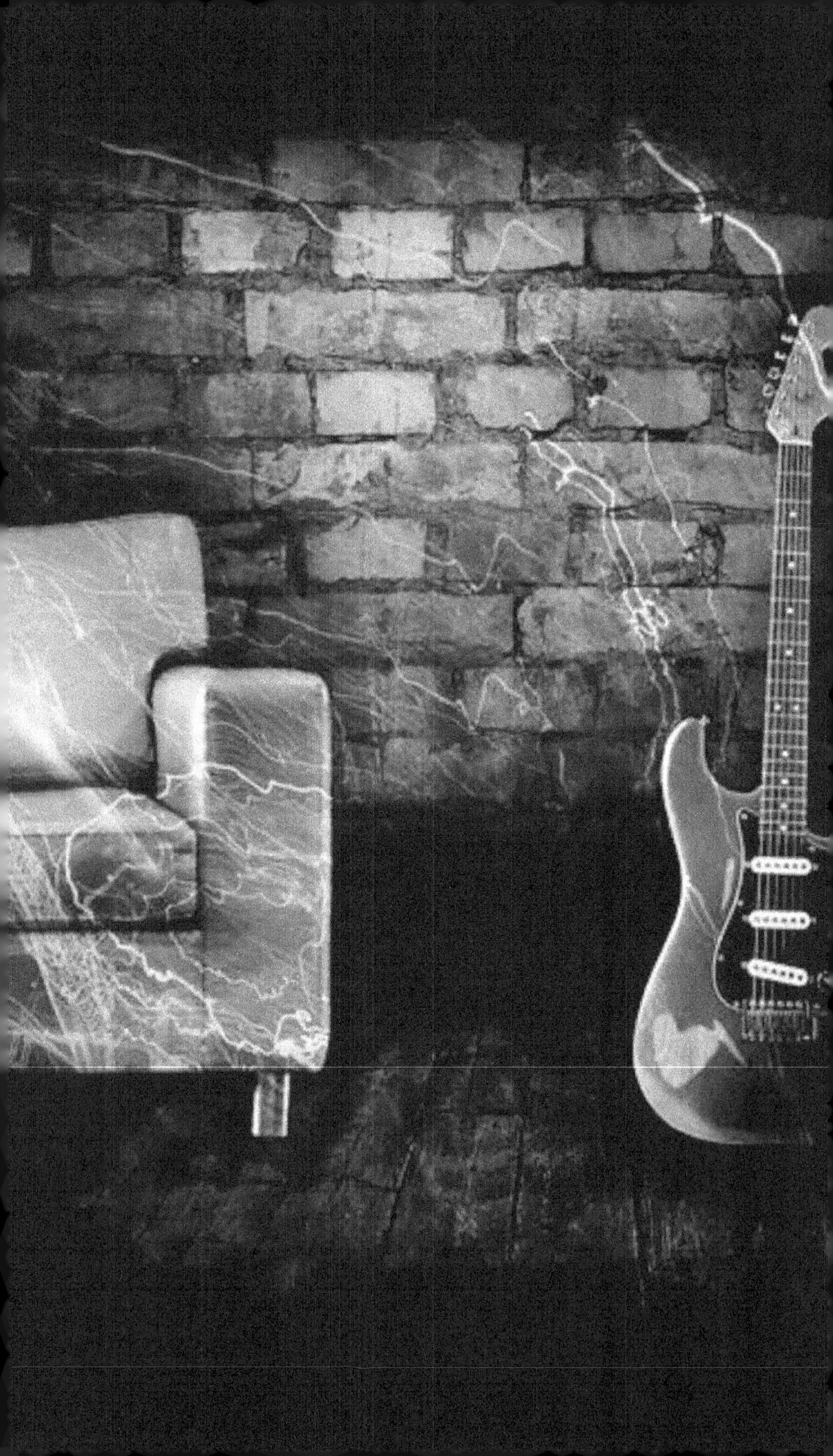

Eleven

The next week proved to be a bit easier. I was mastering my schedule. I still had to deal with Hot Shot staring in every class. Fortunately, if I put my mind to it, I could block out those kinds of distractions. Life on the stage taught me to handle that kind of attention.

Still, whenever our gazes collided the weight of his judgment crashed down on me.

Running had at least earned me a new companion. RJ seemed to head out at the same time each day as I did. He wasn't in Apollo One but in Apollo Three.

There were trails over that way, but he seemed to favor mine.

"Good morning," he greeted me with a quick smile before he went back to his stretches. "Aerosmith, Rolling Stones, or Guns N' Roses?"

It was a fair question. I checked my playlist while I did lunges. "Guns N' Roses."

He gave me a thumbs up, we put in our earbuds, and then we ran. RJ let me set the pace. He had several inches on me and possessed longer legs. It was a no brainer on who was faster, but he moved at my speed. We didn't talk. Usually, just a couple of sentences to start and a couple to end it, and I reveled in it.

There was something so unfeigned about him. Like he'd taken me at my word that I preferred genuine people. I didn't want him to try and impress me. I liked that he treated me as just another person. That was the best.

Despite our efforts to blend, there had already been one incident of younger girls breaking into Apollo One, or at least, attempting to break in, because they wanted to get photos with us. I hated saying no to even one of them, but Aubrey was right. If we didn't set boundaries, they'd keep at it. Harley also had to write those kids up, and I felt like shit about that. But the school had rules.

That, of course, led to some of the girls in our hall being even more disdainful. Love us or hate us, it was kind of like all of our best and worst critics were in the dorm hall with us. Outside of maybe five others, RJ was the only other person who seemed to just see me. Not Torched, not the problem child, not Jennifer and Gibson Crosse's daughter. RJ saw *me*.

I was still grinning when an angry-faced Douchebag Three appeared in my periphery. I glanced over at him because he wasn't passing on the running trail itself. Instead, he'd gone out into the dirt to circle around us.

He was also passing on the right—where I ran—and his scowl didn't encourage conversation, so I just gave him a wave as he moved around us. Then I had a fine view of his ass and legs as he ran away from me. The muscles rippling along his thighs and calves were impressive.

Too bad they belonged to such a raging dick. Then again, if I had to deal with him at all—at least I could enjoy admiring his legs. A laugh escaped me and RJ shot me a look. When I shook my head, he nodded.

See, the guy was great.

At the end of the trail, Douchebag Three waited for us. Or maybe I read too much into him standing there. With hands on his hips and sweat dotting his face as well as darkening the deep blue shirt he had on under the white tank top, he looked grim and unapproachable.

Douchebag Three was a great name for him.

"Problem?" I asked when he didn't move from his blocking position. RJ moved to stand right behind me, close enough that the heat from his body was almost too warm on mine.

Rather than look at me, the road block glared at RJ. "Trail etiquette is *slower* runners stick to the side of the path."

"Really?" RJ replied. "I'll try to remember that for next time."

"Next time, I'll knock you on your ass if you don't get out of the way. Pay attention to where you are and not trying to get into the revolving line-up looking to get into her pants."

"Hey," I protested. "Fuck you."

Douchebag Three spared me a look, his smile thin and his eyes cool. "No, thank you." Then he glared once more at RJ. "Remember what I said."

The absolute rejection in both his tone and attitude rankled. Even more, the dick turned his back on me and stalked away.

RJ dropped his hands onto my shoulders lightly. The touch was brief as he gave me a little squeeze. "Ignore him, Blue," he advised. "Dude's just a dick wanting to impress you."

I snorted. "Hardly. He's pretty much hated me from day one."

My two favorite times of day, now, were my run and oddly my tutoring sessions. TA Malone was as unpleasant as a heat rash, but I *was* learning.

As much as I loathed how much diagramming he had me

doing, the words were beginning to make a lot more sense. If he could just be less of a dick about it, that would be great.

Back-to-back run-ins with Douchebag Three on our daily run had me suggesting to RJ that we change where we were running. I needed to learn more about the campus. I also needed a break from that particular asshole. His presence chafed like sandpaper over skin.

Ignoring him while running was harder than tuning Hot Shot out or only focusing on what I needed from TA Malone. I didn't have to like him to learn from him, and his opinions—whatever they were—were a lot like comments on the internet. Don't listen to them or read them, because sometimes delusion and fantasy were so much better.

The new trail added a quarter mile to my route since I had to go farther to get to the trailhead. Our new path included hills *and* stairs. Lucky us. It was also about a mile longer.

Sweat slicked my neck, and my breathing was definitely coming in more hurried pants. I didn't know if it was the change or the music, but I pushed harder today. So did RJ. He doubled over at the end of the run, hands on his thighs as he caught his breath.

"Remind me not to piss you off," he panted and I rolled my eyes. "Seriously, no one would catch you."

"That's my secret plan," I admitted as I lifted the hair off my neck to cool it. "Don't get caught. Ever."

RJ gave me an amused look. "So, I just have to find a way to get in front of you so that you're running to me instead of away."

I chuckled. "I like the way you think." Nothing discouraged him, and I kind of didn't want to, not anymore. He seemed—*real*. Kind of like Frankie's guys, and who wouldn't want something like that? They adored her. With two fingers, I saluted him and then headed back to the dorm. A little more tired today than normal, but changing routes might be the best thing for me.

It was.

For almost three glorious days. Toward the end of the third day, however, someone called, "On your left." I barely heard them over the music, but it was enough for me to make sure I was on my side of the path. RJ dropped back from next to me to behind me.

When the newcomer ran up, he didn't pass us at all. Instead, he matched pace with me and took the spot to my left, leaving RJ running behind us.

I slowed a fraction, hoping the guy would take the hint. But he seemed to just match my speed. I glanced left and my irritation climbed several notches along with my surprise. Douchebag Three gave me the thinnest kind of smirk.

"Miss me?"

"No." I faced front and focused on the upcoming stairs, 'cause running up them was one thing, but going down them I needed to make sure I didn't break my neck.

Like a bad hangover, the douchebag in question stuck with our run to the end. RJ gave him a dark look, one the dick returned when we got back to campus.

"Thought you didn't want people blocking the trail?" RJ challenged and Douchebag Three just laughed.

"You could have said on your left." Dismissive yet seemingly coldly amused, he glanced at me. "See you tomorrow, Ace."

Not if I saw him first. But I didn't give him the satisfaction. Instead, I focused on RJ. "Thanks for the run," I told him.

"You're welcome. You think you could handle starting thirty minutes earlier?"

I was already getting up too early in the morning, but

what was thirty minutes to my already whacked out sleep schedule?

"What did you have in mind?" I asked as we walked back toward the Apollo buildings.

"There's like a dozen different options for running. We do a different one each day. We start a little earlier so we have time to acclimate to the different routes."

What he didn't say was that if we varied our routes, we could reduce our chances of Douchebag Three interference. I liked it.

"We can start tomorrow?" I offered and he grinned. With the new plan in place, I went back to my room to shower and get ready for classes.

Halfway through history class, our teacher announced a new project. "We'll be pairing up for the next two weeks. You'll each receive an issue that confronted the new American democracy. The two of you will split up the issue, with one of you taking a pro stance and the other a con stance. You will need to make your argument and the counter argument in the same paper. Be creative, but be aware that you should only cite legitimate sources..."

She went over a whole list of rules, including due dates for different parts of the project and the final paper. The work had to blend together; we would have to work with a partner to present a unified work.

I did this with Yvette and Aubrey all the time. I was a collaboration queen. We'd nail this. As Ms. Dimond finished the rules, she handed out the packets with the grading rubric on it before she assigned us to pairs.

At least if she was doing the assigning, we could avoid the awkwardness of trying to identify our own partners. Deidre was the girl to my left, and based on how Ms. Dimond was doing the assignments, I thought we had a good chance...

"Kaitlin, you're with Jonas."

I blinked. Jonas? Who was Jonas? I twisted in my seat to ask her when I met Hot Shot's irritated gaze.

"You're Jonas?" I probably shouldn't have sounded so incredulous, but in my head, he'd been Hot Shot since our first unfortunate encounter.

"Yes," he said, his voice this deeper timbre than I expected with a hint of a rasp. "You're Kaitlin."

"Right, just call me KC." I so rarely went by Kaitlin. "So, we have to split up the work."

"Yes. When we have the issue." He looked pointedly past me and I looked back at the front of the room. Ms. Dimond had finished pairing students off and now stood once more in front of the board.

"So, to keep it fair and to keep it random, I've had other teachers write up the subjects and the issues. One person from each team will draw what their subject is. To be clear, once you have drawn the topic, you cannot draw another, nor can you trade."

"Great," I murmured. So we were stuck with whatever. She went around the class letting kids pull their topic out of the bucket. When it was our turn, I glanced at Jonas and he looked at me. Neither of us moved.

When the teacher shook the bucket at us, I huffed out a breath and reached for inside. If he didn't want to draw, then I could. Pulling it out, I unfolded the little card and stared at the information on it.

"Shay's Rebellion," I informed Jonas. He glanced from the paper to me then back up at Ms. Dimond.

As soon as she stepped away, Jonas said, "I'll take the side of the rebellion, you take the government of Massachusetts."

"Okay, do you want to meet..."

"If you just do your part and I do mine, we don't have to do anything together." He opened his notebook and started writing something, utterly ignoring me.

The whole part of a group project was to work on it like a group. "Look, you don't have to like me to work together. I'll be at the library on Sunday researching this; come and join me and we can write the paper together."

There, offer made.

Jonas said nothing in response. That was how we spent the rest of the class period. While other "groups" talked to hammer out their plans, Jonas and I said nothing.

Good group project. Couldn't wait for more.

I was still turning that over in my head when my phone buzzed and the message was from my mother. It only read, 9-1-1.

Shit.

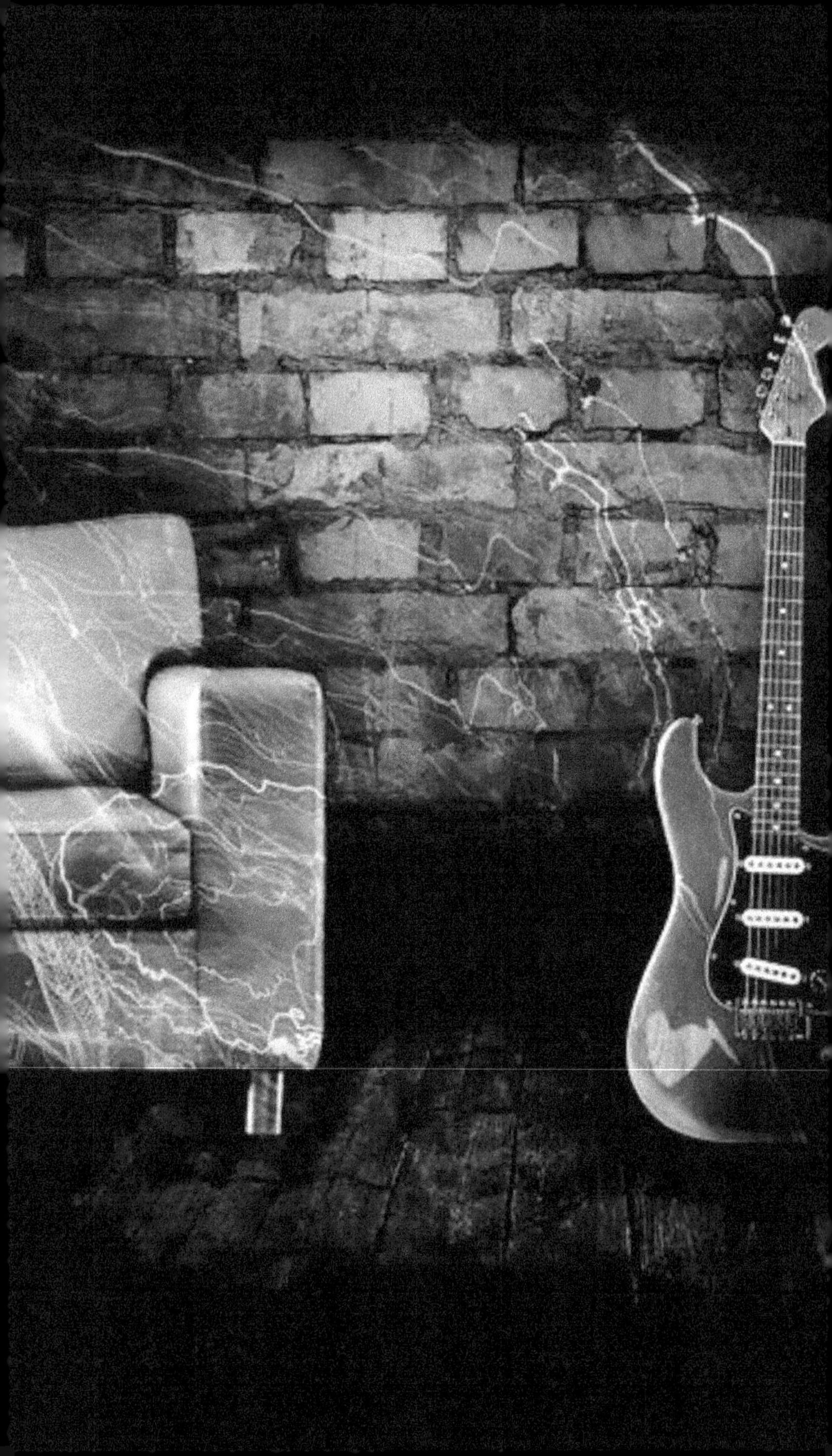

Twelve

I messaged Aubrey, called for an Uber, double-timed it back to our room to pack just the necessities, and then I was out. The Uber picked me up at the administration building. Technically, I was supposed to ask for permission and sign out. Better to ask for forgiveness, so I sent a message to Harley letting her know I had a family emergency.

Hat over my hair and sunglasses on, I'd ditched the uniform. The whole train ride to New York, I kept my attention focused out the window. Mom's 9-1-1 could mean just about anything, from a dress crisis to losing an award to an actual breakdown because her favorite designer didn't have a new collection.

Over the years, there had been a handful of 9-1-1s. Most of the time, Mom was just...Mom. Once or twice, it had been an actual crisis. If she sent that or one of her people did, I would show up—even if I had to leave the tour in Japan to fly halfway around the world and back in the course of five days so we didn't miss any performance dates.

My phone buzzed when we were just fifteen minutes from the city. The message was from Dix; he was at the train station waiting for me. I had no idea when he got to New York from California, and I didn't care. I was so damn grateful that he would be there.

Aubrey's message hit my phone as I climbed off the train. It just said for me to let her know if I needed her and she'd cover for me. Bag over one shoulder, I hurried through the terminal. Grand Central was huge, but I'd been here enough times to navigate easily. As soon as I reached the pickup lane, I spotted Dix leaning against the car.

He opened his arms as I got there and gave me a quick hug. "Hey, Kid, sorry for the interruption."

"It's fine, have you seen her?" I asked as he took my bags and then opened the backdoor for me.

"No, she's not letting anyone but Tricia upstairs and she said she's not opening the bedroom door." No judgment colored his words. Dix had been around long enough to have seen a lot of shit. He didn't ask too many questions and he never spoke to the press. Discretion was a talent worth its weight in gold.

I slid into the car while he loaded my bags into the trunk. In no time at all, he was behind the wheel and we were in the thick of city traffic. It was a thirty-minute drive to cover the two miles.

Dix didn't chatter and I appreciated it. I had to brace myself for whatever I'd find. Sometimes when Mom went off the rails, she went a long way off. My phone buzzed with a news update, but since it wasn't an actual Torched or Problem Child headline, I skipped it for now.

I did fire off a message to Bronson directly that I was on the way to see my mom and I might be MIA for a short bit. He wished me luck and said to call if I needed to scream.

He knew this particular journey well. Bronson was—a great listener and our seven-month age difference seemed to let us bond even though our relationship had basically developed through long distance communication.

That said, he was one of my favorite siblings. As we got to the building, Dix didn't pull into the garage. He pulled right up to the front.

"Go on up, KC," he said over his shoulder as the doorman opened my door. "I'll bring the bags up in a bit."

"Thank you," I said as I reached up to squeeze his shoulder. He caught my hand in his and gave it another squeeze.

"It's gonna be fine," he told me. "We got this."

Stupid as it sounded, I really needed the encouragement. Out of the car and into the lobby, I moved at a normal walking pace rather than running. The doorman murmured, "press," under his breath as he walked me to the door.

I caught sight of a couple of paps, or at least a couple of people who could be paps, leaning against the wall just across the street and another sipping a coffee just twenty feet away at a café on the other side of the door entrance.

At the elevators, I swiped my key to access the private elevator for Jennifer Crosse's penthouse. Mom's place took the entire top floor of the building, having combined all three units that were up there. It even gave me and the girls a private suite when we stayed in the city.

The ride up was swift. The doors opened to shiny wooden floors, deep plush rugs and carpets. The entire sitting room and dining room were done in relentless white that threatened to blind you on a sunny day. Even the knickknacks were white.

The lone spill of color came from a pair of golden statues Mom had won for her work. They sat on the mantel over the fireplace, and there was no missing them when you crossed the room.

Tricia stepped out of the kitchen, her expression more exasperated than troubled.

"Kaitlin, darling, I'm sorry to have dragged you away from school, but it's bad..."

Manager, agent, and my mother's second or third cousin, Tricia St. James, had been my mom's best friend and shield through much of her life. But even she could only handle Mom's temperament so far when a dark episode hit.

I was about to ask how bad as I stripped off my hat and jacket, but the bleeding sound of Coltrane drifted down the stairs. The melancholy and longing rippling along every haunting note made me sigh.

It was *bad*.

"Has she eaten anything?" I asked inside as I stacked my jacket with my hat and sunglasses before pulling my ponytail out and scratching my scalp to ease the pull on it. The delaying tactics would only buy me so much time. As I shoved my shoes off, I turned a few ideas over in my head. I needed to figure out what I was going to do and fast.

"No," Tricia said, folding her arms. "I have managed to get her to have some coffee and a little soup. But not since yesterday. She just leaves the trays to go cold in the hall."

"I'm gonna get her to take a bath and maybe eat. Can you get us some salad, sandwiches, and fruit? Maybe no salad, keep it finger food like."

"Chicken strips? She likes those with honey mustard sometimes."

"Is she still vegan?"

"Only on set," Tricia replied drolly, "so I'll do the real ones."

"Thank you!" I gave her a kiss on the cheek then hurried up the stairs. At the top of the marble steps, I stared down the hall. The carpet up here was also white, too white. I liked my wing better; at least the carpet in there had some blue on the edges.

I walked to the double doors separating her bedroom from

the rest of the suite. Knocking would require her to answer and me to wait for said answer. Just walking in would probably start a fight or, *worse*, a sulk.

At the doors themselves, I hesitated. Open them or not? Knock or no knock...

Fuck it. I gripped the handle and turned it as I knocked. Pushing the door in, I sang, "Oh lay-dee-who..." It was a silly little song she had been singing to me all my life.

I repeated it as I pushed the door wider and stepped deeper into her suite. The white rugs and decor gave way to red—all the red. Red was everywhere. A psychologist would probably have a field day with the bloody effect of all that crimson against marble.

Me, I just scanned for a sign of my blonde doppelgänger who was barely eighteen years older than me. We looked more and more alike with each passing year. Her thirtieth birthday had been tough.

I'd had to fly halfway around the world to attend a *wake* for her youth. It had been so bizarre and kind of funny. I glanced into the ensuite bathroom. The room smelled of her favorite lotions and bath bombs. Honeysuckle, citrus, and jasmine. It threw me back to the first time we went to Costa Rica.

There were a couple of empty bottles of wine waiting on the tile next to the tub. There was also an empty glass with a little red in the bottom.

So, drunk? Maybe.

I continued deeper into the bedroom suite. The sitting room was empty and I continued up another set of steps to the actual bedroom. Light filled the sitting room from the windows overlooking the city, but the bedroom itself was dark and closed off.

The light from the sitting room cut through the gloom and provided the most perfect spotlight to stretch over my mother where she lay on her back, one arm over her eyes and her posture too posed to be relaxed.

Letting out a sigh, I pushed the doors closed and then crossed the room to climb up on the bed next to her. She pulled her arm away and I could barely make out the movement. There was just a hint of glow to the lights lining the ceiling.

"Kaitlin-baby?" Her voice sounded wrecked, like she'd had one too many drinks in a smoky bar after singing torch-songs for hours. Though I supposed it could have been Torched. Mom did like to do impromptu duets when I was there.

"It's me, Mama. Trish sent a message."

"Ugh, I should fire her. I told her to not bother you. You have a tour to finish up." Her groan carried the weight of the world.

"Fortunately," I said, keeping it light as I hooked my fingers together under my head. "We wrapped up the tour over the summer. This is a great time for me to drop by."

"Oh?" Mom rolled over and wrapped around me while tucking her cheek against my shoulder. The scent of wine wreathed her and tickled my nose when she pressed a kiss to my cheek. "I miss my sweet Kaitlin-baby. We should order all the junk food, a masseuse, maybe a tech to do our nails and toes. What do you think?"

Mom sat up abruptly then looked down at me. Her cosmetics were sketchy at best. There were deep shadows under her eyes, mascara that had run with her tears and been smudged across her cheeks. The raccoon eyes weren't artful nor was the redness.

"What happened, Mom?"

"Johnny left me," she said with a sniff then coughed as she studied my arm. "You got a new one."

I had the year before, but it'd been a while since we hung out. I let her lift my arm to study it.

"Maybe I should get one of these," she murmured. "What do you think? Something sparkling and colorful, all over my arms, like one of those painted birds we saw in South America last year."

It was the year before that, but I just grinned. "You can do whatever you want."

"Oh, then let's go…"

"Except you should sober up before you get a tattoo." I kept my voice even, without any rancor or skepticism. Nothing that might make her feel self-conscious. "Alcohol is a blood thinner and you'll bleed a lot if you try to do it now."

"Oh." Her nose wrinkled. "How much blood?"

"A fair amount…"

"Oh." She repeated the syllable with more disappointment before she collapsed on the bed next to me. "I don't like blood."

I knew that but I didn't say anything.

"Maybe we'll just get our mani/pedis done and have a wine brunch. That would be good. Girl time."

"We can do that. Or…" I elongated that last word. "We could get cleaned up, go out into the garden and have real food and coffee. Talk, maybe. Then do some self-care."

While there was only a hint of slurring in her words, it was definitely there. I had no idea how much she'd been drinking, but if she was also doing pills—well, it was better to sober up so we could see how bad the damage was.

"I suppose. But that means going out there and Tricia is just going to mock my choices. Of course he left you, you're an old, dried up hag that doesn't qualify for the ingenue anymore." Mom let out an aggrieved sigh. "I wanted that new role, the action mother, the older woman and former spy—something really meaty that I could sink my teeth into. Think Angelina Jolie in *Salt*. Do you know what they said?"

I braced myself. I was so going to regret asking this. "What did they say?"

"That I wasn't tough enough to be believed in that kind of role, femme fatale or aging femme was all I was good for. I'm an actress for fuck's sake..." She sat up abruptly as she yelled. "I've won BAFTAs and I've been nominated for Oscars. The Golden Globes even asked me to host for them once. How am I not *strong* enough to play a badass?"

The edge of tears was right there in her voice. "Mom..."

But she didn't seem to hear me. "Then Johnny said I was just being ridiculous and dramatic. That I should just embrace what I'm good at." She flung herself back on the bed. "Or maybe...just retire and take the lighter projects for the money."

Oh boy. "Mom, did Johnny leave or did you throw him out?"

"It's all the same thing." She rolled off the bed this time. "I need a drink. And a little pick me up—then you and me? We're going to show the world what we're made of!"

She vanished into her closet and I stared up at the ceiling. Oh, she hadn't crashed yet, but it was coming. This was going to be a long week.

Patience pays off Kissy Kats. Not even two weeks into the new "school" year and who do we see out killing three bottles of wine for brunch? A certain Problem Child is back in the city and she's already making a splash—apparently red is the color choice and the vermouth is quite dry. If this is what rehab looks like, I can tell them what they are doing wrong. Kiss. Kiss. More soon.

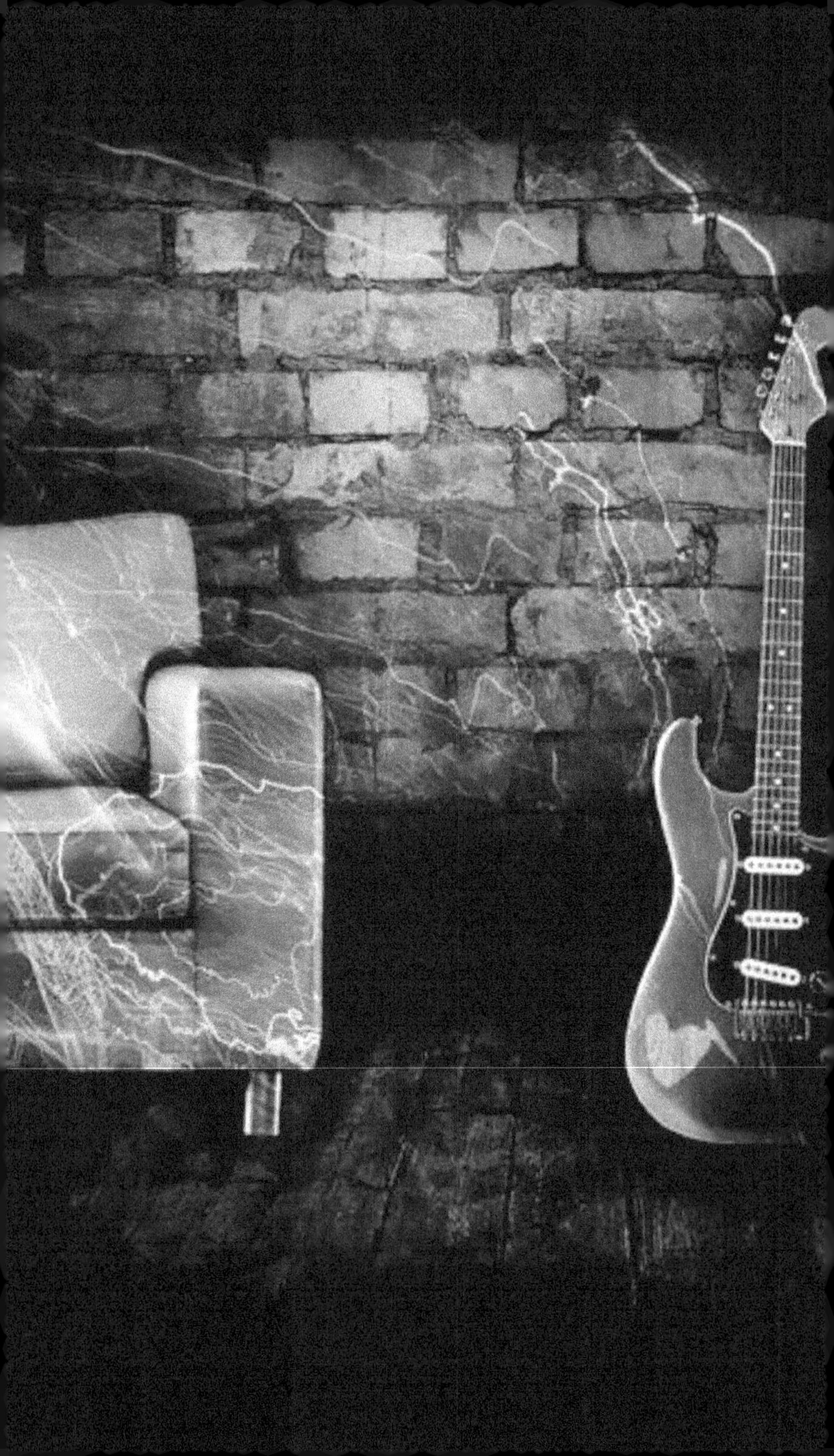

Thirteen

It took the better part of a week to get Mom sober enough to admit that rehab might be a good idea. She'd just finished a movie. Trish said she wasn't due anywhere for at least another six weeks. That would only be for pickup shots. So, the window was at least limited and we had time to cover.

"Are you sure about this place?" I asked. Mom was asleep, I'd been hiding all of the pill bottles and emptying them out as I found them. We didn't need another attempted suicide. We were almost out of wine and Trish had done me a solid by canceling the restock orders.

"Yes," she said without looking up from the phone she was texting on at high speed while Dix looked on. I was so damn glad he was here. Trish was family, but her focus had always been on Mom's appearance in the press and the jobs she got. Her image was everything. Dix, like me, at least cared about making sure Mom was okay.

Maybe I was being unfair. Trish glanced up from her screen when I didn't say anything more.

"Katie-darling, you know I love your mother more than

life, but this place will work wonders. They won't be dazzled by her star status, they won't talk to the press, and they limit outside contact and technology. It's just what she needs to put herself back together."

I studied the information on the Sunshine Retreat. It was located in upstate New York. So we had a bit of a drive to get there, and it was also on a private estate. Dix put a hand on my shoulder and tapped lightly. I glanced at him and nodded to the question in his eyes.

"Excuse me," I said to Trish, but she was already putting the phone to her ear.

"Sorry sweetheart, I have to take this." She didn't wait for acknowledgement, just walked away. I sighed but kept my thoughts to myself while I followed Dix into the kitchen. Mom had staff here, but Trish had kept most of them out. The fewer people who saw her in this state, the better.

Even some of our most trusted staff could make the wrong remark or answer some innocent question, then we would be fighting a media storm. No one needed that. In the kitchen, I opened the fridge and stared inside. Dix had done everything to help since I'd gotten here. When I needed to clean out her pills, he'd distracted her. When I had to coax her to sleep, he'd gone for food. More than once we'd had to clean up puke. At night, when Mom was finally asleep and I tried to do some homework or at least attempt to get the assignments done, he'd sat with her or with me.

"Whatcha thinking?" Dix asked as he leaned against the counter and crossed his arms.

"That I really wish she'd done this while I was on a break, to be honest." I rubbed a hand over my face as I studied the options. Someone had restocked the fridge before her arrival. Or maybe shortly thereafter. I pulled out a bottle of orange juice and opened it. The seal hadn't been broken before.

Good, the quart bottle sounded amazing. Dix gave me a

minute while I opened it up and took a long drink. The cold and the tart were just what I needed. After another couple of gulps, I lifted my head to meet his gaze. I really didn't know how I would have handled all of this without him.

"Am I doing the right thing?" How would Dix know? And why was I dumping this on him? Seriously.

"You have to—"

The chime announcing someone coming up in the elevator sounded, and I reached for my phone. Almost no one had ride-up privileges. The doorman wouldn't let just anyone up without checking with us. I was halfway to the elevator with Dix right behind me when Yvette's message appeared on my phone screen.

Knock. Knock.

Then the doors opened and the feisty strawberry-blonde charged out dressed in the most adorable red jacket, skirt, and boots with a white blouse under it all and a red beret crowning her head.

"I'm here, *mon ami*," she announced in her playful French accent. "We're going to take care of everything."

I met her on the steps down from the elevator and embraced her. The scent of her Christian Dior perfume threaded around me and I sighed. "Oh, I missed you."

"I know," she said with a laugh, squeezing me tightly. "But Aubrey and I flipped a coin. She lost, so here I am coming to the rescue. Tell me everything and we will get your *maman* all settled and you back to normal life."

Leaning back from me, she pulled off her sunglasses. Honestly, Yvette was seriously the best-looking thing I'd seen since I got the message about my mother needing help.

"How bad is it?"

Trish was pacing around on the garden balcony and Dix stood back near the kitchen. "C'mon," I said to Yvette then threw Dix a quick smile. "I'm gonna catch Yvette up...don't disappear?"

"I'll be here, and I'll keep an eye out for your mom," he said with a nod. "Yvette."

She grinned at him and wiggled her fingers. "Hi, Dix."

"Hey."

We didn't say anything else until we made it to my wing. Once in my room, I shut the door and leaned back on it as Yvette pivoted to face me.

"How bad?"

"Johnny and she broke up," I told her. "I really haven't had time to fill Aubrey in on everything. She's been on a bender since I got here, but I think she's finally coming down a little. We've had to sneak the meds out. I don't know where she found the new doctor, but her pharma-bag was definitely full."

Yvette grimaced then sat down on the bed. "So, rehab? Or just going to sober her up?"

"I was trying for sober and maybe clean, but we're having trouble making sure we have all of it. She finally agreed this morning that maybe what she needed was a nice, quiet break, and a bit of a restorative."

Releasing a faint snort, she crossed one leg over the other. "Does this spa place you picked out handle rehab?"

"That's what Trish says," I admitted. "I haven't had a ton of time to research it. Mostly because every time she notices I've 'disappeared,' she gets thirsty."

"Ugh. Okay. What's it called? Give me the details and I'll take care of it. Do you need my help convincing her to go?"

Honestly... "That could go either way. Let me try first. At least then if I take on the role of the bad guy, you can be good cop and all the wonderful things I'm not and persuade her."

"No comment. Okay, name of the facility?" And just like

that, Yvette took over the phone calls while I went to coax my mother into a shower.

The grunting and groaning in her room wasn't live, thank God; instead it came from the television. She sat on the edge of the bed, a cigarette in one hand and a cup of coffee in the other.

As happy as I was to see the coffee mug, I needed to make sure it wasn't spiked.

"This is one of my favorite movies with Johnny," she told me, her expression mournful. "Have you seen this one?"

"Yes," I told her as I crossed the room without looking at the screen. "Pretty sure everyone has seen that."

She wrinkled her nose at me. "Don't be judgmental, Kaitlin. It will age you."

"Is *that* what does it?" I opened up her closet and studied the interior. She had a huge selection to choose from, but we needed to avoid any of the cocktail or formal dresses. Think lowkey.

We had enough here to work with.

"Yes, and you know how fake the stuff is on those sets. Johnny has to pump for hours without coming, which is good. He saves it all for me." From offensive to defensive, though she ended the last sentence on a sigh. "Or he did. Chances are he's going to be feeding all those delicious inches to some other slut now."

I closed my eyes briefly to try and scrub that mental image out. "Really don't want to discuss that part." I pulled out a pair of dark gray yoga pants, and a loose, but slendering top that wasn't a t-shirt but also not something formal. It would be relaxed, yet chic. Also, the red was her go-to color.

"Don't be a prude," she scolded as she put out her cigarette. "Johnny's a gifted lover. Maybe I should have encouraged you to try him out. I'm sure he'd be good for a first timer."

"Mom," I said, just skating right past that highly inappropriate and downright skeevy comment. "Let's get you in the shower. I've got a great outfit for you, Dix is gonna get the car, and then we're all going to take a drive up north."

"I don't know if I want to go." She paused, then looked in her coffee. "Maybe I need a drink and to think about this."

"Maybe," I said, carrying her clothes to the bathroom. "But before that, we have to get you ready. If you want... I'll help you with your hair."

"You will?" Surprise and what I hoped was delight filled her expression. "You haven't helped me with my hair in a long time."

"I know, so I think it would be fun if we did it today. Have some mom and daughter time."

"I'd like that," she told me, her smile warming. "I'd like that a lot."

It didn't take much to persuade her to shower after that. Twenty-five minutes later, she carefully applied a bare minimum of cosmetics while I worked the comb through her hair. My mother's hair was darker than my natural color. But it also gave her this really glossy, classic look in photos.

Personally, I was of the opinion she'd been born to be a 1940s and 50s showgirl with all the looks of pinup to boot. "Do you think I'm still pretty?" The quiet question held a lot of self-doubt and faltering self-confidence.

"I think you're gorgeous, Mom," I told her as I hugged her from behind. Pressing my cheek to hers, I met her gaze in the mirror. "Look at you... perfect skin, perfect eyes, perfect smile..."

At the mention of it, she did smile before she raised a hand to cup my face. "You are precious to me."

That was nice.

"But you really need to get a facial, sweetheart. Have you looked at your pores?"

I laughed. I probably shouldn't have, but I did. "You know, I really haven't. I promise I'll get right on that after I get caught up on missed work this week."

"Oh, where are you touring now?" she asked as I straightened and reclaimed the comb.

"Technically, no tours at the moment. We're taking a well-deserved break and I went back to school, remember?"

"Oh," she said slowly. "I had forgotten that. I suppose it's good research." Still, she eyed me critically in the mirror. "But you should frown less. Frowning ages you prematurely, and you are so perfect right now...perfect skin, perfect hair, perfect eyes..." Somehow the echo of my earlier statement didn't seem as much of a compliment.

She turned to look up at me.

"You will never be as beautiful or as powerful as you are right now," she told me, gripping my hand like this was the most important thing ever. "Don't waste it." Then she brushed a kiss to my cheek. "And don't forget to moisturize."

I did not roll my eyes. But when I glanced up to find Yvette crossing her eyes at me in the mirror, I laughed. Mom caught sight of her and she let out a happy sound.

"Yvette, darling!!"

"Jennifer!" Yvette did the squeal as well and Mom wrapped her up in a hug. "You look sensational, and here I was thinking I'd find you a wreck of a human being."

"Oh, don't believe everything you hear," Mom scolded this time before she patted the cushioned seat next to her. "Come talk to me while Kaitlin finishes my hair and tell me all about that new color of lip gloss. It is new, isn't it?"

I dropped a kiss on Yvette's head before going back to working on Mom's hair. Bless her, she distracted Mom and kept her talking until it was time to put her in the car.

With Yvette and Trish there, Mom was more inclined

toward cooperation and hopefully the trip to the Sunshine Retreat wouldn't change that.

Despite the fact I almost couldn't wait to drop her off and get back to school, I was also reluctant. The past week had kicked my ass. While Aubrey said she'd cover for me, I hadn't even looked at my homework or email since I got here.

Even the night Dix sat up with me to watch a movie because we'd gotten rid of the last drop of alcohol in the apartment and I didn't want Mom ordering any up so I sat up and played guard... I did homework. Yeah, I did as many of my assignments as I could at every chance I got. The split focus didn't help, but I managed two more, but I was so damn tired at that point. Dix offered to keep watch for me if I wanted to sleep, but I was already leaning on him too much.

But he wanted to help and that was why I let him drive me back to Blue Ivy rather than take the train. I also stole a nap in the back of the limo. It was late when we got back and I was definitely worse for wear. I half-stumbled out of the back, gave him a kiss on the cheek and waved him off as I headed inside.

I'd let Harley know when I was on the road that I was on my way back. After I keyed myself in, I signed in on the clipboard hung on her door then climbed the stairs.

Thankfully, it was early in the hours of a Sunday morning. I could possibly get some sleep in before I dove back into so-called normal life.

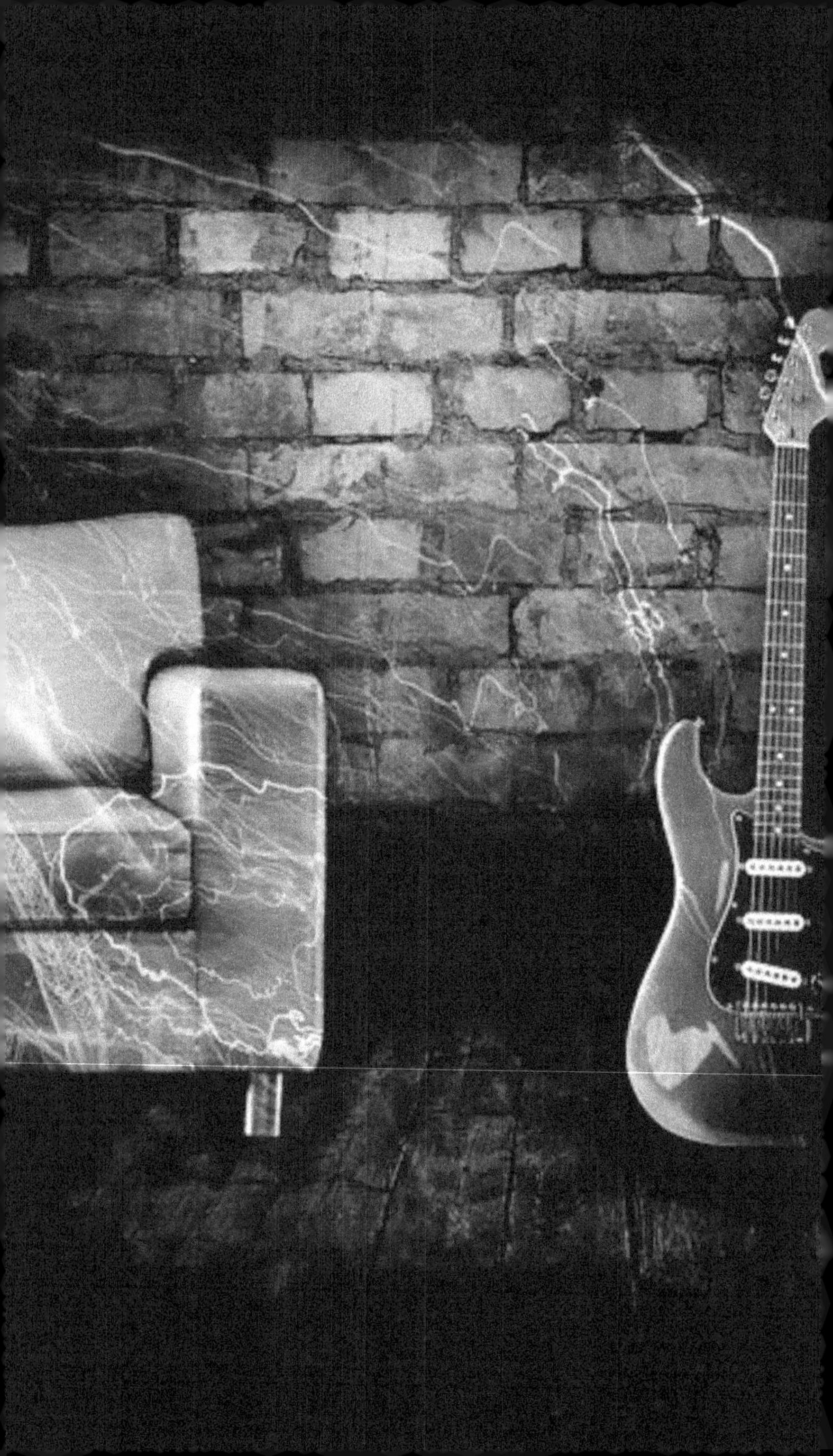

Fourteen

Sunday morning dawned way too early, and as much as I wanted to reclaim my new schedule, I just couldn't bring myself to get out of bed. Instead, I curled back over onto my right side, checked the phone for any emergency messages, and then passed right back out again.

"Come on," Aubrey said sharply as she snapped open the blinds letting sunlight in and damn near blinded me when I peeled one eye open to glare at her. "You need to shower; you smell like you were the one partying, not your mother."

I groaned and rolled over to save my vision before mumbling, "Yvette was amazing, but you know how Mom is."

"Oh, I do," Aubrey assured me with a rub to my shoulder. "But you have homework and I tried to get as much of it as I could."

"I hate my life," I muttered.

"You wanted to go back to school and be normal," she reminded me in a way too cheerful voice. I lifted a hand and flipped her off. "I made you coffee."

"Okay, I think I hate you a little less."

She laughed. "Coffee is in the bathroom. If you want it,

you have to get up and get it. Then shower. I'll go grab us food."

Food. Right. Getting up. "Cruel," I muttered. "But effective."

Every muscle in my body protested as I climbed out of bed, pausing to stretch before I walked toward the bathroom. The scent of the coffee hit me in the bathroom, and it was the right jolt my system craved.

Aubrey followed as far as the door. "Can I trust you to actually shower? You won't like what I do if I come back and you're asleep again."

"Yeah, yeah. I'll be good." I ignored the seriously hard case of bedhead I was rocking. Showering would help. I gulped down the coffee like it was a lifeline.

"I'll be back."

"Hey, Aubrey," I said before she could close the door and she glanced at me, eyebrows raised. "Thank you."

"You're welcome." She blew a kiss. "Now finish the coffee and shower. Then meet at the sofa. We have a lot of work to do."

I saluted, then sagged dramatically, which made her laugh. Thirty minutes later, I was trying to remember that humor as I nibbled at the salmon and cream cheese sandwiches she'd managed to score. There were some with cucumber and cream cheese, too.

Opening my school email had been nightmare-inducing. I closed it and went to work on the assignments that Aubrey had picked up. A few required me to check the syllabi we were handed on the first day for details, and Aubrey helped when I needed to pull facts for one paper and when I was trying to work out the formulas they'd used in another.

Tired KC was not as effective as rested KC. But caffeinated KC was going to win dammit. A girl could do a lot with coffee and determination.

I still had some emails to handle, but by the time we called it a night, I had most of the week's assignments done and turned in via email. Yvette called earlier and we spent an hour just talking, the three of us. I missed her. I missed her even though I'd literally just seen her in New York.

It was still early in California, but I'd been kind of ignoring Bronson while coping with Mom. He didn't have the highest opinion of her. Yet, he always seemed to try really hard not to say anything bad about her.

Tired as I was, I didn't want to get into a debate with him, so I fired off a check-in text and then turned the phone to do not disturb before I collapsed.

I rolled out of bed five minutes before my alarm. Awareness that I needed to get up kept me from sleeping for long or deeply. My routine kept me sane on the road and it would keep me sane here. The week away from school had been grueling, a part of me relaxed now that I was back here.

The run did what the past two nights of sleep hadn't managed: it jazzed up my mood, gave me a much-needed emotional boost, and it was fucking peaceful because there was no Lachlan, "Douchebag Three" Whatever the hell his last name was, to glare and throw shitty comments.

There was no RJ either, but I could handle there not being an RJ. Guilt niggled at me because in the midst of it all, I'd just dropped everything and left. I hadn't called or messaged him —I'd just blipped out.

Shitty thing. I'd have to make it up to him or apologize. My good mood lasted through my shower and breakfast with Aubrey. It carried me through the halls toward my first class of the day and drowned out the "How was New York?"—'cause really not their business—and the "Damn, did the party bus run you over?"—'cause bite me, asshole.

"Hey." The younger freshman stepped right into my path and I had to stop or risk colliding with him. The hallway wasn't crowded, but he stared at me with too-wide eyes that were faintly dilated. The damp brow and hair could have been from a shower, but the distinct body odor said something else. "You're Kaitlin Crosse."

"Yeah," I said, going for the quick smile. "I am. You are?"

He blinked at me like I spoke an alien language. "Can I get a selfie with you?"

Resisting the urge to look at my phone or anywhere else, I tried to focus my attention on him. He seemed so damned nervous and I got that, but...

"You know, sure," I said. "If we can do it quickly. First period is like...now." There hadn't been a chime yet and the class door was literally right down the hall. The kid immediately moved to stand next to me and whipped out his phone.

Years of practice and fan meet-and-greet events had prepared me for a lot of things. Or at least, I always thought they had, but when he pressed his lips right to the corner of my mouth as he snapped the shot, I froze. Instead of jerking away, I just fucking *froze*.

The hum of sound in the hall just faded away, like someone had dialed the volume all the way down. The slam of my heart against my ribs actually hurt and I compressed my lips and resisted the urge to swipe my hand over my mouth.

He grinned at me. "You're even prettier in person. But can I ask for one more thing?"

I just stared at him dumbly for a moment as sound rushed back in and someone hit my shoulder as they pushed between us. The rude movement knocked me to the side and I stumbled back a step.

Hot Shot just glared ahead without even a glance in my direction. Who knew I could be happy to see him? Not only had he made me step to the side, he'd knocked my selfie-stalker back a couple of steps, too.

Taking advantage of the interruption, I shook my head. "No, sorry. You can't. I have to go to class."

I wasn't running to get away from him, but I was walking as fast as possible to get to the classroom. I slid into my seat next to Hot Shot and out of sight of the fuckboy in the hall, I wiped a hand over my mouth.

So gross.

I turned to Hot Shot, relief and exhaustion vying for supremacy. Gratitude actually topped them both. "Thank you," I told him. When he stared at me, his expression almost blank, I added, "For running into me and that guy. You did me a favor. I appreciate it."

He was still staring at me and making it weird.

"So—thank you."

Still he said nothing, so I raised my hands and leaned back. "That's it. I just wanted to say thank you."

With a nod, he twisted in his seat and slapped a paper on the desk in front of me. "Your F," he said. "For the half of the project you didn't do."

Shock locked my lips together. My half of the project...

Oh.

Shit.

"I told the teacher you bailed on it," he continued in his low, gruff voice that had the best rasp to it. I had a thing for voices. And this really wasn't the time to be thinking about how sexy his voice was when he glared at me like I was shit on his shoe or something. "I emailed you four times. But you were too busy partying in New York to be bothered with class."

Goddammit, I forgot all about the project. I'd even forgotten about it the day before in my frantic race to finish things.

But *Jonas* wasn't done. Even as I tried to cobble together an apology, he spit out, "Being a selfish, entitled bitch might not be a big deal to you, but it is when you screw people over. So, enjoy your F."

Yeah. No way in hell I would apologize now.

I should offer it, but he sure as shit didn't deserve it. Fuck, I couldn't believe I'd forgotten all about it. I made it through the class with him ignoring me so loudly it was almost painful.

Like it or not, guilt edged me the whole damn period. At the end, I barely made it to my feet before the teacher called my name.

Right.

I moved up to the front where she eyed me over the top of her glasses. "Miss Crosse, I wanted to confirm with you that you reviewed the syllabus in full on the first day?"

"Yes, ma'am."

"Good, then you understand why the assignments you turned in last night will not receive full marks. The most you can get on the last two is a seventy." She paused to give me a firm look. Her tone wasn't unkind, but she wasn't exactly exuding warmth either. "The third one is an automatic 0 because you failed to turn any of them in on time. I appreciate that you did the assignments, but no one is immune to these rules. I expect you to turn in everything this week on time, yes?"

"Yes, ma'am."

My heart raced and sweat dotted my skin. I did remember the terms—*now*. When I turned to leave, I caught Jonas staring at me from the doorway. He pivoted and stalked away the moment our gazes clashed.

Maybe he enjoyed that scorching review. He pretty much felt the same way she did and they weren't wrong. But—oh, fuck it.

I headed out into the hallway and nearly collided with Payton Webber. Yeah. Not today. When I went to step around her, she cut me off.

"What?" I asked, fisting my temper in both hands and shoving it down as hard as I could. The day that started out great was rapidly swirling down to absolute crap.

"Did you *really* skip class for a week to suck down shots with Tommy Johns?"

I frowned. That was the last question I expected to get. Tommy Johns was an old school rocker who'd actually written a song for us to record once. It had been hella cool, while he was old enough to be my father and had the reputation of being a pussy hound, he never hit on us.

"No," I said, then cut around her before she could ask another question.

Apparently, she didn't need me facing her to throw out, "Oh...so you spent the week sucking down Johnny Pound?"

I pivoted at that name to stare at her. Where had she just pulled his name from... My mother's boyfriend—ex-boyfriend—and I were not close. He was a nice guy, maybe too nice sometimes, but we weren't exactly besties. The minute I spotted the girl in the corner with her phone up but the green light on, I pasted on a smile.

"No, but if I ever need pointers on how to suck someone down like a pro, you'd probably be a better resource than Johnny, right? Must be all that experience." I smiled as sweetly as possible while I resisted the urge to flip them both off and walked away. Bitch.

"Hey!" Sydney glided out of another hall and hooked her arm through mine. "Missed you last week. We still need to grab lunch! But we're doing a mixer this weekend, you have to come."

"A mixer?" Was that a dance? It sounded like cocktails, but I was pretty sure they weren't going to be serving them *at* the school. Then again, the last party we went to had lots of alcohol so what did I know? "You know what, sure. Text me the details? I need to get to class, but I want to catch up."

"Great! I can fill you in on everything." She beamed. "It's going to be amazing!" We parted at the door to my next class.

Jonas waited for me just inside, his attention firmly *not* on me again. So firmly, I swore I could feel him staring. He cut away abruptly and went to his desk.

I paused next to his desk. "If you want a selfie, all you have to do is ask."

Oh, the glare I got for that was almost worth it. I kept right on going, but I was pretty sure he muttered "bitch" in that sexy rasp of his.

Pretty much every class went the way of the first one. My grades took a hit across the board. By the time I walked into Mr. Cohen's lit class, my stomach was in knots.

Thankfully, he didn't say a word to me, we just pushed on with class; more curiously, TA Malone was nowhere to be seen. I didn't want to examine my disappointment about that fact too closely.

Lunch was a breath of fresh air. Sydney pretty much talked all the way through it, filling me in about the mixer. Apparently, this was a new event that Sydney and the drill team were sponsoring. I didn't even know the school had a drill team.

I really needed to pay more attention. I got to see Aubrey for five minutes when she came through the dining hall with a guy hot on her tail. I studied him briefly when she dropped into the chair next to me.

"Don't start," was all she said and I gave her a little shrug. The guy was cute. Dark skin, dark eyes, curly hair, and a killer smile. She could do worse. "We got teamed up for a project, so I'm probably going to be late getting back to the room tonight."

Good for her.

"I'll be right back," Sydney told us as she jumped up to

head across the hall. That girl never stopped moving and she had a kind of sunshine energy that I liked.

"You okay?" Aubrey asked and I summoned up a smile for her and shrugged.

"Long day," I said finally. "I'll tell you about it later. Go get your study buddy. I'll make sure I eat tonight." I held up a hand. "I promise."

"Good girl. See you later..." When she held up her pinky, I locked mine around hers. "Text me if you need me." The last she said was almost sotto voce. "I mean it."

"Same goes for you," I reminded her. I didn't always need them to bail me out. No matter how bad it felt right now.

"I know." She winked, squeezed my pinky and then she was off. I turned back to my grilled salmon and rice, only to lock gazes with Hot Shot Jonas. He was seated at a table with like a dozen other kids, all of them talking—except him.

No, he just sat there doodling with his pencil while watching me. I raised my eyebrows, daring him to say something, but he didn't move and his expression didn't change.

I definitely looked away before he did.

The afternoon definitely didn't improve on the morning, and when I headed to the library, I thought I was ready for TA Malone.

The man waiting for me wore a dark and disapproving expression. "Miss Crosse," he said, closing the door after I was inside. "Take a seat. It's time we had a little reality check."

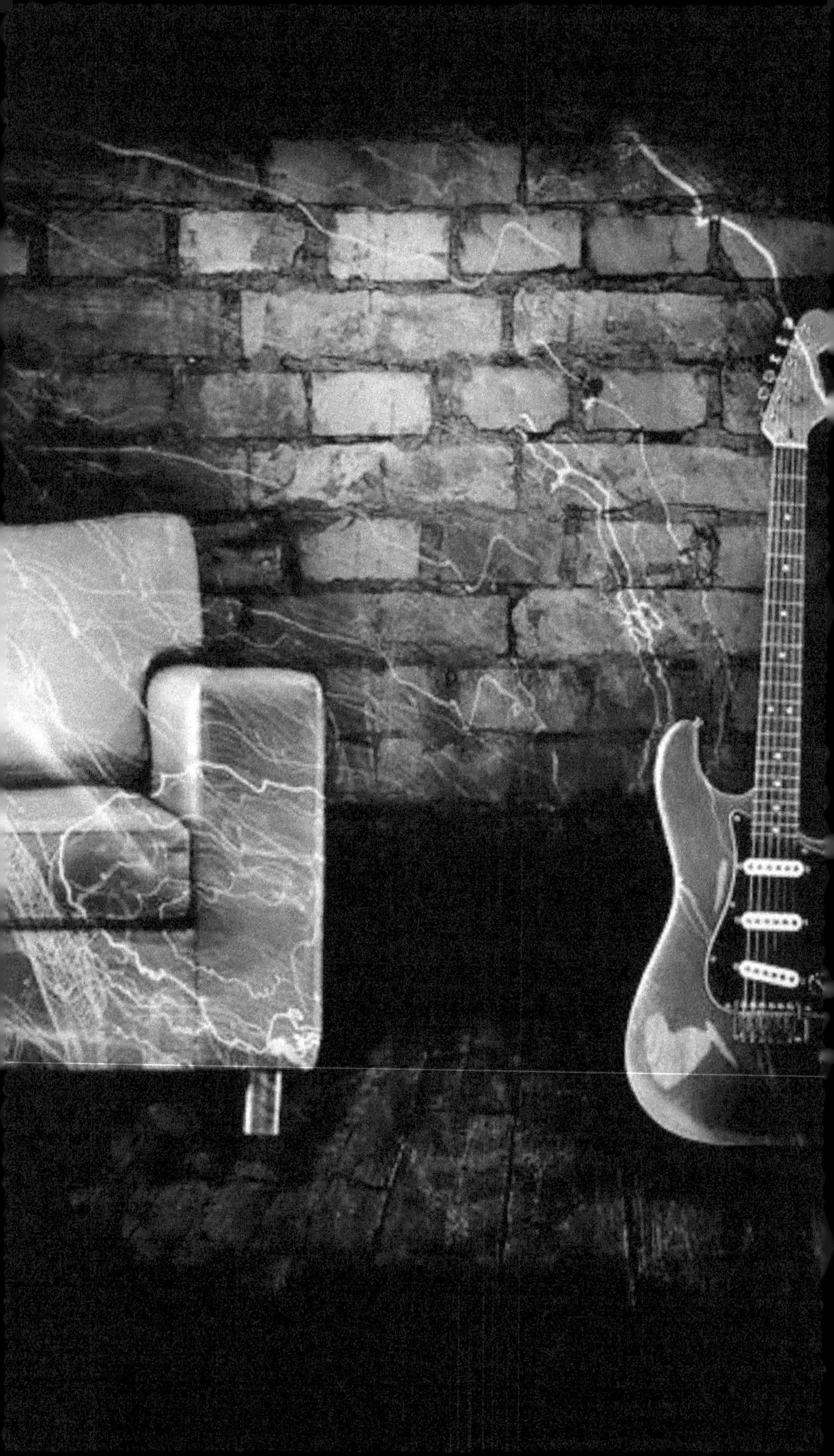

Fifteen

As soon as my ass hit the chair, he planted his broad hands on the table and leaned forward. It was like he took up all the oxygen in the study room. I bit my lower lip as he stared at me. The intensity in his blue eyes kept me pinned in place.

When my stomach bottomed out and my heart squeezed, I tried to lean back in the chair. Maybe if... "I'm—"

"Nothing," he said firmly. "You are absolutely *nothing* here, Miss Crosse. I don't care who you think you are on a stage or in a recording studio or getting plastered in some bar. At this school... in this room... you are nothing."

Just like when I was in the hallway with that kid kissing me for his stupid selfie, I froze. Who the hell did he think...

"You are a student, and based on my observations from the past few weeks, you're a bad one." A slap might have hurt less. "You are here, allegedly, to learn. Jetting off to New York to party is not a part of the curriculum nor does it benefit your education."

I didn't bother to correct him. He didn't want an argument, he wanted to yell.

Did he have to be so hot while he was doing it? And what the hell was wrong with me that I enjoyed watching that vein throb in his forehead and the distinct growl in his voice?

With a sharp shake of his head, he continued, "You are officially on academic probation, Miss Crosse. If you miss classes or fail to turn in assignments again, you can and will be brought before the administrative board for review. Blue Ivy is focused on providing you with an education—*I* am focused on giving you opportunities to improve on an area you are clearly lacking, and instead of taking advantage of it, you're wasting my time."

Eyes narrowing, I tilted my head. "I didn't ask *you* for *anything*, Mr. Malone."

He arched both eyebrows.

"If you'll recall, you *informed* me that I was going to be receiving tutoring. *You* changed my class schedule to make sure I had this hour free, and *you* demanded that I show up."

Straightening slowly, he folded his arms. The act pulled his button down white shirt taut across his chest. It also highlighted the fact he wore an undershirt. It also gave me a peek of tattoo at his wrist.

"Are you quite finished?" The superior tone rankled, but I leaned back in the chair with a long sigh.

"Sure," I told him, waving a hand. "I'm done. I'm here. Are we yelling at me some more or going back to the diagramming of sentences..."

Which reminded me. I opened my bag and pulled out three pages of diagrammed sentences.

"I did do my homework. Granted it's from more than a week ago and is probably only getting a zero, but I did do it."

Maybe it didn't rate a cookie, but I'd never been afraid of hard work or assholes telling me I didn't matter. Everyone —*everyone*—was so damn certain that we would never have gotten a contract to record without our parents being who they were.

Doubters had always been in my life. He could shove his attitude up his ass, but I would prove him wrong.

With a harsh exhale, he dropped his gaze to the papers then pulled out his chair. As he sat down, some of the oxygen filtered back into the room and my heart stopped pounding like it wanted to escape.

The fact I was sweating through enough that I wanted to rip off my shirt wasn't helping. I didn't think this room had been so hot before.

TA Malone handled the papers carefully, like they contained nuclear codes or something. When he picked up his red pen and began to click the end of it, I braced. But he just clicked it again and again.

Oh, this was torture. Folding my arms, I tilted my head back to stare up at the ceiling. I needed the break from his intensity but he kept clicking that pen.

Over.

And over.

"Not bad," he said finally, and I dropped my chin to look at him. "Not bad at all. You're right, it would only get a zero for how late it is—but since this is remedial work and not graded, you get a pass."

Relief swarmed me.

"But don't relax," he continued, his chilly voice brushing against my overheated skin and only fanning the flames. "You missed four days, so now you need to make those up."

Make them up...?

"How?" I asked before I agreed to anything. While I hadn't *wanted* these tutoring sessions, I was here and it already took up a huge chunk of time.

"We'll start with this," he said, pulling a packet out of the messenger bag on the floor next to him and setting it on the table. The thump the packet made hitting the table did not inspire a lot of confidence. "This is everything you should have done last week."

"Okay," I said slowly. "So, you want me to do that packet?"

"Yes," he said, the corners of his lips tipping into a smile that never touched his eyes. If anything, he seemed to become more remote. "You're also going to continue with this week's tutoring. We're starting with today's, so you just need to keep up."

"You're not helping me with this?" I asked as he shoved it over to me.

"No," he said simply. "I was available to help you last week with that. This week, we're moving onto other topics."

And I had a hundred dollars that said this packet was crucial to whatever we were doing this week.

I nodded. "When do you want this back?"

"Last week would have been good." The snarky comment didn't manage to land on any of the open wounds he'd already inflicted earlier. "However, time travel is not an option."

"Right, so I'll get them in this week." I glanced at the first page and then sighed as I moved to put it in my own book bag and then focused on him again.

Sleep was about to become a thing of the past.

"Today we're working on themes," he said. What did themes have to do with grammar?

By the end of our hour, I had a splitting headache and no ego whatsoever. Discussing the meaning behind the story in context with what sentences meant and how grammar could support or distort left my brain aching.

While I understood a lot of it, I really wasn't sure how it connected to diagramming, and I'd bet all the interest on my bank account that I'd find it in that packet.

I was still working on the last paragraph when he rose and

collected his stuff. "I'll see you tomorrow, Miss Crosse." At the door, he paused, "Don't waste my time again."

He didn't wait for my answer and the minute he was out of the room, I dropped my head to the table and just laid there with my arms crossed.

Self-pity was not a place I could live. Not and survive my world. My phone chose that moment to vibrate. There were only three people who could text me when I was in class and it would notify me.

Dragging the phone out I sat up and stared at the screen. The message wasn't from Aubrey or Yvette. It was from Dix.

I hit the contact button and closed the door to the study room for some privacy. Dix answered on the first ring.

"What's wrong?" The question spilled out of me. Granted, all his message had said was "call me when you have a minute" but Dix didn't usually text me when I was gone unless something was wrong.

"Easy, sweetheart," he said, his tone soothing. "Nothing is wrong."

Dropping back into the chair, I slumped and put my hand to my head as I rested my elbow on the table. "Dix, you never text me unless something is wrong."

"Well, we need to fix that." Honestly, that seemed fair. Dix had been doing a lot for me.

"We probably should," I agreed. "Sorry. Hi."

"Hey." His voice softened. "I wanted to check on you. Last week was pretty brutal and you went straight back to school."

"It sucks," I admitted. "But Mom is at the retreat, hopefully sobering up and getting some inner peace." We had a routine: she got clean for a while, bounced back, did a couple of movies and then spiraled again.

"How is KC doing? Are you getting some peace?"

A laugh escaped me, probably a little harsh and abrupt,

but I had to snort laugh. "Not really? I fucked up on the homework, got a few Fs, am now on academic probation, and half the school hates me, the other half wants me for my name, and then there are the people who seem to live to torture me."

"Sounds like high school. But if anyone is giving you a hard time, you call me. I'll take care of my girl."

I smiled at the offer. "I'm a big girl, Dix. I can take care of myself, but thank you."

"Long as you know you can call me."

"I do," I promised. "And I'm going to be great."

"Okay, sweetheart. I'll call you later this week."

"Hey Dix," I said before he could hang up. "Thank you."

"Welcome, sweetheart. You take care of yourself, and I mean it: someone messes with you, get me. Get help. There are too many crazies out there."

Yeah, I knew that, too. Much as it was nice to talk to him, I let him go. It was damn nice of him to check on me. I debated calling the retreat to check on Mom then discarded the idea.

When Mom went to these places, she needed to focus on her. That decided it. I checked the time. The academic day was over, but Aubrey was going to be working on her project and not heading back to the room.

Since I had the study room, I pulled out the hell packet from the previous week and spent the next four hours working my way through every single page.

About halfway through the packet, the diagramming turned to language and literature—a lightbulb went off. I loved the natural melody in words and there was definitely a cadence to each assignment and the more I dug into the word usage and the grammar of the sentences…

It was weird but it was also kind of magical. We did the same things when writing songs. Words had meaning. Everyone brought their own experiences to the table so you had to be able to not only communicate a universal idea that crossed cultural barriers, but also understand how those words worked everywhere.

Fuck.

The assignment was kind of beautiful. It made me wonder what TA Malone would have said if I'd been here for him to guide me through it.

I still made it back to the dorm room before Aubrey and I wrote her a note on the fridge. I was broken and exhausted. I wanted to sleep as hard as I could for as long as I could.

Back in my room and ready for bed, my gaze went to the guitar. It had been a while since I just sat down and played. I needed to make more time for it. My phone rang before I could get up and get it.

Teddy calling was never a good sign. He took care of all our contracts, negotiations, and tour bookings. It had been his job to clear our schedules for the next year. Granted, I wanted to finish high school and that took two more years, but we needed the first year cleared and after that, the second year should take care of itself.

No sooner did I answer the phone than he said, "KC, I need to know where you were last week."

"Why?"

"The *Tattler* has a story that you were in New York partying and doing too many pills, and the excess nearly caused an overdose. That's why you were seen going to a retreat. Where were you?"

"I'm at *school*, Teddy. Chill. It's fine. None of that was me, and I have no idea where they got their story, but I wasn't out partying and I sure as hell wasn't drinking." Quite the opposite; I'd been dumping the alcohol.

"We need to issue a statement, then, categorically denying this."

"Why?" I mean, I got that I hadn't done it. But the gossips were gonna gossip. I didn't have to justify myself to their stories. Categorically denying it would then beg the question of *what* was I doing.

"KC, your mother's rather public breakup with her—boyfriend—is all over the news as is her current location."

He didn't say it and I refused to confirm it. "And?"

His sigh echoed down the line. "And," he continued, "with your mother spiraling and imploding, it's a juicier story if you were joining her on that downward slide, and you're younger and a lot hotter on social media. They are going to get more traction with click-bait stories about you than they are your mother. So, if we don't nip this, that's all that's going to be out there."

I rubbed a hand over my face. "They won't believe a statement."

"They don't have to, we just have to make it. That will help curb some of the reaction and hopefully take the spotlight off of you again." It would take it off me and slam it on Mom. She needed to focus on her.

"I'm at school, leave it alone. I won't explain myself or justify my actions to a bunch of nosey pricks with nothing better to do." Fuck, I was tired.

"Honey," he began and I hated that tone. It was placating and a little condescending. "This is not a smart business decision. Notoriety only goes so far in the music world."

"Goes further than it does in Hollywood." I shook my head. It was no one's fucking business where Mom was and what she was doing. The tabloid fodder was bad enough, but comments and statements just fed the beast. Dad could dick as many women in a night as he wanted and be lauded for it. Mom had any kind of a breakdown and she would be crucified.

Hollywood was not as forgiving as it used to be.

"The speculation on the internet isn't going to stop," he

warned. "They won't let go of the hiatus for the group or the fact the three of you have virtually dropped out of sight."

I laughed. "I haven't dropped out of sight. They're talking about me partying in New York." Whether anyone saw me or not, hot stories would sell, and if I didn't give them anything, then they would just make shit up.

"I disagree with this and I will be talking to Aubrey and Yvette."

"That's fair. We're a democracy, so if they vote for the statement, then I'll even take care of issuing it." They wouldn't. None of us really liked dealing with the press, Yvette least of all.

He didn't linger on the call, and after we hung up, I fell back on the bed. Fuck my life, normal was hard.

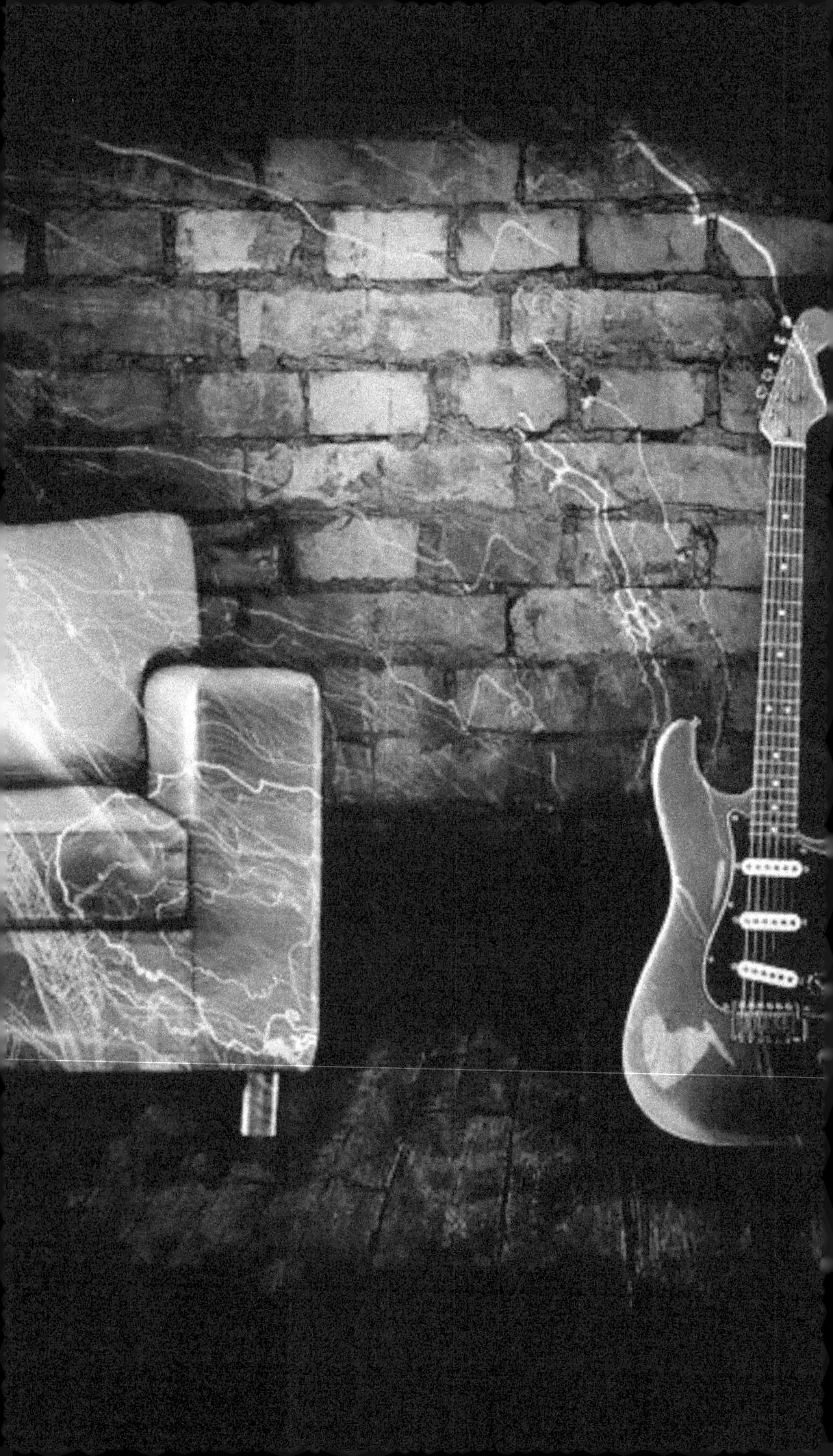

Sixteen

The air was brisk and after a night of tossing and turning, I dragged my sorry ass out to run. I needed to get out of my head. I needed to come up with a plan to deal with—

"Well, well, well." Lachlan, Douchebag Three, waiting to greet me was about as welcome as a stubbed toe on concrete. "Look at you, I heard you were back and that you could even walk."

Head tilted, he gave me a once over. Ignoring him would be nice, but it wouldn't work. So, I just rolled my eyes and ignored my stretches to start running. Granted it was a slow jog, but it would help warm me up.

"Congratulations are in order," he continued, falling into step easily with me.

My ear buds were in so I just scrolled to one of the random playlists on my phone.

"Not even going to ask me for what?" He shot me this cocky grin that not only suited his face, but with the way the light hit him, added about a hundred and ten percent to the sexiness in his charisma.

I hit the first playlist, but the music that came up was too low and sultry, with a low thrumming tempo that was way too provocative for a run.

Worse, it didn't really drown out his voice. Then he swung around in front of me and I had to stop or plow into him. He reached over and plucked one of the earbuds right out.

"You know, it's rude to ignore people."

"Not as rude as assaulting them," I informed him and held out my hand. "Give it back."

Instead of returning it, he popped it into his ear and his expression would have been comical if he wasn't being such a prick. "What the fuck are you listening to you?"

"NOUB." I flexed my fingers in a come hither gesture.

"You have shit taste."

"Good thing no one asked you. Give me the fucking earbud back." I had my thumb on the side of the phone. There were other playlists, and some were a lot more painful than others.

"After you talk to me like a polite human being."

I stared at him. "It's not even six in the morning."

"So?"

"Who the fuck is polite at this hour?"

"Clearly," he said slowly, his smirk growing. "Not you. So, let's call this an education. You want your earbud, keep up...I mean, you can walk after your week of hard partying. Impressive, I like a girl with stamina. Can you run?"

Not waiting for an answer, he pivoted and took off. Did he seriously expect me to chase him? Was I going to chase him?

He wasn't that far ahead, but I glanced down at the phone and changed it to trash metal, then turned it up. The fact he actually flinched and stumbled a step made me smile.

Asshole.

I resumed running, but I kept it to my warm-up jog. At

least for the first half mile. While he stayed ahead of me, he wasn't really trying to get away either. I could afford new earbuds, I didn't have to give in to whatever juvenile torture prank this was.

Instead, I just focused on running. The trash metal wasn't my favorite, but it definitely suited my mood where I pictured him being the target of a brutal beatdown in some action movie.

I actually knew stunt guys and fighters. I wondered if any of them wanted to do me a favor...

Riding the high of that imagery, I failed to notice when he slowed down until I was nearly on top of him and we were hitting the wooden bridge over the pond.

One minute I was passing him and the next, I was flying into the pond. Panic hit me like a brick as I tumbled. Falling was such a horrid sensation. Landing wasn't much better. The water was icy. I went in sideways, which meant I didn't even manage to save my hair. All of me got dunked, and thoroughly.

Thankfully, it wasn't deep, even if it was muddy as fuck. My shoe sank as I floundered to my feet. Chills broke out all over my skin as goosebumps rippled over my flesh.

Water dripped off me and my hair landed in my eyes. I barely stood up before his soft laughter reached me.

"Ha ha," I parroted, even as I flipped him off. "Dick."

I didn't splash around as I made my way to the side and climbed out onto the dewy grass. I was annoyed that my remaining earbud had vanished when I hit the water. A breeze brushed over me and I couldn't suppress the shudder that hit me.

"Huh," Lachlan said from a foot in front of me as he held out a hand as though to help me out of the water. Not falling for that, I shifted direction to finish my exit without his assistance.

I caught him eyeing me and if it weren't for one of the trail lights still being on, I wouldn't have made out the smirk.

"What?" I gripped the hem of my shirt and squeezed it to free some of the water from it. There was no saving my shoes or socks. The longer I stood here, the colder I got. "White shirt in a pond. Very funny. Too bad for you I'm wearing a bra, asshole."

"Yeah," he said, then clucked his tongue before gripping my shirt and yanking it up. Before I could even shift a step, he flicked out a knife and cut the snaps in the front that secured my sports bra. It popped open. "Not anymore."

His smirk grew as he admired his work and chilly air hit my breasts. I jerked back, but he was already letting go of my shirt and I damn near fell in the pond again.

"Not much to brag about there," he said as he slipped the knife away. "White shirt or not."

Still smirking, he pivoted to walk away but then paused to toss the other earbud at me. I caught it on reflex.

"You have shit taste in music, too." Great, he repeated himself now. "Not surprising given the garbage you perform." Walking backwards, he didn't take his gaze off me. "Word to the wise, next time you're hot to party, jump in the pond. It's probably got fewer diseases."

He gave me a mock salute before setting off on his run again, leaving me there bra-less, soaking wet, earbuds pretty much trashed and my hair dripping more icy water down my body.

I made myself wait until he was out of sight before I screamed. Folding my arms over my chest, I doubled back the way we'd come rather than follow him. Surrendering? Probably. Whatever.

I was shivering, and very much trying not to cry. My phone still worked. That was something. The sun was up by the time I made it to the trailhead, and there were more people moving.

The walk hadn't done anything to dry me off.

"What happened to you?" RJ's voice dragged me to the present and I let out a sad little sigh even as relief peppered me.

My greeting died unspoken as I stared at him. He stood at the trailhead, dressed in sweats, but he had on one of those foot boots you get when you're hurt and his right eye was a technicolor mix of black and blue with hints of purple and green.

"Maybe I should be asking you that," I said. He looked like hell.

RJ shrugged with a grin. "Nothing important except missing you." But he sobered almost as soon as his smile appeared. "Are you okay?"

"Sure. Just a bit cold after my morning run."

He leaned back a fraction to give me a once over that held more skepticism than leering. "Maybe don't run in the water next time?"

"Damn," I said with a half-smile and snapped my fingers. "You got me."

As close to tears as I'd been, having RJ right there gave me an audience, and I could mask all real emotions in front of an audience.

Worry seemed to reflect in his eyes as he frowned then took a step forward as his gaze skipped right past me. The less than friendly expression he wore had me twisting.

"Oh," I said as Lachlan strolled up. Sweat dotted his forehead and slicked his hair. "You."

He smirked. "Don't look at me like that. I already told you I wasn't impressed."

Making a face, I shook my head, but it was RJ who said, "Fuck off, Nash. If I find out you shoved her in the pond like some juvenile delinquent...don't think I won't report your ass."

The swiftness of his movements on the trail should have prepared me for how fast he moved when he wanted. One minute, Lachlan was strolling toward us and the next, he had me pinned right up against RJ.

"The black eye is looking a little lonely, Wallach." A muscle twitched in his jaw, but his deep green eyes had gone positively glacial. The mysterious forest plunged into some ice age.

Kind of like my whole body had when I hit that pond. Course, it didn't explain why I was getting so warm now.

Hands landed on my hips, anchoring me in place.

"Hiding behind the little pop princess, Wallach?" Lachlan laughed. "Not sure who is more pathetic." He dropped his gaze to me. "Ace here, giving you the time of day, or you using her as a shield?"

As if to prove how unimpressed he was, Lachlan stepped right into me until I was sandwiched between their chests. They towered over me, their eyes waging war over my head.

This was so not the position I wanted to be in. If they wanted a dick measuring contest, they could do it without my chilly ass even if they were both hotter than hell this close.

To get free though, meant I had to drop my folded arms and push my hands against him. Not that it did fuck all to make him move. If anything, his smirk seemed to grow even if he kept glaring at RJ.

Then he dropped his gaze to my chest.

"Maybe try a different bra next time," he whispered right next to my ear.

Shock and anger vied for the top shelf in my brain as he bit my earlobe.

Fucking. Bit. It.

With RJ right behind me and holding me *still*, I had even less room to escape than I had before.

"Doesn't matter how much you beg me for it," Lachlan continued as he straightened and made a big show of peeling my hands off him. He held them aloft too so he could get another look. "I don't do anyone's sloppy seconds." He paused, then smirked at RJ. "Or their fifth's for that matter."

"You asshole," I snarled but a tittering laugh from the right yanked my attention and fuck my life. Who was standing right there filming us? Payton. Goddamn. Webber.

She lowered the phone to give me a cool look. "You shouldn't throw yourself at other girl's guys. It's cheap. But then...apparently so are you."

Lachlan was almost to her and he hooked an arm around her as he got there and she kissed his jaw all the while staring at me.

If she wanted him, she could have him.

"You should shower," she told Lachlan. "You don't want to catch whatever she might have."

"Class and taste are two things he could use." I was so fucking done. "Next time you swallow his pencil dick, pretend to choke on it."

Behind me, RJ laughed, but I wasn't kidding or trying to be funny. I pulled away from him. He'd managed to spend that whole little standoff *behind* me instead of helping. Or whatever.

"Hey, Problem Child," Payton called out and I glanced over in time for her to snap another shot. "Wet t-shirt looks good on you. Reminds everyone where you're from—they say the whore doesn't fall far from the tree."

Fuck it.

Something in me snapped and I lunged forward. RJ caught my arm and pulled me back even as Lachlan swiveled.

Payton shrank back against him, but he didn't cover her or offer her any kind of protection.

"You're insane," she told me. "I'll go to administration."

"Fuck off, Payton," RJ said. "No one gives a damn about your opinions unless Daddy paid for it."

He tightened his grip on my arm then pulled me back to him. "Come on, KC," RJ said as he wrapped his free arm around my middle. "She's really not worth it. Nothing you say will ever matter, unless you have a dick. Trust me, her blowjobs aren't worth it either."

Red-faced, Payton glared at RJ. "As if I'd ever..."

"Ever?" He chuckled. "Try four times and I got the pictures to prove it. Want to see?"

"Payton, leave it." Lachlan glowered but it was RJ smirking now and all I wanted to do was get the hell away from all of them. I finally pulled myself free.

"Are you really going to let them *talk* to me like that?" Her voice climbed, but I wasn't sticking around for the answer.

Folding my arms to help prevent any more nip pics, I stalked away from all of them. RJ caught up to me a few steps later.

"Hey..." When I didn't slow down, he moved faster to get in front of me. I was really over guys doing that. "Hey," he repeated. "I'm sorry."

"What?" The apology stopped me.

"For that shit back there with Lachlan and Payton. You didn't deserve that...and you sure as hell didn't deserve this..."

He was peeling off his hoodie.

"And I should have offered you this." He was already draping it around me and even if it was damp from where I'd been pushed against him, it was also warm. "Can I take you to breakfast?"

"I need to shower."

"I can wait."

I blinked.

"Really, I can. Let me walk you back to your dorm. I'll wait, then we can get breakfast together. We can catch up..."

A part of me wanted to glance around and see if anyone was watching us. And by anyone, I knew I meant Lachlan and Payton. That realization made me lift my chin and *not* look.

I was probably going to be on some damn blast all over again.

"Say yes, KC." He gave me a teasing grin. "I could even go get breakfast and bring it back to your room if you want."

They probably expected me to go back to my room and lick my wounds. To be fair, I'd been running away a lot. Time for that to stop.

"I'd like that," I told him. "Give me ten to shower and change, then we can go get breakfast. Do you want to go get in your uniform?"

"Nah," he said. "I don't want to miss a minute with you. I can change before class."

He swept his hand toward the building for me to lead and I shoved my hands into the pocket of his hoodie. It was a lot warmer and covered me up. That helped.

The fact the photo made it to social media before I got into the shower didn't.

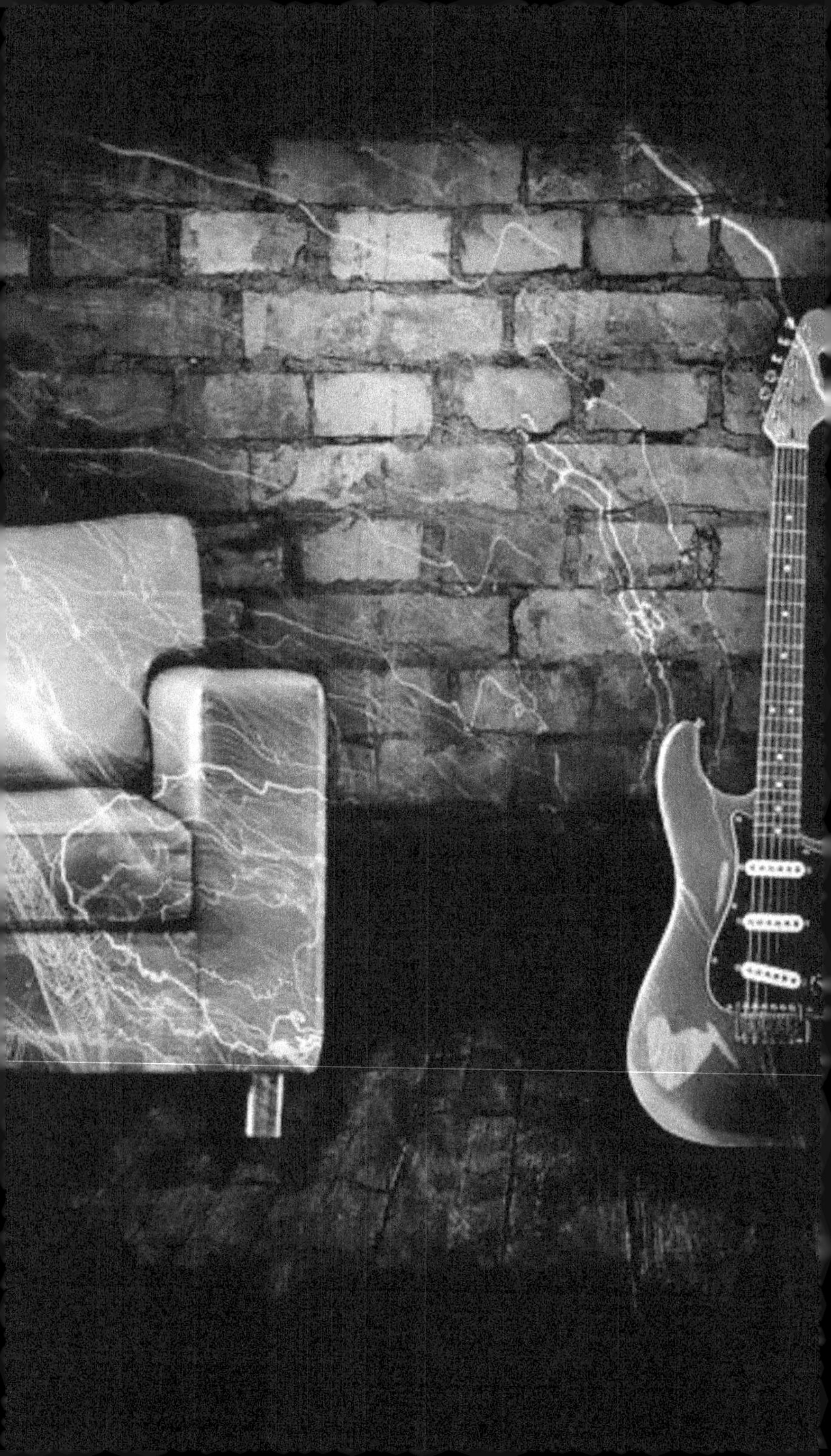

Seventeen

"So he has no idea who you are?" Aubrey asked as she followed me through the mall. Skepticism pervaded every word. Not that I blamed her.

"Not everyone listens to us," I said. "It would be arrogant as fuck to try and pretend they did."

"Right, we're hardly an *unknown* though," she countered, hooking her arm through mine. We'd gotten a ride-share to pick us up first thing on Saturday morning and headed off campus.

I needed new earbuds. More, I needed to be away from campus. We were out of our uniforms, and with my hair all hidden under a dark gray newsboy cap, I'd added a matching gray vest to my long-sleeved black shirt for an arty look.

Tattoos and hair hidden, I blended better, even if the cap got some looks. Aubrey had braided her hair into a crown, and she'd donned a gray vest as well, so only her shirt was white.

"Here's the thing," she said as she took a sip of her coffee.

We were in full-on stroll. We'd been taking our time since we stopped to get bagels for breakfast and then left the little shop with coffee in hand. The mall was rousing awake slowly as we made our way along the first level.

"Let's say he never heard of you before," Aubrey continued. "Fine. Good. Whatever. Weirder things happen. Tell me why he hasn't Googled you or checked out social media? Hell, the whole school knows we're there, and your new stalker Payton has been posting about you pretty regularly."

I sighed.

"Don't make that noise at me," she scolded. "I'm looking out for you. He's cute and he's nice, that's fine. But so far, cute and nice seem to be in short supply at this school, so what is wrong with him?"

"Nothing," I said. "I hope. And look, maybe he did look me up and decided to not do anything about it. I mean, I told him I just wanted to be normal."

She side-eyed me. "You like him, don't you?"

"I don't—not like him," I said then made a face. "He's just...nice. Like Sydney is nice. And Harley." There was a small handful of students I could call nice. Most of them were fucking awful. "You know what's weird?"

"That you keep trying to change the subject off the guy who has a thing for you?" Aubrey asked with a blink of "innocent" eyes. When I gave her a pointed stare, she huffed. "Fine, I'll let it go. But I'm reserving my right to kick this guy in the balls if he turns out to be a sack of shit."

"Deal." I'd take anything that changed the subject.

"Done," she said, touching her coffee cup to mine in a show of toasting. "Now, tell me what's weird."

"I never imagined this being like some bad television drama, you know? I didn't imagine any of this. Like I thought those shows were always just an exaggeration." At least what I'd managed to see of them. But...

"People suck," Aubrey said with a shrug. "We knew it might be hard. Fans can be just as bad as haters."

That was true. "I feel like these people actually hate me. It's like I kicked their dog or something. I don't even know how to defend myself because I don't know what I did."

"Maybe they're just assholes," Aubrey supplied. She was much calmer than she'd been when I showed up at the room soaking wet with my bra sliced. No, then she'd been incensed. "I still think you should have reported them."

"I thought about it, but what good is that going to do? I mean, really? No one actually saw him do it. Anyway...it's done. I just plan to be as far away from Lachlan Nash as I can be. If that means I need to find the gym and use a treadmill to run, then I'll do that."

"Fuck that," Aubrey said as we reached the electronics store. There was another ten minutes before they opened so we found a bench near some planters and settled on it. "I'll get up early and just go running with you. If he tries to shove you in the pond again, I'll be there to help you beat him up."

"Aubrey, you hate the pre-dawn hours."

"So do you."

Well, that was true. "I need to run. You don't. RJ's ankle sprain is gonna keep him from running for another couple of weeks. I'll just use the gym until he's back on his feet. You get to sleep. I get to run."

"Not going to lie. I like the idea of sleeping. But I will not let you keep taking this abuse. You know, maybe I can change classes..."

"I love you," I told her, and when I rested my head on her shoulder she wrapped an arm around me.

"I love you, too. Give me a few days to think about appropriate punishments for Lachlan the Douchebag and Payton the Bitch."

"They kind of have each other; that's pretty much punishment all its own, you know?"

Too bad it wasn't as punishing for them as it was for me.

"Hmm-hmm." Aubrey pulled out her phone and opened up social media. None of us spent a lot of time on there. She pulled up Payton's profile.

"What are you doing?"

"Fighting fire with fire," Aubrey murmured. "We have fans, we could use them."

"No," I said firmly and put my hand over her screen even as a picture of Payton smooshed up to Lachlan popped up. "We don't do that. Remember?"

Fans could be weaponized. We'd seen it. Hell, we'd been on the receiving end of it.

Scowling, Aubrey lowered her phone. "I refuse to let that bitch keep getting away with making bank on humiliating you."

"This is why I love you. Or at least, one of the many."

"I know." Tapping her phone against her chin lightly, she frowned. Finally, she clicked off the screen. "Okay. No fans. You're right. Weaponizing them is not cool. But you need to get better at your phone filming game..."

"Why?"

"How were you born in Hollywood and raised by one of the most gossip-plagued women ever and still ask that question?"

I sighed. "Because I hate the fake shit, I always have. You want me to be ready to film her so we can do to her what she's been doing to me."

"Yes," she said firmly. "And no."

"I'm listening."

"KC, I know you hate the gossips. I know you do everything you can to not make waves and people make them for you. Half the stories that are written about us are blown way out of proportion and the other half are just this side of slanderous lies delivered through suggestion and innuendo."

All true.

"But you have to fight fire with fire. Right now, she's controlling the narrative."

Her stupid TikTok of the drowned blueberry sandwich —that really wasn't any better than problem child to be honest—had gone fucking viral before it had been taken down.

"I'll think about it," I said. "I'm done not fighting back. I've tried to just keep a low profile and get along to go along…"

"Good. And I'm going to have your back every step of the way."

"But first," I said as I stood up. "I need new earbuds."

"Make sure we keep the receipt," Aubrey said. "I want to make sure we nail it to Lachlan Nash's door."

That would be funny. Probably pointless, but a little funny.

The rest of the weekend sped by, but the day at the mall had helped me reset and recover. I spent Sunday playing catchup and getting a little ahead. I'd already done all of the packet of tutoring from TA Malone and I'd gotten another paper written for Mr. Cohen—while also painstakingly trying to vet every sentence for misplaced modifiers and other grammar mistakes.

RJ met me every morning for breakfast, picking me up from the gym. For almost a week, I didn't see Lachlan Nash *at all*. It was the absolute best. Though I couldn't help looking for him every single time I was outside. The leaves were turning amazing colors and I hated not running outside, but I also wanted to focus on avoiding him.

Running at night didn't do it for me, so I kept running on the treadmill in the gym. On Friday, RJ surprised me at the gym with coffee and donuts.

"Hey," I said, wiping the sweat off my face. He didn't usually come in, preferring to wait for me outside. The bruise on his eye had definitely improved. "Am I late?" I checked the time. Running inside was just not as easy for me to track the time spent as the trail.

It kind of sucked, but I had enjoyed the Lachlan reprieve. The whole world getting to see my boobs through a wet t-shirt was not my idea of a good time.

"No," RJ said with a laugh. "But I wanted to make today a little special?"

I sipped the coffee as I followed him out of the gym. I usually went back to my room to shower after breakfast. The cool air helped to dry my damp and overheated skin.

"Did I miss something?" Why was today special? Besides being Friday. Was there something about the date? It was October.

RJ chuckled. "Not that I know of." He led the way down the steps to where there were benches and landscaping that afforded the suggestion of privacy. I loved the pines they had cut and shaped, not that I had any idea what they were precisely other than pretty.

Once we were seated, RJ turned to face me. "So, I've been thinking."

"That's dangerous."

He chuckled. "You have no idea."

"Well, I won't until you tell me." I opened the bag of donuts and chose the glazed. I was the boring girl who liked the plain, regular glazed donuts. Which was great. There was always a lot and I could always find my favorite.

"Nice, logical argument." He grinned.

"Thank you."

RJ had a great smile. The guy was huge, but he also had this open, friendly expression coupled with a smile that just turned him from good looking to purely handsome. He also had a sense of humor and he wasn't a raging dick.

Well, except when he was, but Payton kind of deserved it,

so I'd give him a pass. Not that I wanted to think about the idea of him getting a blowjob from Payton.

Gross.

Right. I shoved that series of thoughts right out of my head. Picturing her giving anyone a blowjob was nauseating. Especially when Lachlan immediately blew in to take up residence in my brain again. It was like he'd carved out his own space even when he wasn't around.

"Anyway..." I said as I tried to shake that thought off. "What's up?"

"I think we're getting good at this friends thing," RJ said slowly, eyeing me even as he lifted his own coffee for a sip. "Yeah?"

"Yeah," I agreed. That seemed obvious but maybe it wasn't. "I think so."

He grinned. "Pretty normal, you and me, just getting to know each other..."

"Uh huh." I raised the donut. "Friends who can run together—when you finish healing up."

"Soon," he promised. "Until then... want to go out with me tonight? Tomorrow? Both? Something fun and low key. I mean, we can do a movie or maybe head over to the game in Hartford."

Game in Hartford... "You're asking me out on a date?"

"Well, I'm trying," he said with a grin. "We get breakfast together every day, we've graduated from the occasional text to running text messages."

Well, that might be stretching it a little. He texted and I answered, but it wasn't like an all day thing. At the same time, a flutter of excitement shivered up my spine.

"Would you like to go out with me?"

"I would," I admitted and his growing smile already had guilt swirling into the space the surprise and anticipation had carved. "But I don't think it's a good idea *right* now."

He frowned. "Why not?"

"Ugh..." I stared up at the sky because I hated telling him no. I hated saying no period. A date sounded like an amazing idea. "Can I tell you something? Just between you and me?"

"Yes." He frowned. "What is it?"

"This is... embarrassing but I got really behind the week I missed and I kind of forgot that I had no excuses on when assignments were due and I'm on academic probation..." I made a face. "The thing is, I've been working on getting caught up and trying to get ahead, but I've got tutoring and a heavy course load. Right now, I can't afford to take the time, as much as I want to."

I'd paid for taking the day on Saturday, but I'd *needed* that time away and Aubrey was right there to back me up on studying Sunday.

"I really have to get my grades up as much as possible because those zeroes are really counting against me right now." I grimaced. "Sorry."

"No," he said slowly. "I get it. You are on probation, need to get your grades up, and once you're caught up or at least ahead, you'd be free to go on a date then?"

"Technically," I answered with a slow nod. "Yes."

"Then, I'll help you. We can study together, I've had some of your classes already, and I know most of the teachers. We'll get you caught up in no time and then we're going to go out and celebrate."

"You don't have to—"

"I want to," he assured me. "Maybe more than you know. So, what's the toughest class? And when do you want to have our first study session? I can come to your room or you can come to mine. We'll have quiet and privacy."

"I currently have a research project that I'm trying to get ahead on, so how about the library? They have all those study rooms." It would be quiet and private—even in public. "And I mean it, studying isn't going to be anywhere near as fun as going out."

RJ grinned as he pulled out another glazed donut and offered it to me. "I get to be with you though, and when we have you caught up and off probation, we're going to have a good time."

I was still grinning as I walked back to my room after we'd finished our little breakfast "date." I was *sort* of dating.

Ok, definitely time to conference Yvette in. I needed some girl time and some advice.

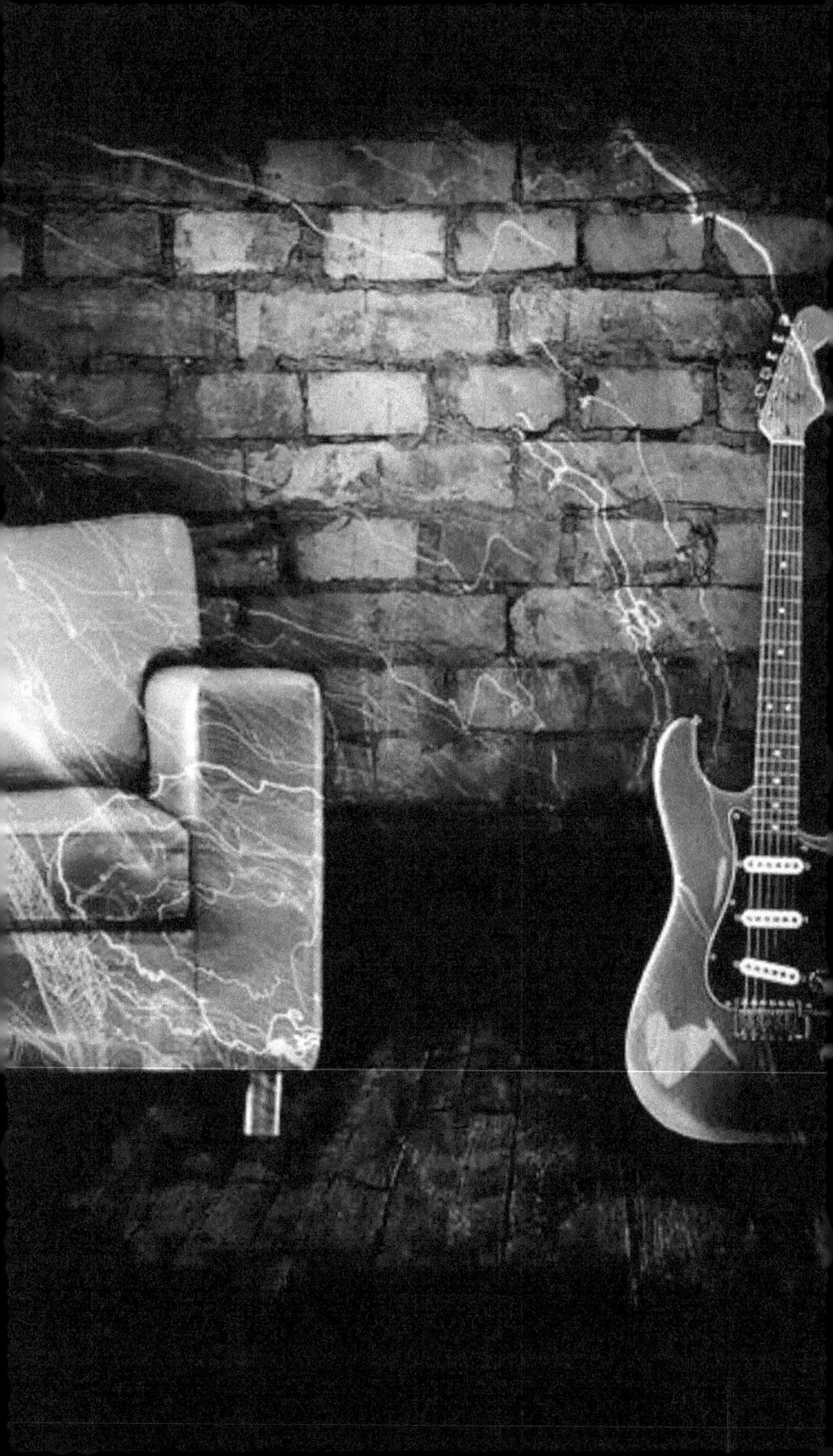

Eighteen

TA Malone practically glowered as I slid in the door. "I'm sorry I'm late," I said, before he could rip into me. "The rain threw me off and I had to have a discussion with Dr. Perry about my assignment. She kept me longer than I expected."

I'd gotten soaked on the rush over to the library. Not as bad as being thrown in the pond, but I hadn't had an umbrella, and my only choice was to run for it.

Setting my bag down, I pulled out a hair claw and twisted my damp hair up into a roll on my head and clipped it in place. It wasn't stylish or even particularly comfortable, but I needed to get the dripping hair out of my eyes. Stripping off my jacket, I hung it on the back of a chair to dry and then faced my nemesis.

"Hmm," was all he said, then motioned to my chair. "You do look a bit like a drowned rat."

I snorted. "Thanks."

"It wasn't a compliment." He pulled out his own chair and sat.

"You know, Mr. Malone..." That sounded really weird for

me, but then he always called me Miss Crosse. "I am doing my best to meet all of your requirements. If you want me to do more, all you have to do is say it."

Personally, I wanted to know what I had to do to dislodge the stick from his ass, but I'd start with being the best damn student he'd ever dealt with.

Bring it on, Malone. Do your worst.

Rather than be impressed by my statement, Malone gave me a bored look. "Let's start with the assignments I gave you yesterday..."

I pulled them out of my bag and passed them over. He liked working on paper, that was one thing I'd noticed. In most of my classes, I could do all my assignments on my laptop or tablet.

Not with Malone. All our lit assignments were on paper, and even the reading was physical books, not digital. I didn't mind, but I guess it was his thing.

"Your handwriting could use some work," Malone said as he went through the pages. "It's very sloppy; your t's and i's could be confused. We might add penmanship to your lessons."

"Really?" I eyed him. "I thought my issue was grammar."

He paused to look at me over the edge of his glasses. That shouldn't be so damn hot, but here we were. "Your *issues* as you put it so succinctly, are a combination of entitlement and inexperience, not to mention, just a hole in your education."

Every word he spoke was carefully enunciated, the syllables crisp and his tone clear. It was both dismissive and patronizing.

Propping my chin on my hand, I watched him go over each page with his pen, bleeding out. There were fewer marks than in the beginning, though.

"Do you practice being arrogant, or does it come naturally?" I hadn't been kidding when I told Aubrey I was done with taking it. Yes, he was a TA, but he wasn't the *teacher* and yet he pulled me into this tutoring then acted like it was a hardship.

He didn't answer right away; instead he finished reading through the last page before he returned the packet to me. "You need to work through these more carefully; the mistakes are careless. I don't care who or what handled your education before Blue Ivy, but this..." He tapped the packet of papers. "This isn't up to our standards. You're already on academic probation," he continued like I didn't know that. "I've been asked to look at your other classwork with you and review where else you need assistance."

A knock at the door prevented me from answering immediately.

"Come in," the TA said as he rose, and the door opened to admit Payton *Fucking* Webber into the room. "Miss Webber, you're running late."

She flashed him a smile as she put a hand to her immaculately coiffed hair. "The rain is causing some issues with travel between the buildings. I took the long way, I hope you weren't waiting on me."

The butter-wouldn't-melt-n-her-mouth tone made me want to vomit. Worse, she was giving him dewy eyes as if she wanted to climb him like a tree. I didn't disagree with how good looking he was, but didn't she *have* a boyfriend?

"Absolutely not. Miss Crosse has so many weaknesses and gaps in her education that we will be doing this for months."

"Oh," she said with a flutter of her hand before cutting me a cruel, tight smile. "How sad for you. Not enough time for a proper education in between binges and sex fests?"

Folding my arms, I leaned back in the chair and met her gaze. "Sounds more your speed than mine, Webber." Focusing on the TA again, I said, "Why is she here?"

"To assist you," he answered before raking a hand through

his hair. "Miss Webber is an exceptional student, ranked third in your class. You need assistance—"

"I have assistance," I cut him off. "And I'd rather gargle with bleach than work with her. Particularly since her hobby appears to be Kaitlin Crosse photos and videos on her various platforms."

Surprise skittered across TA Malone's face. "Excuse me?"

"I will *not* work with her." I enunciated each word very carefully. *She's a total bitch* echoed inside my head, but I bit back the phrase for now.

TA Malone glanced from me to Payton then back. The measuring look in his blue eyes aggravated me. If he was serious about this plan, we were going to have a real issue. Teachers and TAs? Fine. I'd be respectful and do it. But this bitch?

Hell. No.

Half of me wanted to check to see if she had her phone on to record this whole interaction.

"Ramsey," Payton murmured, her voice lowering to something far more intimate than I was comfortable hearing. "I'll do whatever you want me to do."

Gag.

"Even work with..." She spared me a look, a smirk curving her lips. "Her."

"Don't hurt yourself," I suggested. "Or do, but I don't care what he wants, we're not working together."

"No one wants to work with you," Payton informed me. "Ramsey's too polite to tell you—"

"Miss Webber," the reprimand in his voice shut her up, but fuck if it didn't give me shivers. "That's enough. From both of you. Competitiveness builds character. *Vincit qui se vincit.*"

"He conquers who conquers himself." It was the school motto.

"Very good."

"I didn't know you spoke Latin," Payton sneered.

"Payton Webber doesn't know something. In other news, water wet." I made a point of gesturing the letters like I was framing each word on a headline. For a moment, TA Malone's lips tipped upward into the first smile I'd ever seen on his face.

At least in regard to me. As fleeting as the smile was, I still gave myself a point.

"Anyway," TA Malone raised his voice slightly as if to stamp out any more objections. "Strength, courage, vigilance, and leadership are the Blue Ivy way." The words should have been cheesy as fuck, but instead, they resonated in his rich timbre. "My point, ladies, is that you need to overcome this animosity and learn to support each other, and you, Miss Crosse, are not in a position to dictate terms. Between the academic probation and the grades required to maintain your enrollment...Miss Webber is your best bet."

"Yeah, I'd prefer not to put my head in a noose if she's controlling the lever." I met his gaze and held it. "I have a study buddy and support. I also have a friend willing to work with me." Thank you RJ. "So, I'll skip out on the bitch patrol, thanks."

Payton snorted, but the venom in her eyes promised retribution. "I'm sorry, Ramsey, she's probably right. She's too new to our world to fit and she's clearly not that interested in it."

The baby doll tone her voice dropped into was grating like table legs scraping the wood as it was dragged from one side of the stage to the other.

Payton put her hand on *Ramsey's* arm and gave me a dismissive look. "Maybe you shouldn't waste any more time on her. The betting pool has her gone by Christmas."

"Gambling at school is illegal," he said almost absently, but he remained focused on me.

Right. We weren't getting shit done today. I glanced at my phone to see we had ten minutes left in the session. "Speaking of wasting time," I said. "Yours isn't the only valuable one. Since you and *Miss Webber* are so busy being judgmental, I'll let you have the last ten minutes. See you Monday."

I grabbed my bag and the marked-up packet of homework. There was another packet sitting under it. No idea when he added it, and I didn't care. I shoved it all in my bag and headed for the door.

"Our hour is not up," Ramsey said as I pulled the door open. His frown deepened. "We haven't even discussed the next set of assignments or where you are in your other classes..."

Hand on the open door, I faced them both and held up my free hand to tick off the items with my fingers. "One, you chose to invite trouble into the tutoring session so that's a 'you' problem. Two, you were more focused on insulting me and telling me to work with someone who has done nothing but try to sabotage me since I got here—and who has a boyfriend by the way, even if she can't keep her hands off you."

Payton sputtered but Ramsey's eyebrows pulled together in a furious frown. Good. Suck on that lemon, asshole. Despite how much I shook inside, none of it seemed to show up in my posture or my hands. Go stage craft and training.

"And three, I showed up and I was ready to work. I've been as cooperative as I intend to be. You want to tutor me, I'll be here Monday, but if she's here, I'll be leaving. Later."

With that, I walked out and shut the door behind me. Let her jump him on the table or whatever the hell she wanted to do. Maybe they'd get busted by the administration and bye bye TA Malone.

I almost grinned at the idea.

"Well now, I hope I'm the one who brought that sexy

smile to your lips." RJ drifted out from behind one of the stacks as I descended the stairs. He didn't keep his voice low despite the fact we were in a library.

I chuckled. "I didn't expect to see you here. Skipping your last class of the day?" He looked pretty good.

"Maybe," he said. "Or maybe I got a pass to do some research in the library so I could be here when you got done with tutoring. How does a coffee and a talk sound?" The ease in his voice and the way he smiled did a lot to soothe some of the trembling left over from my walking out.

"What are we talking about?" I asked as I went to shoulder my bag, but RJ was already lifting it away from me.

"Anything you want," he said before offering his arm. "I wanted to invite you out to Tate field and the park there, but we have a lounge on the first floor of my dorm. How about we grab a coffee at the Dancing Goats then head back there? It won't be quiet, but we can grab a corner and hang out."

Tempting. So tempting.

"C'mon, I know you're worried about classes and your assignments," he continued in a lower voice. "But I got your back. We can strategize on a plan of attack. Like I said, I probably know all your teachers. Benefit of being a legacy kid here. So, I know the buttons to push."

I was all set to decline when I found a furious Ramsey glaring down at the two of us. Who the fuck did he think he was?

"You know what," I said, looking back up at RJ. "I like that. Can we get pizza delivered at your dorm?"

"We can get whatever you want." He was still holding out his arm, so I looped mine through it. "Coffee, then studying and we'll order pizza."

"It's a date." The bruising on his face had pretty much vanished and...

"Yes," he said with a grin. "It most certainly is."

"The boot is off!" No more bad ankle.

We were at the door to the library and he already had an umbrella open as we stepped outside. I caught sight of Ramsey's reflection in the doors. He was downstairs and still scowling at us.

"Yep." RJ grinned as he wrapped an arm around my shoulders to pull me in tight and keep us both under the umbrella. "Just in time to wade through the fall rain. But worth it..."

Excitement threaded through me. RJ was doing better, which meant I could go running on the trails again and have a buffer against Lachlan the douchebag.

The day was just getting better and better.

Of course, that was the moment my phone lit up with all the notifications.

Dammit.

Tattler Blast

CROSSE SEX TAPE: MOST EXTREME EVER FOR THE ACTRESS

For everyone who was disappointed in last year's sex tape from a certain superhero actress (see, we can be discreet), don't worry, the Jennifer Crosse tape has everything you could want including a well-endowed adult film star partner. Are we seeing a new direction for Crosse's career? Or just a dip back to the wild side?

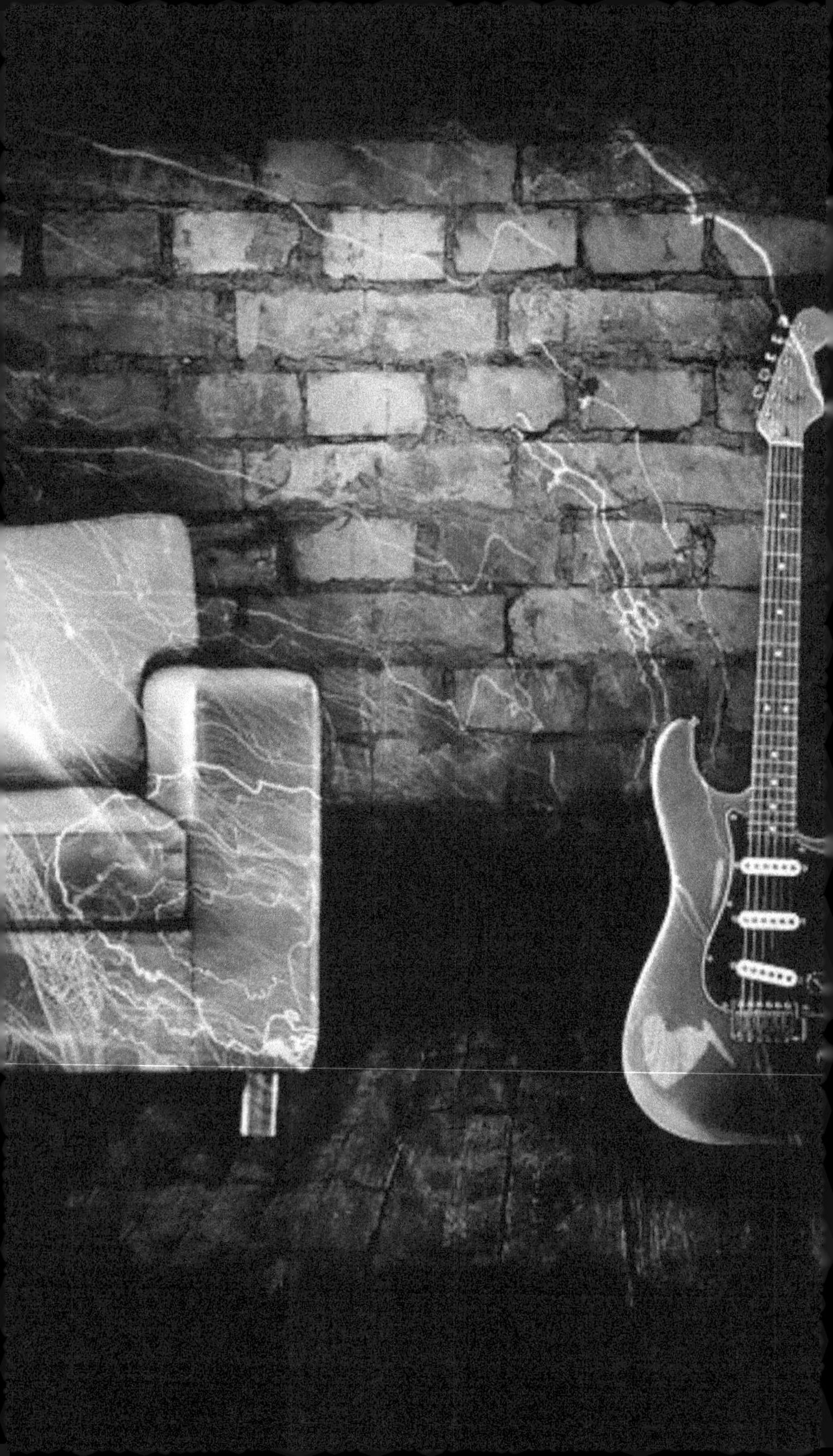

Nineteen

"Oh," a guy said, groaning dramatically from the stairwell as he leaned over. I'd already made the mistake of making eye contact with a pair of jokers in the dining hall as they pitched themselves back dramatically and screamed their faux pleasure.

"Yeah, right there," the guy ahead of me in the hall said as he humped the girl next to him. "Give it to me."

The mock moans and groans coupled with the slapping of hands against hips and asses just added to the overall sex talk. Over the years, there'd been all kinds of stories leaked, sometimes unintentionally, but more often deliberately, that I'd just had to roll with.

A sex tape though?

This was a new one.

Reportedly, there'd been one back in the day between her and my father; I didn't know more about that than it existed and had supposedly been stolen. I also didn't really go looking for it because A, eww, and B, seriously fucking ewww.

This sex tape, however, was different because it was an enthusiastic—apparently *hours* long—session between Mom and Johnny Pound. It was *everywhere.* There were even sound clips trending from it.

Have I mentioned how much I hate my life some days?

A guy slid up behind me, his hot breath on my neck as he gripped my hip and tried to hump me while saying, "So, you like it big like your mama?"

"Not something to worry about with you," I commented and slammed my elbow back into the jackass.

He grunted.

"Aww, c'mon, if you like it dirty—fuck!" He let me go abruptly which sent me stumbling since I'd been trying to yank away.

Some of the catcalls in the hallway ended abruptly, and I twisted to find Jonas standing there, *staring* at the latest fuckboy with the deadest eyes and emptiest expression. It was downright fucking chilling.

Despite having at least three inches on him, the guy who'd been trying to hump me just raised his hands. "Figures," he muttered as he turned away. "The freak is into even more freakishness. You'd think that—"

Whatever else he'd intended to say, never escaped him because Jonas just launched into him. He slammed his fist into fuckboy's jaw. The audible grind of bone on bone even as flesh hit flesh made me wince.

Their bags hit the floor as they collided. Fuckboy might have been walking away, but he delivered a pair of punches in rapid succession. Something hot hit my cheek and I grimaced at the blood.

The eerie quiet erupted into shouts and hooting. The boys were beating the shit out of each other, a shirt ripped, and then they were hitting the ground, but Jonas was on top of the fuckboy and raining punches down.

I jerked my head around looking for help, but the students in the hall were torn between filming it and shouting encouragement or insults. There wasn't a single fucking teacher in sight.

No one waded into the battle. It wasn't a fight when Jonas clearly had the other guy down, and there was going to be an issue if someone didn't stop him. The right side of fuckboy's face was already puffing up, and blood flew from one of the blows.

Should *I* stop it? I didn't even know if I could. I started forward, but a piercing whistle cut through the hall.

I jerked my gaze off the macabre sight where Jonas didn't even seem aware of us, much less the new arrival. The rumbles of the crowd diminished as they split apart. TA Malone stalked through, barely sparing me a glance before he dragged Jonas up and off the slab of meat that he'd rendered almost unrecognizable.

Jonas swung wildly, and I winced when his fist connected with Ramsey's jaw. There was no way that didn't hurt. Ramsey's head snapped to the side, but he caught the next fist and jerked Jonas around until he could pin his arms down.

"Vacate this hallway, now," Ramsey stated in a tone that did *not* match the struggle he was in. The command rippled out and more than a few students hurried off. "Marks," he continued and a guy behind hurried forward. "Take Timothy to the med center. Go."

Jonas let out a *scream* that had me gritting my teeth, but no amount of struggle was getting him free from Ramsey. I took one step forward and Ramsey's gaze locked on me.

"This is not your—" He broke off when Jonas bucked against him and he seemed to need all his concentration to hold onto him.

"Can I do anything?" It was mostly down to just us and somewhere in the distance a bell chimed. The guys' bags were still on the ground and Jonas' panting struggles seemed all the louder in the emptiness.

"You can go to class and let me deal with this," Ramsey said, narrowly avoiding Jonas hitting him in the face with the back of his head. I thought the emptiness in Jonas' gaze had been bad, but the raw fury and wildness in his gray eyes was kind of terrifying.

"I…"

"Just go," Ramsey snapped. "Not everything is about you, Miss Crosse."

I bit back anything more as Jonas seemed to go absolutely feral. It wasn't just his shirt that got torn. He tore at Ramsey's sleeve, and the fabric split, revealing the tanned, tattooed forearm.

Walking away didn't seem cool, not when Jonas had actually done me a favor. Maybe he hadn't even realized it was me, but that guy had been—well, a fuckboy. Right now, Jonas didn't seem quite human.

"Miss Crosse," Ramsey ground out and I raised my hands, backing away. Another bell chimed. I was late to class.

Shit.

Rather than distract him anymore, since Jonas actually managed to catch Ramsey in the jaw with the back of his head, I resumed my path for class. The teacher was just about to close the door, when I got there, but paused to give me a studying look.

"Are you all right, Miss Crosse?"

No, I wasn't all right. Down the hall and around the corner there'd been a loud fight and the students in their chairs all seemed perfectly placid and completely out of touch.

Except for the brunette in the second row who mimed a blowjob at me, and I rolled my eyes.

"Yes," I said, but the teacher gave me another firm once-over.

"Put your things at your desk and then go to the restroom and clean up. You have five minutes then we'll be testing."

Clean—the blood.

Twenty-five minutes later, I was just staring at Jonas' empty chair. The blood on my face had been unsettling. There was some on my shirt as well, but a little strategic repositioning hid most of it.

I worried about Jonas all through the morning classes, right up until Mr. Cohen's class. I was actually hoping Ramsey would be there so maybe I could check in about Jonas, but he wasn't there.

Weirder still, no one talked about the fight in the hall. Except I did manage to find out more about Timothy. He was a junior, like me and Jonas, and he was also a diplomat's son. That—seemed weird. His mother was a U.S. Ambassador.

I heard he had a broken nose and might need surgery to repair his septum. Chances were, he wouldn't be back this week, and I only found that out cause I asked Sydney when I caught her between classes. Bless her for being plugged in.

A part of me felt bad, then some other asshole would begin their moaning and groaning rendition of the tape. That would manage to pretty much kill all of my sympathy. After all, he'd been trying to hump me when it happened.

That was twice Jonas had helped me out. It was going to kill me, but I needed to say thank you. He'd probably spit in my face, but I'd damn well thank him. As it was, I'd collected his homework from our shared classes.

None of the teachers declined when I offered to make sure the assignments got dropped off. I couldn't do anything about the ones he hadn't turned in, but I could do something.

I texted Sydney to find out if she had any idea how I could find where someone's dorm was. She sent me back laughing faces. The social roster for the school listed all of our buildings. It might not list the room, but it would tell me which building.

Huh.

When Ramsey didn't show up for tutoring, I left a note after twenty minutes and headed back to the dorms. It took a minute to find the tab I needed on the school app and to remember *what* Jonas' last name was.

I sucked at names. Luckily, he was the only Jonas on the high school level, so that made it easier.

"Hey," Soren greeted me, holding open the door to Apollo Two. I didn't realize just how close Jonas' dorm was to mine; then again, I'd pretty much not been paying attention to a lot more than getting through the days.

Oh, and Jonas hated me, right.

"Hey," I said as I slid inside.

"This isn't your dorm."

"You're right," I told Soren then held up a stack of papers. "I need to drop these off for Jonas. He missed classes today so I wanted to make sure he got these."

"Cool. You know where his room is?"

"No," I said slowly, with a small smile. "Help a girl out?"

"Want me to clip them to his door?"

Yes. "Thank you!" While I felt guilty about the fight, I didn't need Jonas kicking me for it. As it was, the unhinged display suggested he had more than a few of his own issues. "That would be great."

"Okay." He took the papers. "Why did your mom make a sex tape?" The absolute lack of artifice in the way he asked made it a little more palatable to answer.

"I try to think as little about her sex life as humanly possible." Which was the truth.

"But she's dating a guy who makes adult films, right?"

I shrugged. Not because I begrudged him the answer, but because I tended to avoid all personal commentary on my family and my friends. More than once I'd made the mistake of trusting the wrong person.

Burn me once, shame on me.

Burn me twice? Well, I guess there was a reason they called me problem child. I had some weird need to have faith in people.

"Yeah, okay. I didn't watch the video," he told me. "I got it like four times, but I don't really want to watch it."

"Same. Thanks for that." I nodded to the papers as I backed up. "See you in the dining hall later?"

"Maybe. Bonfire tomorrow."

I paused. There was a bonfire tomorrow. I'd half-forgotten about that. "Harvest Kickoff Event?"

He grinned. "It's not as boring as it sounds. Football season isn't as big here as it is in some places, and even if it was, our team isn't as good as other schools. We do better in soccer, rugby, lacrosse, and polo."

Of course they did.

"But it is fun."

"Well, I'll see you there."

"Okay." With a nod, he turned on his heel and walked away, homework in hand.

Okay, KC, I told myself. You did what you could. He doesn't even need to know it was you. Relieved, I pivoted and ran right into the last person I wanted to see.

Lachlan.

"Lost, Ace?" His smirk was incredibly not friendly. All the air in the hall seemed to evacuate as he loomed a little closer to me. I swore I could feel the heat radiating off of him.

"Nope," I informed him and then moved to walk around him but he sidestepped into my path.

"Then you must be here to see someone."

"Fortunately for both of us, it's not you." I started to step left, but anticipating his intercept I switched to right and cut between him and his friend.

"Why are you running?" Laughter filled his tone and I

simply raised a middle finger in his direction as I got to the door and then out. I sucked in a deeper breath once outside.

Sound rushed back in. Leaves crunched under my shoes. Wind ruffled the trees. The class period chimes sounded from across the quad, signaling the end of the last class of the day.

The hum of students would fill the air along with shouts, laughter, and—a wolf-whistle cut through the air and a guy shouted, "Uh-uh."

Yep, and that.

Ignoring the latest in the litany of porn-fueled applause, I picked up the pace. Hopefully, the sex tape would be yesterday's news tomorrow.

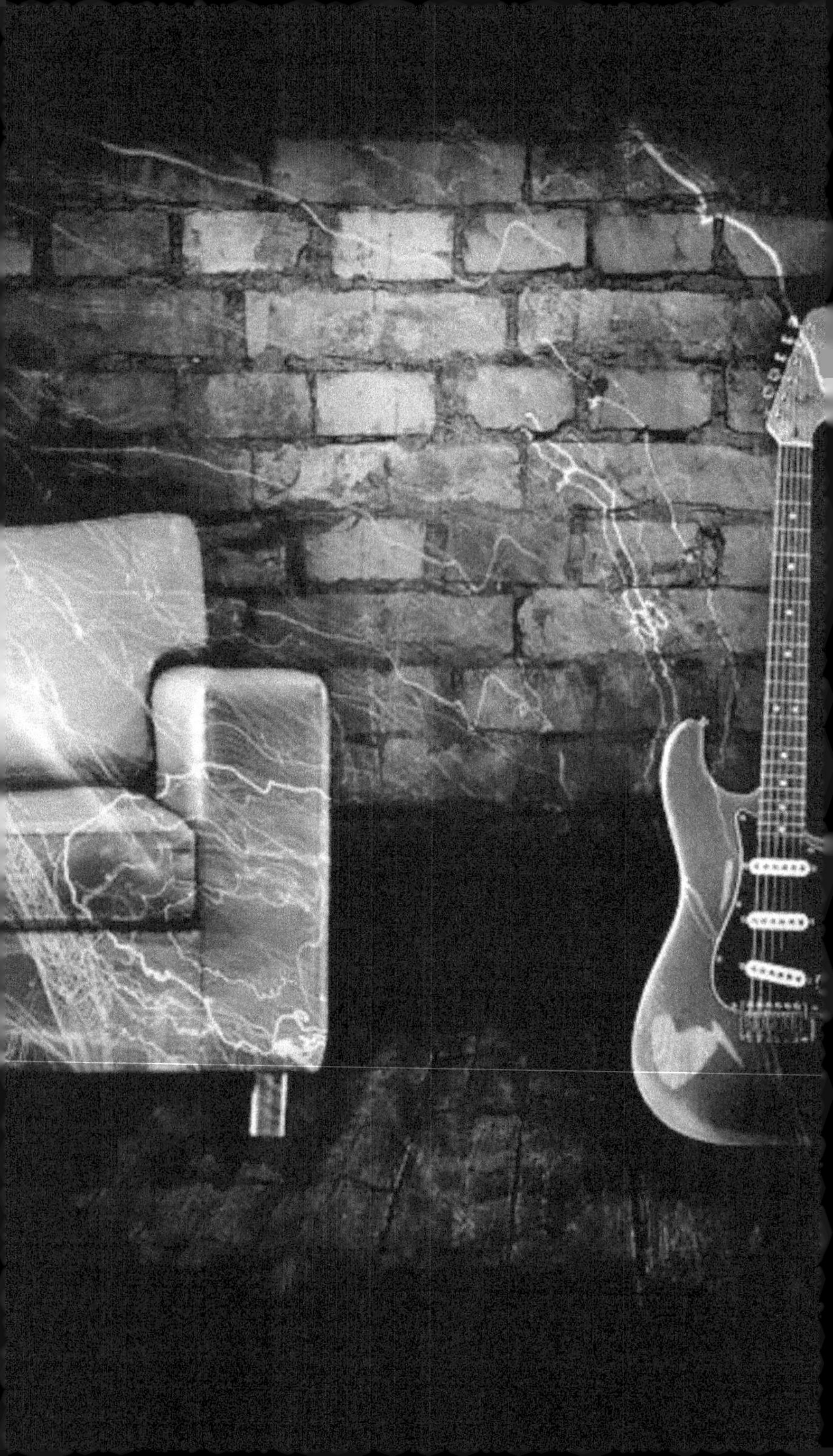

Twenty

Despite RJ inviting me back to his dorm to study, I still preferred the library. Preferred it to my dorm too when he offered to come to me. Aubrey and I hadn't actually invited anyone into our dorm room as yet. I kind of liked it that way. So did she.

Harley had come by a couple of times, but she didn't come in to hang out, and since she had keys we didn't have to be there for her inspections. Yet, she seemed to make sure one of us was present whenever she had to do a room check. It was thoughtful.

Booking a study room had been pretty easy. I chose one on the first floor rather than on the gallery level where I met with Ramsey. It also had a view. The upstairs rooms didn't have windows, at least not good ones.

The ones downstairs did.

RJ was actually waiting for me in the open doorway when I got there. Unlike me, he'd changed out of his uniform and had gone with something more casual.

"We have time," he said as he caught my book bag and lifted it off my shoulder.

"For?" I blinked at him. Had I missed something? It had been something of a busy week and it was Friday.

"For you to get changed," he continued, setting the bag on the table. There were two coffees already waiting, along with a paper bag that smelled suspiciously like croissants.

We were not supposed to bring drinks into the library. We weren't supposed to bring anything consumable in with us, but there he had it on the table in plain view of the open door.

"I'm fine," I told him as I shrugged off the jacket. "This is actually way more comfortable than it looks." I enjoyed the uniforms, even if they were a little buttoned up. But since it was *after* classes, I loosened my tie and dropped the jacket. It was a little stuffy in here.

"Yes, you are," he told me with a slow grin before he reached over to curl a strand of my hair around his finger. "I'm amazed at your hair, I thought it was a dye job but it's..."

"Still blue?" I waited for him to let go before I moved to take a seat and pull open my bag. He moved to slide into the chair next to me rather than across. Probably easier to see what I was working on.

I set out my laptop and the tablet, then pulled out my books. The homework for the weekend was just insane. I had three papers due, a whole worksheet of math problems, and four chapters to read in biology.

"Yeah, don't you have to have it touched up?" He passed me one of the coffees and my gaze landed on one of the black-scrawled names on the side. *Blue.*

No comment. I just took a sip before answering him. "I do, but I also use a color depositing conditioner that keeps it pretty fresh for me. About every twelve weeks, though, I really should get it done." It was every six weeks when we were touring, but I liked the break.

"Huh." He lifted his hand like he was gonna stroke my

hair again, and I quirked a brow. "Sorry, I love your hair. I've been wanting to play with it for a while."

For a minute the statement caught me a little flat-footed. It was and wasn't a compliment. He was just expressing his interest in my hair, but that was almost as good as saying my hair looked great? Maybe?

"Thank you," I said, before shifting to reach for one of my books. "For the coffee. For the compliment. For the help. I mean, I'm sure you have something better to do on a Friday night."

"Bonfire is tomorrow night," he said. "Maybe if we get you super caught up tonight, you'll give that beautiful brain a break and go to the bonfire with me."

"Aubrey and I are going," I promised. "Us and a group of friends. If you want to join us, that would be great."

"It's a date," he answered, then retrieved his own coffee while he eyed the book. "You have Cohen for literature?"

"Yes." I liked him, Mr. Cohen. He was every inch the picture of nerdy academic, but he also knew what he was talking about. Even if I didn't like storytelling and the art of words, I'd have enjoyed the way he waxed poetic about them.

"He's tough." RJ tapped his chin. "But he's also got some easy tells that will let you know if you're on the right track, and he loves it when students engage in debate."

"I'd kind of noticed that, but it's more like he wants you to challenge the ideas presented in the material."

"Sometimes," RJ said. "Other times, he wants you to challenge him. Socratic teaching method is one way to get the information across. To teach ourselves as it were...so, if you know the kinds of questions he'll ask ahead of time, you can prepare for it."

"That sounds a little bit like cheating."

RJ shrugged. "I'm not planning on giving you answers

unless you ask me really nice." His grin was fast. "But I will give you the questions or at least as many as I can remember. What are you reading this week?"

That seemed a lot like splitting hairs to me. But we didn't spend as much time on literature as we did on history and math. Two hours of work left me with a crick in my neck and a much better understanding of lab protocols and preparation. Our coffee was gone and we'd split both croissants.

Despite all of that, my stomach was growling. "We should go get you food," RJ was saying as I cleaned up.

"I don't know if I'm up for the dining hall tonight," I admitted. "I kind of want to just go back to my room, shower, put on PJs and binge watch some trashy television."

Chuckling, he collected our trash. "Okay, now that you've described that, I think I want to do that too. I can grab pizza and bring it back...even get enough to share for your roommate if she's there."

"That's sweet." It was more than sweet. "You've been great this whole time."

"I can be sweeter," he teased, leaning a hip against the table so we were almost eye to eye. "C'mon, KC, say yes. I get that you're worried about your grades, but you just kicked a lot of ass, and it's Friday night."

"Tempting," I admitted. And it definitely was that. "But..." At the last word, he pressed his fingers to my lips.

"No buts. Just give into temptation." He winked at the end of the sentence and I snorted. When he brushed his thumb along my lower lip, I sighed and pulled back a little.

"You are not making this easy."

"Good. Then my plan is working."

I laughed, genuinely. "RJ..."

"Oh, I hear the *but* coming." He gave a very long, if dramatic sigh and folded his arms as he leaned back against the table. "Hit me with it."

"It is tempting. You've been amazing between the running, the homework, and just—" I raked a hand through my hair, finger-combing it back from my face. "You haven't said a word about the tape. You've been a real friend. I appreciate that."

"Then why can't I bring you pizza and binge watch trashy tv with you?"

"Don't take it personally." Even though I didn't like to explain things, RJ had been doing his best by me. "The thing is, honestly, Aubrey and I haven't invited anyone up to the room."

Bag packed, I moved to lean against the table next to him.

"The thing is, we... we've spent so much time touring the last few years that having a space that's just ours—that we don't have to share? It's...it's probably the second best thing about coming to this school."

The best was just the actual break from touring itself. Getting to be people again.

"Second best, huh?" RJ frowned. "What's the first?"

I grinned, but brushed past the question. "The point is, we haven't had a space that was just ours and I think we're going to keep it that way for as long as possible. So, don't hate me, but..."

"I get it," he said slowly, then gave a gentle shrug with a hint of a smile. "Actually, I don't, but—you said you wanted things normal, and it's normal for a guy to ask a girl out or to come over. My room is always available." Then he tipped his head. "But we're working you up to that. So, we'll stick with running, studying, and tomorrow night?"

"The bonfire." A thread of excitement slid through me. "Just don't forget it's going to be a group of us."

"Want me to be nice to your friends?" The low, throaty comment held enough teasing for me to grin.

"I would appreciate it."

"Enough to make it worth my while?"

"Depends," I said, folding my arms. "What did you have in mind?" If he wanted to negotiate, that was fine. However, I never signed the first offer on the dotted line. Fuck that.

"Something simple," RJ mused. "How about if I'm nice to your friends, you agree to a real date with me. Maybe not this week or next—I know you want to get ahead in class. But by Halloween."

Halloween. That wasn't that far away.

"If I said no?"

"I'd probably still be nice to your friends and ask you out again later." The droll response made me laugh.

"That's very thoughtful of you."

"I can be a thoughtful guy for the right girl," he informed me. "Pretty sure you're that girl. So, what will it be, Blue?"

"Split the difference? I'll give you a very firm maybe to a real date by Halloween, provided I'm comfortable enough with where I am class-wise? Does that work?"

"Not as good as a solid yes but way better than a firm no." He held out his hand. "Deal?"

He practically engulfed my hand with his. "Deal," I murmured, but he tugged me forward a step and dipped his head toward mine. I had no idea what I expected—well, yes, I did. From the angle and the movement, it was like he was going to kiss me.

When his lips only brushed my cheek, however, I was both relieved and disappointed.

"Let's get you back to your dorm," he said, squeezing my hand once before he picked up my jacket and held it up for me to slide it on. "Then I'll see you tomorrow morning for a run?"

I loved that idea. I was still riding high on that when we left the library. I was so high on it in fact, I almost didn't recognize Ramsey as he strode up the walk from the direction of the parking lot.

Like RJ, he'd gone for relaxed clothes. The shirt he wore, however, stretched over his shoulders and molded to his chest. He looked positively dangerous in the black t-shirt and jeans. Even better was the art on his arms. I really wanted to get a good look at those.

Right. *Not appropriate, KC.* I gave myself a mental kick and dragged my attention back to RJ as he led the way. The air outside was crisp, cooling rapidly now that the sun had gone down.

There were a lot of kids moving about the campus, most of them out of uniform. Yeah, I stuck out since I hadn't changed. Maybe next time. Well, definitely next time. I couldn't run in my uniform.

Aubrey was just coming out of Apollo One as we walked up. She paused, lifting her hair free from the jacket she'd just pulled on. "Hey, I was going to go grab dinner." She spoke to me, but her gaze tracked to RJ and she gave him a once over. "New friend?"

I resisted the urge to roll my eyes at her teasing. "Yes, and no. This is RJ, we met a few weeks back, and he's helping me get caught up and maybe a little ahead."

Her whole demeanor shifted and Aubrey grinned as she held out her hand. "Aubrey Miller, best friend, band mate, and the girl who will kick your ass if you hurt her."

"Nice to meet you," RJ said with a laugh as he shook her hand. "RJ Wallach, new friend, prospective date if I can get her to agree, and the guy who really likes her, so much that I'll encourage the ass kicking."

"As long as we understand each other."

"We do."

Aubrey nodded once then glanced at me. "Want to grab food with me? Or shall I just bring it back?"

"I don't mind going with you," RJ said, his "deliberate" misunderstanding almost amusing. "However, KC said she wanted to shower, put on PJs, and watch trash television."

"Good to know you found a guy who can listen."

Still chuckling, I reached for my bag and RJ passed it over, although he seemed a bit reluctant. "Let me put my bag up in our room and then we can go." I met RJ's gaze. "Thank you again."

"You're welcome. I'll see you in the morning, bright and early."

"I'll be there."

He stared at me a beat longer before he nodded to Aubrey then let out a sigh before he headed away. A part of me wanted to call him back, maybe invite him to the dining hall with us and at the same time...

"He has it bad," Aubrey commented lightly. "You also failed to mention he was both hot and tall." A deadly combination in her book.

"We'll talk about it after I run upstairs real quick."

She pulled out her phone. "I'll wait for you and don't look at the boxes inside the door. They forwarded over some of the fan mail, and I came down to get it."

"We can work on that Sunday," I decided. "Maybe."

Fan mail was a blessing and a curse. We got a lot of emails and messages through our social media accounts, but we rarely saw those. Only a carefully curated selection were forwarded on.

Snail mail though? If someone cared enough to send us real mail, we liked to see it.

"Agreed, and I told Yvette she was getting the next batch."

I laughed and did a thumbs up as I headed inside. In our room, I set the bag on the floor next to the sofa and stared at the *five* boxes.

Holy shit. Aubrey hadn't been kidding. Right, that was a later-this-weekend problem. Tonight, we were gonna talk boys, eat, and binge watch some bad shows.

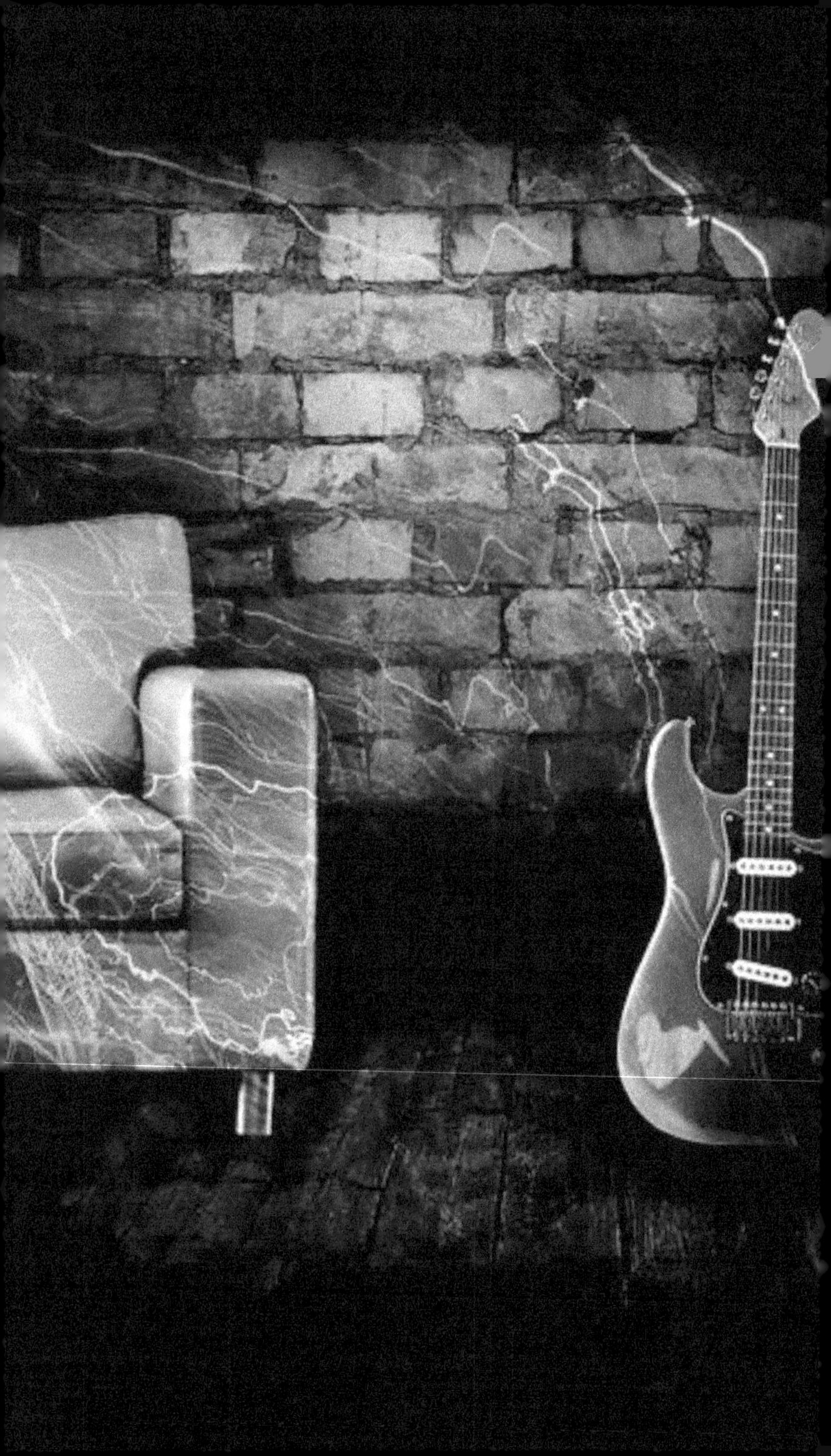

Twenty-One

A shower, four changes of clothes, a blow dry, and light cosmetics later, I was ready to go to the bonfire.

Maybe.

I tugged at the fringe on the ends of my three-quarter sleeves. The dark blue tunic blouse was both comfortable and warm. It also wasn't fitted. The problem? It didn't quite cover all of my arms.

The bonfire, however, was a social event, not an academic one. It was definitely chilly out there, with the evening chasing away what warmth lingered from the afternoon. I wanted sleeves.

The skirt was a lighter shade of blue, closer to my own hair, while the top was dark. The contrast worked. Even better with the dark blue over-the-knee boots. I hadn't had a lot of chances to wear these yet, and they were almost a perfect match for the shirt.

Maybe this was too much? Bonfire, maybe I should go with denim...

"Stop," Aubrey ordered as she sailed out of the bathroom

and into my room. Dressed in a dark gray sweater dress that hit her mid-thigh and laced-up suede boots, she was the picture of elegance. "I can *hear* you second guessing yourself."

"You look fabulous," I informed her.

"Thank you, and I think this outfit is adorable." She toyed with the fringe at the end of my sleeves. "This is a lot more fluttery than I thought it would be."

"I know," I said, then tugged it a little. "It also doesn't cover as much."

"You're not changing again," she informed me. "Cause then I will have to, and we'll end up being in here all night changing and not seeing the bonfire."

I rolled my eyes. "We're not that bad."

"Oh yes, we are. Now, stand still." She aimed her phone at me and snapped a picture and then typed something in. My phone vibrated with a new message and I glanced at it to find she'd messaged Yvette. "See, Yvette agrees with me. That's two to one, we win. Let's go."

I was still laughing when we met up with Sydney and Olivia downstairs.

"Finally," Olivia said when we appeared. "Let's go."

"Don't mind her. We're just impatient, and she likes to get everywhere early." Sydney's eyeroll just added charm to her explanation.

"So do you, smartass," Olivia informed her. "Come on." She tugged her sister's arm.

"Sorry," I said. "I had to try on a few different outfits to find one for this, and now I'm wondering if I picked right." Largely 'cause Olivia was dressed in these adorable denim overalls with a soft beige knit cap and a light sweater with tennis shoes.

Sydney, on the other hand, had gone for an oversized dark red plaid shirt dress with the sleeves rolled up and a pair of boots that came up to her knees. The fat belt just kind of brought it all together.

I had something upstairs—

"Nope," Aubrey informed me as she caught my hand. "No more changing. Let's go!"

Despite Olivia's complaints, we were hardly the last to arrive. There were literally dozens of kids making their ways from the dorms toward the field where the bonfire would be held.

More than one group jogged by; some were dressed all alike, and more had on strange outfits—including feathers in some cases—as they raced past, chanting.

"I don't get it," I said, as I tracked the most recent group of boys—all of them and at least two that I recognized from the hallway fight were dressed in the same uniform. The bonfire was happening over on Bracken Hill. This campus had so many hidden gems and different places.

But at least I knew where this particular hill was because one of the running trails went up it, or at least up the natural steps formed by the rocks, dirt, and tree roots.

Music reached us long before we reached them. A steady beat from drums with some distinctive horns coming in under it and all at once my palms were itching for my guitars. With all the work since I got back from Mom's 9-1-1, I hadn't really had the time to spend with them. Right then, I made a promise to myself that I would spend some time on them the following day. No wonder my agitation level was climbing.

The smell of woodsmoke greeted us as we reached the field below Bracken Hill. The woodsmoke and the flickering firelight all partnered with the music to add a distinctive primal thrum to the air.

Cheers went up as more instruments joined in. The horns added to the pulse pounding, and I grinned. "How have I never heard the band here?"

"You don't go to games," Sydney told me. "The band here is competitive in our division. They are incredible."

She wasn't wrong. Just listening to them roll through several recognizable theme songs with not a single misstep in their transitions had me strumming my fingers against my leg like I was playing.

Aubrey threw me a grin as she held up her dancing fingers, and we both laughed. Right. We needed a jam session. Probably should be doing those regardless. Taking a break was one thing; getting out of practice was another.

The crowd around the bonfire seemed to swell the closer we got. That was when I realized that the marching band was in that crowd, weaving in and out as they played. The groups of guys who'd raced past us in their feathers were also closer to the fire, and they were shouting, hooting, and throwing their fists up as they partied.

"Cider!" Sydney said with a laugh, grabbing at my hand and I gripped hers as she began weaving in and out of the crowd following Olivia. It took us a solid five minutes to get through the throng to where there was a table with hot cider.

Harley manned the table and a broad grin spread across her face when she saw us. "Hey! You didn't miss the challenges."

"Challenges?" I shot a look at Aubrey, who merely lifted her shoulders. "Oh, good. I'm not the only one wondering."

"Don't worry," Harley said, though she had to lean over the table for us to hear her.

I'd gotten fairly good at reading lips during events over the last few years. It was just practical when we were always surrounded by shouting throngs. As long as I could see her mouth, I could follow most of it.

"Really," she continued. "Don't worry. The challenges are all for fun. You don't have to participate. There will be more music and dancing tonight. But first they have to prep the griffins for war."

Her voice climbed on that last word.

"War!" The cry erupted behind us as though in direct response to her and there was an ululating bird cry that climbed in volume as more people joined in. It was hard not to smile or laugh.

The craziness just seemed to escalate from there. Music boomed out from speakers strategically hidden around the area, but it wasn't just the band. Or at least *this* particular blast of song wasn't.

Aubrey and I perched on hay bales that had been strewn out in a wider circle away from the fire. The thing had to be a dozen feet high, and the heat carried to where we were easily.

"I'll be right back," Olivia said before she disappeared. They were saluting their teams now, all of them. Oh, that was why Olivia vanished. She was on the school's golf team. So she went to join them. Blue Ivy Prep fielded a lot of teams, from golf to tennis to football to soccer, lacrosse, and track.

There was a fencing team.

"See," I said, leaning toward Aubrey. "There's a sport we should have taken up."

"Fencing?"

"Yes. So we can be experts when we want to stab people."

She burst out laughing then touched her drink to mine. I caught sight of RJ as he eased through the crowd. His bemused expression just made me smile wider. I was really happy to see him.

That giddy feeling from earlier was back. I bumped Aubrey, nudging her over and she scooted. When I patted the hay next to me, he settled in and wrapped an arm around my shoulders.

"Having fun?"

"Actually," I said, that curious feeling of lightness just

relaxing every part of me. This...this right here was what I was looking forward to. "I am. How about you?"

"Definitely. Especially now that I'm here. And do you mind me saying the out of uniform look is working for you." It wasn't really a question at all.

The compliment echoed in his tone and the way he studied me. A shiver went up my spine, and he tightened his arm around me.

"Cold?"

"Not really," I promised him, and I wasn't. He was pretty damn warm, and this was cozy sitting here between him and Aubrey.

"I'm gonna get us some more cider," Aubrey said with almost a playful look at RJ. "Want some?"

"Is it spiked?"

"Pretty sure it's not," I told him and he chuckled.

"Damn, but I'd love some. Thanks."

With a lift of her chin, Aubrey started away and Sydney bounced to her feet to go with her. A little guilt stabbed at me. I'd told RJ he had to be nice to my friends, and I hadn't really even introduced him.

"Remind me to introduce you when they get back," I told him. It was a little odd to be this close to him. Odd and invigorating. Hair dipped over his forehead, the lock out of place like it was free for the weekend, too.

He'd gone casual in jeans and a dark blue shirt that actually came close to matching mine. It was like we'd coordinated, even if we hadn't. Instead of dress shoes like he wore with his uniform, or running shoes, he had on a pair of hiking boots.

Not that they looked like he'd done any hiking. Then again, I'd never done any hiking either, so what did I know. The temptation to rest my head against his shoulder was there. Not that he appeared to be discouraging it with the weight of his arm around me.

That added another fresh flush of warmth to my chest. It flooded my whole body as I took a deep breath. Beyond the woodsmoke and the cooler air, there was the scent of coffee, pine needles, rain, and just a hint of cedar and musk beneath it all.

Closing my eyes, I tilted my head a little as music and shouts washed over us. The cacophony of the gathering reminded me a lot of a concert. There was so much emotion when you walked into the venue. The anticipation. The hum as equipment powered up and the lights came on.

Then the people. The people brought their own energy. It was electric and licked over like you were gripping a live wire. I *loved* that feeling. When you added the anticipation to it all, my stomach would bottom out and I would shiver.

The anticipation surging under my skin tonight wasn't for a performance or even the bonfire. It was for the guy with his arm around me who looked at me with such warmth in his eyes, who made me laugh, and seemed willing to roll with my rules and didn't seem remotely deterred by my putting off a real date.

Then again, what was tonight? I opened my eyes to find RJ right there. He studied me, and the way the firelight played over his face had the shadows dancing. I could make out one of his eyes perfectly while the other, wreathed in shadows, stayed hidden.

It was kind of perfect. For a moment, his gaze dipped to my lips and back up again. I found myself mirroring the gesture and when our gazes locked, he narrowed the distance. His breath was a whisper across my lips when something collided with the hay bale, or maybe they hit RJ.

Either way, one moment we were up, the next I sprawled as paint was dumped over me, my shirt, my skirt, and my brand new boots. It was cold, sticky, and—tasted foul.

Feathers rained down and the band started up again, the music rising as people laughed and cheered.

I blinked against the paint that had managed to hit my face and wiped my eyes. Not that the action helped much. Feathers clung to my hands and to my cheeks. One glance at RJ said he'd not fared much better than I had.

His expression though gave me a serious pause. Anger flashed in his eyes. A kind of raw fury that killed what anticipation hadn't already been doused by the paint. Not that I blamed him. Laughter rose up behind me, and I already knew who would be standing there before I even glanced.

Lachlan gave me a saucy little wink as he grinned wider. The whole lacrosse team let out a booyah and a chant before they marched on.

Fucker.

"Welcome to Blue Ivy," Payton said as she sauntered past, her smirk firmly in place. "*Vincit qui se vincit.*" Her laughter, like Lachlan's, followed in her wake.

Now it was war.

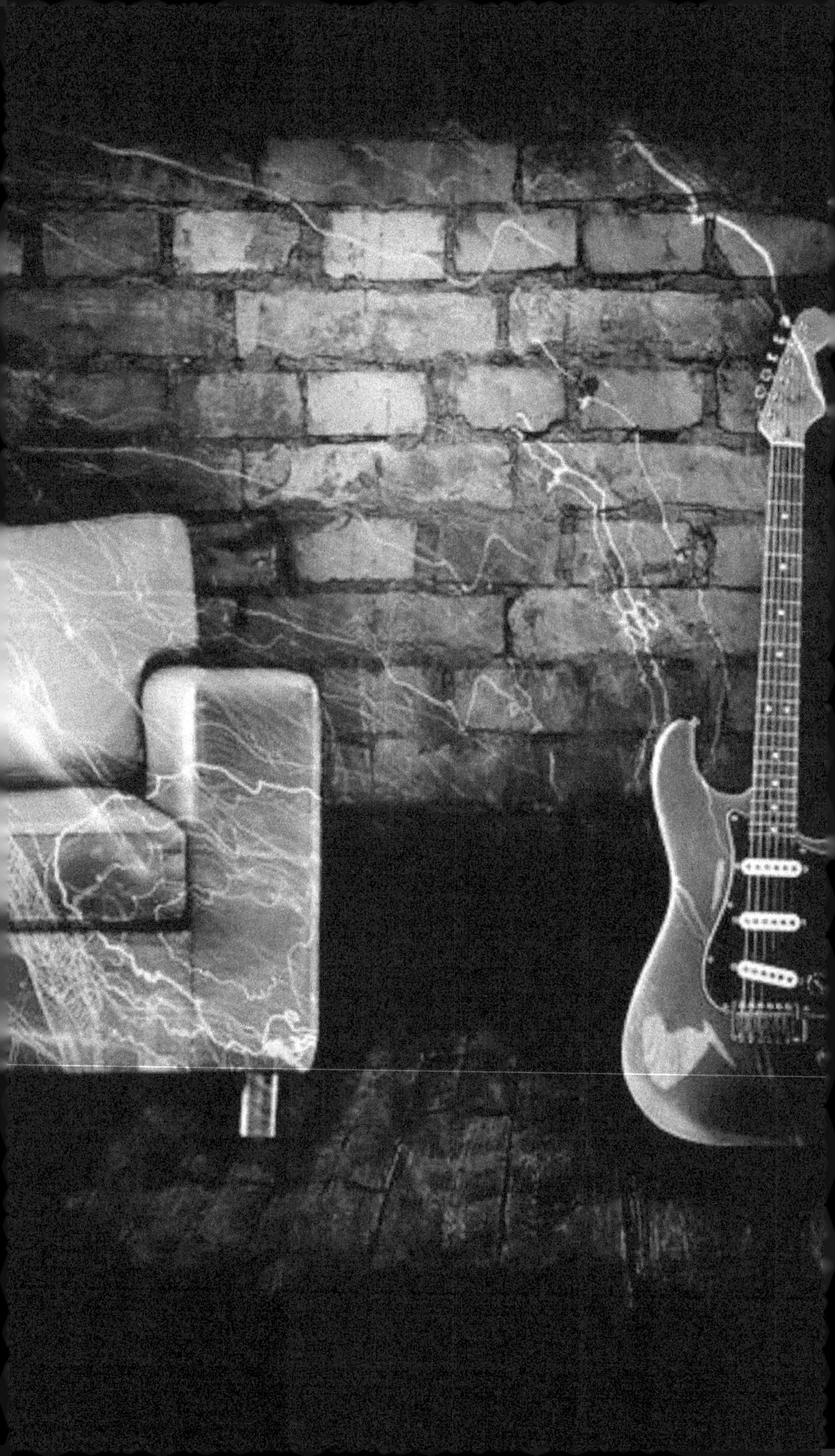

Twenty-Two

Halloween was fast approaching and my life at Blue Ivy had taken on a kind of surreal normalcy. Runs with RJ at least three times a week. The days he couldn't run, I hit the gym and used the treadmill.

After the paint and feather debacle, RJ had been *incensed*. Aubrey had been pretty pissed off, too. We weren't the *only* students who got "painted and feathered," but it didn't matter. The crap took forever to get out of my hair, and the boots were a lost cause.

I was angrier about the boots and the fact RJ's mood had nose-dived after. The rest of the night had been kind of a bust. Sydney had been so upset, because the paint wasn't supposed to be real, but food dye in water. The feathers were a griffin tradition.

There was no mistaking the fact that the paint they'd dumped on me had been real. Monday morning, I still had flakes of it I was trying to work free. The weather had turned much chillier after Friday night.

Much. Chillier.

Monday dawned dark, gray, with the promise of rain in

the air. When I went out to run, there was no sign of RJ. I debated texting him, but he'd always been on time. If he wasn't here now, then he probably needed the sleep. I gave him ten minutes while I stretched.

Then I put one earbud in, turned up the music, and ran. One in to listen, the other out so I could be aware of my surroundings. I needed a plan. Aubrey was ready to rip right into Payton and the others. Problem being, they'd masked their actions with the "rituals" for bonfire.

Cute.

The choice to dump real paint on me had to have come from Lachlan, Payton, or both. My money was on both. They were like the Jack and Jill of bitchiness. No, Jack and Jill were siblings. Clearly, Payton and Lachlan weren't.

Payton needed a lesson or she'd keep this shit up. It was only escalating, and I'd meant it when I said I was done. The paint hadn't been the last straw. No, that had come before. This?

This was the first salvo in a new war. It could not go unaddressed. But, the question was *how* to address it. Aubrey would just punch her. Whether she punched her in the face or the tits was debatable. She might do both.

I loved that about Aubrey. She was direct. Confrontation didn't scare her in the slightest. If anything, she thrived on it. I swore it must be genetic. Like me, she had ties to the entertainment world. Her father was an old school rocker from a band that did really well in the seventies and eighties and had a resurgence in the late nineties.

Her mom, however, was an attorney. She thrived on conflict. Or at least, that was how Aubrey described it. Debates at their dinner table were often vicious, and you better show up prepared. That was when they had dinner.

Still, I wanted to do this. *I* needed to give Payton a dose of her own medicine. At the same time, plotting to actively get someone was a new one for me. Yvette and Aubrey would be better at it, and they would have tons of ideas.

While that might be true, this was on me. The sound of a second set of shoes slapping the ground as their owner ran warned me that I wasn't alone.

The trails were dark pools of shadows between the lights along the way. Tons of places for ambushes. Being out here with Lachlan wasn't high on my list of things I wanted.

A twinge hit me for going on the run without RJ, but I needed to think. Needed to deal with Payton.

That said, I also needed to deal with Lachlan. He came up on my left-hand side, right on cue. Face forward, I pretended not to see him even as I braced for whatever came next.

At least there were no ponds on this route. We made it a whole three minutes.

"Where's the boyfriend?"

I spared him a glance. "Where's your girlfriend?"

He flashed me a grin. "She doesn't run."

"Shocking." Payton probably needed an appointment to have a thought.

"Didn't answer my question," he said after another minute.

"Glad you noticed." I had my run down. I could push it, but I ran because I needed to burn off this energy. The problem with Lachlan was he incited me so much, the running barely seemed to touch the edge.

"Aww," he said with more than a hint of smugness. "You're not mad about the feathers are you? You looked fantastic. We got lots of photos."

Oh, I was aware. They'd taken great glee to post some of those or at least get them out there. I'd seen more than one so-called funny TikTok that included each moment in stop motion as RJ leaned in to kiss me and they approached with the paint.

In another lifetime, I might even look back at it and laugh. Today was not that day.

"Ace," Lachlan said abruptly, cutting me off and I had to stop or plow into him. We were between two of the light posts and Lachlan was way too damn close. "You shouldn't be out here running all by yourself."

"Currently," I said, keeping my voice even. Tonal modulation was a thing. "I'm not alone. Also, it's none of your business what I do. The only problems I run into are usually you and your girlfriend."

Not one hundred percent true. Since the incident in the hall with Timothy, Jonas had been absent from class. It was weird. He'd been gone the whole week. I'd collected his homework, and Soren had made sure to get it to his door.

But that didn't have anything to do with what was happening *here*.

Head cocked to the side, Lachlan began to smile. "Yet, you're still standing here talking to me."

"Not willingly," I said, then snapped my fingers. "Thank you for reminding me that I have a choice."

I went to go around him, but he blocked me again. "Don't rush off. We have time to talk."

"About?" I raised my brows. The last thing I wanted to do was talk to him. "I came out here to run, not socialize."

"Well, maybe if you socialized a little more, you wouldn't have so much trouble fitting in." The smug condescension in his tone had me narrowing my eyes. "Communication," he continued, lifting two fingers to brush my cheek. "It's important."

"Don't." I slapped his hand away, and I swore his smile just got wider. "You know what, just fuck off, Lachlan. If you want to run, run. Clearly, I can't stop you. But I don't have to talk to you or make nice."

I made it two whole steps before he caught my arm. When

he pulled me back to him, the song playing changed to something more primal.

"You keep running," Lachlan warned. "That just makes me want to chase."

"That sounds an awful lot like a you problem," I told him. Even in the dark, I could see his eyes, but I couldn't read them. The haunted forests were cloaked in shadows.

"You like being chased," he said, his voice lowering to a whisper that had the hairs on my arms rising. "Don't you?"

This close, there was no missing even a single breath of his because it brushed against my skin. A faint chill raced over me, and I tried to brace against the bizarre combination of apprehension and anticipation.

"Is that what you think?" I dared him, because he was still gripping my arms.

"Yeah," he said, and I swore his nose brushed mine. "It is... more, I think you like being caught." That low, husky growl was not doing me any favors. The douchebag had no damn right to be sexy.

None.

Zip.

Zero.

"Why is that?" I did my best to breathe through my mouth. His nearness and scent were as overwhelming as his arrogance and bullshit.

"Because you're still here," he whispered, then pressed a kiss behind my ear.

"You have a point," I admitted and he slid one hand from my arm to cup my chin. The move forced my head up.

"I'm glad we're on the same page," he said. Those were some famous last words. I needed to save it for the song I could write about this crap. His head dipped and I swore he was swooping in for the kiss he'd denied me and RJ Friday night.

Asshole.

I didn't have paint, but I did have a knee. I slammed it up between his legs as hard as I could. His hands spasmed as he let me go, and a soundless groan escaped him.

"Nope," I informed him as he put a hand over his nuts and gagged. "We're not even in the same library. Toodles."

I pivoted and took off. My run this time was definitely at a much faster pace. I had no idea how long it took a guy to recover from having his nuts smashed, and I didn't want to find out.

The song list rolled over to Queen, and a real laugh escaped me. Appropriate as hell. I rode the high of that for the rest of my run. Luckily, I didn't see Lachlan again. He was probably still holding onto his balls.

Maybe it was just a little thing, but I enjoyed that triumph. Not to mention, he really deserved it. Shoved me in a pond. Cut my bra. Dumped paint and fucking feathers on me.

I was still wrestling with the Payton problem. She didn't have nuts I could smash; besides, she deserved something else. Lachlan had made his harassment physical and intimidating. She'd just been a bitch who enjoyed the gossip.

Well, that and she was Lachlan's girlfriend. Ugh. I really didn't know what was worse. That they were dating or that he tried to kiss me *while* he was still dating her.

"KC," Aubrey said as she stuck her head in the room. "I've got a study date before class. You good?" She'd been worried about me the day before, and it had taken both of us to get the paint totally out of my hair.

"I'm great. Go have fun." If I needed her, she'd stay. "I'm just gonna hit all my classes and maybe play this afternoon." I motioned to the guitars. The day before I'd tuned them, but I hadn't really settled in to play.

"Got the itch?" Sympathy marked the question and I nodded.

"More than a little."

"I'll be back by dinner. We can have a jam session."

I grinned. After she left, my smile faded and I stared at the guitar. Double-checking my book bag, I pulled the little silver-wrapped chocolates out of the side pocket. Hell, I'd forgotten those were in there.

What Payton needed was some humiliation. I was not going to take pictures of her boyfriend or her. I wasn't going to start a rumor.

I hated all of that shit. But what could I do...

My phone buzzed and I pulled it out. There was an update about an assembly that morning. We would not be having class for the first three periods as we had a series of guest lecturers coming in for the whole junior class.

That meant sitting in the auditorium for several hours. Right, coffee on the way. It wasn't until I was in line at the Dancing Goats that it hit me. Payton was about a dozen people in line behind me and talking loud.

"It was just perfect, she looked like that girl Carrie without the blood..."

Bad movie reference. Carrie got even with those assholes. Soren was working making the coffee, and I grinned at him when I got there. "This is new."

"They were hiring," he told me. "Want a free coffee? I don't like it but I get a free one each day I work."

"I don't mind paying, but thank you."

"You're welcome." He beckoned for me to step out of line, so I did and moved over to where he was making the coffee. Opportunity. Means. Cover.

Keeping my focus on Soren and not on Payton, I smiled. "Can I ask you for a favor?"

"Yes."

"Would you mind helping me get back at someone?"

He stared at me for a beat. My voice was low; it wouldn't

carry very far. The espresso maker was loud as was the milk steamer.

"What do you want me to do?"

When I told him, he looked from me to the line then back. I waited while he finished making my coffee, and when he handed it to me, he nodded.

"I can do that."

I was going to owe him big time. "You need anything, it's yours. I'm going to owe you." I passed him the chocolates.

"Just smile," he said. "It makes Sydney happy. She doesn't like it when you're down."

That was wildly sweet. "Thank you, Soren."

"You're welcome."

"You know," Payton said from behind me. "The line isn't getting any shorter and you're not that important. Maybe let the rest of us get coffee."

"Sure thing," I told her and grinned. "Have a great day."

Her eyes narrowed, but I kept right on smiling as I left the coffee area and headed to the auditorium. I really hoped I had a good seat for when the laxatives kicked in.

Payton was about to be *really* miserable.

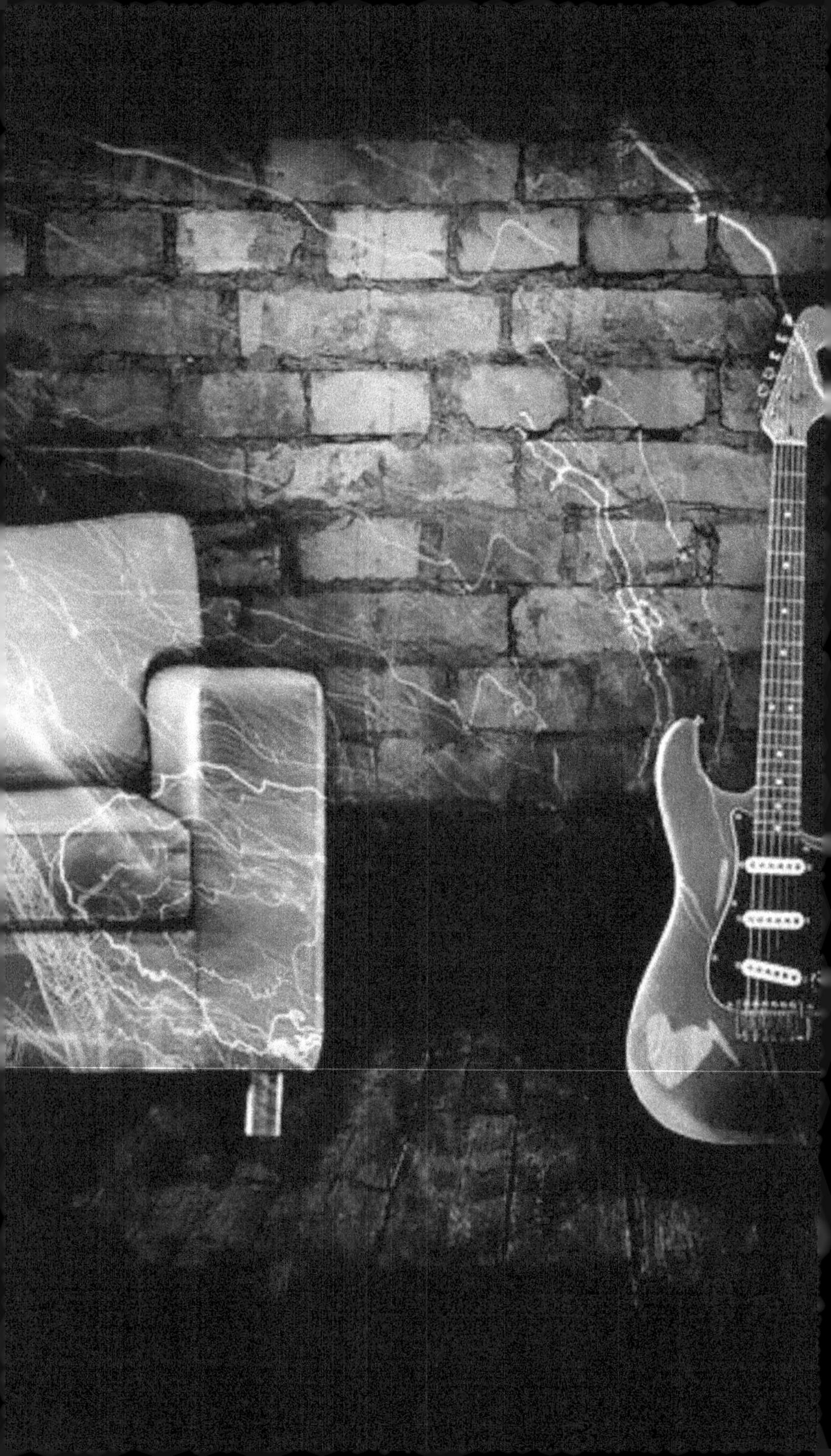

Twenty-Three

Since I got to the auditorium early, I took a seat in the back and on the side. I wanted the best vantage. If Payton reacted predictably, she was gonna be front and center.

Right on cue, she entered the auditorium with her little clutch of friends. They chattered their way to the center of the row closer to the front. Aubrey entered a couple of minutes after them, and she found me where I'd set up in the corner.

"Hiding?" she asked as she scooted over to take the seat next to me.

"Nope," I promised her with a grin. At her pitiful look, I shared my coffee. "Just wanted a good spot."

Aubrey side-eyed me for a moment then twisted to look around the slowly filling auditorium. We were early, but we weren't the only ones. "Thank you," she said as she took a drink. I knew the moment she spotted Payton, because her whole posture went stiff. After a beat, she leaned closer to me and dropped her voice, "Why are we watching *her*?"

The corner of my mouth kicked up and I took a sip of my

coffee to try and get my grin under control. "Do you remember Brazil?"

Eyes narrowing thoughtfully, Aubrey frowned. "Vaguely. Didn't we have to reschedule dates?"

"Yep," I said before raising my cup. "Yvette made a mistake about the silver-foiled chocolates in my bag." It had been an absolutely miserable twenty-four hours for her, but we'd all learned something valuable.

"Oh," Aubrey whispered. "Shit." She glanced from Payton to me then back again.

"Not yet." I hummed a happy little tune. Aubrey gawped at me, then let out the richest laugh as she bumped my shoulder with hers. I let my gaze wander as more juniors filtered in for the presentation.

Hopefully, I'd see RJ at lunch. I'd sent him a message, but he hadn't answered yet. Then again, he missed the run so he might be tied up elsewhere. I probably should have called him after the bonfire, but I'd not been in the best mood either.

Goosebumps raced over my skin, and the feeling of being watched crept through my amusement until I let myself glance around the auditorium. The feeling was unsettling at best.

It wasn't Payton; she was still talking a mile a minute to the group of sycophants around her. Considering they glanced in my direction more than once, well... I could guess about the topic of conversation.

Skipping them, I continued my slow scan of the rapidly filling space. It took me a moment, but I finally found the source of the agitation seeming to vibrate in my bones.

Jonas Dekkar sat at the end of the row in the middle directly opposite where me and Aubrey were sitting. He looked...better. I hadn't really seen him after the fight in the hallway—okay it was more a massacre for Timothy—and I hadn't gotten to thank him. I hadn't seen Timothy either.

Rumor had it, he'd had to go get his nose fixed as well as something with his jaw.

Whatever it was, he hadn't been back to the school. Not that I would have noticed one way or another. I hadn't even seen him before the day he got all touchy feely in the hall. Hadn't missed him since to be honest. Sydney, however, knew most of the gossip, and she'd told me.

Instead of looking away, scowling, or dismissing me—all of which he had done in the past—he just...stared. The hostility I'd gotten kind of used to was absent. If anything, his expression was bemused. He didn't get me.

Well, that made two of us. I didn't get him either. Hot Shot and I had definitely gotten off to a not so stellar start, but maybe we could have detente now.

Maybe.

The scratch of a microphone cut through the various conversations, though it didn't silence them. Feedback had me wincing, and when I refocused on Jonas, he wore a hint of a smile. It was the first one I'd ever seen on him. It softened some of the harsher lines of his face, lifted the dark brooding in his eyes, and really...

What the hell was I doing?

I shook my head and when I focused on him again, he wasn't looking at me anymore.

He also wasn't smiling. Aubrey elbowed me and I resettled in my seat, facing forward. My earlier amusement regarding Payton was half-forgotten. Jonas Dekkar almost smiled at me.

And I liked it.

I shook my head again. Maybe I had finally lost it. Still. The laxatives worked better than I thought they would. About a third of the way through the presentation, I caught sight of Payton squirming in her seat.

She didn't make it another ten minutes. I did my best to

not stare, but when she made a frantic run for the door, there was no point in not watching—everyone else was.

Aubrey shot me a look, hand over her mouth, and the suppressed sound of her laughter just made happy sigh. I didn't smile though. Nope, I schooled my features as I tracked Payton's exodus. It wasn't until my gaze collided with Jonas' again that my lips twitched.

He tilted his head, like he had a question. As much as I might want to answer, it would only indulge my curiosity and I'd already been burned.

By afternoon, the campus was buzzing with stories about Payton's "accident" during her rush to get to a bathroom. To say I was above enjoying it would have been disingenuous. Aubrey cackled every single time our gazes met at lunch.

RJ was back at lunchtime, too. "Sorry," he murmured as he slid into the chair next to me. He was in his uniform but also wearing sunglasses. "My only excuse was I drank too much. Party. I know better but...yeah, so sorry I wasn't there this morning. Did you just go to the gym?"

"Nope," I said with a shrug. "I wanted a longer run outside so I risked it."

He grimaced, before whipping his sunglasses off to reveal bloodshot eyes and enough luggage under his eyes to declare his hangover had come for a long visit.

"You should drink more water," Aubrey told him as she passed him an unopened bottle. We always picked up a couple. "Hydration is your friend in the face of a hangover."

Squinting at her, he said, "Yeah, I drank some already when I took some painkillers."

"Drink more," I nudged him and then pushed the bottle

to him. "The only thing you missed besides the run was the junior assembly. Not that you'd have been there."

"Nope, I would have skipped that anyway. I did skip it last year," he informed me. "Trust me when I say they are never worth it."

I caught Aubrey's eye and grinned. "I enjoyed today's." Not that I could tell you what the actual assembly had been about. "But the sleep probably helped you more."

"Surprised you didn't invite KC to the party," Aubrey murmured and I cut her a look. Her bland expression said, "What? You don't want to know?"

"I wanted to, but she's made her priorities clear." RJ drained the water bottle, then slid his sunglasses on before he brushed his fingers down my cheek. "Since they are important to you, they are important to me. I'll meet you in the library after classes?"

My heart did a little fist bump with my ribs. "Only if you're feeling up to it."

"I'll be there. Get you caught up, then you can take a break and go out with me." He lifted his chin to Aubrey then strolled off.

"He still should have asked you," Aubrey muttered and I glanced over at her. "What? He should have. Or skipped it. The guy wants to date you but he goes to a party and gets hammered without you?"

"A," I said slowly. "He's a friend. Dating has been broached but also tabled for now."

"Broached. Who says broached?" Her nose wrinkled, but her lips twitched.

"People with a vocabulary," I reminded her and she chuckled. "Besides, the point is—he's my friend. He doesn't owe me any explanations. Even if he'd asked, I'd have said no."

"Okay, this school is killing all the fun in you."

"Pfft." It wasn't the school. "I'm still lots of fun."

"Fine, I'm getting us a party invite and we're going. Harley said all the fall parties are coming up...the bonfire was one of the first. Now, before you remind me that you went and it ended badly, we're prepared now and I have your back."

I couldn't argue with that. "We'll see."

"Yes, the party," Aubrey said. "Because all work and no play makes KC unhappy, and we didn't come here for you to suffer."

No. Then again... "Frankie did say that high school was both the best and the worst."

"Exactly. We've had some of the worst. We need some of the best."

"Okay, I'll think about it." That was the least I could do.

After lunch, we split up to get to our classes, but my phone buzzed with a message from Bronson.

Pen at hospital. Mom and I are on the way.

I skidded to a stop, then diverted from the building and hit his contact information. He answered on the first ring.

"I don't know anything more than that, and I was typing that in when you called."

"They didn't tell you *why* she was in the hospital?" Penelope was a *baby*. Babies shouldn't need to go to the hospital.

"Mom is down as an emergency contact."

Bless Jackie.

"So when they brought her in and couldn't get ahold of her mom, they called us."

I closed my eyes. "Tell me what you need."

"For you not to panic," Jackie said, her sober tone carrying over the line. "This might be nothing, but until we get there, I don't know what it is exactly. It's not life or death critical."

I sagged.

"That much I know," Jackie continued. "Go to class. Bronson will text as soon as we know anything..."

"If there's a cost, use the card I gave you." Then, because Jackie was an adult, I tacked on, "Please."

"We'll sort it out," she replied, her tone softening. "I know you're going to worry, but let me do that for now, and we'll keep you in the loop."

"Thanks."

"Hang in there," Bronson said. "Seriously. I'll text you as soon as I know anything."

Then there wasn't anything else to say. I stared at my phone and then at the building. I still had to get to class, but all I could think about was how little Pen was. She wasn't even able to walk yet.

I absolutely hated the idea of her being in the hospital.

My phone buzzed again. This time it was Trish, and I answered the call immediately. "Is Mom okay?" Trish and I never really talked unless it was about Mom.

"She's fine, or so she says. She sounded fine. But she's decided to stay at the retreat for another thirty days. If you're up for it, she'd like you to go there for Thanksgiving…"

Oh, sure. 'Cause that sounded like fun. "Okay, thanks for telling me."

"Of course, and don't worry about your mom. She really did sound a lot better." Trish didn't linger on the phone, and I sighed. The problem with telling me to not worry about Mom…it just made me worry.

"Miss Crosse."

Ugh.

Ramsey.

I pivoted to face TA Malone where he stood by the open door. "Mr. Malone?"

"You should be in class," he informed me. "Receiving calls during the day is typically not a good idea."

"But not against the rules?" Like Jonas, I hadn't really seen much of him since the incident in the hallway. He'd missed a handful of tutoring sessions but left me with work to do.

Folding his arms, he gave me a hard stare. "Why are you here?"

"I'm sorry?"

"Why are you here?"

I slid my phone into my bag and then shrugged. "I'm here because I got a message. It was important, so I paused to answer it."

He didn't roll his eyes, but I swore disapproval rolled off him in waves. "I don't mean right here in the courtyard." He motioned to the area around us. "I meant this school. Why are you here?"

"To get an education," I told him, and when he kept staring at me like he was trying to drill holes into my soul, I spread my arms. "I'm sorry if you don't like the answer. But that's what I have. I came here to go to school."

And I'd step on my own tongue before I told this disapproving prick I came here to be normal. I could just imagine the comments.

"That's the only reason you came here?" He continued studying me like I was some science experiment or something.

"Pretty much," I informed him. "Why else would I be here?"

The bell sounded, signaling no matter what I chose now I would either be late to class or absent.

"You should go," he told me. "I expect you in the library at the end of the day." With that, he turned his back on me and walked away.

"I've been there every day," I called after him. "Even when you weren't." Since he wanted to just drop his little snarky comments and leave.

Taking a page from his book, I walked away. Granted, I hadn't gone after he tried to pair me with Payton, but then there was the fight in the hall and it just went downhill from there.

Huh, Jonas and Ramsey back on the same day. Maybe my little run of good luck had all been spent on Payton.

Worth it.

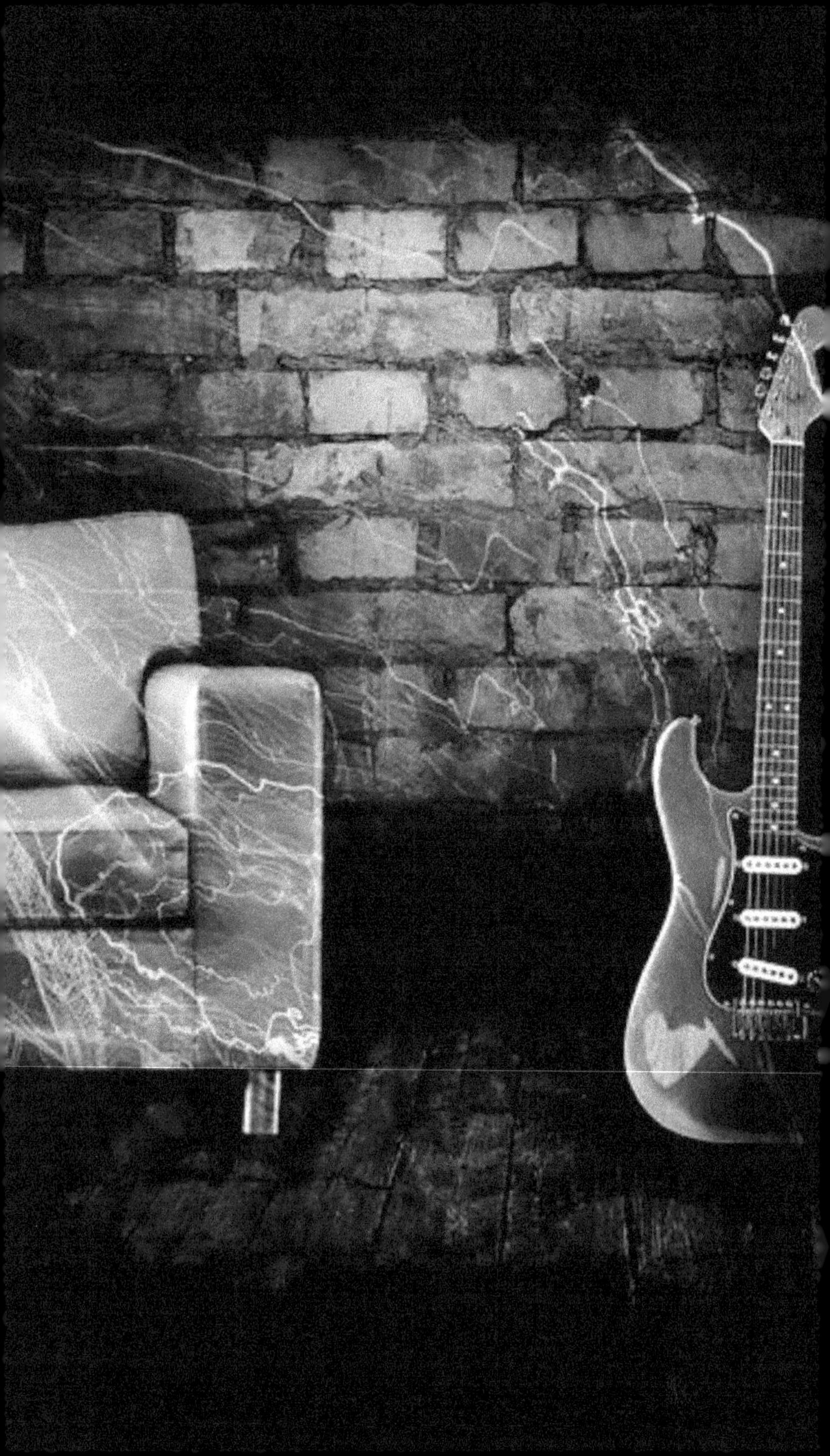

Twenty-Four

"I got it!" Aubrey announced as soon as I was in the door from studying with RJ. After missing the run because of his hangover, he'd not missed a single one since. Nor had Lachlan.

At least, he kept his distance so far. Not that we managed a single run without him putting on an appearance somewhere. The way he watched me made me damn glad RJ was there.

The animosity between the pair crackled. Oddly, the energy made me want to capture the *feel* of it in music. While I was usually better at writing the lyrics, I'd been working on the music for the last week.

At Aubrey's announcement though, I paused with my fingers on the strings. "Got what?"

"The invitation you've been waiting for," she said, her tone smug and her eyes dancing with laughter. "Aven set us up."

Aven. I didn't know Aven. "Wait, isn't she the girl in your film club?" Aubrey had been expanding her interests, and she decided to join a film club because we were always working on new ideas for videos. She'd gotten into an AV class, too.

I envied her on that, since *someone* had gotten my art class removed. Thank you TA Malone, for tutoring.

"Yes, she is." Aubrey dumped her bag and came to sit on the sofa where I was perched, bare feet propped on the table while I worked my way through the different keys to find the minor key that would work best to underscore that tension. "She's also connected, like connected-connected. There's going to be a Halloween party and masquerade off-campus the last weekend of the month."

That was *next* weekend.

"Off-campus, where?" Because anything *not* on campus already sounded better to me. There'd been no sign of Payton since her—incident. The fact she shit herself *before* she made it to a bathroom was something I was going to savor for a while.

"At the Windsor Estate. It's about twenty-five minutes from here in Old Brook."

Old Brook. Classy.

"Who's throwing the party?"

Aubrey gave me a long look.

"What? I just want to know."

"Uh huh. It's a *party*, KC. A party you and I desperately need."

"I don't know that I would go so far as to say *desperately* need it."

"I would," she retorted, twisting to sit sideways as she pulled her tie loose. I'd ditched the uniform as soon as I was back. Hair in a ponytail, I'd pulled on an old band t-shirt and sweats before settling in.

The weather had been getting decidedly colder, and Halloween was only a few days away. We were also coming up on the nine-week mark, and I would hopefully see an improvement across the board for my grades.

Some of my teachers had been more supportive than

others. Some. Though to be fair, I liked Mr. Cohen *way* more than his sexy bastard of a TA.

"Look, call Yvette if you don't believe me, but you need some high-energy events. You've been running more and more, don't think I haven't noticed just how much you're running, and it's not always helping."

Not twitching was hard, but I leaned forward to snag my pencil and add a few new measures to the sheet. It gave me something to do and bought me a little time to consider that.

"It depends on whether I run into that dickhead or not." Douchebag Three, Lachlan—something. I knew I knew his last name but right now I couldn't place it. "But," I said, raising a hand with the guitar pick in it before she offered her first rebuttal, "I see your point."

"Yes!" She raised her fists to the sky. "I like winning without presenting my argument."

I laughed. "Look, I get it. We took the break so we could have fun and study."

"Exactly. I can't think of something *more* fun that getting dressed up, going to an off-campus party, maybe have a couple of drinks, dance, and just be someone else."

How were we going to be someone else? "Oh. Costumes." I grimaced.

But Aubrey wasn't remotely dissuaded. "Exactly. We're going to look fabulous, keep up the masquerade…" Then she tilted her head to look at me. "We need to get you a really nice wig."

Wigs were so damn hot. But she had a point. I was currently the only one with blue hair. "The party is this weekend?"

"Yep. I'm going to see if we can get a ride from Forrest to a costume place tomorrow. So, can you skip studying with RJ? That will give us more time."

It would. I rubbed my thumb against one of the strings thoughtfully. "You mind if I ask RJ if he wants to go with?"

"Considering he's been trying to talk you into a date for weeks?" Aubrey smirked. "Of course not. Now I'm gonna get changed. Play me what you have so far on whatever that is you're working on."

I laughed. Picking up my phone, I sent a text to him and then a second one to Bronson. Pen was out of the hospital. Her mom hadn't shown up for three days, so Jackie took her home with them. But now she was back, and I was kind of hoping she'd either just fall all the way off the wagon or get on it.

One or the other. In the meanwhile, both of them were at Bronson's place.

She's good. He texted back. *Whatever fever she was running they think was just a virus.*

He included a picture of her. Penelope with her mop of dark blonde hair, pale blue eyes, and wide smile. She only had a couple of teeth, but she was downright precious.

Our baby sister was about as close to perfect as you could get. Six months old and just—precious as hell.

Let me know if you guys need anything. Then a thought occurred to me. *What is she going to be for Halloween?*

A dalmatian puppy. Came his immediate response. *Mom is going as Cruella and I'm gonna be Jasper or Horus—or maybe one of the other dogs.*

I cracked up.

Pictures or it didn't happen.

He just sent me a middle finger and then said he had to get to class.

Penelope was fine. Mom was at her retreat getting clean and sober. Classes were going well.

"What do we want to be?" I called out.

"I had some thoughts on that," Aubrey yelled back. "Make us coffee and I will share."

Laughing, I rose and set my guitar down on the stand to the side before I headed toward our little kitchenette. I couldn't wait to hear what her ideas were.

While I waited for the shots to brew, I sent a message to RJ letting him know we were going to the party and whether he wanted to go with or meet there. Meeting there was less pressure date-wise, so I kind of preferred it.

His response was swift. He would definitely be there and what costume was I wearing so he could coordinate. I promised to let him know as soon as I did and that Aubrey and I were going costume shopping the next day.

Excitement threaded through me at his thumbs up response. This was going to be so much fun.

The weekend could not come fast enough. Aubrey and I had a ridiculously good time trying on costumes. Forrest, as it turned out, had excellent taste. He also had his eye on Aubrey and flirted every chance he got. It was downright adorable. The fact Aubrey flirted back just made my whole day.

They also coordinated their costumes. She was a bone countess while he was a bone daddy duke. It was both adorable *and* hilarious. The black of their costumes offset by their face paint and masks was going to be so striking.

The masquerade portion of the costume party suggested a little old-world style to go with the masks themselves. I'd tried on both a gothic black swan costume *and* a corpse countess.

Aubrey voted for the black swan, but I kind of liked the corpse countess better. Forrest said, "You wanted to wear a wig, right?"

"Yes," I said as I turned in the gray and white ripped dress that was both elegant and kind of spooky. It had taken a few pulls from Aubrey to help me tighten the bodice so I could get the full look of it.

It even managed to give me boobs, and that was impressive. The fact it covered more than it revealed gave what it revealed a little more emphasis.

Forrest held up the French court wigs that would more than cover my hair.

I shot a look at Aubrey and she nodded. "Shoes."

"And makeup." If I was going as a corpse countess, I needed some shimmery white ghost makeup to truly add to the effect.

Adding a silver masquerade mask to the pale costume, makeup, and cosmetics would wash me out almost completely. From bold color to black and white. The drape of the sleeves threatened to reveal my tattoos so I went with elbow length white gloves that would leave my fingers bare.

The closer we got to the weekend, the more the hum in my system accelerated. Aubrey was right. We needed a party. A real one. I'd let RJ know what I was dressing as and he said to keep my eyes out for my Day of the Dead duke. He would be on the hunt for me.

I was more than ready. My upbeat mood lingered through every class and tutoring session. I even managed to smile at TA Malone on Thursday because I would be partying the next night and I couldn't *wait*.

The party was in full swing when we arrived. Not only did Forrest take us to get costumes, he also drove us to the party. The guy was a doll and completely besotted with Aubrey, something clear to anyone with eyes. I was so happy for her.

The Windsor Estate had been completely tricked out for

the party, from the pumpkin guards at the gate to the skeletons serving as valet service.

Lights shone from nearly every window in a multitude of colors. The Connecticut country-style mansion was also bedecked in dark and white lace, and blood red accents with dry ice creating a misty fog that invaded everywhere.

Haunted mansion on crack. I loved it. The music's pounding beat throbbed in the air, and I was already dancing in place while I waited for Forrest and Aubrey to head up the stairs.

"You want to wait for RJ?" Aubrey asked, but I shook my head.

"I sent him a picture of me," I said. "He'll find me." Even if I hadn't, I didn't think I could stand to wait outside. They had a Queen song on, but it was already segueing into Killer Bees. The gothic feel to the mansion was not reflected in the music, and that was fine. It was a total vibe and I was here for it.

"Go on." I shooed Aubrey with a wink. "Go dance. I'm right behind you guys."

She wasn't about to be sent away, so she snagged my hand even as she gripped Forrest's arm. "Forrest can dance with both of us."

"Me dancing with two gorgeous girls?" Forrest said with a slow smile. "Please twist my arm."

I was still laughing as we got inside. There was a guy at the door who offered to take our coats if we had them, but we'd all skipped it. Between my heavier costume and the heat I'd generate by dancing, I wasn't the least bit worried.

Forrest led the way through the downstairs to the first ballroom—there were three—and the whole place was done up in black lights, which lit up Aubrey and Forrest's makeup perfectly and added to my haunting appearance.

Even my gloves looked like they were glowing. While I

started out dancing with them, it wasn't long before RJ appeared. He looked amazing in his red and black suit and wearing lifelike skull makeup. The slicked back effect to his hair just added to the appeal.

When he held out his hand to me, I was more than ready to grip his fingers and let him tug me to him. The volume of the music seemed to increase when my chest collided with his. Grinning, I squeezed his fingers.

Aubrey was right.

This was *exactly* what I needed.

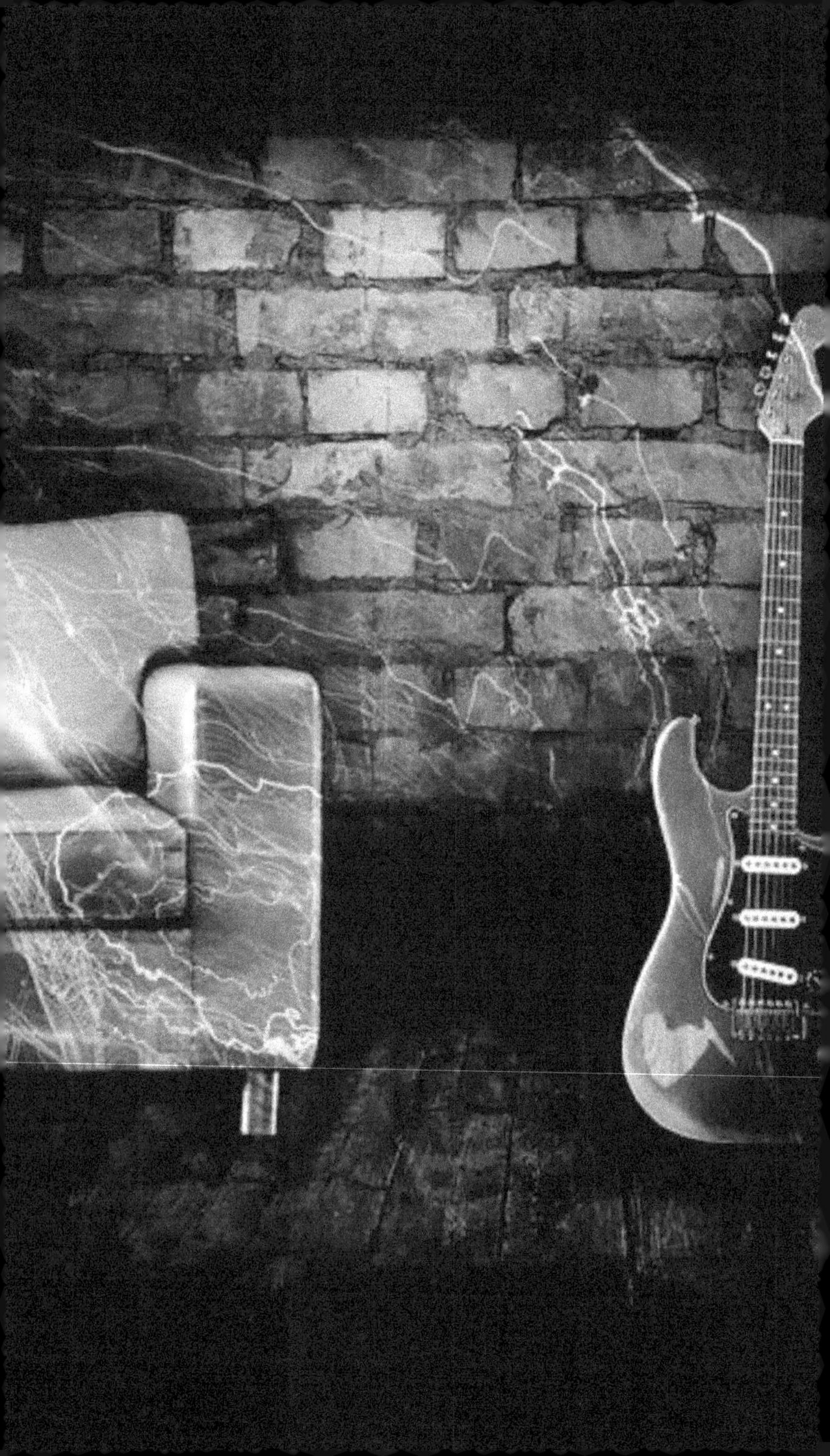

Twenty-Five

The pulsating music filled the darkened ballroom with its red and blue lights, dancing ghosts on the ceilings, and hints of sticky faux spiderwebs everywhere. Throw all the directions in with the dry ice fog drifting over the floors and it was the perfect atmosphere.

The fog created a chill that was perfect for dancing, and damn could RJ move. While he still had one of my hands in his, he'd looped his free arm around my waist and it didn't matter if the beat was fast or slow, he didn't leave any space between us.

Even better, no one was looking at me sideways, or if they did, I never saw them. The black lights illuminated his skull makeup. It probably made my face paint glow, too. We were hardly the only dancing ghouls in the ballroom doing the monster mash.

Laughter bubbled up through me when the music shifted again. I thought *I* had eclectic taste. The DJ went from modern rock to punk to classic rock before diving into some grunge stylings. The best part was that it gave me time to catch my breath as RJ twisted me around, loosening his grip to let me pull away, only to haul me to him again.

Adrenaline surging, I threw my head back and laughed. I had to hold on too because he picked me right up off the ground and twisted to spin me around.

There were other rooms for dancing, food, drink, and more. As curious as I was about the other ballrooms, I didn't want to abandon this one. Not when I knew the songs they were playing and I was more than happy to dance and sing along. Maybe when the latest song ended, we could take a cool-down break.

That sounded like a plan, except, when the song ended, a Torched song blasted from the speakers. First album. One of the first ones we'd written.

Dark Heart, Wild Soul.

Between the flashing lights, the beat rioting from the speakers, and the fact RJ kept dragging me into him, I let myself go. I wanted to move to the familiar rhythms, like we were on stage performing.

I'd already been in the mood to sing when we'd first gotten in here, but now I just went with it. This song both ripped out my heart, and put it back together again. It was all about our families, the fact we never felt we had a place in them.

It was about breaking away from their expectations as well as all their baggage and building our own future. It was the first song of ours to hit the top of the charts and it had *stayed* there for weeks, only getting knocked off by a second hit.

A hip bumped mine and RJ twisted so I could see Aubrey. We leaned into each other, singing the chorus together before our respective dates pulled us apart. The earlier laughter turned into this giddy rush.

They followed up that hit with the Big City Rockets and then Pink Disciples. I was breathless when RJ lifted his chin toward the side and I nodded. A breather was probably a great plan.

"Water?" While I could *barely* hear him over the music, I could read his lips, even if they were painted black and white with the skeletal face.

"Please," I said, fanning myself as he let go of my hands. The dry ice chill had long since failed to cool me down. We might have to go outside.

"Hey," Aubrey said as she caught me in a quick, if humid, hug. "We're going to find a room."

The words were spoken right into my ear and I blinked as I leaned back. But there was no denying her smile or the gleam in her eyes.

For real? I mouthed the sentiment rather than say it aloud because Forrest was right there, just a step behind her. Damn, he couldn't keep his eyes off her. It was sexy *and* sweet.

She nodded and her smile seemed to grow exponentially. I lifted my pinky and she hooked hers to mine.

"You okay on your own?" Yeah, I was totally fine on my own. "I didn't want to abandon you but..." She glanced in the direction RJ had gone.

"I'm good," I promised her. "Take care of you and be safe." Another hug and she grinned, her delight practically shimmering in the air around her. I watched her go with a real smile. Aubrey *looked* happy, and that was everything.

I barely had a minute to fan myself before RJ was back with a huge bottle of water. Condensation ran down the side of it and he twisted it open right in front of me, cracking the seal.

That was...really fucking thoughtful.

He also offered it to me first for a drink and I downed several gulps. Cold and wet, it was perfect. When I passed it back to him, it gave me a thrill when he took a drink after me.

When he finished the bottle, he tossed it into a trash can I hadn't even noticed. Holding out a hand to me, I swore he looked at me as if he could read my soul. The corner of my mouth kicked a little higher when he raised his eyebrows.

Despite the lighting, or maybe because of it, his eyes seemed to be daring me to take a leap. A flutter filled my abdomen as a thrill chased up my spine. The last few weeks had been a series of brutal downs with a few ups thrown in to keep me sane.

RJ had been amazing through all of it. Even when I turned down his date offers, he'd taken it like a champ and just offered to help me. From running to the library to breakfast treats—RJ had been the best.

I clasped his hand and laughed when he hauled me toward him. The music vibrated around us, but I was only half aware of the other dancers. That was bullshit, I wasn't aware of them at all. It was the hard chest against mine, the calluses on his fingertips where he traced along the sides of my pinkies that had my full attention.

The thump of his heart seemed to reflect the pounding beats and it sent another thrill of excitement racing over my skin. I shivered despite the heat in the room. I wasn't cold at all. Head dipping toward me, he murmured something, but I was too busy looking at his eyes to read his lips and I didn't hear it over the pound of my pulse.

The idea of kissing a guy was one of those things I'd always flirted with then retreated from. It was terrifying. What if I couldn't do it right? What if our teeth hit? What if—

Curiosity surged through me as he leaned in closer. I rose up on my tiptoes to meet the suggestion of the kiss, mental fingers crossed I wasn't reading the movement wrong. Then his lips brushed mine. The contact was brief, but the combination of my cosmetics and his had our lips clinging together almost like they'd sealed, and then he pulled back a fraction.

Pulse racing, I dug my fingers into the back of his neck and then his mouth slammed down on mine. The force crushed all my fears and burned away the tentativeness. At the single press of his tongue, I opened up to meet the thrust of his tongue with my own.

It was like we had to fight our way through the kiss and it was—fuck it was *everything*. Groaning, I tried to scoot closer. The layers of costuming made it harder to feel him, but he looped an arm around my waist and then lifted. It put our faces even, and even if my feet dangled, I didn't care.

Desperate for oxygen, I lifted my head and he was still right there. We were moving with the beat and there were people all around us, but it was like they couldn't touch us. Or at least they didn't dare touch him.

A smile burst out of me and he gave me a squeeze before our mouths collided again. There was a scrape of teeth, and a hint of peppermint on his breath. He tasted like—nothing I'd ever sampled. It made me hungry for more.

The music changed and he twirled me around, then my back was to a wall and our mouths fused as I gripped his jacket. A wild heat burst through me, and if we weren't in the colorful, fog-filled room, I'd worry I was in danger of a sunburn.

We lingered there, dancing with our tongues even as the music rose and fell. Only when a slower song kicked in and the lights playing against my eyelids changed did he lift his head. I couldn't help but swipe my tongue against my lower lip where the taste of him remained.

The roughness of his fingertips traced along my throat to where my pulse leapt at the contact. His eyes seemed so dark, like the pupil had swallowed all the color. The makeup on his lips had come away some, but it only added to the effect.

I was made up much paler than him, so did I now have his darker cosmetics on my lips? A laugh escaped me and at my smile he tilted his head. The moment he dipped his gaze to my lips, I moved. I wanted to kiss him again.

And again.

We moved with the music, kissing, teasing, and kissing some more. When he squeezed my ass, my whole body jolted but rather than push him away—I dragged him closer.

I wanted...more.

Time ceased to have meaning. Even as the songs shifted and changed, we just kept dancing, kissing, and then kissing some more. The next time we broke apart, a laugh escaped me and he studied me again.

The sad truth was I had no idea if he'd said anything because between the music and the racing of my heart, I really couldn't hear anything. I was a lyricist. Words, the way they shaped and formed the music to help propel the emotion, were something I understood.

Yet, here I was, wordless with wonder and half-drunk on the heated kisses that left me craving more. When he traced his fingers from my throat to my cheek, I leaned into the contact. One light tug and I was back in his arms. I had no idea who reached for who first, only that I desperately wanted more of this kiss.

While there had been many starts and stops, it had all been one, long intoxicating kiss. When he pushed a leg between mine, I arched into the contact. My skirt was long and full. There wasn't much in the way of real force, but I could imagine it.

My heart squeezed with pleasure that left me shuddering. When he abandoned my lips to kiss along my jaw, I sighed. Eyes half-open, I took in the scene around us. Costumed bodies writhing as they danced. Corpses. Ghouls. Ghosts. Vampires.

His lips tickled along my earlobe and his hand closed over my breast as his thumb skated over the swell of it. The urge to grind against his leg held me captive as his breath feathered over my ear.

"Fuck me, Ace, you're hot."

There was no imagining the ragged groan beneath his words even as their content registered.

Ace.

My eyes opened abruptly and I jerked back to meet his slow smirk. Beyond him, just stepping into the ballroom was another guy in a black suit with lifelike skull face paint and hair that looked like he'd been running his hands through it.

Lighter colored hair.

Lighter.

Colored.

Hair.

I jerked my gaze back to the guy I'd been making out with while we danced.

Not RJ.

Horror crept through me, because the guy I'd been clinging to and panting over was Lachlan.

Lachlan. Fucking. Nash.

I'd been making out with Lachlan Nash.

What the hell was wrong with me?

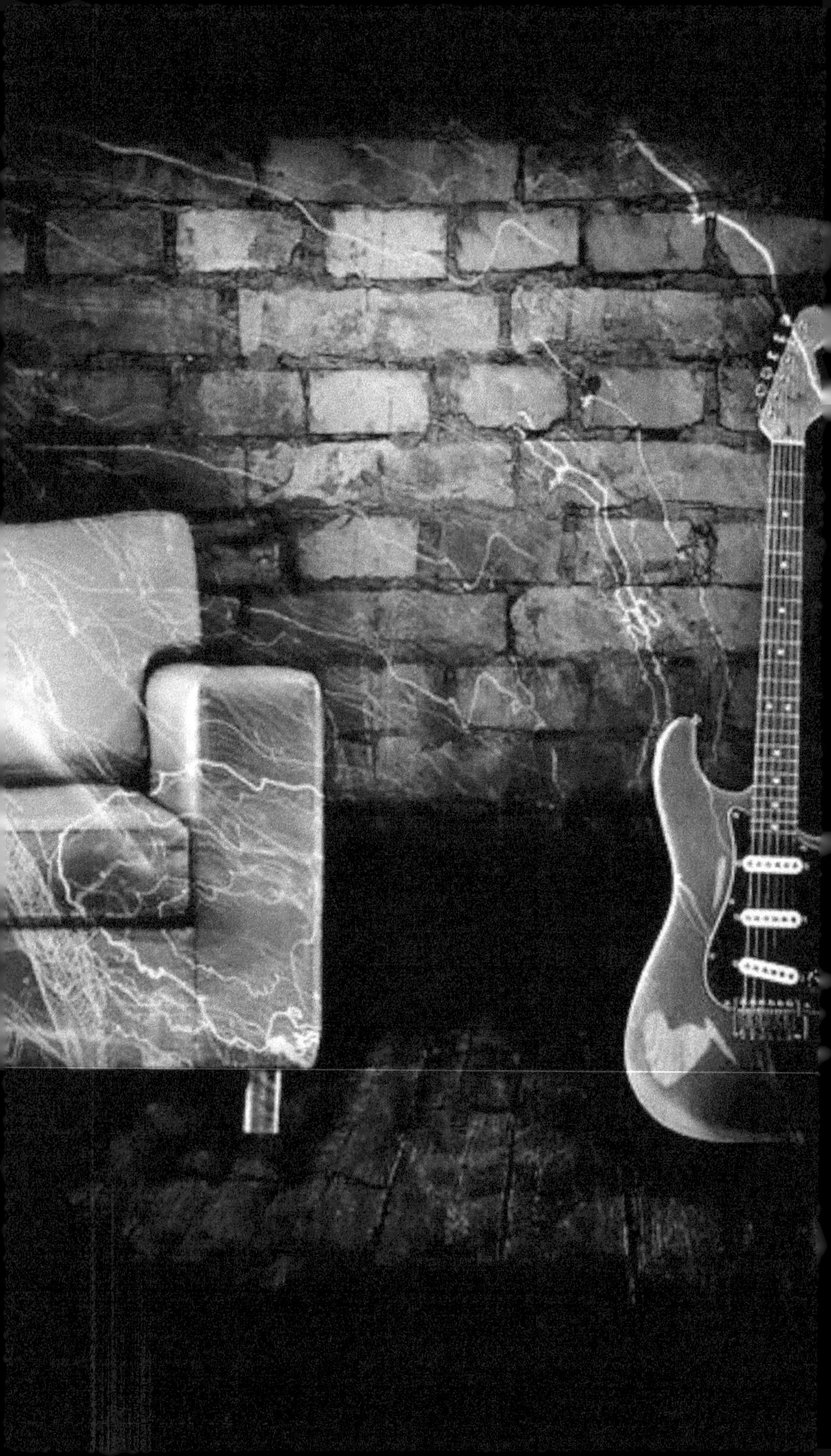

Twenty-Six

"I can't believe he did that," Aubrey said, her tone less disbelief and more raw fury. She was late getting back, later than me. That part made me happy. I'd gotten a ride-share; thankfully the app worked anywhere.

It also meant I had to dump out on RJ and for that—well, I was a coward. I could not imagine telling him that I'd just made out with Lachlan thinking it was him. Especially when the kiss had been all I'd dreamt about all damn night long.

"He's such an ass," I said, pacing the room. It had been eating at me but I didn't want to dump it all into Aubrey's lap the night before. When she'd come back, she'd been almost floating.

"He's worse than that." Scowling, Aubrey had her phone in her hand. "Why didn't you tell me last night? All you said in your message was you were tired and wanted to head back early."

Pausing mid-pace, I pivoted to face her. "I didn't tell you because you were with Forrest and I was really hoping you were having a good time."

Her expression softened, the scowl fading briefly even as

her eyes brightened. "We had an *amazing* time." Then she shook her head. "But this is the kind of thing I should have been there to back you on. I thought he was RJ when I left and you looked...*happy*."

I had been happy. The music, the dancing—he'd been a great damn partner. When I thought he was going to kiss me, I just went for it. A shudder began at the base of my spine and rocketed up and down. It left me both cold and overheated just thinking about the way his lips had felt against my own.

My first *real* kiss.

Interlocking my fingers together behind my head, I fought back the urge to scream. First kiss and it had to be *him*.

"You had plans," I said, circling back to her comment. "You were with Forrest and you had an amazing time..."

"I haven't even told you yet," she decried my description with a frown.

"Your joy had wings." To be fair, the fact that it did helped soothe the scorch marks left behind following the realization of who I'd been kissing. "That is everything."

Aubrey's smile grew, then she gave a little shivering shrug. "It was...a lot and magical and more than a little uncomfortable at times, but totally worth it."

"Good." I meant it. I wanted everything for her. Just like I wanted everything for Yvette. "So, are you and Forrest like officially dating now?"

Her soft snort just made me grin. "You've been wanting to ask that."

"Yes and no. I figured you'd tell me when you got to it." Privacy was the gift we gave each other. With so much attention on us out there, when it was just us? Yeah, we butted out.

Most of the time.

"And yes," she said, "we are. Maybe I'll ask him about beating up this Lachlan Nash dickhead."

Ugh. And we were back to Lachlan. "No, I already kicked him in the balls."

"You should do it again," was her advice, and I had to laugh.

"Don't tempt me."

"Oh, I don't need to tempt you." Aubrey nodded at me. "If I see him first, I'm totally getting him in the balls. He wants to keep putting his hands and lips where they don't belong, then I'll give him something to hold onto."

A second laugh escaped me and I dropped my arms to face her. "I love you."

"I know."

The next morning, RJ was waiting for me as I left the dorm. He glanced at my shirt and grinned. It was officially November and the air was damn chilly. They had been talking about snow this week, but so far, none had made an appearance.

"Hey," he said as I zipped up my hoodie to cover the shirt's saying: *I have never faked a sarcasm. Ever.* "You didn't answer my texts yesterday."

When he held his hand out to me, I sighed and slid my palm into his warmer grip. "Sorry, I was...I was exhausted yesterday and kind of just burrowed down and watched movies with Aubrey."

It was mostly the truth.

"Okay, you ducked out of the party pretty fast and right after I got there." It wasn't a scold, but his tone definitely held an element of dislike in it.

"It was...not as fun as I thought it would be." Liar.

It had been amazing right up until I realized *who* I was kissing. Just like that, I could feel Lachlan's lips on mine. Heat flushed through me and I glanced away from RJ, grateful that our early hour meant it was still dark enough to hide my embarrassment.

He squeezed my hand. "Did something happen?"

A chill wrapped its way around me despite the flushed state of my skin. "Can we just run? I'm sorry I bailed on you. I'll make it up to you, I promise."

I owed him that much. Especially after...well after I made out with another guy thinking it was him.

Not glancing at him, I tugged my hand free to start stretching. He didn't maintain his grip but he didn't join me either.

A low whistle cut through the darkness when I was bent over and I wanted to either sink into the ground and vanish, or have a brick I could throw.

"Fuck off, Nash," RJ said with a hell of a lot more heat than he'd displayed previously. "Don't you know when a girl isn't interested?"

"Ignore him," I said, not bothering to look at the douchebag in question. "He just wants attention." And I was *not* going to give it to him.

"Awww, c'mon Ace, that's not what you were doing at the party."

"Shall we?" I said to RJ and he glanced from me to Lachlan and then back.

"Don't know if he wants to after all, Ace. The man has questions."

Pivoting, I scowled at Lachlan. "Aren't you dating Payton? Why don't you go make out with her and leave me alone."

"Payton and I have an understanding," he said with a slow smile. The shadows draping him didn't remotely disguise the knowing look on his face. "Something the boyfriend there already knows, isn't that right, Wallach?"

RJ snorted. "I don't fuck crazy," he commented.

"Nah, you just let it suck you off." Lachlan slid a look at me. "Or do you not do that yet?"

I punched him.

I put every ounce of my weight forward and struck his nose. It was a glancing blow, but it still made my hand hurt.

"Fuck," I swore as I shook out my hand. Lachlan, the whackjob, put a hand to his nose and then stared at me a beat before he started laughing.

"Ace, you really need to work on getting all that pent-up frustration out. If Wallach isn't doing it for you—"

It was RJ's turn to swing this time, only Lachlan seemed ready for him. He caught the fist and then retaliated. His blow was a hell of a lot harder and it staggered RJ.

Shit.

It was the hallway fight between Jonas and Timothy all over again. Only, RJ wasn't deterred or down. We also weren't in a hallway. The crash of his fists into Lachlan echoed with the soft thud of flesh on flesh.

Neither shouted or cussed. They barely even spoke. It came out more in grunts, blows, and harsh exhales. RJ shoved his arm up and over Lachlan's shoulder, they went from trading blows to a full grapple.

Then they went down the hill and I wasn't sure how much was them falling or fighting. Probably both. When they hit the bottom, Lachlan was down with RJ.

RJ twisted, then he was up on his feet and he went to kick Lachlan. I opened my mouth to say something, but Lachlan caught his foot and twisted.

The snap echoed through the cold air and I flinched. A harsh pained sound came from RJ, and he rolled to the side. Half-stumbling down the hill, I collided with Lachlan and shoved as hard as I could to push him away from RJ.

"Stop it."

Getting between them wasn't going to do much if I couldn't get Lachlan to back off.

The fog of our breath collided as I faced Lachlan, he stared at me for a moment, the light from the nearby trailhead leaving half of his face in shadow. He cut his gaze past me to RJ then back again.

"Keep him the fuck away from me," Lachlan warned. "Or next time... he won't even be able to limp away."

"Well then stay the hell away from me," I retorted. "We were here first."

That stopped him in his tracks and he chuckled softly as he stalked back to me. "Actually Ace... I was here first." Nothing could have prepared me for what he did next. He gripped my arms and dragged me forward before he kissed me.

His mouth slammed against mine. I tasted the hint of coffee, a slice of orange, and something coppery that had to be blood. It took a split-second for all of that to register.

Like a match against dry kindling, I was going up in flames. And I didn't even like this asshole, but fuck—it was the kiss at the party all over again. Another half-second for me to slam my knee upward even as heat spiraled through me.

I bit his lower lip even as he avoided my knee. I hit his thigh, he grunted but when I dug my teeth in—he finally yanked his head away.

Laughter huffed out of him as he stared down at me. "I like a girl with teeth. I like one who knows when to use them, too."

He wrapped a hand under my chin, not quite around my throat as he stared down at me. The blood under his nose and trickling from a cut on his cheek didn't seem to faze him in the slightest.

"Lose the dead weight, Ace. Stay away from Wallach or next time, I'll do more than break him."

He dipped his head in again like he was going to kiss me, tightening his grip to keep me from yanking away.

"Until next time..." The whisper of his words lingered in my ear even as he released me abruptly and headed for the trail.

Then he was gone and I stood there, heart racing and a little breathless. My lips tingled and I stared after him like some kind of idiot. A groan from behind me jerked my attention back to the present.

"RJ..." I moved to help him, but he jerked his hand away and shook his head. "I'm...I'm sorry."

"Yeah, you looked sorry kissing him like that," RJ said with a scowl as he dragged himself upward. I winced at the dislike icing every word. He wasn't wrong...

When he would have stumbled, I slipped under his arm to brace him upward. He let out a string of curses as he hobbled. "I'm sorry," I murmured. "I know you were trying to help..."

"Yeah, pretty sure he fucking broke my ankle this time."

This time.

I frowned. "He hurt you last time?"

For a minute, RJ just stared at me and then shook his head. "Don't worry about it."

How was I not supposed to worry about that?

"At least," he continued, every word coming out a pained huff. "I know why you took off from the party and who you were making out with..."

Who I was...? I winced.

"Saw the pictures," he told me, as he leaned on me. RJ was not a small guy and it took some effort to steady him.

Pictures? "I'm sorry," I managed again, though it sounded particularly flimsy. "Let's get you looked at..."

"Miss Crosse?" The very last person I expected to run into in the dark had to be the first person we encountered at the top of the hill. "Mr. Wallach."

Ramsey glanced between us then down at RJ's ankle. "What happened?"

"Fucking Lachlan," RJ said before I could comment. "Trust me when I say the prick isn't getting away with it this time." He glared at Ramsey with such venom it made me cold. "You should warn him, I'm going all the way to the board this time."

This time...

"Miss Crosse, let me escort Mr. Wallach to the infirmary. You should go back inside. The temperatures are dropping..."

Were they? "I want to help."

"No," RJ said abruptly and I blinked as he pulled away from me. "Go to the gym and run. Stay off the trails and away from that asshole until I can get back out here."

Ramsey didn't say anything, not even when RJ paused to press a kiss to my cheek. Thankfully, he didn't go for a real kiss. Especially not with Lachlan's touch still tingling on my lips.

"I'll see you later," RJ said, his tone firm. "I haven't forgotten our study dates."

RJ limped away from me and shook Ramsey off. The TA glanced over his shoulder at me with a frown and I folded my arms, then looked away because honestly, I didn't have any explanations for the last few minutes.

My hand still hurt, too. As much as I wanted to just go for a run on the trail, I didn't want to run into Lachlan again. Not now.

I also didn't want to go to the gym. My adrenaline was already surging. Back in our room, I opened my phone to check for the latest on social media and there it was, bright, bold and huge on Kissy Kat's gossip site.

Fuck.

The photo was definitely me and Lachlan, all done up in our costumes and fused together. Heat swept through me as I stared at the picture. It was high-definition too. Someone had taken that picture at the party.

Then they'd sent it in.

The only person who'd known it was me in that costume had been me, Aubrey, Forrest, RJ—and Lachlan.

Son of a bitch.

Caught - Problem Child's gone wild. Pop princesses might be born at the top, but they are more than capable of sliding down into the muck and climbing back out all by themselves, no matter who they have to drag down with them to do it. So, who is Problem Child's new paramour?

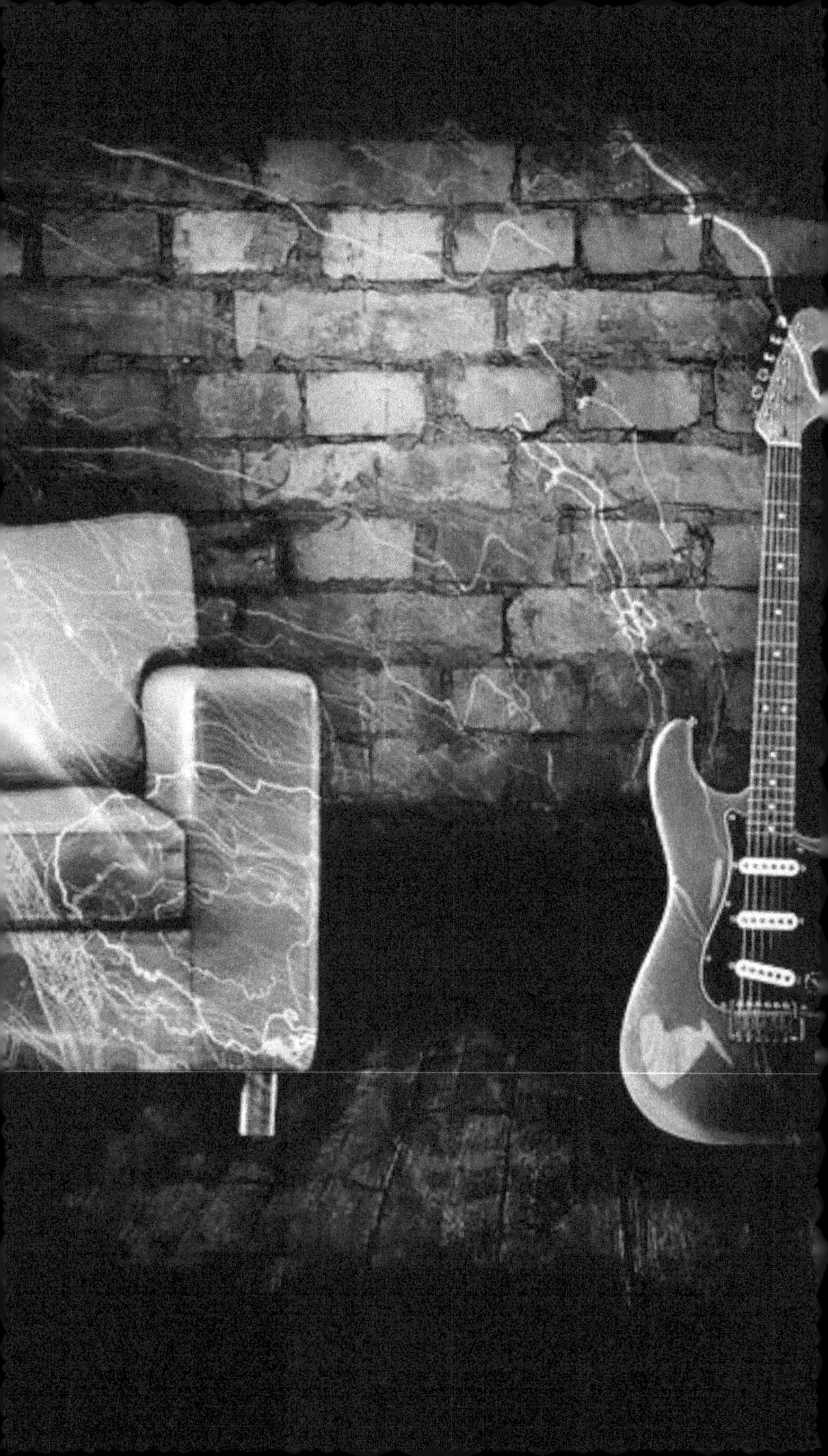

Twenty-Seven

The first few days after the Halloween weekend were not the most comfortable. Lachlan had managed to surprise me between the dorm and the gym, stealing a kiss before I'd even begun to process it was him. When I would have slapped him, he snared my wrist, then kissed the palm before he wandered off whistling.

Such a dick.

Worse, it left my lips tingling and me *thinking* about the son of a bitch. I could not get him out of my head for more than five minutes it felt like.

Ramsey didn't bring up the incident with RJ and Lachlan. What he did do, however, was begin showing up at the study sessions RJ and I had at the library.

"I thought you had other things to do," I challenged him when he settled at the table where RJ and I were working. The downstairs study room was booked every day after classes for two hours. We didn't always need the whole time, but RJ had been a trooper.

Especially since he had more than a wrenched ankle this time. It was a break. Faster to heal, but he would not be running anytime soon. So, back to the gym I went. The fact I had to choose a different venue irked me with RJ, with Lachlan—hell, even with Ramsey.

I wanted to *run*. I needed it. The treadmill was *not* the same as the trail. Just like having Mr. "My time is valuable" intruding on my study sessions with RJ. If he kept showing up *now*, why couldn't we have done this before? Then I could still have my damn art class.

A class I was missing. Particularly when I caught sight of the sheet music in Jonas' stack the other day. The school had an art of music club, and apparently Hot Shot was in it. It was like the whole universe heard my plan to be *normal* and just scoffed at me.

"I do," Ramsey responded to my earlier comment before fixing RJ with a look. "I would prefer that my work with you isn't a waste of time." Then he refocused on me. "Also, Mr. Wallach is not in any of your classes, so you're relying on knowledge gleaned from a previous academic year by a less than stellar student."

So much for his time being "valuable."

RJ snorted. "Not all of us pretend to be high-functioning freaks when it comes to academics. Being a TA doesn't make you better than anyone else. It just means you kiss more ass."

A headache began to pound behind my right eye. "Look, I'm still showing up for tutoring. I'm using this time to make up for the late assignment grades I received and to get ahead again. You don't need to hang out."

"Not a problem," Ramsey told me as he pulled out a stack of papers from his messenger bag. "I have plenty to do and I am available for any questions you might have." At RJ's scoff, Ramsey fixed a cool eye on him. "Mr. Wallach, your presence is not remotely necessary. If you're having trouble with staying busy, I'm sure I can help out there."

"Why don't you go fuck yourself, Malone?" RJ asked him in a tone that bordered on amusement but sank into disdain.

The next hour didn't improve the temperature in the room or the climate between the two men. Neither seemed to take notice immediately when I stopped working, until I began packing up my bag.

"Hey," RJ said, his tone far more solicitous. "Are you done? We haven't even done half the work you had planned."

"No," I said, agreeing with him as I stood. "But this room is vibrating with everything you two aren't saying and I need to work so—you two have fun with whatever this is." I delivered the last bit with a wave at the two of them as I shouldered my bag.

RJ's eyes narrowed at my dismissal. Guilt raked through me. He certainly hadn't invited Ramsey to join us, but he also seemed determined to antagonize him. When I flicked a look at Ramsey, I found him watching me, though his head tilted like he was reading the words on the page.

"I'll text you later," I told RJ, then gave his shoulder a squeeze. "I just—I need to get these grades up. Okay?"

He sighed, then cut a cold look at Ramsey. "Go on, sweetheart." He covered my hand with his. "I'll talk to you later."

"Thank you." Relieved more than anything else to escape the room swelling with all that toxic testosterone, I didn't even bother to tell Ramsey goodbye.

He invited himself. He could also bid himself farewell. I skipped dinner in the dining hall and ordered pizza after I got back to the room, and there was a message from Aubrey that she was going out with Forrest.

At least one of us was having a great time. That thought just made me smile. One of us *was* having a good time. I ordered the pizza after I sent a message to Harley and offered her one.

She declined but said she'd message as soon as it was there. In the meanwhile, I spread out my books and went to work.

The next two weeks passed nearly identically. I could avoid Lachlan for a couple of days, but then he would find me. I tried to vary my times at the gym, though early mornings were my preferred time slot. If I didn't get an early morning run in, it was like I had a beehive buzzing beneath my skin.

However, when Lachlan caught me—one time tugging me into a utility closet and another, just pinning me to the wall outside the gym, he left me buzzing for an entirely different reason.

Weirder still, he only ever said, "Miss me, Ace?" if he said anything at all.

The guy was driving me crazy. Ramsey was just as bad as Lachlan but for an entirely different reason. He showed up for every single study session with RJ. They spent more time glaring at each other than they did working.

Worse, Ramsey had added to our tutoring sessions, and it wasn't just grammar but seemed to be incorporating more from my other classes. When I pointed it out, all he'd done was given me a bland stare and reminded me that academic probation was for the entire semester and we still had a little under six weeks to go.

Whatever.

RJ kept trying to help but when I cut the study sessions from two hours to one—sorry I could only take so much choking testosterone—he offered to come by the room. Aubrey and I were still keeping it our safe space, so I'd offered to meet him in the media rooms on the first floor or in the dining hall.

The fact he didn't like those options made me even more reticent to invite him to my room and then I'd get annoyed with myself. I *liked* RJ.

Most of the time.

But get him around Lachlan or Ramsey and he just turned into this—well, dick. To be fair, Lachlan broke his fucking ankle, but I couldn't fix that. No matter how much I would like to help him.

Then there was fucking Payton. I swore, she was turning into some form of paparazzi. I couldn't even use a restroom without her suddenly appearing, like my own personal stalker.

Bronson and I had been playing message tag for a few days. He was underwater at school, but they still had Penelope with them, and I'd called my accountant to make sure they sent Jackie more money to help cover Pen staying there.

Friday morning before the Thanksgiving break, Trish called and left a message while I was in classes. "Hey hon, your mom is settled in at the Sunshine Retreat. I spoke to her for about fifteen minutes and she sounds good—real good. She's not planning to leave the retreat just for the break, but she said you're welcome to come up to see her if you want but you should wait until Christmas. Have a good break, sweetie!"

That was that.

When I played the message for Aubrey, she grinned. "Good. You can come with me up to Yvette's. Mom and Dad are in South America for the next three weeks climbing Machu Pichu or something. I don't know, I didn't ask. But Yvette says the guest rooms are ready."

Twist my arm.

So Friday afternoon, bags packed, we called a rideshare, checked ourselves out, and left. Yvette's place was an adorable top floor apartment with three full bedrooms and a view of Boston Harbor.

The first snow hit while we were there. I don't think we slept the entirety of the first weekend in between pizza and Netflix binges, but we crashed sometime on Monday morning.

The week was exactly what I needed. I finished two songs,

played, and we even watched the Macy's Thanksgiving Day parade on Thursday morning.

Rather than starve, we ordered buckets of fried chicken, mashed potatoes, veggies, and biscuits. We had pies delivered, too, and by afternoon, we were all flat on our backs on the floor, nursing food babies and exhaustion.

That was when I basically told the girls about everything. Aubrey knew a good chunk of it, but I hadn't told her about the continued ninja kisses or the weirdness between RJ and Ramsey.

"What a bitch," Yvette muttered when I finished the last about Payton. "There's a lyric for you."

I laughed, probably harder than the joke really needed, but that said, I rolled my head to look at her. "I feel like writing *any* song about her gives her way too much credit. I'd rather forget her than immortalize her."

"What a bitch," Aubrey and Yvette chorused in the same tune and I giggled.

Yeah. Payton was a bitch.

Our week of respite ended way too soon. But I'd taken some of the time during the week to keep studying, and when we got back to campus, for the first time since Mom's emergency message sent me racing to Manhattan, I was back on track.

Enough that when Monday morning rolled around with fresh powder on the ground, I bundled up and went running. The cold crisp air, the snowladen trees—it was a fucking post card.

I loved it.

Hell, I even laughed when I caught sight of a surprised Lachlan on my way back to the dorm. I didn't slow down, just flipped him off as I climbed the hill. It was the perfect way to get back to school.

A fresh start.

The welcome back buzz continued all day. I had lunch with RJ and he apologized for being so distracted with family over Thanksgiving. He should have called.

Yeah, I hadn't really noticed that he hadn't, and that only served to make me feel guiltier about it. So, I promised him it was all good. I didn't go so far as to tell him I was sorry I hadn't called him, but I did regret that we hadn't connected.

"You know," he suggested as we walked together toward the academic building after lunch. "I can do better. I owe you a date, a real one. I know the Halloween party didn't work out, but what do you say to going out with me this Friday? For real?"

My stomach did a little flip. I was caught up. Finally. The current assignments didn't seem so challenging. "Yes," I told him before I could change my mind.

He'd been patient and supportive.

"It's a date."

His grin made me smile, and the swift brush of his lips against mine caught me off guard. It was a blink and you'd miss it kiss, but it was still a kiss. "I'll plan everything," he said. "We're definitely going off campus, too."

Okay then.

I was floating on that news all the way back to our room after tutoring. Since I was caught up, no study date was required. RJ promised to meet me at the gym the next day and hang out while I ran.

Aubrey was in our room when I got back, staring at more boxes.

"Holy shit," I muttered at the five new cartons that had been added to the previous stack we'd picked up.

"Right?" she said, staring at me. "When Harley told me we had more, I wasn't imagining this."

Nor was I.

"Did we get this much mail on the road?"

We exchanged a blank look. We did fan mail continuously on the road, but most of the time it had been streamlined between the three of us.

"I think Yvette should be getting boxes, too." Aubrey dragged her hair up and tied it up into a neat knot on top of her head. "Get changed, I'll make coffee. You start on one end and I'll start on the other? Maybe an hour a day?"

"Until we're done?" That was intimidating. "What about two hours?"

Two hours later, we'd barely made a dent, but between us, we'd written up about two dozen responses. Personalized.

"Maybe we should have someone go through the letters for us," I suggested, not that I really meant it. As exhausting as it was, I liked answering the kids, and so did she.

"Two more," Aubrey said. "Then we get dinner."

With a groan, I stretched forward to snag two letters from the top of my stack. They were addressed to me via Torched. Some of the letters were addressed to us individually and some just to all of us.

KC,

Missing your tour appearances and social media shenanigans. While I can listen to you and watch old concert videos, it's not the same. Miss your face.

When will you be back on the road?

Your Forever Fan

Right. Okay. I checked the return address but there wasn't one. Setting it aside, I moved on to the next. Across from me, Aubrey was writing out a response. The next was a postcard from a little girl in Baja California. She wanted to dye her hair blue and wanted to know if I could send her a note telling her mom it would be cool.

The note I wrote was that blue hair could be cool, but it took a lot of work. I had to use color depositing conditioner and get it touched up every few weeks. There were times when I had too much growth that I'd have to get the roots bleached. Even with my blonde hair.

Then I added blue wigs were the best, so maybe try that for a while to see if she liked it. I'd signed it and addressed it. A glance over at Aubrey showed she was reading another letter so I reached for one more. At this rate, we were still gonna be on these boxes when the Christmas break got there.

> *KC,*
>
> *I need to see you. It's getting ridiculous that you're not doing any appearances. What about a talk show? A podcast? Don't you have a TikTok? I know the band has one. Just go live and say hi to your forever fan.*
>
> *I need you.*
>
> *Your Forever Fan*

Right...

"That's not creepy." I didn't mean to mutter it aloud but Aubrey glanced over at me so I passed her the letter. She made a face.

"You have a couple of those in this stack too..." She dug through it and passed them to me.

They were more of the same. My Forever Fan was beside themselves with my lack of appearances.

"No return address," she said.

"Same here. I mean, I get it. They miss us, but—not like I can do anything about it."

"Same."

We did two more then set the stack for mailing off to the side. "We should pouch those back to LA," I told her.

"Let's send it overnight on Thursday? That way we can get as much answered as possible?"

Worked for me.

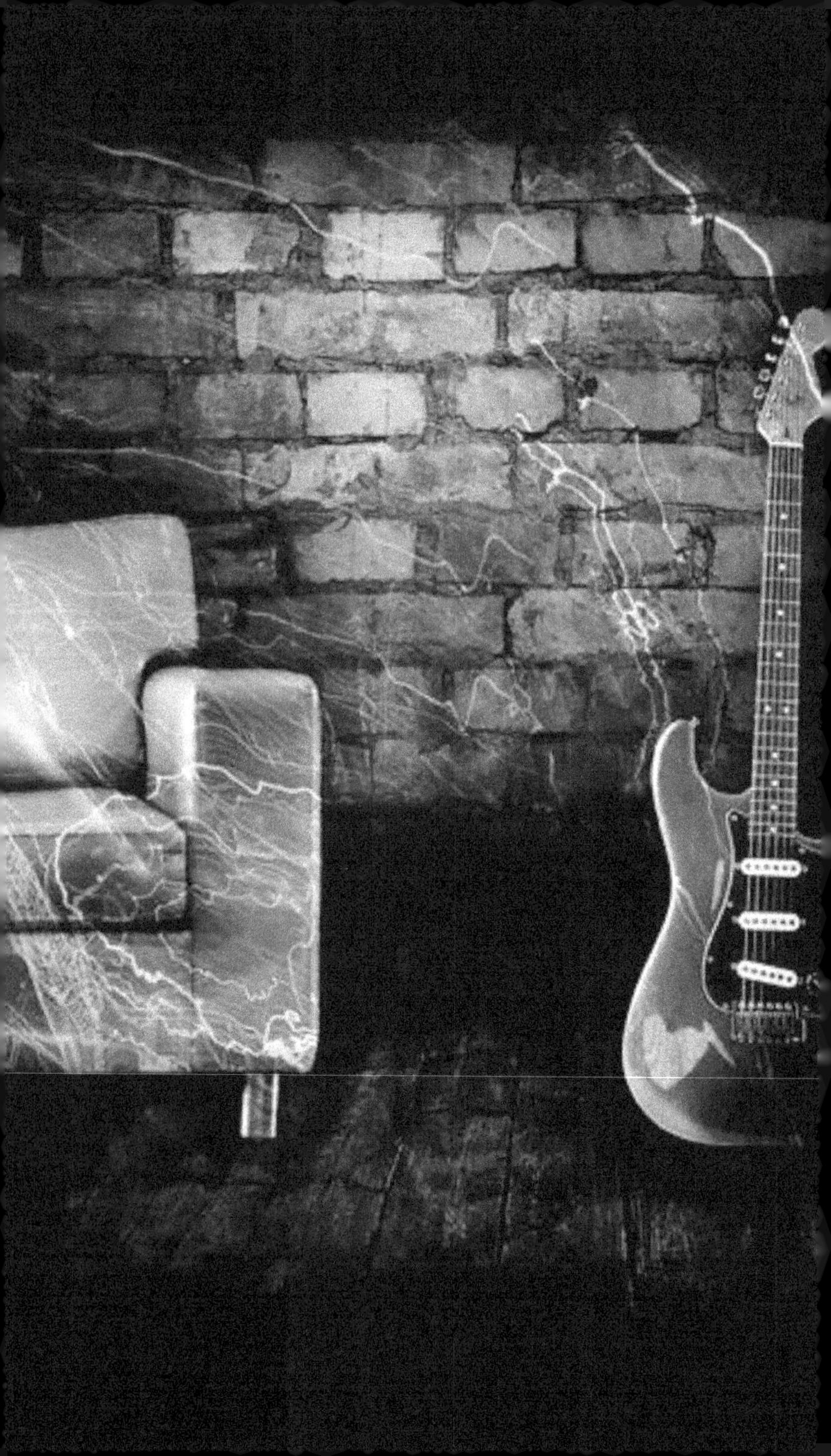

Twenty-Eight

Aubrey hit the edge of my bed and bounced me. I woke with a snap as she landed and sent me up again. "Happy! Happy! Happy! Day-ay! Hap-py! Hap-py! Day-ay-yay!"

My groan turned into a laugh as she elongated the notes to the song.

"Hap-py! Hap-py day that brought you to me."

Her grin was positively incandescent. She wrapped me up into a hug before I'd even fully sat up. December birthday baby, go me.

"Hap-py day! Happy da-yay. The happiest day that brought you to me. Don't forget," Yvette sang. "Don't ev-ah forget..."

Aubrey whipped out her phone to show me Yvette sitting up in her own bed, hair in a thick braid. "She can't forget," Aubrey sang.

"Oh, no," I joined in on the third-line melody. "She can't forget."

"No way can she forget," Yvette dove in. "Because today is our da-yay to celebrate."

Then we all did a wild version of an air guitar before we burst into laughter. Flopping back on the bed with Aubrey, I stared up at her phone where Yvette grinned at us.

"Happy birthday, bitch," Yvette told me. "You're our bitch and don't you forget it."

I saluted, still laughing. "I missed your face."

"I know," she said, her French accent seasoning the words. "That is why I am a gift to all who know me."

"Oh my god," Aubrey said with a groan. "You are something."

"Don't hate, you know that distance makes the heart grow fonder; therefore, I am the special one. However, today is not about me," she added the last few words like a gentle reprimand. "It's for the bestest bitch ever."

I grinned. "You're just saying that cause no matter how old I get, you'll always be older."

"True," Yvette agreed with a smug grin. "But I've always believed in letting the best lead the way..."

"Huh," Aubrey muttered. "I thought we saved the best for last."

That made me laugh for real. "I think we're all the best and this conversation is going to drive us crazy."

"Accurate," Yvette said as I rolled off the bed. "C'mon, KC, it's your birthday. You cannot be going out to run in the frigid cold."

"Yes, I can," I said. "Running has absolutely kept me sane this semester. Based on my moods *with* running, Aubrey would have smothered me in my sleep already without it."

"You're not wrong," Aubrey declared as I dragged on my gear. "It's also fucking freezing out there."

"That's why you run," I told her over my shoulder. "So you can warm up."

"I hate my life right now," Aubrey intoned.

"Hey, you wanted to be here with me," I reminded her as

Yvette said, "You picked going to school with our favorite girl over being roomies with me."

She flipped us both off.

"Fine, I'll get changed, then coffee for your birthday and we'll do something fun…"

"Yes," I called after her. "Classes."

Yvette cracked up 'cause Aubrey had left her phone. After pulling my hair up and tucking a knit cap over my ears, I picked it up.

"Miss you."

"Miss you, too. I wish you were coming up here for the holidays."

"I would—but you said you needed to see your parents since they would be back in the country."

Yvette made a face. "Well, they will be in Canada. But close enough."

I grinned. "Yes, you are going to spend Christmas with them, and Aubrey is going to see her parents."

As if summoned by the mention of her name, Aubrey appeared in the doorway. "I can totally cancel."

"Oh, so can I!" Yvette immediately volunteered and I grinned at them.

"I love you both."

"But we should still go because we made plans," Aubrey finished for me then sighed. "I know, but I'd rather just hang with you two."

"Same," Yvette said almost mournfully.

"Cut out early if it sucks? We'll do something for New Year's?"

That cheered them both up. "All right, Yvette, I'm going running with KC for her birthday. If I don't survive—know I went out doing my best."

Yvette rolled her eyes as I laughed. "I'll talk to you both soon!"

As soon as we hung up, I studied Aubrey. "You don't—"

"Don't even. It's your birthday. You love running. Ergo, I will go running with you and help you take out Mr. Ninja Kiss."

I almost stumbled at that description. When I gaped at her, Aubrey just smiled and held up a small bottle of pepper spray.

"Hoes before bros."

I was still laughing when we got outside. The cold air was a slap in the face. A dusting of snow lay everywhere, but it wasn't deep.

"Oh, it's a good thing I love you," Aubrey informed me as she began to jog in place, and I grinned at her. "Cause my nipples are going to freeze the fuck off."

That made me laugh harder. "C'mon. Running will keep you warm."

The best part of running with Aubrey was singing with her. It started off with drinking songs then we segued into a decade hop from the sixties to the seventies and eighties, finally to the nineties. We might have thrown in some Taylor Swift, but who didn't love her?

Well, I could think of a few but they could get fucked regardless. Running and singing took a hell of a lot of energy and oxygen. My birthday was off to an amazing start.

After the run, we both showered and changed. My phone lit up with a message from Jackie and Bronson wishing me a happy birthday.

"Oh my god," Aubrey said as she leaned over my shoulder to watch the video of them singing me happy birthday. "Pen is huge."

"She is," I said with a laugh. "She's gonna be one soon, and it feels like I just found out about her a couple of days ago."

She had gotten so big. Her eyes were the same color as

mine. The same as our father's. The one actual physical attribute of his I'd gotten. I didn't mind so much that they were Pen's eyes, too.

Bronson looked more like his mother than us, and that was cool too. From his dark hair to his dark eyes, he was this picture of calm. No one my age should be so serene, but I swear, he was.

The fact that he crossed his eyes and stuck out his tongue at the end of the video cracked me up. It buzzed with more messages—if I checked my inbox there would probably be other birthday wishes from the label, our manager, the stage people, and the crew.

There were a lot of people in our lives who always remembered. Which was more than either of my parents. Mom was at the retreat and Dad was—well, he was wherever he was.

Zeke and Cam both sent text messages. It was definitely way too early in California where Bronson lived and had sent the message, but not in South Carolina or Florida—where they were. Allie was—I had to think about it for a minute—in South Africa. Her mother had gotten a teaching position at a university there.

Allie was also only ten, so I wasn't too worried about whether she remembered or not. But I set a reminder to send her a note after classes. We had a group chat, for all of us. That was where some of the birthday messages were coming in.

I was still smiling as I read the adorable message from Dix. He'd even included pictures of flowers and coffee with a note that said, "Keep your eyes out for the surprise."

Debating the answer, I didn't even see Lachlan before I collided with him and he dragged me into a—a closet? No, it was a little office, not that I got to see much before he filled my vision after he pushed me back against the wall on the other side of the closed door.

"You've been hiding from me, Ace." The chocolate-dipped warmth softened the huskiness in his tone as he crowded right into me. The tease of his breath on my cheek turned the anticipation electric where it eddied over my skin.

The moment his head lowered, I twisted away so his lips collided with my cheek rather than my mouth. "You really think a lot of yourself..."

"Do I?" Laughter danced in between the two syllables. He crowded right up until he had a hand around my nape and could angle my head back.

There was no missing the scent of snow, linen, and something muskier—maybe an aftershave. It was a heady combination. Most of the time I could ignore how much bigger than me he was, but right now? When he filled my whole view and kept me trapped against a wall, all I could consider was how to get away.

"You have a girlfriend," I reminded him.

"Where?" A smirk curved those sinful lips and when he swooped in this time, I had nowhere to go. I could nail him in the jewels again or head butt him, I supposed, but I just locked my gaze on him and that seemed to slow him down. "You see me right here, don't you, Ace?"

I raised my brows.

"I don't want there to be any mistakes about who you're kissing..."

"Who said I was kissing you—"

I didn't get to finish the question before his lips fused with mine. The contact sent a real buzz through me.

There were times on the stage when between the lights shining, the electric feeling in the air, and the static generated by sliding across the stage as I danced and sang, that I thought I would get a shock from gripping a microphone or lifting up my guitar.

Lachlan's kiss held every single one of those elements. He pressed his thumb against my jaw and my mouth opened to him. His tongue swept in to tease mine. Liquid heat raced through my veins and pooled in my center.

"Don't ever forget who you're kissing, Ace," Lachlan ordered, and I yanked my eyes open at that proprietary tone. "Do you understand?"

"Sure, RJ," I whispered and he jerked like I'd slapped him. It was almost more effective than physically hitting him. The swiftness with which he released me might have stung, except he was the one offended.

His scowl deepened as he glared at me, and I couldn't resist patting him on the chest.

"Burns to be used in the place for someone else," I told him. "Doesn't it?"

Then I yanked the door open and slid out before he could respond. As it was, my lips were tingling and my legs were shaking. I was definitely unsteady when I slid into my first class of the day and half-worried everyone would notice my swollen lips or my flushed face.

It felt like a huge neon sign glowed over my head, but I tried to shake off the effect and focus. I made it all the way to our third period of the day before Jonas and I had to sit next to each other.

Beyond a word here or there, he'd been steadfastly ignoring me since returning after he beat the crap out of Timothy. I kind of wanted to thank him, but the last time had gone so poorly that I just kept the words to myself.

The door to the classroom burst open and everyone jumped, myself included.

Ms. Dimond frowned as three guys slid inside, all dressed similarly in school uniforms, but they also had a speaker and a microphone.

"Gentlemen—"

But she never got to finish her statement as the three of them snapped to attention, facing the class and then one of them lifted the microphone. They started off with a rock-meets-rap version of happy birthday.

At which point, I just wanted to die.

They ended their little performance with a slide down the aisles to where I was seated, and the whole class let out a burst of spontaneous applause.

Kill. Me.

I tried to summon a smile, but it faltered as the guys grinned at me. One of them lunged forward like he was going to kiss me. He didn't even make it a half-step when he lurched and if he hadn't caught himself, he damn near ate shit against the floor.

He glared at Jonas, but Jonas just stared at him with that empty-eyed expression that left me chilled and intrigued. I'd barely seen Jonas shift his leg, but there was no mistaking he'd nearly tripped the guy.

"That's enough, gentlemen," Ms. Dimond said as she tried to get control of the classroom back. Clapping her hands, she ushered them out and I scrubbed a hand over my face.

"Happy birthday," the guy in front of me said as he glanced back at me.

"Thanks," I said quietly. When he opened his mouth to say something more, he paled and then jerked around to face front again.

A glance to my left told me why the guy paled. Jonas currently stared at him like he was sizing him up for a coffin. That shouldn't be hot, but I still had to suppress a shiver.

Class dragged, but it came to a record-screeching halt at the words *team project*. Especially when she went down the rows to let people pick their partners and Jonas picked me.

He. Picked. Me.

I cut a look at him as Ms. Dimond moved on.

"Why me?"

He just shrugged and I glanced down at the project rubric.

We'd need to meet in the library and pull research. I could probably Google search a lot of it, but we were going to need examples...

"I have a study time booked in the library," I volunteered. "If you want to meet then..." RJ would hate it, but I'd make something work. Hopefully, I wouldn't have to deal with Ramsey in the middle of this, too.

"It'll be great if you can take time away from your adoring fans and partying to do the work this time."

What a dick. I ground my teeth together. "Do you want to meet or not?"

I hadn't abandoned him last time, even if it seemed that way. This time? This time I was gonna stick it to him.

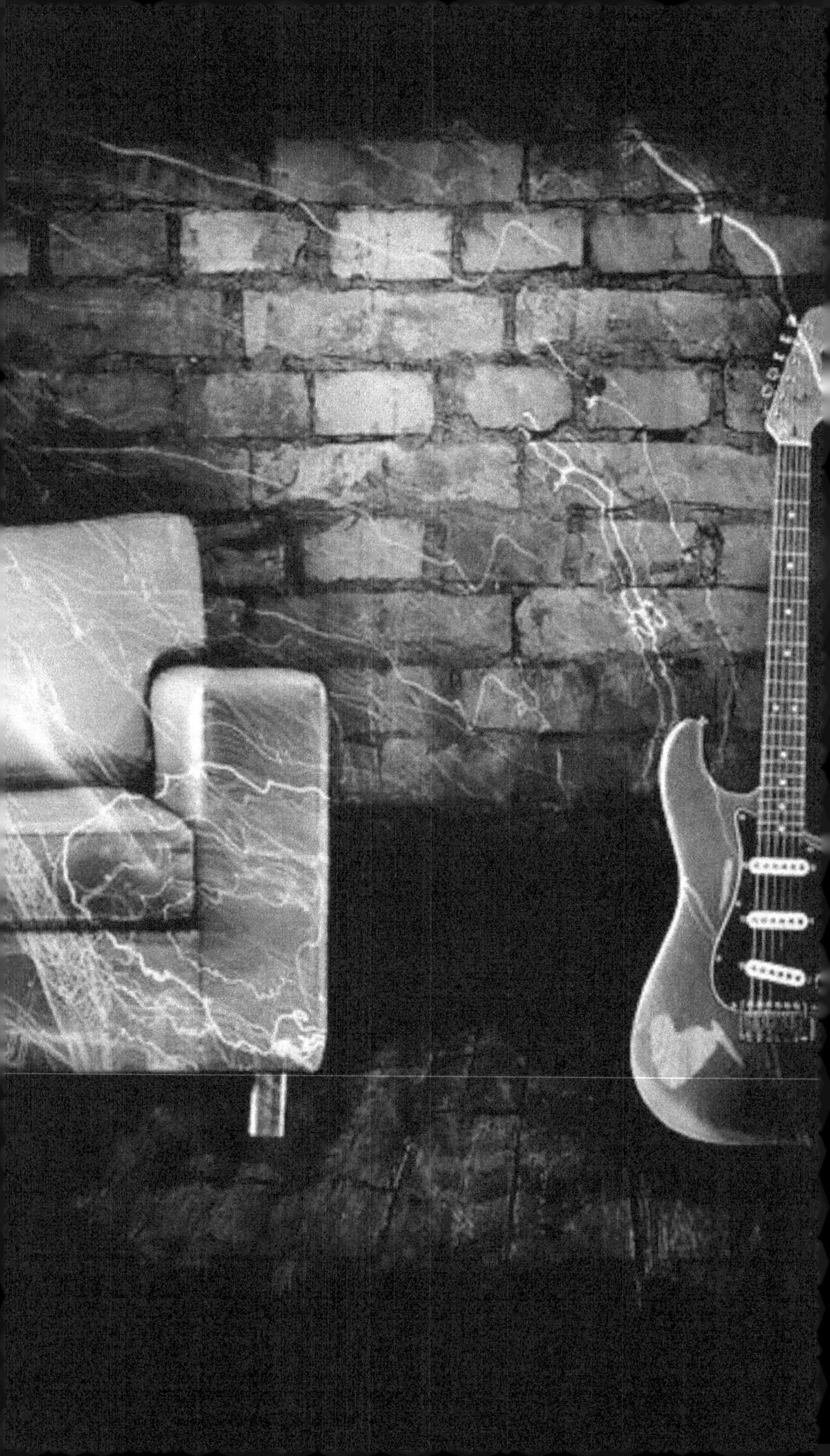

Twenty-Nine

With less than ten class days to go before we were free for winter break, I spent every free moment in the library working on our project. Jonas didn't show up the first two days, leaving it until Wednesday before he put in an appearance, and then he showed up only fifteen minutes before my reservation time ended.

He slid into the chair opposite me, and I glanced at him over the stack of reference books I'd pulled. The assignment was at least interesting. We'd been assigned a historical event and we needed to reshape and reframe all the information on it into something digestible for today's media audience.

"I was thinking about a TikTok," I told him as I gestured to the images in the books. "See if we can condense it to sixty seconds or less, hit all the high points along with a link that would take you to a longer article for more in-depth details."

I glanced over to find him just staring at me. Rather than throw a pen at his face, I pulled my hair up into a messy bun on my head. It had been snowing when I came inside and I'd brought a jacket because it had gone from chilly to fuck me it's cold out there.

"Thoughts?" I finally asked.

He shrugged. Then my phone buzzed as the time was up. Not saying a word, he got up and left. I stared at his retreating back. What the hell was his problem?

Fine, he thought I was some kind of party animal. I'd apologized for before, the time really had gotten away from me. But it wasn't like he did me any favors. So why was he being such an asshole—I closed my eyes and tilted my head back as the tired hit.

I barely had time to keep my shit together, and I really couldn't do this for someone else. When I opened them, I was still alone in the room and all my research was spread out around me.

I straightened it up and stacked the books together on a cart in the corner, then left the note on them like I was instructed. For now, the room had to be open to others, but I could keep my research there as long as I tagged the books "Don't re-shelve."

The following morning, I hit the gym because it was snowing like hell. It should have surprised me when Lachlan hit the treadmill next to mine, but I just turned up my music and ignored him.

We weren't alone in the gym. There was an entire sports team in there working out. More than a couple of the guys tried to get my attention. I gave them a firmly polite smile and that was it.

Lachlan? Him I just flipped off as I was leaving. His laughter followed me. The guy was—nuts. There was no other explanation for it. Even if he kissed like some kind of god, he was so much more a devil.

And you like him...

I shoved that annoying little voice back into its box. Liking Lachlan was kind of like picturing what it would be if I jumped off a stage or a bridge. Just because I could imagine it didn't mean I had any business doing it.

Kissing him, for example, was too damn intoxicating to be good for me. Especially when I spotted him in the dining hall with Payton hanging all over him. I was in line for coffee, but the angle gave me a direct view of the table he was at with a ton of other people, including Payton. But since he was wearing her like an accessory—yeah.

I jerked my brain back to our table where the topic was all holiday plans all the time. Olivia and Sydney were going home. Soren and Finley were also flying out early to meet their families. Aubrey had gotten an early dismissal for the same reason.

Everyone had plans. I loved hearing about them. Tutoring with Ramsey was more of the same, though he seemed more relaxed today than he had the whole semester.

"With the holidays coming up, I thought I'd go ahead and return the tutoring hour to you," he was saying when I zeroed back in on the conversation. "You've gotten caught up and you've pulled your grades up."

"That sounded suspiciously like a compliment," I mused aloud and he gave me a bland look.

"Inference and implication are not the same," he reminded me.

"No, one is a conclusion and the other is a statement," I said, "which is why I said it *sounded* suspiciously like one and didn't imply that it was one."

The corners of his lips twitched. The movement absolutely fascinated me. When I raised my eyebrows, he just chuckled and shook his head. "Take advantage of the offer, Miss Crosse."

"Think we can keep the library time?" If Jonas wasn't going to participate in the project, I could use the extra study time.

"For?" Ramsey asked, studying me rather than the paper

of mine he'd been reviewing. The fact it wasn't bleeding red made me pat myself on the back.

"Well, for research and studying. What else do people use the library for..." No sooner did I ask that, then I held up a hand and said, "You know what, don't answer that. I've got a project for history and I need to do a full breakdown, and my partner isn't all that interested in the work. So, I want to do the best I can on it."

He frowned. "Every student at Blue Ivy is required to pull their own weight. Even group projects require individual exceptionalism. If your partner isn't doing the work, then turn them into the teacher."

"Whether I turn them in or not," I said, not that I'd asked his advice because that was exactly what Jonas had done to me. "I can't turn in a half-completed project."

"No," he said slowly, his frown deepening. "You can't." He rubbed at his jaw, and there was the faintest rasp of stubble against his palm.

"So does that mean I can keep the hour in the library?" The sooner I got this done, the sooner I could focus on semester finals. I already had a plan for my first week of holiday break—sleep.

"Go ahead," Ramsey said after a long moment. "I'll work here for the same hour if you require assistance."

"Thanks," I said, meaning it as I flipped closed the notebook for tutoring and pulled out the one for my project along with my laptop. "I appreciate it."

The silence that greeted my statement had me glancing at him. For a moment, he wore the exact same expression as Jonas when he stared at me. More shuttered than empty-eyed stare, but the effect was the same. Chills raced over my skin. It was...unnerving.

Shaking it off, I got to work. With the addition of the tutoring hour, I actually had a solid outline and the details laid out for the TikTok, as well as the paper to support the information for the video, by the end of the week.

Jonas had also not bothered to show up. I dropped him an email to his school account. Everyone had one; we were required to submit all assignments via these accounts. Mine had a bit of a spam issue, but there were also notes from some of the students at the school that would come in.

A couple had come from the lower-grade kids that had managed to get into their dorm. They wanted to know if we would sign a copy of our last album for them to take home.

It wasn't a big ask, and at least they didn't break in this time. I forwarded it over to Aubrey. We didn't have CDs on hand most of the time, but we did have some leftovers in our luggage. I wasn't even sure which of us packed them.

We'd take care of that over the weekend and drop it into the campus mail. The rest of the emails were pretty standard. Comments on assignments from teachers. A summary from Ramsey, including a recommendation that I continue tutoring in the spring.

I grimaced. Really? I thought I'd managed to bootstrap my grades up enough to not need that. Then again, I had a free hour that I would have to fill if we didn't meet.

Right, finals first, then I'd worry about that. I might be too late to add a class to my schedule anyway. The weekend blew past me. RJ had messaged a couple of times, but like me, he was getting ready for finals.

He also would be graduating at the end of the spring semester so he didn't have a lot of wiggle room. We had another couple of boxes delivered with fan mail. I grimaced when Harley snagged me in the hallway.

"Sorry," she said. "I didn't realize they would keep sending them this close to the holidays."

"It happens. We got behind, so I'll try to make up for that

over the next couple of weeks." Which reminded me... "Did you get my notice about the break?"

"I did, and thank you for sending that. I will not be here for the whole break, but there will be at least two other RAs staying over the holidays. You can reach out to them if you need anything. Deliveries should go to one of their buildings, too."

That made sense, but I grimaced regardless.

"And, the dining hall will be closed for three days in each week, but I put in the order for packed meals to be made so you can pick those up and store them in your room."

"You're a goddess," I told her and she laughed. Thankfully, she even took pity on me and helped me carry the boxes up to our room. "If I don't see you before you head out next week—have a great holiday."

"You, too." She winked as she closed the door behind her.

The weekend flew past, I left the boxes of letters for after the break started. I recorded the video, talked to Aubrey about a couple of parts and she helped me re-clip them and then we did a music sample so we could really highlight the bullet points.

It was ridiculous and fun. The paper was ninety percent done, but I still hadn't gotten a single reply from Jonas. Hot Shot apparently had better things to do this week. I turned Ramsey's advice over in my head on Sunday night. I could turn in the project and state that Jonas hadn't done a damn thing or I could just turn it in for both of us and get on with my life.

I finished the last ten percent of the paper, checked the citations, then watched the video one more time before I turned it all in. I CC'd Jonas so he'd know it was turned in and we'd both be getting credit for it.

See, I wasn't a petty bitch, and he could suck it.

Monday after sixth period, he cornered me in the hallway.

I was supposed to be on my way to tutoring and instead, I was facing off with a seriously pissed Jonas.

"Why?" The growl of that word in his raspy voice sent a pulse through me even as it irked me.

"Okay, Hot Shot. I'm going to need more than a single syllable. Why what?"

"Why did you turn it in with both of our names on it?"

Seriously? This was what he was angry about?

Fuck guys, man. Just fuck them.

"Because it was a joint project and you picked me for your partner." I shrugged. "I turned it in. It's done. If you have a problem with the research or the video, you had plenty of time to object—or even, you know—show up. But you were too busy doing whatever it was you were doing."

Note, I didn't accuse him of being a partying douchebag.

I was tempted, but I didn't do it.

He scowled. The fierce expression riveted me to the spot. "That's not a reason."

"No," I countered, because fuck you buddy. "That is a reason. It was my reason. You don't have to like it. Hell, you don't even have to believe me. I don't care. Trust me when I say you've beaten the give a shit right out of me this semester. It's done, it's turned in. If we fail, we fail together. If we get an A, we get that together, too. You want to be a dick—knock yourself out. I have better things to do."

With that, I circled around him and headed for the library. Just because I didn't have tutoring didn't mean I couldn't use the study time to get ready for finals. The fact Ramsey stood at the end of the hall, perfectly placed to witness that fiasco, just didn't help.

I continued past him, intending to push open the door and head downstairs, but he held the door for me and then followed.

"I take it that was your partner for the group project," he

said, almost conversationally as we descended the steps together.

"Sure. Project is done and turned in. All taken care of." I kept my tone light. "Nothing to see or worry about."

He continued to walk with me, then popped open the door at the bottom of the stairwell to hold it before sliding around me to hit the door to the outside. Okay, if he wanted to be a doorman, I wasn't going to stop him.

"Would you like some advice regarding Jonas?" The question caught me off-guard and I slowed to face him.

"Excuse me?"

"Jonas, your study partner."

"Project partner," I corrected him. "He'd have to show up to be a study partner." Then, because it was cold out here and I only had my uniform jacket on, I folded my arms and faced him. "The project is done, classes are over in a few days. So, not sure I really need advice about him."

"Maybe not," Ramsey said slowly as his brows tightened. Sometimes he looked young, and other times, like now, he seemed beyond adult. The man had hot professor vibes for days. It was—unnerving. Especially when I had another semester of dealing with him ahead.

"What you should know or at least take into account," Ramsey said slowly. "Jonas has never been good about change and you're a huge one."

"How am I a huge one?" Fresh anger kindled in me. "I didn't do a damn thing to him. I'm a student in the class, just like he is." While I did miss that project, I *had* tried to apologize.

"Miss Crosse, look at yourself. You have flouted dress code a couple of times without censure. You maintain your blue hair despite it not following school policy, unlike other students enrolled here. You left campus for a week with barely a word to anyone, failed to turn in assignments—"

"Woah there, Captain Crunch," I said, holding up a hand. "I got permission to keep the hair. Unlike a lot of the other students here, I have a job—a full on career—one I've been engaged in for almost five years now. If there are interviews or promo we have to do—the blue hair is a trademark. As for the rest of that...well, that sounds more like a you or a him problem than a me problem. All I've tried to do is get along and get things done."

I started to walk away because why the fuck was I explaining this to him.

"You know," I continued, pivoting to face him again. "Maybe you should consider that deciding to judge someone based on press coverage, then telling me I need to cut some douchebag a break because he doesn't like change, is pretty fucking hypocritical."

Then, because I probably shouldn't be swearing at him, I added, "Not to mention the fact, I *have* faced consequences. He turned me in for failure to help on a project and that got me a zero. Most of my work, which I did while gone, was marked several grades lower because I failed to turn it in on time. And you know what—that's on me. I messed up and I got academic probation."

The anger he'd ignited had me panting and I finally just shook my head.

"You know what, I don't care. Judge me. Don't judge me. It won't change anything for me. It never has."

It never would.

We stared at each other for a couple of heartbeats longer, then I turned on my heel and walked away. Well, it looked like I got the last word for once.

Too bad that didn't actually feel like a victory.

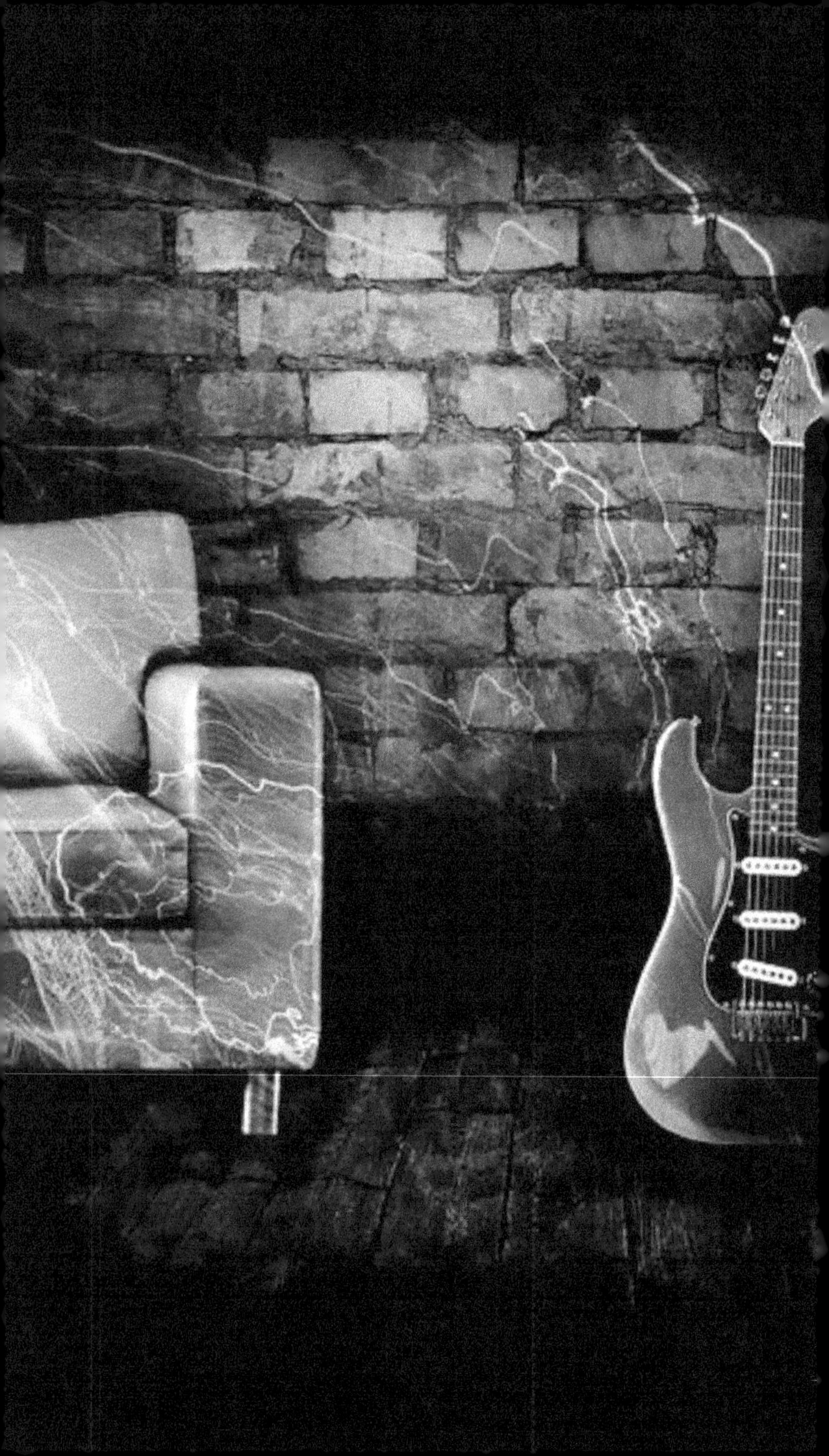

Thirty

Wednesday night, I was hugging Aubrey goodbye as we waited for her car to pick her up. Forrest had come by to give her a kiss farewell and then it was me and her boyfriend staring after her car as it pulled away. I kept my smile firmly in place.

"I wanted to say thank you," Forrest said as the car continued down the driveway. I wrapped my jacket a little tighter as I folded my arms and glanced at him.

"For what?" Don't get me wrong, I liked Forrest. Mostly because he made Aubrey smile. I needed to make an effort to get to know him better, but the most important thing I already knew—Aubrey was crazy about him.

"You nudged her to go," he said. "She was worried about leaving you here by yourself and said you didn't want to go with her. She hates leaving you here alone and at the same time—"

"You don't have to thank me for being her friend. I'll always be that." I suppressed a shiver. "The thing is, I don't do well with family, and she hasn't gotten to spend any time with them in a while. So, I get some downtime, she gets her family, then we're back here for spring semester."

Forrest studied me for a long moment then nodded. "Well, I'm here for another couple of days. My flight is on Saturday. If you need anything..."

"Have a safe flight," I told him. "And Aubrey loves goldfish."

"Like, actual fish or the cracker?"

I grinned. "Do you have any idea how tempting it is to make you guess?"

He threw his head back and laughed. Look at that, the guy had a sense of humor, too. Definitely a checkmark in his favor.

Because of that, I threw him a bone. "She loves any kind of cheddar cracker, so the crackers are definitely on the list. But she loves koi—which are kind of goldfish on steroids."

"Thank you very much for that inside info." He looked thoughtful.

"Good luck with it," I told him as I headed back inside. The breeze had turned positively frigid and my face was numb. Okay, one point that the road had in favor over the school—we had chances to travel to much warmer locales.

Fuck.

I stomped my feet off to clear the snow as I headed inside and rubbed at my arms as I climbed the stairs. Sydney and Olivia grinned at me as they were heading down the stairs with bags over their shoulders.

"We're out," Olivia said while Sydney gave me a hug. "We're gonna bring back a huge basket of treats and stuff. We told Mom you were staying, so she said we had to bring you a little of everything. If you're allergic to some food, just text Syd."

"I can do that," I said with a laugh. "But you guys really don't have to..."

"Oh, yes we do," they chorused, while Sydney slung her

arm around me. "Mom wanted us to bring you home with us, but I told her that would be a little weird. Next year—you're probably getting invited."

"We're saving you," Olivia promised. "See you next year!"

Then they were gone. The floor was almost quiet; not that it was especially loud, but there was a hum that filled the building. That hum had been there practically since the day we moved in and with over half of the dorm out tonight and a good chunk leaving tomorrow, I was going to be one of the only students present.

At least the sex tape scandal had died down over the last few weeks. It had only really been awful that first couple of days. While I got some shit and heard some comments, the worst of it had ended the day Jonas lost his shit in the hall.

Back in the room, I turned on the television for some background noise then went to grab my guitar from the bedroom. A note waited for me and I recognized Aubrey's handwriting.

Don't forget to fuck off, sleep in, and binge watch shows. The holiday break is still a break. But I bet Yvette you'd write lyrics for at least three songs because you can't help yourself. She thinks it will be five. Who wins? I can't wait to find out. - mwah

I burst out laughing. Because I already had plans to work on putting together some of the lyrics I'd been writing over the last few weeks. The music was in my head, and now that I wasn't so slammed, it was exactly what I wanted to do. My girls knew me well.

I spent the rest of the evening shopping online and giving my dormant credit cards a workout. I also emailed our business manager 'cause when the bills came in, I didn't want him to have a heart attack.

Trish had sent me a text the previous weekend about Mom staying at the Sunshine Retreat through this holiday, too. Well, if it was working to get her sober then I was all for it.

I made sure to send her a card there. Even though it was a retreat, a card said I was thinking about her and it would cut off any possible recriminations later. It wasn't until I was getting ready to sleep that I stared at the boxes waiting for me to work on fan mail.

Not feeling it, I left it alone. The next morning, I rolled out of bed to fresh snowfall and temperature warnings for the wind chill.

I bundled up, snugged a knit cap down over my ears, and pulled on a neoprene mask. It was like armor against the wind and ninja kisses. Hard to kiss me if he couldn't get to my mouth.

No part of me wanted to be a little thrilled at the sight of Lachlan by the start to the running trail. Everything from his posture to the way he was dressed said he was waiting. Maybe giving myself a little too much credit that he was waiting for me, but he straightened at my approach.

"I thought you'd have already left, Ace," was his greeting.

"Sure, that's why you're down here waiting," I said. "Unless...oh, you dog. Got some other girl you like to harass and tackle kiss on a regular basis?"

His expression darkened and his eyes narrowed. "What is that supposed to mean?"

"Pretty sure I didn't stutter," I told him before I rolled my head from side to side. "Enjoy your run." Then I set off. I had to wonder was he actually waiting for someone else or would he linger to prove he hadn't been waiting for me? There really didn't seem to be a good answer to that.

Not that he chose that option; he was after me in a second. His steps struck the snow, crunching lightly just like mine. Someone had already cleared the trails, snow-blowing the thing. It meant I wasn't sinking into the snow, but it was still falling pretty fast.

"What are you still doing here?" he asked.

"I go to school here," I told him. "I enrolled this autumn, and I'll be here through graduation—or at least, that is the plan. Remember?"

"Funny," he commented, the sarcasm in his voice making a lie out of his words.

"Thank you," I told him as I began to increase my pace. The one thing I'd gotten damn good at this semester had been bettering my running times. I'd also been building my stamina. I could go further and longer, I'd never had this kind of time to devote to running before.

"Seriously, Ace," he said, as if he needed an answer to the question. "Your roomie left, so shouldn't you be going, too?"

I didn't stumble or trip, but I did cut him a look. "Adding stalking to your repertoire of ambushes and insults? Or trying to line up the next time you dump food or paint on me?"

To my own amusement, he actually missed a step and slid. I pulled ahead and chuckled. Maybe he would get the picture. Maybe he wouldn't. The fact he caught up to me before I'd gone more than a dozen strides said he was definitely not giving up.

"Most students leave for the holidays. It's a skeleton crew here on campus..."

"So I've heard. Still doesn't tell me why you want to know."

He cut in front of me. Rather than run into him, I cut around him, even if it did sink my shoes into the snow and leave it crusted on my sweatpants.

"You are so damn stubborn," he complained as he caught up to me again.

"Says the guy who keeps following me and trying to corner me every chance he gets." The neoprene kept my face somewhat warm even if my eyeballs were stuck dealing with the cold. It also helped me to take warmer breaths. Not much warmer, but I'd take what I could get.

"Why don't I put this a different way," he said, matching me stride for stride. "Staying on campus isn't the best idea. You're too public."

"Awww," I said, putting a hand over my heart. "You're killing me with the caring."

This time when he cut me off, he grabbed my arm to keep me from going around him. Instead, I slid and impacted his chest. He tilted his head to stare down at me.

"Straight answer, Ace. When are you leaving?"

"When I feel like it," I told him, bending his thumb back. It made him loosen his grip on me and he jerked his hand away. "You don't like it, too fucking bad. No one asked you."

So close.

I was so close to getting away, when he hauled me back and jerked my neoprene mask down. The tear of the velcro ripping in the cold air seemed preternaturally loud. Especially with how hushed the world was. His lips were cool, but his tongue was hot when he kissed me.

A groan tangled with a protest as he wrapped an arm around me. When he dragged my lower lip out, I shuddered. I half-expected to see steam rising off my skin. Pure fire had flashed through my system. The ninja kisses were turning into something addictive.

I enjoyed them almost as much as the banter surrounding them. It didn't change the fact he was an asshole most of the time.

"Are you done?" I asked, resisting the urge to lick my lips. "Because kissing me into submission to get your answers isn't going to work either."

I yanked my mask back from him while he glared at me.

"Stubborn," I reminded him, then cut away after putting the mask on. It didn't take him long to catch up, but I ignored him and, thankfully, he let me.

The dining hall was cavernous. Not only were most of my

favorite people gone, but so were the assholes. I caught sight of Jonas eating breakfast, and I detoured to go to the far side where I could have my coffee and muffin in peace.

A peace Ramsey sabotaged just as I bit into the blueberry muffin. "You're still here..."

I glanced up at the TA and raised my brows. His hair was askew, like he'd raked his hand through it several times. For the first time since I'd met him, he had a five o'clock shadow at seven in the morning, and he wasn't sporting a tie.

Button-down shirt, sleeves buttoned at the cuff and dress slacks, but the top two buttons at his throat were open and there was no tie in place. He was like...the most disheveled I'd ever seen him.

That counted the day he was Mr. Grumpy in the parking lot when I was moving in. It was a ridiculously attractive look on him. Shaking off that thought, I said, "I keep hearing that. Sorry to disappoint."

Not really, but I took another bite of my muffin then washed it down with coffee. Ramsey continued to stare at me, and I met his gaze questioningly. There were literally two days of classes left; all due dates had been Monday or Tuesday. I had everything in, I was taking one extra credit test in bio so I could add a few more points to my grade, but otherwise it should be quiet.

"Right," I said when Ramsey didn't say anything more. I stuffed the rest of the muffin in my mouth—attractive, I know —before I grabbed my bag and my coffee. "I'll see you next semester, Ramsey, assuming you won't be in Mr. Cohen's class today."

He hadn't been for the last three days, so it seemed a safe bet. With a half-wave, I headed out into the cold to walk to my first set of classes. The number of students still around was impressively quiet, so that was nice. No hustling in the halls, no kids making out or yelling insults, compliments, or, my least favorite, dirty jokes.

It was kind of weird, the school which had become, at times, a little *Lord of the Flies* meets *Mad Max*, was downright peaceful. I was still grinning when Jonas showed up at our first class. It was him, me, and four other kids. That was it.

But it was nice. His frown just made me smile wider. Honestly, it was the first time since I'd gotten to the school that it felt like what I'd been wanting from the beginning. Normal.

Okay, it was challenging, but normal.

Awareness skittered over me when the teacher gave us leave to start on the reading we needed to do over the break for the first week back. I stole a look to my left and sure enough, Jonas stared at me like he was trying to get inside my brain.

I shook my head and focused back on the book. Just two more days, then everyone would be gone and I would have some blissful quiet.

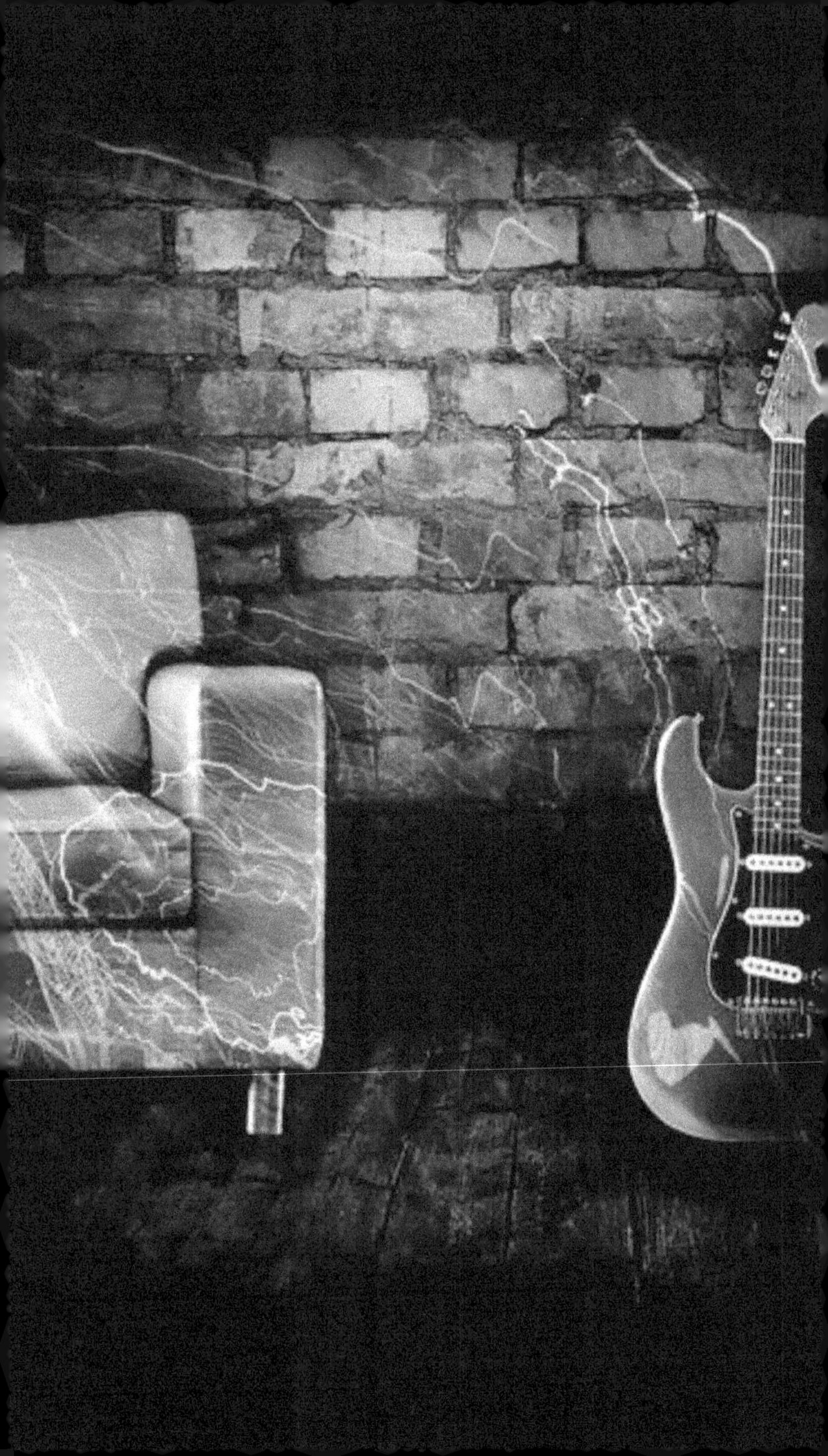

Thirty-One

Saturday morning, I got up early because I'd gotten into the habit and pulled on my running clothes. I had every intention of going *back* to bed when I was done, but I'd get my run on. It was like a postcard outside, the perfect New England winter. Not the kind on the holiday channel with the fake snow and the city girl who goes to the country to discover all she was missing in life was baking gingerbread and the sexy lumberjack.

The whole image just made me laugh. No, it wasn't like that at all. But it was still pretty. I took a couple of pictures before I went through my stretches, jogging in place for a few minutes to warm up before I took off. Even running through the woods on the trail was a magical journey. The hush seemed almost deeper now with the campus practically empty.

As glad for the solitude as I was, it had been a bit of a stomach-bottoming-out moment when I realized that Lachlan wasn't there. He probably wouldn't be for a few days. Shaking that off, I turned up the music and just focused on my run.

Jonas was coming out of the door to my dorm when I returned. He paused when our gazes locked, but then he stuffed his hands in his pockets and stalked away. "Have a merry Christmas," I called after him. "You asshole." The last part I kept quieter, not that he glanced past at the shout.

I stomped the snow off my shoes before I headed upstairs. Granted, I pulled the knit cap and mask off as I got to the top of the steps. Jonas had just been inside the dorm—how did he get in here without a key?

He could have tailgated in on someone who was leaving late. I hadn't exactly done a headcount to see how many people were actually still here. Harley left the night before, and I had the number of the RA for Apollo/Volusia Four. She was the only one for all four of these new buildings.

When I texted her, she just asked that I send a daily check-in, otherwise, not to worry. Even better in my book. When I got to the third floor, I glanced around the corners before passing them.

Call me paranoid, but the idea of being pranked even when no one was around didn't seem far-fetched. Especially because it was Jonas.

I grimaced. That wasn't entirely fair, but the guy was such a bag of crazy contradictions. Nothing happened, thankfully, except there was a bag hanging on my door. Stuffing my hat and mask into my pockets, I pulled it off. No note, no address, just a bag with a folder inside it.

Sheet music.

With care, I flipped through the pages. It was all sheet music, handwritten, with each bar and key mapped out. The faint writing on the edge was definitely Jonas' handwriting. I'd seen it in class enough to recognize it.

Jonas brought me sheet music?

I glanced around, half-convinced I was about to be punked, but there was no one there and Jonas was gone. Or maybe he'd just gone back to his dorm.

Maybe, like me, he was going to be here for the holidays.

That was weird, but...this was nice. I let myself into the room and locked up. I tossed the music onto the table while I went to shower and change into dry clothes.

Pajamas and Netflix were my plans for the day. I had some reheatable meals in the fridge. I spoiled myself with some coffee before I pulled up the first show to watch. But my gaze kept going back to the sheet music.

No lyrics, just music. Pausing the episode, I grabbed my guitar and then played out the song. It was almost four minutes long and had a gorgeous rhythm and chorus section. I took it down a key and it was this dark, broody piece. Up a key and it was almost effervescent.

But the key he'd written it in gave it this kind of moody, unpredictable vibe. I liked it.

Even after I put the guitar up and went back to the show, I couldn't get the music out of my head. It stuck with me while I shopped online and played Santa for my siblings. I made plans to video chat with them at different points on the holiday.

Another perk of having an open schedule: I could video chat South Africa in the middle of the night and not worry about waking anyone up here. It took me a while to find a present for RJ, and I ordered it to come here. I couldn't send it to him because I didn't actually know where he lived.

Though he texted me back when I checked on him. He'd left earlier than planned because of the broken ankle. But he planned to be back for New Year's if I wanted to do something.

I told him I'd let him know since Aubrey, Yvette, and I might have plans. He offered to join us, which was just all kinds of hilarious no. I didn't need them spending all of New Year's interrogating him or testing him when we hadn't really had a full-on date yet.

So you do want to go on a date with me. Good to know, Blue. I'll see you before the ball drops.

Cute. The fact he still wanted to date after everything that happened with Lachlan. Ugh... Lachlan and the ninja kisses. Those needed to stop if I was going to date RJ.

Disappointment curved through me. I just wasn't sure if it was thinking about dating RJ or giving up the kisses? I didn't ask for them...and he constantly seemed to enjoy grabbing me and kissing me.

Treated me like crap the rest of the time, not that I'd seen that much of him beyond the kissing ambushes. Ugh. I shoved all thoughts of boys and everything else out of my head.

Break time meant a break from them, too.

The next couple of days went much like the first one. I made a point of running, savoring my time on the trail until there was ice glittering everywhere, and then I sucked it up and went to the gym.

I divided my days up into music time, homework time, and binge-watching time. Messages popped in from Aubrey and Yvette regularly with blow-by-blows of how their family holidays were going.

Staying at school was looking better and better to me. I used some of the binge watching time to go through the stacks of mail. There were Christmas cards in this bunch...

The RA in the other building alerted me to new mail having arrived, only I had to haul over to the mailroom proper to get it. This was mail from the manager and stuff addressed to me here.

Not that many had my address here. There was a holiday card from Sydney and Olivia. I laughed at the message they'd written inside it. Another from Yvette and one from Aubrey. Frankie had sent one, too, and I chuckled at the messages.

Life had been crazy for her. I really should call and check on them at some point, too. In the box from our manager were more fan letters, some cards, and one that was actually from Johnny.

Oh shit, Johnny sent me a Christmas card. What the hell? I slit it open and a letter slid out along with a photo. The letter wasn't addressed to me but to Mom. Okay. I tugged the card out before I flipped over the picture and then slammed the picture face-down again.

Did he really send me a damn dick pic?

I peeked at the photo again. Ugh. Yep. Dick pic.

Shaking my head, I stared at the unhappy snowman on the card and when I opened it, he'd scrawled a handwritten note inside.

It's too hot to be without you was the sentiment and I almost threw up in my mouth, but the message he'd written was on the other side.

Kaitlin,

Sorry to send this to you but your mother has been avoiding me for weeks. I've been calling her, sending flowers, doing everything I can to get her attention. Nothing has been successful. Is she really serious about this break-up? I don't want her to be serious. The letter is for her and so is the picture. This is asking a lot, I know, but could you forward them to her?

Thanks so much. If I can do anything for you just let me know. Hope school is going well, I know you said this was what you wanted, but I looked up the school and dude, you picked a tough one.

Merry Christmas and all my best,

Johnny

A dick pic in a holiday card. It was absurd and so damn Johnny. And Mom initiated the break-up, of course she did. I sighed. With care, I stuck the dick pic back in the envelope where I couldn't see it. How much brain bleach did one need to forget that image? I tucked the letter in there, too, and didn't read it.

It was several pages long. Flopping back against the sofa, I stared up at the ceiling. Mom was still at the Sunshine Retreat. My options were to hang onto it until she was out or send it to her there.

This would be almost three months soon. Surely, she'd be leaving there sooner rather than later, right? I put both the letter and the photo into a different envelope and set it on my desk in my room. I'd deal with it later.

The Christmas card was sweet—in its own way. I added to the others I'd been taping to the edge of the television. We didn't have a tree in the room so that made it a little less festive.

The day before Christmas, another round of mail arrived along with a surprise delivery of a hot Christmas meal. Aubrey and Yvette cracked me up. They were dealing with their families and took the time to send me a turkey dinner with all the trimmings and pie. Granted, it was basically two plates all pre-prepared, but it was also wonderful.

One of the boxes that arrived came via our manager and it was from Dad. I stared at the brown paper wrapped box with the return address of his manager in Chicago.

Yeah.

I shoved the box in my closet and left it there. It was probably another snow globe or something equally ubiquitous and impersonal. His manager's office sent that. Not Dad. They probably had a spawn list and sent out a present to each of us.

Definitely didn't want to waste his time on actually knowing his kids. Between that and the fact Mom sent nothing, also not a surprise, my mood plummeted and I shoved it all away.

I wanted to enjoy my holiday and that meant eating the dinner the girls had sent, then I sent them messages thanking them. The presents I'd sent for them should have arrived already.

The rest of the night and into the morning, I spent on video calls to the siblings. It was well after four in the morning before I crawled into bed. My Christmas present to myself was to sleep late and not go running.

One day off.

By noon, though, I was bored with Christmas movies and homework. I'd started on the fan mail, but there was another letter from my forever fan that had me side-eyeing it.

When are you going to come back to me? I miss you. Months without a new release, a new video, a new...anything. Where are you?

Your Forever Fan

Yeah, that wasn't creepy. I needed to go through all the mail and see how many more this person had sent.

After I put those away and reheated my second Christmas plate, I stared at the folder with the sheet music in it. I didn't even make it through the whole meal before I pulled Jonas' music over and let it run through my head while I ate.

Finally, I grabbed the guitar and a pencil. The music was amazing, but he needed lyrics. It took me most of the day and into the day after Christmas to finish, but I had it ready to slide under his door when he got back.

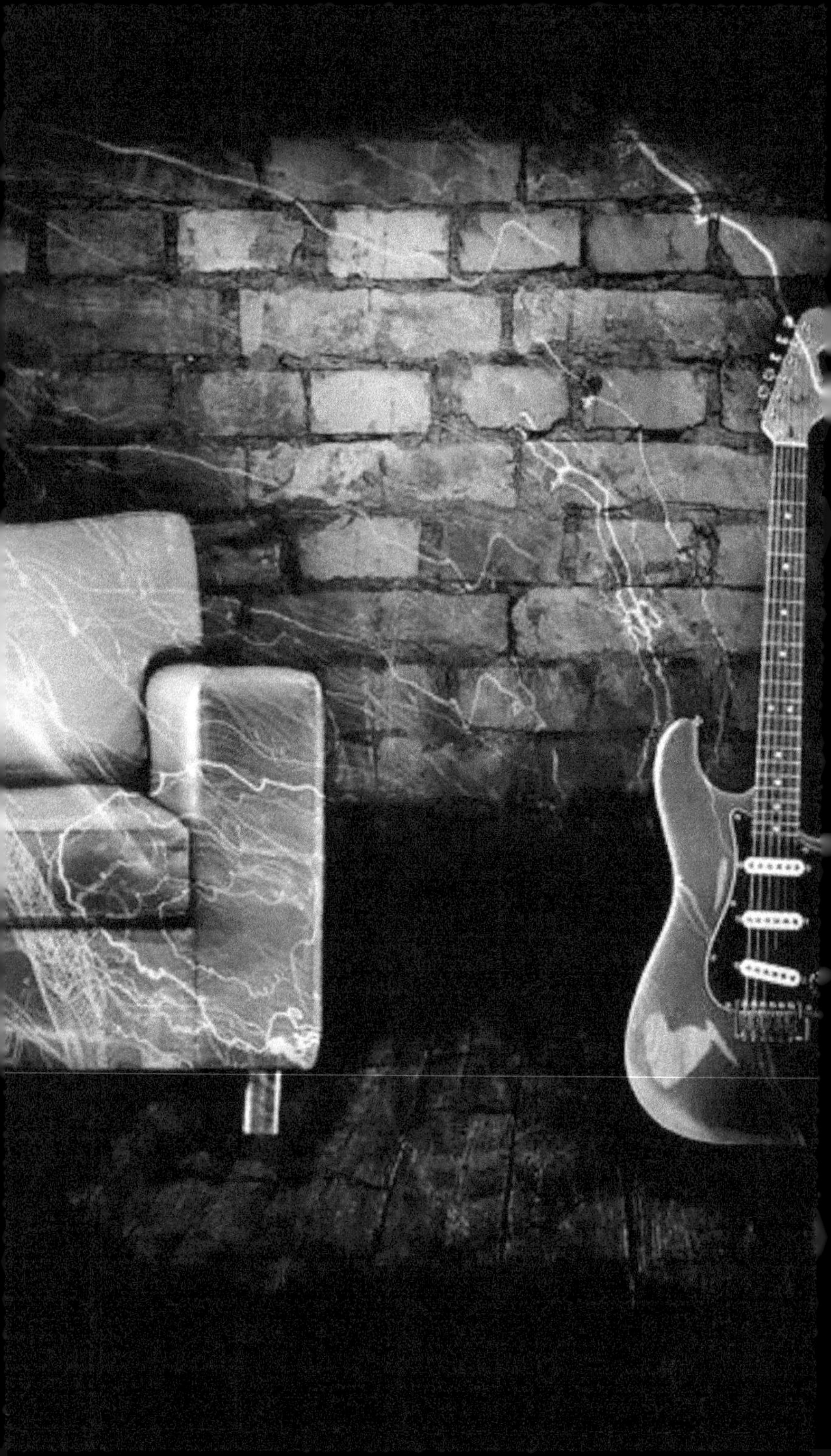

Thirty-Two

Yvette and Aubrey made it back for New Year's. Instead of staying on campus, we grabbed a hotel room in the city so we could watch the fireworks over the harbor. We almost didn't get one, but we scored a last-minute cancellation. The girls brought me back gifts too, which they didn't have to do.

Of course they didn't, but Yvette had loved her cashmere sweater and the alpaca socks I'd sent her, while Aubrey was thrilled with the classic LPs I'd managed to find for some of her favorite groups. Comfort and music. You couldn't go wrong with those.

New running shoes, however, really killed it. They were teal blue and would match my hair. I loved them. I also laughed at the running pants that said, "If you can read this, get off my ass."

"We love you," Yvette reminded me. "Even if you think endorphin dumping via running is a good idea."

"Aww, you're just saying that because you'd rather break your own leg than go running with me."

Yvette grinned. "Absolutely."

Too soon we had to say goodbye. "Spring break," she reminded us. "Let's do something fun."

It sounded like a great idea. We'd survived the first semester. The second semester had to be easier, right?

Somehow, I didn't think so.

Somehow.

Back on campus, I delivered the sheet music to Jonas' room via Soren. RJ was waiting when I got back from dropping off the music. He was still in a boot.

The chances of him running anytime soon were pretty slim. "Friday night," he told me. "There's a party on Greek row in Mansfield. It's not gonna be a huge thing, but it's the first party of the year and it could be a lot of fun."

A frat house party. That was—normal. "Can I think about it?"

"I was trying to come up with something to make you more comfortable. I know you like to dance, and we really didn't get to enjoy the Halloween party."

My mind flashed back to thinking I was dancing with him. How much fun I had and then when Lachlan kissed me and I still thought it was RJ.

Guilt stabbed me. I should have told him about it, but considering the animosity between RJ and Lachlan, maybe not. Speaking of...he said he was going to report him, but I hadn't noticed anything with Lachlan, and RJ hadn't brought it up again.

Did I remind him by asking? Or leave it alone?

"I'd like to go," I said slowly, "but since we're just getting back to classes…"

"I won't be offended if we have to make it a study date, but can we skip the library and the killjoy that is Ramsey Malone?" The offer kicked it up with real irritation on the end.

"You don't like him," I said slowly.

"What gave it away?" RJ asked.

I laughed. "Nothing. And yeah, if we need to do a study date, maybe we can do it over coffee somewhere."

"That's my girl," he said, then glanced past me and I twisted to look but I didn't see anything and when I faced him again, he was right there. When he dipped his gaze to my lips, I debated the wisdom of kissing him or letting him kiss me.

I'd been all for it on Halloween, but two months of ninja kisses later and I still didn't know what I was doing. However, I met him halfway when he dipped his head. His lips were cool, and a little dry. I winced a little for him because they were also a little chapped.

"Sorry," I murmured when I pulled back.

"For what?" His smile was genuine, and it relaxed some of the tension backing up in my spine. "I've been wanting to do that for a while." When he lifted his hand, I didn't withdraw as he cupped my face. "Friday night, you and me..."

"A date," I told him firmly. "Just a date."

"Or a study date," he said easily. "Don't worry, KC." His voice dipped a little. "I remember that you want to just get to know me for me and you for you."

I did. But that wasn't quite what I meant...

"I'm not making any assumptions." When he trailed his fingers down to my shoulder, I frowned. "I'm also not going to say no if we drift in that direction."

"We'll see," was about all I could say to that. Frankly, the way my stomach dropped at his pronouncement didn't make me feel better.

"Yes, we will." He swooped in and kissed me again, this time lingering in the moment.

The pressure was there and the movement, but none of the zing. I was almost too aware of how dry his lips were and how long it actually took before he lifted his head. Relief, not desire, flooded me when he let me go.

"I need to go," he said with an element of regret. "If I'd realized that we'd be having this much fun, I'd have rescheduled the college interview."

Interview? "You should not reschedule it. College is important."

RJ shrugged. "It's a formality. I know where I'm going. That was decided a long time ago." He blew out a breath. "Dammit, I really wish I had canceled it now." He kissed me again, the swift contact over before it even started. "To be continued..."

I touched a hand to my lips as I turned to go back into the dorm. The air was still cold and my cheeks were definitely stinging, but shouldn't the kiss have been more like those electric entanglements I kept getting into with Lachlan?

I liked RJ. I couldn't stand Lachlan.

What the hell?

The idea chased its own tail through my head. It was like it couldn't let go of any of it. Aubrey glanced up from the stack of fan mail when I came in. "It's about time. I thought you were just gonna drop something off."

"I was," I told her as I stripped out of my jacket. "Ran into RJ."

"Oh yeah?" She patted the floor next to her. She had created stacks on the coffee table for us to work on. "By the way, the next two box loads are going to Yvette. They haven't sent her any."

"Yeah," I told her as I opened one of the envelopes.

"Good run in or bad run in?"

That was such a good question, if only my answer could be offered as easily. "TBD," I said and she canted her head to the side.

"Yeah?"

"Yeah." The fact it was TBD didn't bode well.

The first day of actual classes had me both dreading and anticipating getting back into my routine. I'd skipped the run for the day, mostly because I'd been up late the night before when Jackie called to tell me that Pen was back in the emergency room with a high fever.

She wanted to look into getting custodianship of Pen. While she didn't say anything about Pen's mother, she didn't have to. I wasn't a lawyer. I didn't even know what we'd have to do...but she was a social worker so she did know, and I had lawyers I could access.

"I know my age immediately disqualifies me," I said, "but I can be the financial support." Neither one of us brought up Dad. That would be a dead end.

"Not asking for that right now," Jackie assured me. "And I know you would, sweetheart. I wanted to warn you, because she is sick, and these fevers don't seem to have a direct cause. They keep saying viral but...it bothers me and it bothers me that her mother keeps disappearing every time she gets sick."

"Whatever you need," I promised. "Does Pen need to see a different doctor?"

We'd talked for another half hour, but after I got off the phone with Jackie, Bronson and I started texting. He was a lot more colorful than Jackie about the shit condition their apartment had been in.

They'd gone there looking for Pen's mom, and it had been unlocked. That was just a whole other headache. I had money set aside for all of my siblings, but especially little Pen. I hadn't really gotten to know the others right after they were born. Most of them I hadn't met before we formed Torched.

Penelope was the first one, and I adored every inch of her adorable face. Even when she screamed—and the kid had lungs for days. She'd probably be a rock star.

It made me laugh, but even after I hung up with Bronson, I hadn't really been able to sleep. That made skipping the run more a matter of survival because I needed to stay awake for classes.

Lachlan was in line for coffee when I got to the dining hall with Aubrey. Payton was leaning against him, chatting away with her phone in her hand. Yeah, I'd give up drinking coffee before I got in that line.

Sydney and Olivia were back. We'd seen them the afternoon before, and they both looked half-asleep at their table when we got there with our breakfast. Finley was there, but Soren was absent. I hadn't seen him over at the coffee shop.

"I love going home for Christmas," Sydney complained through a series of yawns. "I hate having to get back on schedule."

"Dark chocolate covered espresso beans," I told her as I downed some water.

Aubrey laughed. "They definitely work. That's a tour secret."

"Not so much a secret as a method of coping when we had back-to-back shows and not enough sleep. They definitely give you a jolt and get you moving."

"We need to find some," Sydney said around another yawn. "Cause I'm dying."

Oddly, even without the run, I wasn't. I was kind of excited about getting back to class. I'd enjoyed the silence over the break, but I was so ready for familiar faces and catching up with people.

And I definitely didn't look toward the coffee line at that thought.

Jonas was waiting at the door to the building when I got to it. He pulled the door open for me, and I blinked slowly. He was holding it and staring at me when I didn't immediately go through it.

"Don't take this the wrong way, but you don't have like a bucket of pig's blood or something waiting to dump on me inside, do you?"

Head canted, Jonas squinted at me. His pale gray eyes seemed a little warmer today. "No," he finally said when I made no attempt to continue through the door. "Was I supposed to?"

The corner of my mouth quirked upward. "No, and I'd be really grateful if you didn't."

He nodded then walked in the door, holding it open for me still, so I finally followed him.

"Thanks."

He spared me another nod and then we were walking together toward class like we did this every day. I half-expected Jordan Peele or Rob Serling to pop out and start narrating that instead of walking back into a new semester, I'd actually arrived in the Twilight Zone.

Personally, I hoped it was Jordan Peele, cause Serling was dead and that would just take this to a whole other level of creepy. The absurdity of the thought made me grin.

Jonas took the desk next to mine when I sat down in the last row.

"Good morning, welcome back from break. Thank you all for taking your new seats. They will be your assigned seats for the rest of this semester..."

Oh. That was why he'd moved. I glanced over at him but he had his notebook out and a pen in hand. So I focused on the teacher too.

Had we finally achieved detente? I was almost afraid to push it at all, given the fragile balance we'd developed. The truce seemed to last through all of our first three classes together. He didn't have fourth with me, so we parted ways, but before he left, he handed me three sheets of music.

"Thanks," I said but he was already walking away.

Curiosity broke out like a fever in my system. I wanted to go back to my room and play this. Just humming the first couple of bars had me intrigued.

But we were still in classes and I stowed the music away safely for later. Ramsey was in the classroom when I entered, and he gave me an almost pleasant nod.

Okay. That was it, someone had kidnapped the douchebags and replaced them with pod people.

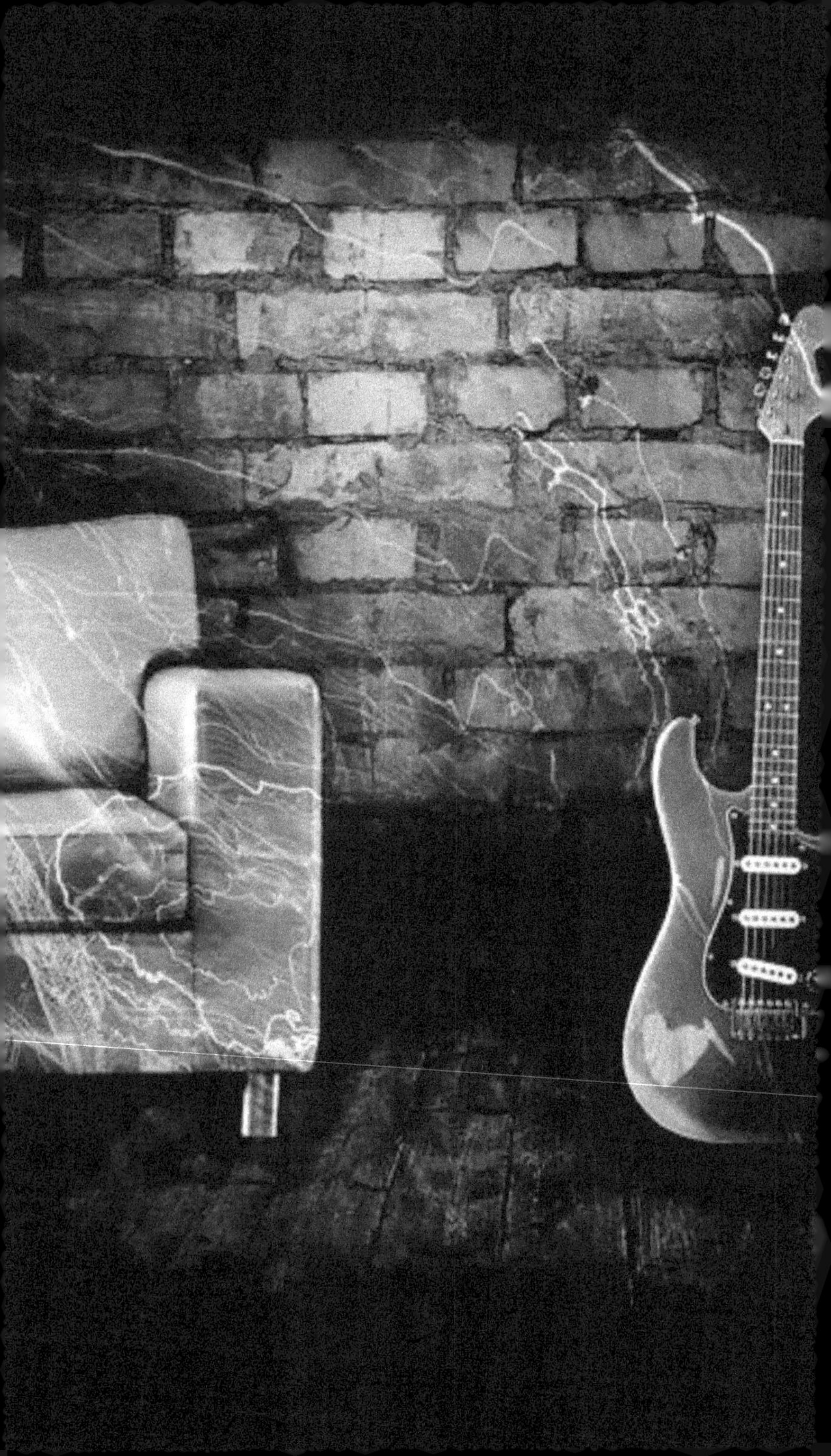

Thirty-Three

Ramsey's good mood lasted all the way to our tutoring session, where he asked me to go over all of my classes with him.

"Why?" I said as I flipped open the notebook. "Not to be offensive, but they lifted my academic probation." That email had come in during my last class. I turned my phone to show him. "See?"

I wasn't the slacker he'd accused me of being. The corners of his mouth quirked a little higher. I knew he could smile. I'd seen him smile at other students. On one occasion, I could have sworn I'd seen him grin. It was a good look on him.

"Yes, Miss Crosse, you successfully proved yourself," he said, each word measured as if their weight had impact. The thrill I got from him saying I had succeeded coursed through me. "The new semester gives you the opportunity to start fresh. To get ahead as it were, instead of fighting to catch up."

"I hear what you're saying, but are you planning to tutor me in all of these classes?" I didn't really need one for history, for example, or for science—despite my distaste for cutting up dead animals.

"Let's call it applied study methods. You've been working through the homework assignments, then applying them to both your classwork and during our sessions. Have they been helpful?" Genuine curiosity seemed to inhabit the question and I leaned back in the chair.

As much as I might hate to admit it, they had helped. "I think so," I said, resisting the urge to commit fully. The guy was arrogant, kind of dickish, and definitely didn't think much of me. The fact none of it seemed to decrease his hot professor vibe was infuriating.

Was I really nursing a crush on the teacher? The words drifted through my head and my fingers twitched. I needed a pencil to write all of this down.

"But?" he prompted me and I canted my head.

"Truthfully?"

"I would appreciate that," he said, the way his voice slid over the word appreciate was just... dammit stop thinking about him like that.

Teacher's assistant or teacher, it didn't matter. Not for me. "You don't like me," I said bluntly. "Can't say I'm terribly fond of you either." *Even if I'm sitting here wondering what the rest of the ink on you looks like and that I'd like to rumple that fresh-pressed and buttoned-down look of yours.*

"Go on."

"Does it need to be more?"

"Well, Miss Crosse, let's be clear—in life, you don't always get the choice of who you work with to get the job done. You choose the best people and hope everything works out. Whether I like you or not should have no impact on how well we work together."

"Bullshit," I said.

His eyebrows skyrocketed and the facade of cool academic cracked. The flash of irritation in his blue eyes made me happy.

For someone who preferred honesty, he definitely affected a mask.

"Excuse me?" He threw those two words down like a challenge.

"I've lived in the real world and in life. I've built a career. Yes, you encounter people you don't like, but you don't invite them into the bubble. You don't make their challenges a part of your work, because there are already challenges." I blew out a breath. "I get what you're trying to tell me."

And I did. He wanted to help and the offer was both kind and irritating. Hard to decide between the two, so I didn't try. He said nothing as we stared at each other. I had to wonder if he was regretting making the offer already.

"Do you really want to help me with my classes?" Simple question.

"Yes." Simple answer.

"Why?"

"Two reasons—you have proven to be an adept and capable student. Your lack of foundation in some subjects has less to do with your intelligence than your experience."

Well, that was something. "Yay, I'm not stupid."

The withering look he shot at me just made me grin wider.

"The second reason...you need someone objective and not using your study sessions to score points."

RJ.

"You really don't like him." He didn't try to hide it.

"No," Ramsey said, "I don't. Miss Crosse, I can't tell you who you should or shouldn't choose as a friend, but when it comes to your grades and academic standing—cut that dead weight and let me fill in the gaps."

"Call me KC."

"What?"

"Call me KC. Or Kaitlin if you want, but Miss Crosse is so

prim and proper. We're not in a Dickensian or Jane Austen novel. I'm KC and you're Ramsey—"

He frowned. "That's not appropriate."

"Split the difference, in tutoring sessions we're KC and Ramsey. In class, we're Miss Crosse and TA Malone."

Not that Miss Crosse sounded any better in a classroom. If anything, it sounded even more old-fashioned.

"Then you'll agree to go over the whole semester with me and your classes so we can build a study plan for you?"

"Call me KC and you've got a deal."

His frown tightened for a moment, but he finally nodded. "KC…"

"Atta boy, Ramsey, I knew you had it in you." I was almost proud.

"Hmmm."

I couldn't tell if he was amused or if he was regretting his choices. I pulled out my tablet, my laptop and the rest of the folders in my backpack.

"Where do you want to start?"

It was Wednesday before I got to head out for a run. I'd been up late Monday night talking to Jackie about Penelope. They'd also filed a missing person's report for her mother. Five bucks said she went to score and forgot to come back.

I hated everything about the situation. But Jackie had already filed the emergency papers. Bronson and I were not legal age, but we could support her. Bronson, cause he was there physically to help, and me, because I had the money.

Tuesday night, there had been nothing to report. No changes. Her fever seemed to have abated and they hadn't tracked down the causes for it. That made me wonder if it was neglect, drugs, or something else…

The whole thing was enough to make me scream. Restlessness had plagued my sleep along with some bad dreams. I didn't care what the weather or temperature was today, I needed to run. I hadn't broken in the new running shoes yet, but I would.

Right now, I just went with what was reliable. I descended the steps rapidly, my earbuds already in. I needed something violent and fast-paced. I hated the idea of Pen suffering. I hated it even more because I was out here and not there.

Jackie kept telling me that I couldn't do any more there, so I had to go to classes and stay focused. *"I'll keep you in the loop, I promise."*

I believed her, but it didn't fix this for Penelope. She should be growing teeth or learning to walk or whatever little rug rats did at that age.

Hitting the door, I jumped when it was caught by a hand and held open. Lachlan stood there, a faint smirk on his face and a jacket hooked over one of his arms. Not that he wasn't already wearing one.

Like me, he'd bundled up, ready for the weather. "Hey there, Ace, I was wondering if I was going to have to come in and roust you."

"Roust me?" I raised my eyebrows. "Pretty sure you've been doing that for weeks."

A smile flashed across his face and I shook my head. Pod people. They were all pod people.

"Look, I get that we have this hate-hate relationship going on. Normally, I'd be down for the push-pull, though I'd like to skip the dunking in the pond, frozen or not. Today, I'd rather just run. Okay?"

He studied me for a beat. "Put this on." He thrust the jacket at me and I stared at it then him. "It's a jacket, put it on."

"I know what a jacket is." Also, the fact my lips and cheeks were freezing. I pulled my neoprene mask out and slid it on. Then I took the jacket.

No ninja kisses for you.

It was soft, lighter, but insulated.

"Put it on over your sweats. It's moisture wicking, but it will keep you warm while you run and not soak you in sweat."

Oh.

"This is—"

"A jacket," he told me with a half-smile. "Clearly, it's not a present."

"Oh, well that's good. Presents are for friends."

"Exactly."

So what the hell did that mean?

He spread his arms. "You putting it on or freezing? Cause there's snow in the forecast and I'd rather run before the packed snow gets slushy."

It wasn't like I asked him to wait, but here he was.

"C'mon, Ace. Time to go. You've been hitting what, three miles? Five? We need to get a move on if you're planning on coffee and croissants today."

I pulled on the jacket. Non-present or not, throwing it back in his face seemed kind of childish. Now, did I check the pockets to make sure there wasn't poop or a stink bomb in them?

Yeah.

I did.

He frowned as I did, then shook his head as he pulled his knit cap down and donned his own neoprene mask. We looked like a pair of criminals about to make a heist.

The image cracked me up, but I shook my head and motioned him toward the trail. "After you..."

"Aww, you're wounding me, Ace. It's like you don't trust me or something."

"Or something," I called but only his laughter drifted back.

"Are we doing trash metal today?"

"Like that, did you?"

"No, but I wanted to know if you were going to be deaf when this was over."

I rolled my eyes. "Trust me, you haven't felt deafened until you've done a performance in front of mega-amps and had the beat thrum through you until even your heart needs to hit the same cadence."

With that, I cranked up the volume and followed him. He spared a look back at me but I pointed to my earbuds. As he yanked his mask down, a grin flash-fired over his face again and he pointed to me, then to him and mouthed, "Stay with me."

When he checked me again, I shrugged and waved him onward. We could argue or we could run. Right now, I *needed* to run. As if he heard those thoughts, he set the pace. It wasn't grueling, but he gradually increased it the longer we ran.

The mask helped with the icy air as I tried to regulate my breathing. It was still a bit of a burn with every inhale, but I craved that burn. Just like I needed it in my legs and my arms. I needed to exhaust myself.

I needed to shut up the voices in my head.

Jackie was right, I couldn't do more than I already was, but it didn't make it better or easier. We did the outer loop, it wasn't near the pond—that was a point in its favor—and the snow had been packed pretty neatly. My shoes didn't sink with every stride.

Lachlan stuck with me every step until we were back at my dorm. "Later, Ace."

Then he was gone and I still had the new jacket. I stared after him and shook my head. Pod people.

They'd left for the holidays and they'd all been replaced. Ugh, which meant I needed to watch for the other shoe to drop. I double-checked my pockets again on my way up to the room.

Paranoia was healthy.

The next morning, Lachlan was there again. The day after that. But Friday afternoon, the weather turned vicious. RJ had canceled our date after I promised him a raincheck. Lachlan, however, instead of meeting me outside, *knocked* on the dorm door.

"How the hell did you get up here?" I demanded.

With a shrug, he just offered me a lazy grin. "Blizzard conditions today, Ace. We're gonna need to go to the gym to run."

"Since when did we become friends?" Because every day, he'd been there and while RJ couldn't run—courtesy of Lachlan—it had been nice. But this felt a lot like a trap.

"We're not friends," he informed me before pushing me up against the door. One moment I was inside the room half-dressed, the next Lachlan had his arms around me and his mouth fused to mine.

It was the first ninja kiss of the year. The heat of his mouth against mine was a direct contrast of his chilly hands on my cheeks. Then he slid a hand back into my hair as he walked me backwards.

We really shouldn't be— His tongue thrust against mine and I swore the tingles radiating through my whole body pulsed like we'd found our own personal beat. When his hands landed on my hips, I pushed against his chest.

A low groan escaped before I finally managed to get my head back. I stared at him, a little dazed.

His eyes were heavy-lidded. The forest of secrets he held in his eyes seemed to lure me in. I wanted more of that kiss. I wanted more of the way he dug his fingers into my hips.

Hips that were only covered by pajama bottoms.

Shit.

I yanked backwards. "I can't believe you did that."

"Missed me, Ace?" He grinned, then gave my ass a slap that stung. "Get dressed...or stay undressed. Either way, we're getting a workout."

Heat flooded through me and I pointed to the door. "Out." The word lacked some force considering the way my voice quavered.

With another chuckle, he winked. "I'll be right outside the door. Just let me know how you want to—" He gave me a once over. "—work up a sweat. It is cold outside after all."

Fuck.

As soon as he was out of the door, I shoved it closed, locked it, then leaned against it. My breath came in panting little gasps, and I was as far from cold as you could get.

"He has a girlfriend," I reminded myself. "Even if she's a raging bitch."

The kissing really had to stop.

I licked my lips and hated myself a little.

I didn't want it to stop.

What was wrong with me?

KC,

Quick update for you. I spoke to your mother briefly. She is not interested in leaving the Sunshine Retreat anytime soon. Apparently she feels better than she has in a while. We might need you to fly out to California for the Critics Awards to accept in her place.

Will let you know.

Tricia

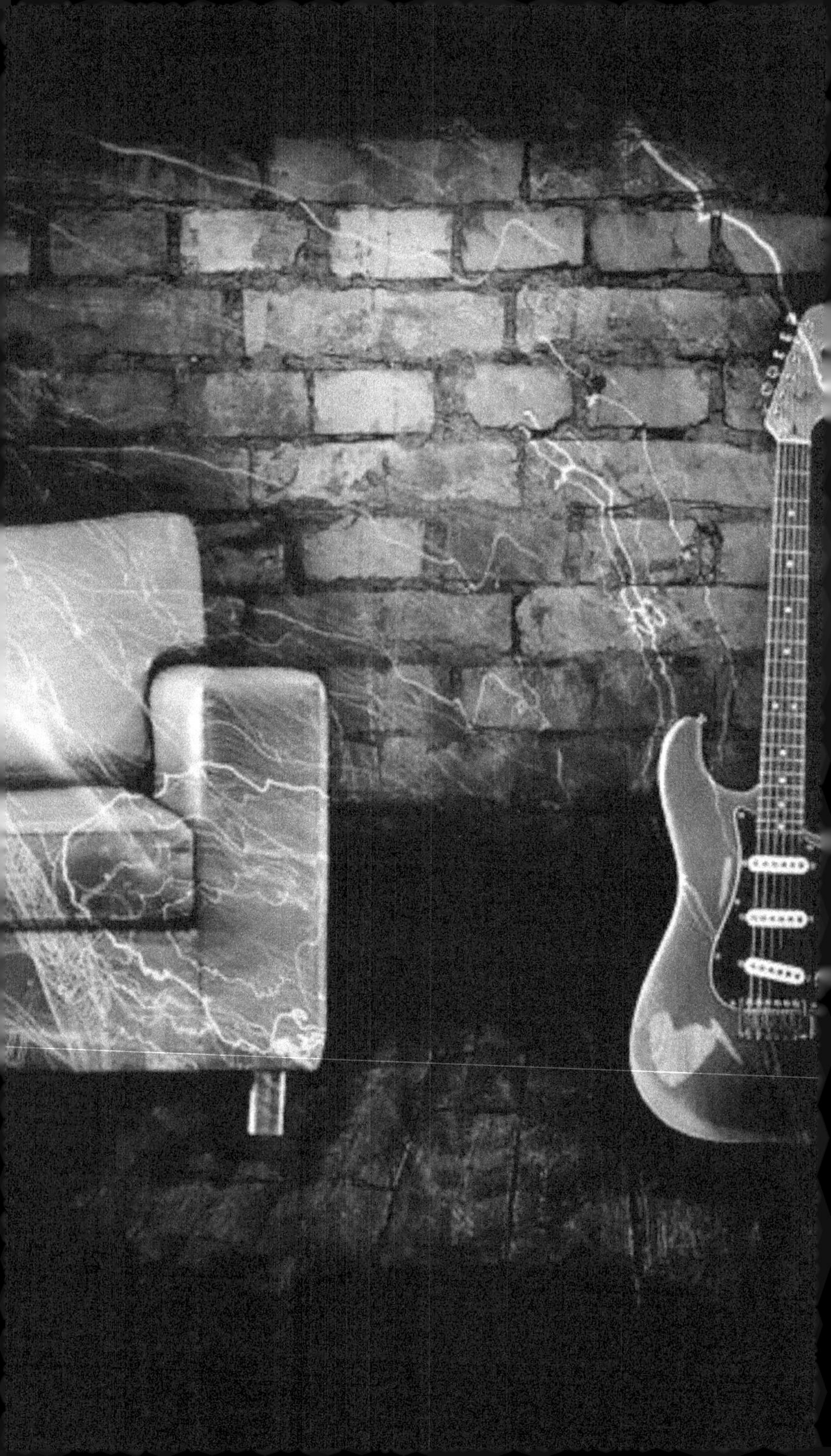

Thirty-Four

January slipped into February before I knew it. The first six weeks grades were posted along with class rankings. I didn't care about the rankings as much as I did the grades themselves. As soon as I slipped out of sixth period and headed for tutoring, I paused to get the grades to load up on my phone.

One. Two. Three...holy shit. Four. I kept scrolling, then had to scroll back to verify before I went to the bottom.

I did it.

Excitement flooded through me. Twice more, I scrolled every single class's grade. As. All of them. There were numerical scores, but they were all right in the range of 94 to 96. Solid As. Not A-minuses or A-pluses. As.

The first six weeks had seen me hit barely passing with a C, particularly with how much work had been cut off. Fighting to catch up, I'd pulled the grades for Bs and gotten myself to a respectable B-plus for the first semester.

Kicking this one off with As? I wanted to dance! As it was, I did a little jig as I jogged into the library. The wind had picked up and while *some* of the walkways between the buildings were covered, not all of them were. While we didn't have snow up to our eyeballs, it was definitely *cold*.

I'd actually pulled on tights today *and* thick over-the-knee socks. The skirts were comfortable, but I liked having feeling in my lower extremities.

At the top of the stairs, I did a little hop before I fired the text off to Aubrey and Yvette. Yvette's "Yaaas bitch!" arrived with a lot of heart eyes and smiley faces. It might take Aubrey a hot minute, since she was in class, but I was going to ride this high.

Not only was I off academic probation, I was kicking ass. RJ was due to lose the boot for his ankle and he would be doing physical therapy. And I was still running every day with Lachlan. Avoiding his kiss ambushes had become something of a game.

One I probably shouldn't enjoy as much as I did, but it was still fun.

Ramsey was at the table like he always was. His jacket was hung on the back of a chair, and he had his sleeves rolled up, showing off the pair of tats on his forearms. And they were some gorgeous forearms, from the golden hair against his tanned skin to the way the muscles moved and flexed as he wrote.

He was making these neat, little concise notes on a page in his notebook. Something I'd noticed about Ramsey, he did all of his note taking by hand. No laptops, tablets, or phones for him.

I preferred to write my lyrics with a pencil, so I got it, but it was also kind of fascinating to watch. Even with the excitement bubbling through me, I lingered in the doorway. It was rare I got a chance to study him unobserved.

It was hard to reconcile the idea that he was a teacher's

assistant and someone who also graded me. He didn't seem quite so fierce or unapproachable at the moment. The pair of black bands on his right forearm held me riveted.

They typically meant mourning.

But mourning for what?

There were feathers on his left arm and a clock, but the angle didn't let me study them as closely. The ink thrilled me. So many people didn't understand the stories you could tell in the art you wore. I literally had my heart on my sleeve if you knew what to look for.

Was Ramsey the same?

He paused mid-stroke on the page, lifting his right hand to brace his chin as he read something from the book he had open.

Fuck.

I still had my phone in my hand, if I angled it, could I get a photo of him like that?

The moment that thought slid out, I shook my head. That was creeper behavior. I cleared my throat and he glanced up, his candid expression shuttering swiftly.

"Hey, Ramsey," I said, trying to play off against the fact that I'd been leering in the doorway at him like some horny groupie. "Guess what?"

I grinned as he raised his eyebrows. "What?"

After pulling up the grades on my phone, I set it on the table and pushed it over to him. "Straight As."

Flipping the book he'd had open closed, he picked up the phone and scanned the grades. "Well done."

"Thank you," I said, some of my enthusiasm spilling over in the smile stretching my cheeks. "For real, thank you. I know I didn't ask for your help and I've pretty much resented it more than been grateful for it, but you have done a lot for me."

He set the phone down to push back to me as I spread my arms.

"This semester, between working with you and staying on top of everything—it's really made a difference." I'd started with the thank you, but I wasn't sure those two words were enough to convey how grateful I was. "I get I'm probably not a joy to work with, but I really do appreciate everything you've done."

The awkward silence that filled the room when I finished made me twitch. Instead of replying or even showing a hint of pride, Ramsey studied me with a tense frown tightening his brow.

"That's it," I tacked on rather lamely. "I just—wanted to thank you."

I blew out a breath. Maybe I shouldn't have said anything.

"You know what these grades tell me?" The quiet question raked over me. Then not waiting for me to answer, he continued, "That when you spend less time obsessing about yourself and your career, you are open to new ideas and focused work. When you take time away from being in front of everyone and in their face, you'd notice the other people around you."

What. The. Fuck.

"Are you for real right now?" The question fell out before I could rethink it. "Are you really scolding me to work harder when I've already been busting my ass?"

His entire expression turned cool and remote. "I'm telling you that you are capable of more, you just have to stop being such an entitled brat."

Brat.

Entitled.

"You know what, bite me," I said. It was only slightly politer than my initial response. "Actually, I take that back. Fuck you. I don't want you to bite me or anything else. I'm trying to thank you for being a tremendous teacher and admit that I was wrong to not want anything to do with this, but you're basically embracing the douche canoe."

He rose. "Miss Crosse..."

"Don't you Miss Crosse me," I countered. "Fuck no. You've had a hard-on hate for me from day one and not a damn thing I do is going to change that. Thank you for pointing out that saying thank you just blows up in someone's face. Fine. You're here to do a job and so am I."

I dropped my book bag on the table.

"Let's forget all about the thank yous and the appreciation. You don't want them, clearly," I stressed that last word. "And I can't be fucked to offer them if this is gonna be the response."

Yanking my homework notebook out, I flipped it open to the day's assignments and slammed it down.

"Are you quite finished?" Oh look, he found the stick to ram up his ass again. This was TA Malone, dismissive prick.

"Sure, I need to go back to being entitled and failing to notice other people. So make it snappy." We'd made progress, or so I thought.

At the moment though, all of that progress seemed to be rushing down the drain. Fine. We didn't need to like each other. The sense of camaraderie that had developed over the last few weeks had probably just been my imagination.

People show you who they are, I reminded myself internally. They show you with all their actions and their responses. TA Malone disliked me intensely. He'd been demonstrating it from day one and whether the dislike was real or not, his disdain definitely was. The man didn't think anything of me.

Made me question his motives for offering to help at the beginning of this semester. He could have just made due with the tutoring we already had, but whatever. Burn me once, shame on you.

Burn me twice? Well, not happening.

"Miss Crosse," he said, rising to face me, so I stayed standing. Like every other male in this school over the age of fifteen, he was taller than me. I wasn't giving up an inch of ground by sitting now. "Your attitude is appalling."

I snorted. "Try saying that three times in a mirror, you might catch a clue." I pulled the sheet out of the book and slid it over to him. "Tutoring started five minutes ago. We have less than an hour left."

Something hot burned in his eyes, melting away the frost as he actually glared at me. "You think you can just walk in anywhere and say what you like?"

"Nope," I told him gamely. "I think I could come in here offering platitudes and sweetness and you'd still insult me to the best of your capabilities. Nothing I do is good enough—silly me for trying to look beyond the hostility. Don't worry, I won't make the mistake again."

Instead of beginning, we stood there and glared at each other. A muscle ticked in his jaw, and I kept my gaze focused on his face and not his sexy fucking forearms. Cause douchebags and fuckboys came in all shapes, sizes, and terms of sexiness. Didn't make them less douchey or fuckboyish.

Planting his hands on the table, he said, "Perhaps we should begin again."

"Nice offer, but no. If we're studying, let's do it, otherwise —I'm out." No more trying to connect on a personal level. I probably shouldn't have been anyway. Stupid me for thinking we could get past whatever his preconceptions were.

I'd made the mistake of the smooth sailing from the last few weeks as a positive. Forgot to look for the traps.

When he still said nothing, I nodded and shut the notebook. "Have it your way. I'll see you tomorrow." Maybe. I left the last word unsaid. I was pissed.

I knew I was pissed.

Anger helped me. Most of the time it gave me the strength to keep tears at bay. Right now, I needed all the help I could get. I'd been genuinely fucking proud of myself before Mr. Ramsey "The Fucking Buzzkill" Malone reminded me that I was just...

The door closed before I could get to it and I jerked my head up to find Ramsey blocking the door.

"Not a good move," I told him. "Especially right now."

"You're not just storming out of here." He ground out each word. Anger vibrated in each syllable. "Not again."

It was like dumping a lit match into kerosene. "Get out of my way, *Mr. Malone*. This is a school, not a prison. You're a teacher's *assistant*, not a warden."

Not to mention a class A asshole.

Hey, look, another A.

His scowl darkened. "Miss Crosse, you're not helping your case."

I snorted. "Nothing I say or do would help my case. You've made that abundantly clear. I'm sorry my excitement triggered you. I forgot for a moment the roles you assigned us on the first day of school. Now get out of my way."

"You," he said through gritted teeth, "are the most infuriating woman."

"Good," I told him. "Then you got something right. Move." Then because he was still a teacher's assistant, I tacked on, "Please."

He turned to the side so I went for the handle, but he planted his hand against it. "Miss Crosse—"

I glared up at him. "Get out of my way."

All the air in the room seemed to evacuate, leaving me lightheaded and still furious. This close, I could see the hint of gray flecks in his blue eyes. They were—

He wrapped a hand around my nape and dragged me

forward. Words failed me when his lips collided with mine. This wasn't Lachlan stealing a kiss. This was—complete and total control. Ramsey's lips were firm, warm, and so damn soft. They fused with mine like we needed to be one to breathe.

It made me dizzy. At the first brush of his tongue, I parted my lips and the world went electric as all the hairs on my body stood up. My heart slammed so hard I could feel it everywhere, and then he made a low, soft groan and reality splashed against me like ice water.

Between one breath and the next, I just reacted. I slammed my knee into his crotch and unlike Lachlan who'd been getting good at avoiding it, Ramsey let out a soundless scream as he staggered back.

His teeth scraped over my lower lip as he fell against the wall. I tasted a hint of copper along with the sweet butterscotch warmth that had been his kiss. He stared at me, still gasping and if I wasn't so fucking mad, I might have laughed at his shocked expression.

"I'm really fucking over people grabbing and kissing me like it's their right. Keep your hands and your lips to yourself."

Then I yanked the door open and stormed out. I didn't slow down or look back as I descended the steps and out the front doors of the library into the icy air. My face was so hot, I barely felt the change in the temps or the way the wind rushed against me.

I pressed my fingers against my still tingling lips as I double-timed it across the campus—thankfully not as busy with the final class period still going on—all the way to the dorm and I didn't slow down until I was inside, behind the locked door, and then in my own room with that door closed.

The shakes hit as I sank to my knees. I could still feel the way he'd kissed me. My teacher—teacher's assistant—kissed me. He kissed the hell out of me and I liked it.

Then I assaulted him.

Well, to be fair, the kiss and the door blockade meant he started it.

But holy shit.

He kissed me and I tried to geld him.

Maybe I was a goddamn problem child.

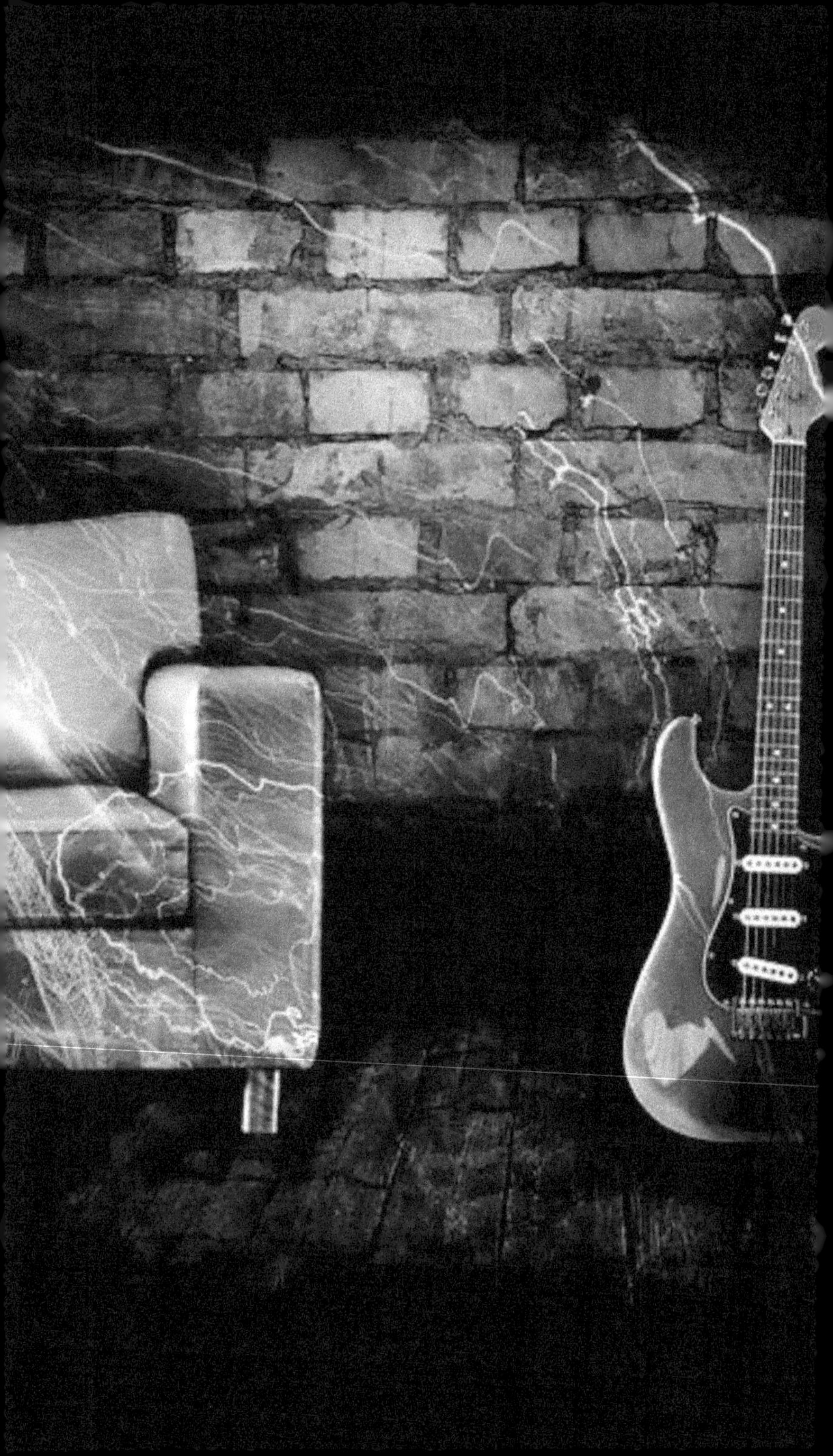

Thirty-Five

I did *not* go to classes the next day. I didn't go running either. Honestly, I didn't even get out of bed. It was almost no time until spring break and at the same time it seemed a million years away.

"Hey," Aubrey called as the door closed behind her. "I brought you lunch."

I groaned but dragged myself up as she let herself into my room.

"Wow, you do look like crap," she offered. Then, being the best friend that she was, she pulled out her phone and took a picture of me. My messy bedhead and middle finger were absolutely no deterrent. Not that I thought they would be.

Then she held up her peace offering in the form of broccoli cheese soup and garlic bread. There was a huge cup of coffee from Dancing Goats, too. My stomach grumbled at the combination of scents.

"Hot and fresh from the dining hall. Sydney grabbed it and ran it out to me so I could run it over here."

Now I felt like such an asshole. "You guys didn't have to do that." The croak in my voice made me sound even worse than I felt and considering that I felt like absolute crap. "Thank you."

Aubrey waited for me to settle back against the pillows and straighten up the tangle of sheets and blankets. The night had been spent tossing and turning. I half-expected a summons to the administration building or for the dean to basically kick my ass out because I assaulted a teacher.

Yes, teacher's assistant. I wanted to bind and gag the voice in my head. Mute it forever. Didn't matter. I'd definitely done some damage.

"I'm worried about you," Aubrey said, studying me. "You've been crying."

I closed my eyes, it was hard to hide anything from her. She knew me too well. Then again, I knew her and Yvette the same way. "Just stressed," I admitted before taking a sip of the coffee. It was just this side of scalding and soothed over the rough cracks in my throat.

"Talk to me?" The offer immediately plunged me back into a vat of guilt. "I can't help if I don't know."

Leaning my head back, I stared up at the ceiling for a long time. "Ninja kisses and asshole TAs, then there's the boy who keeps giving me music but won't actually talk to me." That was part of it. "Mom is still at that retreat." Months she'd been there now. Almost six of them. "Poor Johnny doesn't know what to do, he's been writing me almost weekly and I finally emailed him because I really don't want any more dick pics to take to Mom."

The last came out somewhat mournfully, and Aubrey grinned. "You know, I'm starting to get curious about his movies now."

I gagged. "Please don't. He sleeps with my mother. That's literally *all* I need to know. Even if he is a sweetheart." And he was. A bit of a himbo, but then he meant well. There was nothing arrogant about his sexuality and as far as I'd seen, and he didn't hit on everything that moved.

Then again, how interesting could sex be if that was what you did for a living?

Grimacing, I tried to scrub that from my head. Especially when my first thought was the way Ramsey kissed me. There was no ignoring the way it lit me up or the fact that I'd actually begun to anticipate Lachlan's ninja kisses.

"Well, I am glad he's a sweetheart." Aubrey studied me. "Are you hiding in here from those boys?"

"No," I said almost immediately. Then... "Yes, but it's not for what you think. Or maybe it is. Fuck, I don't know—" My phone buzzed and I flipped it over to see the message from Jackie on the screen.

Call asap.

Holding up a finger, I hit her contact immediately and it rang through. Aubrey's frown tightened.

"You didn't have to leave class," Jackie scolded in a somewhat harried voice that carried absolutely no recrimination. If anything, she sounded... tearful. "First, Bronson is fine and Penelope is going to be fine."

My heart dropped.

"What happened?" Don't freak out, I told myself. No amount of self-lecturing could slow my heart's rapid, staccato beat.

"Pen developed another fever. It's not teething, it's not viral, I don't care what those doctors said." Her voice turned fierce. "We went back to the hospital, and this time, I didn't let them just ignore every single symptom. This has been persistent."

She wasn't wrong.

"The head of pediatrics came down to look at her case and they ordered a whole battery of tests. They just called me with the results..."

I was going to throw up. I knew I was.

"We have an appointment with a pediatric oncologist in a week."

It was like my heart accordioned as I fisted all of my control. "They think it's cancer."

"Her symptoms fit, her age—yes. We're going to tackle this." Firm conviction filled her voice. "We have temporary custody; there's a hearing next month to determine permanent custody."

"I'll be there if you need me."

"I know you will, but we have this…Kaitlin, sweetheart, I'm telling you all of this because I know you're going to worry. But this isn't on you to fix."

What could I do? Throw money at the problem? I couldn't cure cancer. "I don't want it to be cancer."

"No one does," she said, her tone definitely soothing.

Aubrey's hand found mine, and she squeezed my fingers. She'd moved to sit beside me and had her head pressed to the other side of my phone. She hadn't missed a single word.

"We start with getting a diagnosis. Getting her real help. We're doing that. We're taking care of getting her custody settled, and I saw how much money you had put in my account, young lady. Trust me, we will be discussing it later."

Tears burned in my eyes. "For my baby sister, nothing is too much. Not for Bronson either. You're not so bad, yourself, you know."

Her soft laughter pulled a smile from me. My problems were pretty fucking paltry compared to this.

"I do know," Jackie said. "Now, back to class. Focus. Work on those grades, and as soon as I have any more information, you and Bronson are my first calls."

"Jackie," I said, keeping my tears in check. "Thank you."

"It's going to be okay," she said, the promise fierce, but

there was no hiding the worry beneath it. "We're going to take care of this. Talk soon."

Then she was gone. Aubrey wrapped an arm around me, and I sighed. This was just the crappy cherry on the shit sundae.

"You know we'll do anything, right?" Aubrey reminded me, and I nodded.

"I do know."

"Okay, I have to get back to classes," she said with another squeeze. "Finish the coffee, eat the soup, then shower—you smell."

I laughed at her last little dig, but she was gone and I was left staring at the soup. I managed about half of it, then I checked my email.

Bronson had sent me a message, basically freaking out while not freaking out. Then there were more emails from Johnny, including one about Mom still being at the retreat.

Why was she still there? I'd put in a couple of calls to Trish, but she hadn't answered. At all.

After looking up their number, I called the retreat itself.

"Good afternoon, thank you for calling the Sunshine Retreat. I hope you're having a blessed day. How can we facilitate your needs today?"

The chipper voice was a little *too* bright and a little *too* happy. "I'm calling for Jennifer Crosse. This is her daughter, Kaitlin. She is a patient there..."

"Jennifer is a sister of the light, not a patient. Those terms offer a shackle to the progress of the mind, body, and soul." The correction was gentle if patronizing.

"I need to speak to her, please."

"If you'll hold on one moment, I will check to see where she is. Thank you." She didn't wait for my response before she clicked away.

Sister of the light. What crock of crap was that?

"Kaitlin, sweetheart," Mom said, her voice warm and effervescent. "I'm so glad you called."

"You are?" Then because it was true, I added, "You sound amazing. How are you doing?"

"I am—filled with light here. It's taken the darkness in a chokehold, and we're thrusting it out. No more suppression of my soul."

Uh huh. "Okay..."

"Ever the skeptic my beautiful darling, you should come up to see me. You have some time to take off? I've graduated to a full suite so you can stay with me."

Graduated... "Mom, what's going on? You've been there for weeks." Months at this point.

"I am transitioning from a life of darkness and bad choices to one of enlightenment. No more shadows to mar the path, we face everything, chins up and our eyes on the future. Oh, my sweet baby, you have to come. This place would be so good for you. I don't think I've ever been happier."

As much as I wanted nothing to do with that place, I said, "I have next week off. I can leave on Friday. I just have to get a driver."

"Call Dix, baby. Tell him to come get you and bring you here. I haven't seen him in forever either. Having all of you together will be wonderful." Someone called her in the background and she covered the phone, muffling her reply. "I'll be there in a moment." Then the volume increased and grew clear when she continued, "I need to go. It's a meditation hour and it's important to keep my soul and mind in balance with my heart. I'll expect you Saturday? Mwah. Love you."

Like the woman earlier, she didn't wait for an answer before she hung up. What was going on? Trish not returning my calls wasn't that unusual, but Jennifer Crosse had been off the map for months and she was *still* in rehab?

Fuck.

I finished my soup, then made myself get up. After a shower, brushing my teeth and fresh clothes, I wasn't quite human yet but I was definitely several levels above the craptastic mess I'd been before.

After straightening my room, I made coffee then settled with my laptop. Even though I missed classes, I made sure to turn in all my work, then I emailed Harley to let her know I would be leaving on Friday for a week.

I fired off messages to Yvette and Aubrey. They needed to know where I was going and for how long. Next, I called Dix and began to scroll my email while I waited.

OPEN THIS

The subject jumped out at me.

Inside were a pair of photos.

One was me kissing RJ. That was the other week, not that we'd talked as much since then. I needed to stop blowing him off.

The second picture was me running by myself.

In the snow.

In the dark.

That...

"KC sweetheart," Dix said when he answered the phone. "Finally tired of the wrong coast and calling me for a rescue?"

I laughed, the sound might have come out a little hollow, but I did mean it. The laughter made me feel better. So did his sardonic comment. "I miss you," I admitted.

"I can be there in a few hours," he said. "I just need to book a flight."

"Charge it to us and get it first class," I said and there was dead silence for a minute.

"Really? You want me there...now?" Why the surprise?

"I talked to Mom and she's still at the retreat. She wants me to come up..."

"And you need a ride." Understanding seemed to cover the

hint of disappointment in his voice. "Jennifer doesn't always think these things through."

"If it was just a ride, I could book a car service." All true.

"What do you need?" Sobering, Dix became all business. "And how fast do you need me there?"

"By Friday, if you can. I'll leave right after school. We can stay at a hotel near the retreat, not sure about being at the retreat that late. But I need you there so if it's all as weird in person as it was just now on the phone, I may need help getting her out."

"I'll be there. Don't leave without me. I'll get a car and text you Friday."

Relief trickled through the fingers of icy panic gripping me. "Thank you."

"Don't worry, sweetheart. We'll make sure everything is okay."

It wasn't until we got off the phone that I refocused on those photos.

One of these is okay. Not the other.

The first photo appeared below the line, but with RJ ripped out of it.

Don't disappoint me again.
Your Forever Fan

Yeah, that...that was creepy. I sent that off to Teddy and the team. Along with a few others and I mentioned the other letters.

I frowned at the photo of me running again. That wasn't that long ago that I'd worn that outfit.

A shudder went up my spine. The rattle of the door made me jump, and I strode over to glance out the peephole. Jonas stood there, arms up like he was putting something on the door.

I pulled it open, and it was his turn to jump. He stared at

me a beat, then handed me the music sheets. New ones. Only when I went to take the pages, he didn't let them go.

"Are you all right?"

"Yes," I lied, then tugged the music to look at it. "Thank you for this."

He nodded but didn't say anything. When he backed away, I took a step forward and he paused.

"Um...I'm going out of town for the break. So it might take me a few days to get this back to you."

A nod, then he turned and walked away.

If only I could abandon my irritations and problems that easily.

Retreating into the room, I didn't fight the urge to get my guitar. My head swirled with information, images, and worry. Mom. Penelope. My Forever Fan.

Not to mention Ramsey, Lachlan, Jonas, and RJ.

The image of us kissing was older than the running pic, but how did they get those photos at all?

And was that creepy fan actually here at the school? For a moment, my mind leapt to Jonas and then I looked back at the music as I settled the guitar on my lap.

No...Jonas had been pretty violent with the guy in the hall; if he'd seen me and RJ kissing, I had a feeling that he wouldn't have been taking a picture of it.

That was probably the last thing he'd do.

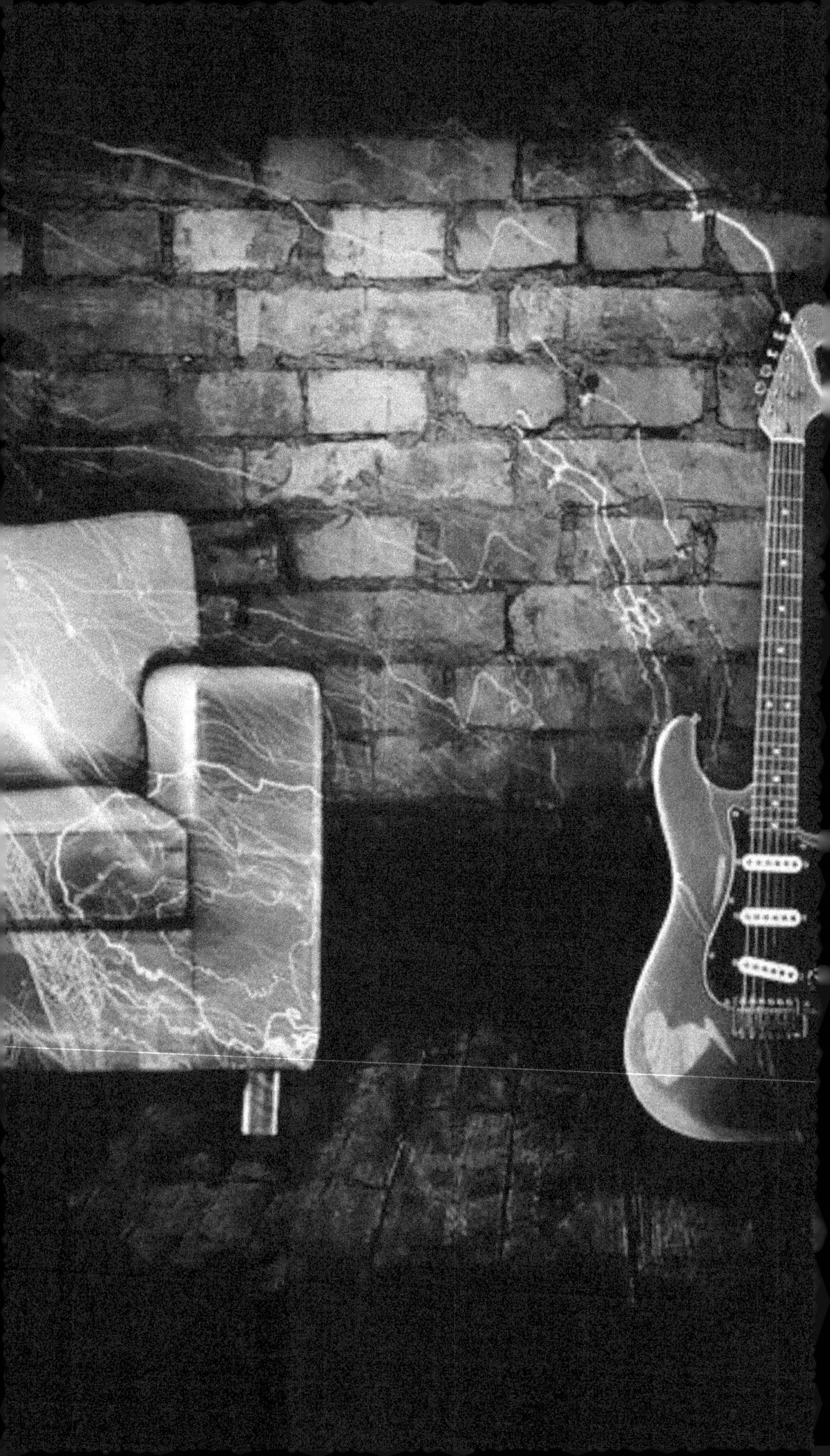

Thirty-Six

Not even twenty-four hours into my stay at the Sunshine Retreat and I was ready to leave. Dix couldn't stay on the property, so he'd gotten a hotel room. I texted him to pick me up the next day. I would come out and see Mom, but staying there at night was giving me the creeps.

Serious creeps.

"It's time for Session," Mom said as she pushed open my door. I'd woken up an hour earlier, but I was still checking emails on my phone. There was one from Ramsey that I didn't want to open and another from Lachlan. Yeah, I'd skip that, too.

Coward?

No, but I had only so many battles I could wage, and Mom's was the most pressing. I fired off a quick text to let Aubrey and Yvette know I was alive before I focused on her.

"Session?"

"Yes, session is amazing. Our guide leads the sessions, and it allows all of the sisters of the light to work together. It's an important step toward self-actualization."

"So, group therapy?"

Mom's nose wrinkled, but her smile didn't diminish at all. Dressed in white silk pajamas and a robe, she looked—well, she looked amazing. Peaceful. Granted, she still had on some cosmetics, but the glow was all her from the shine of her hair to the sparkle in her eyes.

So. Weird.

"Not at all," Mom informed me. "We don't do *therapy*. Therapy implies something is wrong."

Um...

"What we do is let someone open us to enlightenment, then we can follow the path."

Right.

"Do I have time for coffee before this?"

"Coffee is a crutch. It has a suppressive influence on our ability to just enjoy life and thrive. You are far too young to be the victim of that. It's part of the reason I wanted you to come here."

"Mom," I said slowly, "if I have to go to some enlightenment session on my week off from school without coffee, I will cut people. Do not test me on this."

She sighed. "I have instant. It's considered contraband, so do be a dear and don't mention it."

"Deal."

The instant coffee was ass, but it also proved to be the elixir I needed to get through a *four*, count it, *four fucking hours* long "session" for enlightenment.

The women in the group ranged in ages from a little older than me to older than mom. One grandmother with a skin care regimen to kill for, smiled beatifically at us when we arrived.

"This is my daughter," Mom said, putting a hand on my shoulder. I'd dressed in jeans and a t-shirt with running shoes. Oh, did I miss running already. I stood out like a sore thumb amidst all the white flowing pants, tops, jackets, and dresses. "She's going to be with me all week, so I thought I would bring her to sessions so she can discover the light with us."

Oh, I was discovering something.

After four hours of self-reflective ruminating—guided meditations led by the grandmother type—as well as each person discussing where they were before the light and where they were now, I was ready to pull the ripcord and get out.

Everything about this place made my nerves jangle. Lunch was served in a quiet room. Even the meals were silent, served by waif-like figures who floated in, set the bowls of soup and rice down and then drifted out again.

More than once, I opened my mouth to say something and Mom would just put her hand on mine and shake her head. There was no mistaking her serenity, but to be honest, I wasn't looking forward to nightfall. Did they do blood sacrifice somewhere?

Maybe that wasn't fair.

After we escaped the creepy quiet of lunch, Mom and I went for a long walk. It required bundling up. Upstate New York was still snowy, and spring was a promise in the early afternoon but not totally committed.

"What are you doing, Mom?" I asked her as we walked. It was the first time since we woke in her suite that we'd been alone. The cold air slapped at my cheeks, and tasted like freedom. The compound where the retreat was located hid a much larger facility.

The building we'd dropped Mom off at was in the front. It was also where Mom went to meet with her sponsor, but once you'd gone through immersion, you moved to the nicer facilities out here. None of this was in the pamphlet she'd shown me.

I was going to kill Trish.

"I'm cleaning my soul and developing my inner strength

so I can become the person I've always been meant to be," Mom said, giving me a soft smile. "I've let too many people dictate how I should look, feel, act, or even think for too long. David has truly shone the light on how I was sabotaging my own happiness by looking at the steps I needed to take, rather than apportioning blame."

"Okay," I said slowly as we climbed a path toward a rise that looked out over a beautifully snowy field bordered by thick trees. "Six months? What about your career? Your houses? Your friends?"

"What is a career but a distraction," Mom said with an airy wave. "If it is meant to be it will be there. For now, I need to focus on me." That made sense, except...

"Are you focusing on you?" I studied her. "You've basically cut yourself off from everyone." I hadn't heard from her at all. Not really. "When was the last time you spoke to Trish?"

"Trish and I don't speak anymore." She said that like it was the most natural thing in the world. "David felt that she was a suppressive influence, particularly calling me weekly with auditions and potential roles. Also, she came here and we had an awful row. I was in the darkness for days after..."

She sighed, the disappointment almost tangible in the air around her.

"He suggested that the only way to cleanse the darkness and truly shine the light was to remove that suppression threatening to smother me."

"What did you do?" I kind of wanted to know where all the exits were.

"Fired her," Mom said, and for a moment, real sadness swept over her face. "From the first day of my career, Trish has always been there..." Another long sigh. "But she encouraged some of my worst decisions, and her need to control me just..."

"Her need to control you? Suggesting you get help?"

The sadness vanished behind a shutter, and Mom turned

to me. When she put her hand to my cheek, I studied her. She looked like Mom and almost sounded like her, but I felt like I was being punked and she was just preparing for some role.

Because the alternative that this was *real* was a lot more terrifying.

"She also called you whenever she could not get her way and summoned you to me. Using my feelings for you to emotionally manipulate me into getting her way." Real regret shone in her eyes. "That's why I couldn't see you at Thanksgiving or Christmas."

I frowned. "Because Trish emotionally manipulated you?" That wasn't tracking.

"Because you're a part of me, granted a part that is forever tangled with Gibson, but I think you're more me than you'll ever be him. I need my light to be stronger. I know you mean well, but you can't believe everyone, sweetheart, and I should be the one guiding you after all."

"Is alcohol as much contraband as coffee is?" Because I could use a drink.

Mom pressed a finger to her lips. While she didn't answer, she did pull out a bottle of wine in her suite later. Dinner was there and not with the rest; apparently that was only for the sisters and brothers of the light, and I wasn't even a member yet.

Fine by me.

The next three days passed much the same, and I really didn't sleep well, but Mom *seemed* happy and content. Mom's melodrama might not be everyone's cup of tea, but that loud, bombastic, over-the-top woman was the woman who'd raised me and this—serenity just seemed unreal.

On day five, I planned to leave. I still needed to get back up to school, and I had homework to do. I'd worked some in the evenings, though we couldn't turn the music up and absolutely no singing was allowed.

Yeah, this place was hell. Did I belt out a song in the shower on my last day?

Fuck yes.

"Dix will be here in an hour," I called to Mom as I zipped closed my suitcase. Fortunately, there was no session today and I'd already had a cup of contraband coffee. "I have something—"

I broke off as I came out of my room to see Mom with a guy I hadn't met yet. Like Mom, he was dressed all in white. His dress shirt and slacks didn't have that floaty feeling of her silk pajamas and outfits. Did these people have a personal grudge against some color?

"Kaitlin, sweetheart, I want to introduce you to David Ranier. He's been my guide since I came here..."

The man had dark brown hair and brown eyes. There was something—off about him, but I couldn't put my finger on what it was. He pressed his palms together as he crossed the room toward me.

"Good day, Kaitlin, it's a real pleasure to meet you." When he held out both of his hands to me, I eyed them then him.

"Mr. Ranier," I said by way of greeting, then folded my arms.

Mom frowned, but her "guide" held up his hands. "It's fine, Jennifer. Be at peace, sister. Remember, we can only light the way, we cannot force anyone to follow the path."

"I worry about Kaitlin."

When Mr. Ranier turned and put his hand on her cheek, I shook my head and glanced elsewhere. Yeah, this guy just gave me bad vibes. Truthfully, the whole place did. Mom's Stepford wife role was creeping me out just as much.

"I know you do," he said to her. "But Kaitlin seems well, despite the wild and troubled life she's leading." Then he glanced at me, the corners of his mouth lifting into a bit of a smile. From his long hair to his perfectly tailored suit, the man was a mismatch of contradictions. "Are you well?"

"Depends on who you ask," I quipped. "But I wouldn't believe everything you read, or hear for that matter."

"Sarcasm as self-defense," he said, his voice gentling. "You've had to shield the flame of your light too much, and now it's guttering in the chill. Don't be afraid to let it shine."

"Okay." Then I looked at Mom who stared at me imploringly. Yeah, this wasn't some big time producer or studio executive she wanted to charm and trotted me out like the show pony to brag about. I wasn't going to make nice with him. "Actually, if you wouldn't mind excusing us. I wanted to spend this last little bit of time with my mother."

"Kaitlin," Mom snapped, but David took her hand and stroked it like she was some kind of pet.

"It's quite all right," he said in a perfectly calm tone. "Be the guide and shine the light, but don't try to force the path."

"Of course," my mother said, and I did my best not to roll my eyes.

Then he looked at me and reached out to grip my biceps. "It is a real pleasure to meet you, Kaitlin. I would love to come up to your school. Jennifer has told me about how dedicated you are to reinventing yourself, and I would be more than happy to come to you and visit."

"Thanks," I said without an ounce of sincerity. "We're really not allowed visitors on campus. It's closed and secure."

And I would lie through my teeth to make sure that happened.

"Of course, of course. Maybe on your next visit then." He gave my arms a squeeze and it took everything I had not to shrug him off of me.

So. Gross.

Then he let me go before leaving the room. Mom turned

to me, her eyes blazing. "How could you embarrass me like that?"

"This has nothing to do with embarrassment," I countered. "You want to drink the Kool-Aid, that's one thing. I'm not so sure."

"Kaitlin, baby, of all of us, you've been the most trapped in this world that wants to chew us up and spit us out. The light—it's right there. Even David sees it."

"I'll keep that in mind." Then I reached into my back pocket and pulled out the thin stack of letters I'd rubber banded together. "I brought you something."

Mom blinked at the mail. "Where did you get those?"

"Johnny's been sending them to me at the school. He says he hasn't had any luck getting to you, so he wanted me to bring them to you if I could."

She traced her fingers against the lettering.

"For what it's worth, he sounds pretty miserable." I skipped the dick pic parts. She could find those on her own. "And I know you were missing him."

She blinked rapidly, then held the letters to her chest. "I'm not supposed to have contact with the outside world...it's potentially detrimental to the progress I've already made."

"Well, apparently coffee and wine aren't on their acceptable list, along with music. Don't mind me if I don't think much of them."

For a moment, a small smile escaped her. "Thank you for bringing these to me."

"You're welcome." Then because I couldn't not ask, I said, "Are you sure I can't convince you to come with me? There's a whole world out there..."

"Thank you darling, but no." When she opened her arms, I went into them and hugged her. "I'm where I need to be. Maybe you can come back over the summer."

Hell no. "We'll see," I said, not promising anything. It

wasn't long before Dix was there and he grabbed my suitcase for me and loaded it.

Instead of climbing into the back, I slid into the passenger seat. Mom didn't linger outside, vanishing back into the facility as soon as she'd bid me farewell.

"All good?" Dix asked. "I half-expected you to call me to come get you for the hotel."

"I thought about it," I told him. "Sorry, I know I said I might and that basically just made you wait for me."

He put a hand on my leg and gave it a gentle pat. "I'll wait for as long as you need. Always. Now tell me, what's wrong?"

"That's what I need to figure out." Did I try to get her out of there? Did I report it to someone?

What the hell was I supposed to do?

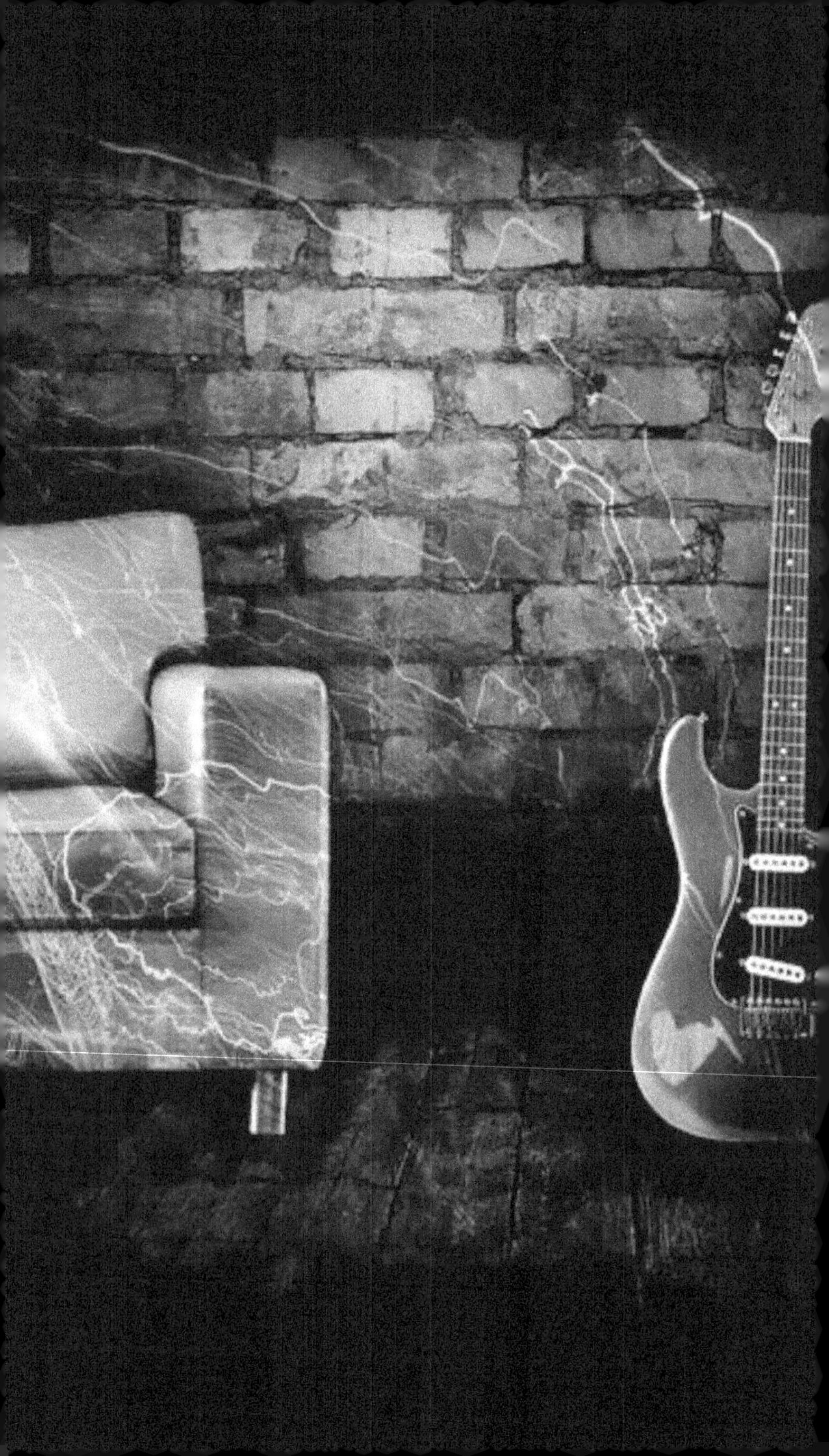

Thirty-Seven

As soon as I was back on campus, I found that my request to end the study sessions and tutoring had been declined. There was no explanation other than we could revisit for the following autumn term, but for now, I would have to go back to those hours in the library.

Fuck.

After briefing Aubrey and Yvette about the Sunshine Retreat, they'd both been horrified but they weren't sure what we should do any more than I was. I'd also put another call into Trish, but she wasn't answering.

My mood was pretty bleak when I remembered I had the music from Jonas to play. I tried to add lyrics to it but it was just not coming. Jackie had no new updates, just the doctors were running tests.

Lots and lots of tests.

Monday morning, the first day back after the spring break, I headed out to run. I needed out of my head. There was just so much noise and it was blocking all of the music.

I collided with Lachlan as I came out the doors, and he

gripped my arms to steady me as we both slid a little. I glanced down at the ice on the sidewalk then back up.

There was ice on everything.

It was—beautiful and really fucking irritating.

I wanted to stomp my feet and scream.

"Hey," Lachlan said jerking my attention to him. Vapor from his breath added another illustration to how cold it was out here. He frowned as he studied me. "Where have you been?"

"None of your business," I replied, before glancing at the sheen of ice heading up the hill to where the trail started. "Is the gym going to be open if it's all icy out here?"

"Even if it's not, I have a key."

That startled me. "You have a key?"

"Lacrosse team trains regularly, particularly as we head into spring. Running is vital to staying in shape for it."

"Right," I said slowly. "Lacrosse team." Had I even seen a lacrosse game? Like ever?

"Are you okay?" Lachlan asked after a beat and I focused on him again.

"No. It's icy and I need to run, so I'm going to check the gym out." It was cold as fuck out here and my cheeks burned from the bite in the air.

"I'll go with you," Lachlan said and I just shrugged. It wasn't like I could stop him. "We need to talk."

"I'm not in the mood to talk," I told him. "I just want to run."

He frowned and I swore he searched my eyes like he was looking for nuclear secrets. Unfortunately for him, I was all tapped out at the moment. My head was almost too full.

Pivoting, I headed up the path and tried my best to not bust my ass. It was early, maybe that was why they hadn't salted yet. Or maybe they were working on it.

I didn't care.

To my surprise, he didn't say anything. Instead, he followed me all the way to the gym and when the door was locked, he produced a key and opened it.

"As promised," he murmured.

"Thank you."

"That wasn't so hard was it?"

I just rolled my eyes and stripped off my jacket because it would be too warm to run in here with it on. "Look, Lachlan," I said as I put my earbuds in. "I need to run and I just need to run."

"Answer one question for me?" The fact he even asked rather than ordered said something.

Sighing, I asked, "What question?"

He held up his phone and there was the picture of me and RJ kissing. "Was this before or after I broke his ankle?"

"Not answering that." I shook my head. No way was I going to be responsible for Lachlan hurting RJ more or Lachlan getting kicked out of school or whatever. Not that anything seemed to happen, despite RJ's threats. "Honestly, I just want to run."

"Then it was after. Good to know, Ace. Now get that sexy ass on the treadmill and we'll run. But—" he caught me before I made it one step and pulled me to him. "You and me…we're a thing. You're not kissing RJ again. You better not let him kiss you."

I snorted. "You don't own me."

The corners of his mouth twitched. "Who said anything about ownership?"

"Do you still have a girlfriend? You know—about my height with a bitch on wheels attitude who seems to delight in my misery?"

Lachlan's smirk died and his expression blanked.

I patted his cheek. "Then have a little more shut the fuck up in your life."

Why did everyone think they had a right to tell me how to live?

"Are you going to tell me where you disappeared to last week?"

I spared him a look before I turned up the music. "No."

Then I just drowned everything out and ran. I ran until I was shaking and dripping sweat. I ran all the while aware of him on the treadmill next to me and that he kept glancing at me. I ran until I could empty some of the crazier thoughts out of my head.

More of his teammates showed up while we were running and I took advantage of his distraction to leave. It was still cold as hell out there. So much for spring. Then again, maybe winter wanted one last blowout.

I kind of got that.

Aubrey was awake when I got back. She waited for me to shower and change, then we went for breakfast. I still hadn't figured anything out, and I still hadn't written Jonas' lyrics.

Despite my best attempts, I drifted through classes. At least I had my homework done and I was on target for things.

"Hey, Hot Shot," I said as I caught up with him leaving our last class of the day together. "Sorry about the lyrics. Still haven't been feeling it yet. The music is—intense."

He frowned, and I tried to summon a smile.

"And by intense, I mean in a good way."

With a slow nod, he gave me a long look. "Are you okay?"

Did I have a sign on my head or something? "I'm great." I lied. Faking it until I made it was the name of the game. "Perfect. Don't you know?" I smiled and pointed to it. "See? All good."

Yeah, he didn't look like he believed me either.

"I need to go to tutoring," I said, making a face. That realization just had my stomach sinking all over again. "I'll see you later?"

I don't know why I phrased it like a question, but Jonas had been trying and I hated that I'd been letting him down.

"I'll find you," he said finally. "Later."

That made me smile for real. Leaving him, I headed for the library. The ice from earlier seemed to have begun to melt and despite the frigid early morning temps, Mother Nature seemed to recall that it was supposed to be spring.

Ramsey was standing when I came in, and he straightened immediately. Despite the fact it had been more than ten days since I kicked him in the junk *after* he kissed me, he looked better than I expected.

"KC..."

"I think you were right the first time around," I told him. "Miss Crosse would probably be better." As it was, I didn't want to be in here. It was one thing to nurse my personal silent crush on him, but the fact he'd kissed me after he tore into me?

Yeah, I just couldn't do that right now.

Or pretty much any time.

He let out a sigh. "Agreed, Miss Crosse, however, I owe KC an apology."

"Okay, you're sorry. Great, can we just focus on classwork and nothing else?"

"I kissed you," he said slowly.

"No shit, Sherlock. I was there. Got the t-shirt." I bit my lip in order to shut up before I let another stream of random bullshit spill out. Honestly, I couldn't tell whether he was annoyed or frustrated.

I cobbled together some semblance of dignity and said, "Mistakes were made. I say we let it go and just focus on what we're here for. I won't try to impress you and you don't try to kiss me. I'll do my work. You can tell me how utterly ungrateful I am, as well as how privileged or whatever, and I can mock you for being a stuck-up prick. Deal?"

I didn't wait for him to respond.

"Deal." I dropped my bag on the table. "Where do we start?"

Ramsey stared at me for a long moment; the faint twist in my gut left me nervous and jumpy. I was already agitated, I might as well have not run at all today for how much my heart was racing.

"All right," he said finally, taking his seat. "Let me see your work from the break..."

Gratitude swarmed through me that he was going for it. I wasn't sure I could handle any more of this today. Academics I could do.

The next hour flew by and we kept our conversation and attention on the work. I was already repacking my bag when the bell went off and I was out of the room like a shot.

I made it down the stairs and almost out of the building when a hand caught mine and hauled me into an open study room. Stumbling, I turned to face my assailant, ready to fling fire when I found myself pressed up against Lachlan's chest.

"You were a bad girl and ran away this morning, Ace," he murmured. The warmth of his breath feathering over my lips sent a shiver through me.

"I'm really tired of you boys all grabbing me and kissing me..." I told him as he crowded me back against the wall.

"Don't you worry about RJ," he promised, violence threading every word. "He's not going to be a problem."

"He is—" I didn't get to finish the thought because the next moment, his lips fused to mine and heat swept over me. The soft, silken pressure of his lips were as intoxicating now as they'd been the first time he kissed me. It was like he needed to touch every part of me, but everything connected where our mouths met.

The bag slipped down my arm as Lachlan wrapped his hand around my chin, the pressure of his thumb pushed my mouth wider. He thrust his tongue against mine, as though demanding I let him play. It sent shivers cascading down my spine.

"Ace," he whispered against my lips before he pushed me against the wall and the world vanished in the fierceness of his kiss.

One minute he was there and the next, he stumbled away. No, he'd been jerked away. Jonas stood there, his gray eyes stormy as hell and his expression dark and foreboding.

The ice that slithered through me this time was more apprehension than desire.

"What the fuck, Jonas?" Lachlan growled. "Get the fuck —" He never finished the sentence because Jonas hit him. I winced at the crash of flesh on flesh and bone on bone.

Not a sound came out of Jonas as he attacked Lachlan in a fury of fists. "Shit," I whispered. "Jonas—wait..."

But I couldn't get near them and Lachlan wasn't just letting Jonas hit him, he delivered three sharp jabs that staggered Jonas. While Lachlan seemed bigger than Jonas, it was more in bulk than height. His shirt tore or maybe it was Lachlan's.

A chair crashed into a table and I narrowly avoided being caught up in their tumble as Jonas drove Lachlan into a corner.

"Stop," I tried again, but I didn't dare grab one of them. That was a good way to get punched. "Guys..."

A whistle split the air, loud enough it made me wince and then Ramsey was there, wading between the two. "Knock it off," he ordered, as he seized Jonas. He wrapped both arms around him and pulled him off his feet.

Lachlan went for another shot but Jonas caught him in the chest with both feet.

"Enough," Ramsey snarled, half tossing Jonas behind him and pointing a finger at Lachlan. "I mean it Lach, back off."

Then he turned and slammed a hand into Jonas to push him back against the wall. "Calm the fuck down."

Blood dotted Lachlan's face where it trickled from his nose. His jacket and his shirt were both torn. Jonas' tie was missing and three buttons were gone from his shirt. He glared at Lachlan with pure malice in his eyes.

"What the hell is going on?" Ramsey demanded, glancing between them before he focused on me. "KC?"

"I—"

"It's not her fault," Lachlan snapped. "Jonas came in here like a damn psycho. You need to play sports and burn some of that edge off baby brother, that left of yours sucks."

Baby brother?

"You were *kissing* her," Jonas said, his expression still filled with rage. "Shoving her against a wall and kissing her."

At that Ramsey snapped a look to Lachlan and then me.

"You knew and you did it anyway..." Jonas was so angry, he seemed to be shaking from it.

"You weren't doing anything," Lachlan said, his grin a little less cocky. "And Ace likes it when I kiss her..." He looked at me. "Don't you?"

"Baby brother?" I countered and that was when Jonas pushed away from the wall.

"Ten months," Jonas said. "Not that much younger."

"You're brothers..." I looked from one to the other, then Lachlan gave me a wry grin.

"Yeah, but don't judge too harshly, Ace." He motioned to Jonas and Ramsey. "I didn't ask for my brothers who were emo or academic overachievers."

I stumbled back a step and looked at Ramsey. "You're their brother, too?"

What the...

He sighed. "Yes, we're brothers. If you don't mind, KC, I'll take care of these two."

Take care…oh the fight. He didn't want me to report it.

Yeah. Sure. Whatever.

I grabbed my bag and hauled it over my shoulder. They were brothers and I'd missed it. Completely.

"I'm going to go."

"Hey," Lachlan said, but Ramsey stopped him and I met Jonas' gaze and the disappointment in those eyes cut through me. I wanted to say sorry and I had no idea why.

I needed to just go.

It would be better.

I'd been kissed by brothers.

Brothers. They didn't even have the same last name—ugh.

Fuck, this wasn't fair.

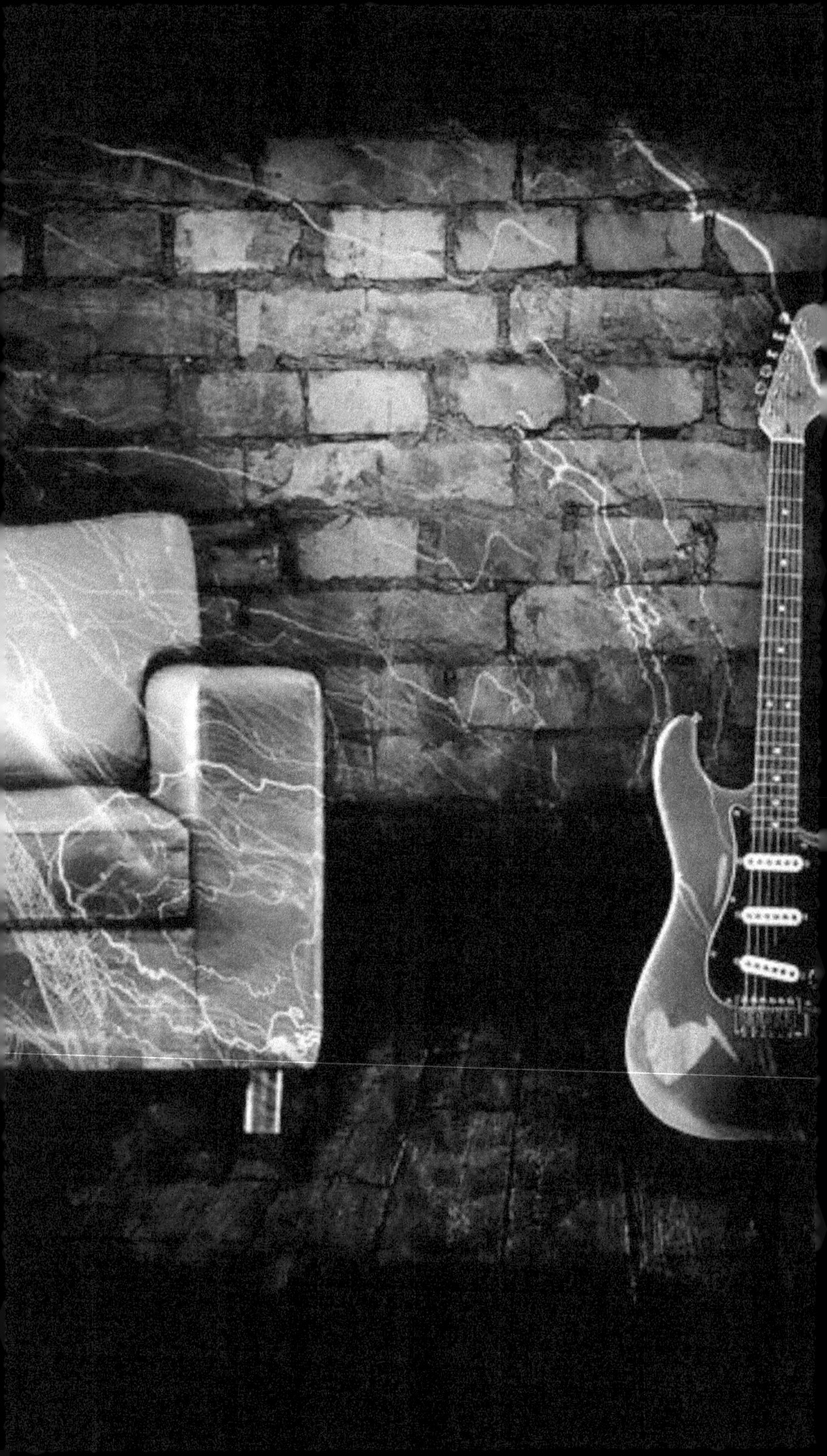

Thirty-Eight

Brothers.

Douchebags One, Two, *and* Three were all brothers. I hadn't seen it. Nor had any of them mentioned it. But at the same time...

It made so much sense. All the little things I'd seen—Ramsey pulling Jonas off that guy in the hallway and taking care of it. RJ shouting at Ramsey that he was going to report Lachlan this time.

RJ knew they were brothers. The whole fucking school probably knew. Payton definitely knew. Did Lachlan know his girlfriend was hitting on his brother?

I had a headache pulsing behind my eye.

Brothers. What a cluster fuck.

Aubrey's reaction helped. She was pissed. Absolutely incensed.

"I don't even know why this is as annoying to me as it is —" I admitted. "I can't stand them most of the time. Except—Ramsey helped, a lot and he didn't have to. Then Jonas...he's been bringing me those music sheets. It's like I get him on that level."

"And Mr. Ninja Kiss?"

"He's a dick." There was no doubt about it. "But... Aubrey, I like his kisses, what the hell is wrong with me?"

"I hate to say it," she said as she joined me on the sofa. "But nothing is wrong with you. The guy is good looking and apparently knows how to kiss. He's also got a thing for you, even if he's being a dick about it."

"He's also got a girlfriend."

"See the second part of my comment about him. He's a dick."

I sighed. "I hate this." Mom. Penelope. Now these guys.

I hated all of it.

The next three weeks passed in slow-motion. Every single minute of every day seemed to drag. Jonas had gone back to just icily ignoring me again. I still needed to work out the lyrics for that last song.

Maybe I could use that as a peace offering. I didn't know Lachlan was his brother so I wasn't sure why he was so angry with me for kissing him or maybe he was angry for another reason.

The guy didn't use words much.

Ramsey and I had come to a very armed truce where tutoring was concerned. We'd moved out of the private room to a table in the library proper. We were *never* alone and I liked that.

Lachlan still tried to run with me, but I did my best to ignore him and avoid his ninja kisses. Fortunately, he seemed to have backed off on that part. Then one of the gossip sites posted that picture of RJ and me kissing.

The one my forever fan had sent. The one that somehow

Lachlan had also ended up with. RJ Wallach was identified as the problem child's boyfriend.

I really didn't want to deal with that. For all the reasons I'd come to this school, the drama and the angst hadn't been on my list. I desperately needed a break. Mom was back in the trades though; she was going to be in a new film and it began shooting in under a month. She'd also been photographed at the Santa Barbara Film Festival *with* Johnny.

Okay, so maybe she dipped out from the Sunshine Retreat and reunited with Johnny. He sent an email a couple of days after that news broke to thank me for getting his messages to her.

Well, that was a relief.

Penelope had a diagnosis, too, and while we knew what it was, the battle was far from over. Jackie also had full custody of Penelope—apparently, they'd reached out to Dad but he'd just asked where to send the checks.

I hated him some days.

Really hated him.

As soon as school was out, I was going to see her. In the meanwhile, Aubrey and I worked hard to wrap up the academic year. Forrest ran interference for us. Sydney and Olivia, who'd also known that Lachlan and Jonas were brothers and assumed I'd known, also pitched in. I was never alone.

It made it a lot harder for Lachlan to corner me and kiss me. Soren and Finley helped, too. It was like I had my own personal group of allies. RJ had been suspiciously absent for a while. At first I just hadn't been paying attention, but when I texted him, there hadn't been an answer and I hadn't seen him since Lachlan made that vague—well, not so vague—threat.

At the end of the semester, there was a parents' open house presentation weekend. It was literally the last weekend of school, post finals. I had zero intention of sticking around, until Aubrey mentioned that her parents were coming.

"Seriously?"

"I know." Aubrey looked as startled as I felt. "But when we were together over Christmas, Dad said he'd like to see the place and he liked what I'd been doing."

"I'll be here," I promised. "I'll have your back."

She wouldn't ask it, but then I never asked them to help with Mom either. The girls just did. So I wouldn't leave her on her own.

"Should we call in Yvette?"

"Backup plan," Aubrey suggested. "Especially if we need to do a fast escape, we can say we have to meet her."

"Good plan."

That just meant making it through the last two weeks of finals, including final papers, and projects. Jonas and I almost got paired again, but the teacher changed her mind about partner projects and just gave us individual assignments.

I was both disappointed and relieved. But I'd also been working on the lyrics. They were almost done. I worked on it every chance I got in between studying, homework, and long calls with Jackie and Bronson about Pen.

When I went to California, I'd get tested too. They needed bone marrow matches for Penelope, just in case. Bronson wasn't a match. We were all half-siblings so we might not be one, but I had to try. Anything to help her.

Following my last final, I slept about twenty-four hours. Not really, but it felt like it. I was exhausted, but we'd done it. I finished the second semester with straight As.

I also finished the lyric sheet and posted it to Jonas' door by way of apology. I probably wouldn't see any of them before the next year—if at all. Lachlan was a senior, so he had to be graduating, right?

Then again, Ramsey was a TA so he might be there, but I didn't need to think about that for a few months. Aubrey and

PROBLEM CHILD

I packed up everything so it was ready for when Dix and his movers arrived to empty our room.

Shockingly, Aubrey's parents were not late. Even more shocking was the guy arriving right behind them.

"Johnny?" I said when he came strolling up. Dressed in a suit and tie, he looked good. His grin was open and friendly, and it was both weird and not weird when he gave me a hug.

"Surprise?"

"Yeah," I said, then looked past him. "Is Mom...?"

"No, she's on location filming. But we got the invitations and she was sad she couldn't come. So, I told her I would be your parental support unit for the day." He grinned. "You did me a favor, so it was the least I could do."

Laughter swelled up in me, but at the same time... "Thank you." I glanced to where Aubrey gave me a little grin. "We're going to show Aubrey's parents around... Would you like to join us?"

"Absolutely."

Johnny turned out to be a great asset on the tour. He asked questions even when Aubrey's parents looked like they weren't sure what to say, and he made some droll comments about the other parents we encountered.

It didn't escape some people's notice that he was there, and I'd clocked more than one phone pointed in his direction.

"Ignore them," he murmured when I shifted at one point. We were all making our way to the dining hall where there would be lunch served and some speeches. "We can't control what people think or do, only our reactions."

"I just hate the idea that you'll be tabloid fodder."

He gave me a shit-eating grin. "Kaitlin, I've been tabloid fodder since the day I asked your mother out. Then they found out what I did for a living. I don't make apologies for being who I am or for loving who I love. You don't have to make any either."

"I like the sound of that."

The dining hall was organized chaos. Sydney waved from where she and Olivia were already seated at a full table, and I lifted my hand. I'd lost sight of Aubrey at some point, so Johnny and I made a beeline for the coffee.

Three steps from the coffee counter though, I froze. It had been a long time since we were in the same place and if not for his profile, I might not have noticed him right away.

Dad.

A tall man, he stood out amongst the group he seemed to be in conversation with. My heart bottomed out. His hair had changed; the wild blond mane that hung past his shoulder blades had been replaced with a shorter cut, and there was a definite touch of silver amongst the golden hair.

His face, weathered from years of partying and sunshine, crinkled as he smiled and shook some other guy's hand.

"You okay, kiddo?" Johnny asked as he came back to where I'd taken root. Then he followed my gaze. "Is that…"

"I didn't know he was coming," I said slowly. He was a lot leaner than he'd been; some of the paunch from drinking had disappeared, and he wasn't as red-faced. Maybe he was getting clean and sober like Mom?

"Do you want to go talk to him?"

Did I?

The internal debate raged through me. I kind of wanted to and at the same time—why hadn't he said anything to me? Maybe I should? I took a single step forward when he turned to a woman who strolled up and slid an arm around him.

"Oh, the new wife. Linzi—something." Johnny tapped his chin. "Linzi—oh, what was her last name?"

I hesitated again. They'd gotten married during our last tour. A part of me had blocked it out. The invitation hadn't arrived until the last minute and either they hadn't planned ahead or maybe they'd just forgotten me. Either way, they were married less than a month before Penelope had been born.

"I'll be right back," I told Johnny and he nodded as I worked my way across the hall. I'd almost made it to them when Linzi's face lit up with a smile.

"There's my boy," Linzi said as she greeted Lachlan with open arms. Jonas was a half-step behind him and he looked more uncomfortable with her hug than I was watching it. "All of my boys."

She was all hugs and smiles for them and Dad... Dad clapped their shoulders and shook their hands. Then Ramsey was there and Dad welcomed him with a smile before wrapping an arm around his shoulders.

"They're the picture of a perfect family," Payton said, and the words barely registered as she came up beside me. "Aren't they?"

Her smile was as cold as it was cruel.

"Yeah, picture perfect," I said.

Brothers.

No wonder I hadn't known Dad was coming.

Ninja kisses. Asshole TAs. Moody musicians.

Not only were they brothers.

He hadn't come for *me*.

He'd come for them—*my* stepbrothers.

Tears burned in my eyes as I stared at them, then I turned and walked away.

From all of them.

KC will return in Mad Boys.

Mad Boys

Preorder Now

The pop princess with her bright blue hair, pouty lips, haunting eyes, and the voice of a siren... She's always been too busy for us. Music seems to be the one language we both speak.

It's not enough. For her. For them. For anyone.

I'm not enough.

My brothers want her, the world owns her, and everyone else is vying for a piece of her. At the end of the school year, she walked away and didn't give us a second look. Discarding us like she had her father.

Now, I can't decide what I want more—for her to come back or to never see her again.

Afterword

Deep breaths. You made it to the other side. Poor KC, she was not expecting that. I can't wait to see what happens next in Mad Boys, book 2 of Blue Ivy Prep. Are you ready?

Do you have theories? Thoughts? Feelings? I love to hear from my readers, be sure to join us on Facebook in the reader and spoiler groups.

See you soon!

xoxo

Heather

Reader group: facebook.com/groups/heatherspack

Spoiler group: facebook.com/groups/teammadatheather

About Heather Long

I *love* books. Not just a little bit, but a lot. Books were my best friends when I was growing up. Books didn't care if I was new to a town or to a class. They were always there, my trustiest of companions. Until they turned on me and said I had to write them.

I can tell you that my own personal happily ever after included writing books. I've always said that an HEA is a work in progress. It's true in my marriage, my friendships, and in my career. I am constantly nurturing my muse as we dive into new tales, new tropes, new characters and more.

After seventeen years in Texas, we relocated to the Pacific Northwest in search of seasons, new experiences, and new geography. I can't wait to discover what life (and my muse) have in store for me.

Maybe writing was always my destiny and romance my fate. After all, my grandmother wasn't a fan of picture books and used to read me her Harlequin Romance novels.

Friends to lovers, enemies to lovers, friends to enemies to lovers, you name it, I love them and love to write them. I started with Earth Witches Aren't Easy, the first in the Chance Monroe trilogy, but my characters and I have traveled a long way since I created that urban fantasy world.

One of the series I hear my readers recommend the most is the Untouchable series followed in quick succession by the Vandals, and that just delights me. No lie, whenever one of my readers brings up my wolves, I do a little a fist pump.

I'm active on social media, and I love hearing from readers.

Feel free to tag me with a question about any of my books, or just say hi!

Follow Heather & Sign up for her news and updates:
www.heatherlong.net
TikTok

Also by Heather Long

82nd Street Vandals

Savage Vandal

Vicious Rebel

Ruthless Traitor

Dirty Devil

Brutal Fighter

Dangerous Renegade

Merciless Spy

Always a Marine Series

Once Her Man, Always Her Man

Retreat Hell! She Just Got Here

Tell It to the Marine

Proud to Serve Her

Her Marine

No Regrets, No Surrender

The Marine Cowboy

The Two and the Proud

A Marine and a Gentleman

Combat Barbie

Whiskey Tango Foxtrot

What Part of Marine Don't You Understand?

A Marine Affair

Marine Ever After

Marine in the Wind

Marine with Benefits

A Marine of Plenty

A Candle for a Marine

Marine under the Mistletoe

Have Yourself a Marine Christmas

Lest Old Marines Be Forgot

Her Marine Bodyguard

Smoke & Marines

Bravo Team Wolf

When Danger Bites

Bitten Under Fire

Cardinal Sins

Kill Song

First Chorus

High Note

Chance Monroe

Earth Witches Aren't Easy

Plan Witch from Out of Town

Bad Witch Rising

Her Elite Assets

Featuring:

Pure Copper
Target: Tungsten
Asset: Arsenic

Fevered Hearts

Marshal of Hel Dorado
Brave are the Lonely
Micah & Mrs. Miller
A Fistful of Dreams
Raising Kane
Wanted: Fevered or Alive
Wild and Fevered
The Quick & The Fevered
A Man Called Wyatt

Going Royal

Some Like It Royal
Some Like It Scandalous
Some Like It Deadly
Some Like it Secret
Some Like it Easy
Her Marine Prince
Blocked

Heart of the Nebula

Queenmaker
Deal Breaker

Throne Taker

Lone Star Leathernecks

Semper Fi Cowboy

As You Were, Cowboy

Magic & Mayhem

The Witch Singer

Bridget's Witch's Diary

The Witched Away Bride

Mongrels

Mongrels, Mischief & Mayhem

Shackled Souls

Succubus Chained

Succubus Unchained

Succubus Blessed

Shackled Souls (Omnibus)

Space Cowboy

Space Cowboy Survival Guide

Untouchable

Rules and Roses

Changes and Chocolates

Keys and Kisses

Whispers and Wishes

Hangovers and Holidays

Brazen and Breathless

Trials and Tiaras

Graduation and Gifts

Defiance and Dedication

Songs and Sweethearts

Legacy and Lovers

Farewells and Forever

Wolves of Willow Bend

Wolf at Law

Wolf Bite

Caged Wolf

Wolf Claim

Wolf Next Door

Rogue Wolf

Bayou Wolf

Untamed Wolf

Wolf with Benefits

River Wolf

Single Wicked Wolf

Desert Wolf

Snow Wolf

Wolf on Board

Holly Jolly Wolf

Shadow Wolf

His Moonstruck Wolf

Thunder Wolf

Ghost Wolf

Outlaw Wolves

Wolf Unleashed

CPSIA information can be obtained
at www.ICGtesting.com
Printed in the USA
LVHW040840160223
739598LV00008BA/560